THE
CLUES
IN THE
FJORD

Satu Rämö moved to Iceland twenty years ago as an economics exchange student but quickly shifted her focus to Icelandic culture, literature and mythology. Alongside forging a successful career as a blogger, writer, coach and mentor, Rämö has published numerous bestselling, prizewinning non-fiction titles in her native Finland. *Hildur* is her fiction debut. She lives with her Icelandic husband and two children in the small town of Ísafjörður in northwest Iceland.

THE CLUES IN THE FJORD

SATU RÄMÖ

Translated by Kristian London

ZAFFRE

First published as Hildur by Werner Söderström Ltd in 2022
Published in the English language by arrangement with
Bonnier Rights Finland, Helsinki, Finland

First published in the UK in 2024 by
ZAFFRE
An imprint of Bonnier Books UK
4th Floor, Victoria House, Bloomsbury Square, London, WC1B 4DA
Owned by Bonnier Books
Sveavägen 56, Stockholm, Sweden

A CIP catalogue record for this book is
available from the British Library.

ISBN: 978-1-80418-840-8

Also available as an ebook and an audiobook

1 3 5 7 9 10 8 6 4 2

Typeset by IDSUK (Data Connection) Ltd
Printed and bound in Great Britain by Clays Ltd, Elcograf S.p.A.

Zaffre is an imprint of Bonnier Books UK
www.bonnierbooks.co.uk

BEFORE

Chapter 1

Summer 1550, Mosfellsheiði

Sleipnir's thick brown mane tossed to and fro as his gait quickened. He was foaming at the mouth, and his eyes burned with the fire of forward momentum.

Sitting astride his fleet-footed steed, Haraldur inhaled the cool late-summer air. In his right hand, he held the reins. From his left, a rope led to the halters of two spare mounts galloping at his side. A knife lashed at Haraldur's waist slapped against his right thigh in time to Sleipnir's canter.

As he exhaled, Haraldur blew a low, long '*ǫǫ*' through his thick chestnut beard. It was meant to calm the stallion, but the beast's urge to run would not be restrained, even by exhaustion.

A good horse wanted the best for its master. It wanted to show what it was capable of. But Haraldur didn't want to ride his favourite mount into the ground, as the long Mosfellsheiði ascent still lay ahead.

Three hard days had passed since Haraldur had readied the three horses and set out from his home at Fellsströnd on the shores of the Broad Fjord, Breiðarfjörður. He had left the Westfjords behind and was headed south.

He was on his way to warn his friend.

Haraldur had caught wind of a band of cutthroats from a rival clan plotting to murder Njáll. Njáll was one of the most prosperous landowners in southern Iceland, and as such, wielded great influence. But money and power attracted enemies who found ways of helping themselves to the wealth of others.

Njáll and Haraldur had become fast friends as boys because they were cousins through their mothers. Haraldur had set out the moment word of Njáll's peril reached his ears.

The evening sun stained the land orange. Autumn was in the air. The birds no longer chattered as they had during the mating season, and the meadow grass was fading from green to golden. As the sun set and dusk fell, Haraldur reached the final stop on his journey, a *sæluhús* on the Mosfellsheiði plateau. He reined the horses in outside the modest peat cottage and dropped from Sleipnir's back. He watered his horses and led them to a walled pasture to rest.

Haraldur opened the door and stepped into a dim, low hall. He wanted to stretch his limbs for the night and continue his journey early the next day. He had no more than a half day's ride left to reach Njáll's farm on the banks of the wide, fast-flowing Ölfusá.

A young woman in an undyed wool skirt appeared in the central hall, lamp in hand. The soft glow of the burning oil deepened the green of her eyes.

'Three horses and one man, just for one night.' Haraldur shifted his weight as he growled through his beard. His long red hair framed a strong-jawed face. 'Can you lodge us?'

'There's a room in the back,' she said with a flick of her head. 'Payment in the morning. And no tricks.'

Una was approaching her thirtieth year and hailed from the south. She spent winters as a servant at a farm on the neighbouring fjord. During the summer, she looked after the guesthouse that stood on her master's land. All those travelling between west and south broke their journeys at this *sæluhús* for the night.

Una took a long look at the handsome man standing in the hall. Much longer than the glance she usually granted guests. 'Are you hungry? I can see what I can find in the cook room.'

They shared a fillet of dried cod and broke off hunks from a loaf of seaweed bread. Haraldur spoke of the horses travelling with him and his sheep farm on the Broad Fjord, which was dotted with so many islands no man had ever counted them. Una said she was a quick hand at shearing.

It was not often Una invited strangers into her bed, but tonight she chose to make an exception. Haraldur seemed different. Special. He spoke to her as an equal. He asked her views, listened without interruption, and shared everyday stories from his life.

The next morning, as Haraldur was preparing to leave, he asked Una what she would say if he came to claim her on the return journey.

'If you don't tarry too long, I just might go with you,' Una replied, then remained braiding her hair as Haraldur departed. The rays of the morning sun penetrated a narrow window in the turf walls. The strip of light seemed to split the room in two. Una stood in its glow, shut her eyes, and basked in the warmth spilling over her face.

Haraldur reached the banks of the Ölfusá before the outlaws did. Njáll was pleased to see his friend, and the two of them celebrated their reunion long into the night. Njáll hired a pair of stout workmen from a trustworthy neighbour to maintain a constant watch over his person and guard his life. As Haraldur took his leave, Njáll handed his friend a leather pouch filled with coins struck from silver and copper, *klippinge*.

The *klippinge* clinked in Haraldur's pocket as he rode up to the *sæluhús* two days later. Una packed up her few belongings, mounted the young mare owned by this handsome traveller, and left for the west, for the Broad Fjord and its countless islands.

She and Haraldur ought never have met, but they did. And they had an exceptionally large brood of offspring.

Chapter 2

November 1994, Ísafjörður

The wind was flinging the snow back and forth outside the living room window. A storm was rising.

Lóa's belly felt velvety and warm under Björk's palm. *It's as soft as silk*, she thought as she steadily stroked the drowsy animal. The cat purred quietly. A plough drove past, its orange-yellow flashes sweeping across the living room. The big machine was clearing the road, pushing the snow into piles in the empty plot next door. The clank and screech of the ground-grazing vehicle carried indoors.

The cat woke and stretched its front paws against the corduroy couch, opened its eye-slits as little as possible, and glanced at its young caretaker in satisfaction.

Björk was sad she couldn't have a cat of her own. Her mum was allergic. A dog was a no-no, too. Horses they had, but horses were always outside and you couldn't play with them like this on the living room couch.

And so Björk had been delighted when Mum's old friend Jón had asked her and her sister Rósa to mind his cat. He'd had to go to Reykjavík to buy glasses because there was no place in the Westfjords that sold specs, let alone an optometrist. The six-hour drive south and a couple of nights in an affordable hotel on the outskirts of the capital wouldn't have suited old Lóa. She didn't like riding in her carrier in the back seat. She always got car sick.

Björk and Rósa had come straight from school to look after the cat. They'd given Lóa a couple of codfish tongues and measured out dry food for her bowl. There was a cat flap in the door; Lóa came and went as she pleased and did her business outside.

Björk couldn't bear to leave the napping cat. She was so soft and warm.

'Come on, we really have to go,' her sister nagged. 'We're going to miss the bus.'

'I just want to scratch her for one more sec. She likes it so much. Look how she's pushing her head into my lap. Kiss kiss kiss.'

Eight-year-old Rósa stood in the entryway with her red My Little Pony backpack over her shoulders, impatiently shifting her weight from foot to foot. The bus to their village on the other side of the mountain would leave the school in five minutes, and Rósa knew the driver didn't wait for stragglers. But Björk was only in Year One and didn't have a very good sense of time yet. To her, five minutes and fifteen minutes were the same thing. At least Rósa was in Year Three.

Luckily, Jón lived right next to the school. Mum had told them he had another house as well, an old summer place out in the countryside. Lóa preferred the country, too, since she could frolic in the grass without having to worry about passing cars.

'I'm going. You can stay if you want,' Rósa said, turning toward the front door. She tried to coax her sister along one last time: 'Mum promised to make *lummur* today, remember?'

Björk loved *lummur*. Small but scrumptiously thick pancakes you poured syrup over and topped with spoonfuls of rhubarb jam. They were Björk's favourite. And Mum could even make them in the shape of flowers and hearts.

Björk rose slowly from the sofa and petted the cat one last time. 'OK. I'm coming. I just have to go to the bathroom first.'

Rósa pressed the front door shut behind her and made sure she heard it close. A strong gust might push it open otherwise and let snow in the house.

The girls trudged across the banks of snow that had formed in the yard. At least half a metre had fallen over the last two days. They marvelled at the windswept shapes and talked about going sledding on the hill behind their house.

As they approached the road, shoes full of snow, the school bus zoomed past. Rósa chased after it a short distance and waved for the driver to stop, but it was no use. Either the driver didn't see her or didn't care.

'We have to get home. What are we going to do?' Björk asked anxiously. Her voice was thickening with welling tears. 'There's snow in my shoe. Mum says I'll catch a cold if I'm outside with wet feet.'

Rósa looked thoughtful. The school was closed. The other children had gone home or been picked up. The bus had left. Mum was outside feeding the horses right now, and it would be at least an hour before she was back inside. And Dad was at sea. His fishing boat wouldn't return to harbour until the weekend.

'Should we go to someone else's house?' Björk suggested. 'Mum's going to be cross if she has to come and get us,' Rósa said.

And then Björk had an idea. 'What if . . . what if we just walked?'

She knew walking home was forbidden. They could get lost in the snowstorm, and the fancy new tunnel wasn't open yet. Besides, you weren't allowed to enter the tunnel on foot.

Over the past few years, a tunnel had been dug under the mountain to connect Ísafjörður with the nearby villages. A few kilometres long, it would shorten distances and make the trip safer. Soon there would be no need to use the steep, winding mountain road that was dangerous to drive, especially during winter storms.

'We're not allowed to go in the tunnel,' Rósa said in alarm. 'It's not finished yet.'

'I heard Mum tell Dad you can already get through the mountain. The road's finished,' Björk insisted with a six-year-old's certainty. She fixed her gaze on her sister. 'I'm positive.'

'I suppose we do have to get home somehow,' Rósa reflected. 'And if the tunnel's not open yet, there won't be any cars in it.'

But now Björk was having second thoughts. 'I'm afraid of the dark, though,' she protested. 'And the tunnel's really dark.'

'We'll go slowly. I'll go first and hold your hand the whole way. I won't let go until we're home. We'll walk along the edge of the road,' Rósa said. 'Just think about those pancakes.'

Björk's resistance melted, and she took her sister's hand. They started for home.

As the girls walked along the paved shoulder towards the cavern in the mountainside, the snow began falling again. The afternoon light was fading, and darkness was falling fast. Soon it would be just as dark outside as it was inside the tunnel.

'Luckily it won't be snowing in the tunnel,' Rósa said, urging her little sister along. 'Come on, let's go.'

Rósa and Björk entered the tunnel hand in hand. The last sign of them was a red My Little Pony backpack being swallowed up by the shadows.

And then they were gone.

NOW

Chapter 1

October 2019, Ísafjörður

The sea moaned softly. The waves had travelled an immense distance. A storm in the seas off Greenland manifested a few days later in rollers that crashed into the craggy shores of Iceland's north-west coast. The water churned into white foam as it broke on the rocks, spraying the mouths of caves formed eons ago by volcanic eruptions.

Everyone needed occasional contact with the bedrock that kept their life stable. For Detective Hildur Rúnarsdóttir, that foundation was surfing. The sea was fickle; no one could foresee its movements precisely. There was always that cold, dark place that evaded prediction. Demanded caution. The risk was beguiling. Playing with this cold place was Hildur's way of managing life.

Hildur tightly knotted her long braid into a bun at her nape, allowing her neoprene hood to fit snugly over her head.

She estimated the temperature of the water at five, at most six, degrees Celsius. Her full-body wetsuit was the thickest model. It had full legs and sleeves, but the neoprene there was a couple of millimetres thinner because her legs and arms needed more freedom to move. She also used gloves and booties designed for cold-water surfing.

The black suit fit like a second skin. If it were loose, it would let in too much water and her body would cool too much.

An overly tight suit made it hard to move. Riding a surfboard required agility.

The grey, late-October light drizzled through tattered clouds. The village saw no sun in the winter; the surrounding mountains kept it out of sight from November to February. This was the time of year when the sun vanished, not to return until winter waned.

Hildur reached an arm around her green surfboard and stepped into the water. Her neoprene booties had hard rubber soles, but she could still sense the jagged volcanic rock underfoot. After a few wary steps, she lay on the board and started paddling toward the open water. Her muscular arms rhythmically ploughed the sea; her breathing came faster.

In the sea, one can venture only as far as the mind allows. Today Hildur wanted to venture as far as possible. The waves were low but long, typical remnants of a Greenland storm. Paddling into them was exhausting. And that was exactly why Hildur loved scooping her way through the waves. As she expended energy physically, she somehow generated more of it in her mind.

The board sliced through the sea, and Hildur's breathing grew more laboured. She noticed a jet-black raven flying overhead. And in the instant it took to glance at it, the sea seized her. Just one breath with her face raised, and a fistful of saltwater found its way into her lungs, sparking a violent coughing fit.

After paddling a few hundred metres, Hildur turned the board and waited for the next wave, which she intended to claim. The shore was empty. There weren't many surfers in her town of a couple of thousand residents, and today the sea was hers alone.

An hour later, Hildur took her board and walked toward the Arnarnes peninsula, where she'd left her four-wheel-drive SUV. Taking a break from everything had done the trick again. Her anxiety that morning had been crushing, and although she no longer felt as agonised as she had when she woke, she could still sense she'd be receiving bad news soon.

Hildur headed up the missing children's unit for rural Iceland and worked at the Ísafjörður Police Department as a detective, the only detective in the Westfjords.

As she walked up to her vehicle, she heard her phone ring. Hildur unrolled her skintight surfing gloves, opened the car door, and reached for the phone flashing on the front seat.

'This is Hildur,' she said, out of breath. She wiped the saltwater from her brow and removed her thick neoprene hood.

It was Hildur's boss Beta, with an urgent matter. The call came as no surprise to Hildur.

'I'll be there. I'm on my way. I'll just drop by my place to change.'

Most people were able to anticipate good things. That felt strange to Hildur. For her, *good* meant not needing to dread future events: that things would just happen, and life would safely roll on. The instant she felt any anticipation, it foreboded something bad, some misfortune.

This sense hadn't always been so unnerving. When she was a child, she'd been capable of anticipating good things. She'd taken pleasure in Christmas, classmates' birthday parties, weekend horseback rides, the first snow of the year.

Then everything changed

She threw a thick towel under her backside and climbed into the leather driver's seat. Then she started up the SUV and sped off, tyres squealing, for the tiny town of Ísafjörður, where she lived and worked.

Chapter 2

The plaid upholstery felt coarse under Pétur's fingers. The living room floor was beige laminate. When the synthetic soles of his Vans came into contact with it, it made a nasty squeak.

Pétur pulled down his black beanie and tried to relax by fixing his gaze on the square Ikea bookshelf opposite. There was no rhyme or reason to its contents. Haphazard piles of paper towels, advertising flyers, and empty pizza boxes had been crammed in its shelves. Porcelain cows and Halldór Laxness's novel *Salka Valka*. A sticky coat of grime covered by a skim of dust.

Pétur was hungry. All he'd eaten in the last two days was a strawberry yoghurt he stole from a service station along the way. But thinking about eating was impossible right now. He was too agitated.

Luckily that young doctor had pulled over and promised to drive Pétur all the way to Ísafjörður. Some Pole who hadn't lived in Iceland long and didn't speak the language. That was fine with Pétur. Pétur's English was good. He hadn't learned it at school; he hadn't even finished primary school. YouTube and online discussion forums had taught him what he needed to know, and he'd had no trouble conversing with the Polish doctor. He was glad a foreigner had picked him up. A foreigner wasn't going to recognise him. Icelanders had kin in every fucking fjord. Hitching with them was always risky.

Pétur stirred and shot a surreptitious glance at the dining table in the middle of the room. An old man in a red flannel shirt that was too tight at the gut sat there, packing marijuana into the bong bowl. The old man was evaluating his handiwork through chipped reading glasses. The furrows in his scarred forehead deepened as he peered at the bowl.

'You sure kept me waiting. It took you a while to get here, don't you think? Why did it take you so long?' he asked Pétur as he fit the bowl into the stem. 'I'm pretty disappointed in you.'

The old man set down the bong and the lighter on the coffee table, in front of Pétur's roving eyes. 'But no worries, kid. You're a good guy. I'm sure we'll think of something to cheer me up, don't you reckon?'

The old man returned to his seat, folded his hands behind his neck, and leaned back. He stared at the teenager in the armchair, evidently relishing the moment. Eventually, his penetrating gaze elicited an answer from Pétur.

'Yeah, well. It was a pain in the ass sneaking out of that place. The people who work there are sharp as fuck.'

'Lucky we're sharper, don't you think?' The old man smirked, with a nod at the bong.

Pétur immediately reached for the pipe. This wasn't his first time. He took the bong in his lap, lit the bowl, and started sucking furiously on the mouthpiece. The room filled with the quiet burble of the water pipe and the old man's heavy breathing. *Finally*, Pétur thought. As his lungs filled with the cool vapour, tranquillity spread throughout his limbs. The itch in his arms faded.

'Go ahead, give that pipe a good, long suck. Take your time. It'll get you nice and relaxed. Don't you think?'

The old man ogled the teenage boy smoking the bong and slowly, slowly, started undoing his belt.

Chapter 3

Hildur pulled up outside the police station and sat there, tapping the wheel of the Škoda Octavia. She had a view of the car park through the windscreen, and she was watching a man in a lightweight blazer and gelled hair climb into a particularly expensive-looking Range Rover. The SUV had custom wheels and a personalised plate. Hildur wasn't sure what model it was, but assumed for the price of a ride like that she could buy two one-bedroom terraced houses and still have enough money left over for a couple of trips abroad. Then the black Range Rover blurred into the grey surroundings, the well-dressed guy at the wheel melted to mush, and eventually both faded from view.

Hildur flicked on the wipers. They glided lazily across the windscreen every few seconds. The rain had come. The brisk south wind promised in the forecast almost always brought precipitation, so Hildur would be waiting a while for clear, crisp weather. In this part of the world, autumn was long and dark.

Hildur turned on the radio as she waited for her superior. Police Chief Elísabet Baldursdóttir, otherwise known as Beta. Beta was the first boss Hildur had truly liked. Beta had moved to Ísafjörður a few years before. Her husband Óliver, a software engineer, was originally from the area. After their twins were born, Beta and Óliver had dreamed of relocating to a small town, so when the position of Ísafjörður station chief opened up, Beta had applied for and secured the job. Óliver worked remotely for a company in Reykjavík, and the twins attended the local daycare.

Beta was work-focused but wonderfully down to earth. No unnecessary drama, no overly close connections to local politicians. Hildur knew Beta didn't even attend the weekly meetings of the Freemasons. Not that she could have, anyway; only men were accepted as members. And when Beta had started in her new position, she'd made it clear to all that she wanted to remain the police chief of a small department and had no interest in competing for a seat among the top brass at the national police organisation. She'd come to Ísafjörður so she could work with the public and do honest-to-God police work despite her supervisory status.

Hildur, in contrast, hadn't chosen Ísafjörður; Ísafjörður had chosen her. She'd been born in this remote place.

The mountainous Westfjords were in north-west Iceland, far from cities, traffic lights, bowling alleys, and international airports. An old folk-tale had it that at the beginning of time, two raging trolls had tried to tear the Westfjords away from the rest of Iceland, but the sun had risen before they finished their labours. Because trolls cannot survive the sun's rays, they had frozen into mountains on the spot, and the Westfjords remained attached to the main island by a seven-kilometre peninsula.

Two torturous mountain passes linked the Westfjords to the rest of Iceland. Not that they were heavily trafficked. The Westfjords made up a fifth of Iceland's land area, but less than 2 per cent of the population lived at the end of the narrow road – about seven thousand children and adults, all told: fishermen, teachers, truck drivers, those who made a living from tourism. And a handful of police officers.

Hildur looked around and sighed. The patter against the windscreen grew louder and louder. When it rained here, it really rained. And when it was windy, the wind tore mercilessly through the open expanses and wailed in the fjords. Iceland was a long way from everything. Thousands of kilometres from Europe and the United States. A small, solitary island, all lava and glaciers, in the middle of a frigid sea. And someone had decided to establish a settlement in the remotest part of that island. How had it ever occurred to anyone to move here, a place so far from everything?

Hildur tapped at the steering wheel and reached back into her memory. If it served her correctly, the area's first inhabitant was a man with Norwegian roots, Helgi. About a thousand years ago, Helgi had scoured the vicinity for empty land where he could establish a home for his family. He had found this fjord, deemed it habitable, and seen a seal harpoon bobbing in the shallows. Helgi had named the place Harpoon Fjord and made himself at home. Later a church was established on the same shores, as was a marketplace christened Ísafjörður.

Helgi had stuck in Hildur's mind from a history class that covered the settling of Iceland. She'd always been fascinated by old stories and people's pasts. The first big book she'd read had been about the outlaw Eyvindur of the Mountains, who'd roamed the wilds of Iceland during the 1700s. She'd found the book on her parents' bookshelf as a girl and devoured it from cover to cover. Hildur could still spend hours absorbed in a biography or old news stories about people she knew. When she travelled around Iceland, she made a habit of stopping at every heritage museum she came across and harassing the summer workers with questions about local minutiae. For Hildur, the past was a solid wall she could lean against.

Not surprisingly, she'd ended up studying history at the university. She'd been born in the Westfjords and spent her childhood here with her sisters and parents. When tragedy struck, she'd moved in with an aunt who lived nearby. After high school, she'd headed to Reykjavík and found a small studio west of the centre. Nowadays the neighbourhood was one of the city's most expensive. Housing prices were so high in downtown Reykjavík that with her police wages, she'd had no chance of living on the block where she'd once rented as a student.

Hildur had initially found her studies in history at the University of Iceland rewarding. But after earning her bachelor's degree, she realised that although she enjoyed analysing societal changes and the impact of past events on the present, an academic career held zero interest for her. She'd begun craving activity, action – feeling more of a draw to sweaty gyms and the frigid sea than lecture halls or making a name for herself as an expert. Hildur had discovered surfing through her boyfriend at the time. The waves had literally carried her away. She'd fallen in love with the idea of taming the sea, beguiled by the notion of briefly possessing part of it. And so she'd headed out surfing after lectures, on weekends, and on every vacation day she had.

Gradually, the thrill of physical exertion had taken precedence over studies. When Hildur began skipping lectures to improve her surfing, she realised she was headed into the wrong profession.

One summer she'd decided to apply to the police academy. On the first day of her studies, she knew she'd come to the right place. She loved the intense team spirit and rigorous physical training.

After earning her degree, Hildur had spent a few years on the Reykjavík police force, where she collaborated closely with child protection services. In crimes involving children or troubled adolescents, Hildur had served as the liaison to child protection services and child psychologists.

She felt like she was doing something meaningful when she helped children. Maybe she was trying to compensate for the tragedy that happened so long ago. She supposed she must have thought if she didn't even try, things would remain so much harder.

More funding was acquired for the missing children's unit in Reykjavík, and the model Hildur had helped pilot was gradually introduced across the country. So when the Ísafjörður Police Department was looking for an officer who could work part-time with the missing children's unit, Hildur knew her chance had come. She applied, got the job, and moved back to her hometown with her surfboard strapped to the roof of her SUV.

Nearly ten years had passed since then. She enjoyed the slow pace in the tiny town and was particularly happy about the superb surfing conditions.

Hildur snapped out of her reverie when the driver's door flew open. Short, energetic Beta climbed in, forcefully pulled the door shut, and let out a deep sigh. The rain had flattened her curls, but Beta never paid attention to such things.

Hildur waited for her boss to buckle her seatbelt before saying, 'So what's up?'

'We're heading to Fjallavegur. Both patrols are nearly an hour away on calls. We'll be handling this one ourselves.'

Hildur nodded and waited for Beta to fill her in.

'I got a call from the southern youth shelter that a Pétur who'd been detoxing there left the shelter last night. They suspect he came here to Ísafjörður for drugs.'

'Why here, of all places?' Hildur asked, starting up the car. Ísafjörður wasn't on the way anywhere, and there was no ending up here by accident. To get to the Westfjords, you had to travel here on purpose. The drive from the capital took hours.

'Pétur's mobile phone had been confiscated for a few days because of some minor infraction, and an old man from Ísafjörður had tried to reach him several times by calling the shelter landline. The staff at detox guessed right away who it was.'

'Goddammit. Did he go to that old perv's place?' Hildur asked as she sped from the station to the road skirting the village. It was really coming down now, so Hildur had to turn up the wipers to see the road ahead properly.

Everyone who'd been in Ísafjörður for any length of time knew the dodgy guy who lived at the far end of Fjallavegur. A lonely man coming up on seventy, Jón Jónsson had received a number of charges over the past twenty years for possession of narcotics and lewd behaviour. He'd spent a little over a year in prison, but that had been back in the early '00s. At the time, Jón had been found in possession of half a kilo of hash. Since then, his rap sheet showed nothing but fines, even though he clearly exploited troubled youth. He promised them free drugs if they'd watch him masturbate.

Hildur couldn't wrap her brain around such lenient sentences. Why were those guilty of financial crimes sentenced to years in prison and substantial damages, while a violation of another person got you nothing more than damn community service? She huffed and tightened her grip around the wheel to restrain the rage smouldering within her. 'We just paid the asshole a visit last summer about this stuff. Isn't there anything we can do about him?'

'Not really. The kids seek him out voluntarily because they can get drugs from him. They either won't admit the molestation or it can't be proved. The most Jón is going to be charged with is possession of marijuana,' Beta said, although she knew Hildur already understood this.

The Škoda glided from the traffic circle onto the road leading past the hospital and the library. Fjallavegur was the longest street in the quiet neighbourhood on the mountain's lower slopes. Its long row of white terraces dated from the 1960s, while the oldest wooden houses had been built before Iceland declared independence during the Second World War.

Hildur kept the speedometer at thirty and surveyed her surroundings from the driver's seat. The locals valued their privacy: curtains had been drawn across all the street-facing windows. Some displayed framed homilies bought from the supermarket, embarrassingly insipid banalities. *Happiness lives here. Home is where the family is. Happiness is a lovely home.* Almost every backyard sported a large gas barbecue, where the middle-class residents conveyed their middle-class happiness to their neighbours by flipping lamb chops on weekends. The wealthiest homes had hot tubs. This happy street continued for a couple of kilometres.

Leaving the houses and terraces behind, Hildur and Beta entered a sparser neighbourhood made up of cabins. Over the decades, numerous summertime structures had sprouted on the slope. Some were small allotment cottages; a few had big yards and covered patios. Overnight stays here were only allowed between early May and early November; the nearby mountains and snow-heavy winters placed the area squarely in the avalanche zone. Even a small slide could destroy a home, which made the cottages unsafe for winter occupation.

Hildur and Beta had paid Jón many visits. The old man's tactics always followed the same pattern: he would befriend troubled youth online, promise them free drugs, and let them stay with him. In return, he would expose himself to them, masturbate while they watched, paw at them. A lot of kids struggling with addiction sought not only drugs from Jón but also safety, because they had no one else.

Hildur pulled up outside a little green cottage. The paint was peeling, and rain was spilling over along the entire façade. Apparently, the sagging gutters hadn't been cleaned in a while.

Hildur opened the rusty gate, and she and Beta climbed the steps to the front door. Beta took the lead and rapped on it with her knuckles. No response. Beta rapped again, this time more loudly. No answer.

'There are lights on in the kitchen, and Jón's old Suzuki is parked right there,' Hildur said. 'He never walks anywhere. I'm sure he's home.'

She spotted a ground-floor window that was open and stuck her head in. 'Open up! This is the police,' she bellowed, slamming her palm against the windowpane. 'We know you're in there and others are in there too. Come and open this door right now or we're going to take that Suzuki of yours down to the station. You're late with your MOT.'

Sometimes Hildur was like a shepherd driving her flock down the mountain, waving her hands and roaring until her throat ached. That was how you got sheep to run in the desired direction. But when dealing with people, a little more tact was sometimes useful. After completing the academy training, Hildur had applied for detective work because, in all honesty, constant interaction with the public wasn't her thing. The mandatory patrols of her early years in law enforcement had been a grind; the daily breathalysing, questioning, and detaining of dozens of people had truly grated on her nerves.

A moment later, there was a rustling at the door. It creaked open, revealing a dishevelled, frightened-looking man in the gap between the door and the jamb. He had a sizeable scar

25

on his forehead. Some said Jón had got it as a child from running into a bakery window. His red flannel shirt looked like it hadn't been washed in months, and his jeans were unbuttoned. A musty smell wafted out, assaulting the police officers' noses.

'*Jæjja* Jón,' Hildur said. *Jæjja* was a local exclamation, the meaning of which depended on the context. Right now it meant: *cut the crap and let's get down to business.* 'We have reason to believe Pétur, a runaway from Reykjavík, is here.' Hildur tried to peer over Jón's shoulders into the gloom. She flicked her head toward the Suzuki and eyed Jón stonily. 'I guess we'll have to call in a tow truck.'

Jón rubbed his perspiring bald patch and looked around in dismay. A bead of sweat rolled down the scar on his forehead.

He glanced past the police officers to make sure his car was still there. Then he cleared his throat, signalling surrender. 'The kid's in the living room. I'm not keeping him prisoner. He came here of his own free will and didn't want to leave.'

'Just like the rest of them,' Hildur said. She asked Jón to move aside. 'Is there anyone else in the house?

'No, no . . . You're not going to take my car, are you?'

Beta stayed at the front door with Jón as Hildur entered the filthy cottage and walked to the end of the hall. There was a little bedroom to the left; the living room was to the right. Hildur stood at the narrow doorway to the living room. A fifteen-year-old boy was snoring in a threadbare armchair. He looked exactly like the description sent by child protection services: slim, black hair, black clothes, nose ring, glasses.

Hildur walked over to the armchair and gingerly shook the boy by the shoulder, trying to rouse him. 'Wake up. Can you get up?'

The young man muttered something unintelligible. He seemed half-asleep.

'You need to wake up,' Hildur said a little more forcefully. She patted the boy lightly on the cheek.

The boy opened his eyes in alarm and shouted: 'What the hell!'

'No, I'm not from hell. My name is Hildur Rúnarsdóttir; I'm a detective with the Ísafjörður Police. Child protection services called, and my colleague and I are here to pick you up. Are you all right? Did Jón do anything to you?'

From the glassy eyes and sweet funk, Hildur could tell Pétur was stoned. This deduction was confirmed by the empty bong on the coffee table.

'I was just resting for a sec,' the boy mumbled.

'Did anyone hurt you?' Hildur asked.

'No, no one hurt me. Like I said, I was just resting here for a sec.'

Hildur eyed Pétur, and at least superficially he looked fine. He was dressed and there were no signs of violence. She led Pétur out of the cottage to the patrol car. Before following them, Beta confiscated a baggie of dark-green hashish from the table.

'Don't take my car, OK?' Jón called from the door.

'Not this time. But be sure to bring it in for inspection right away.' Hildur said. As she steered Pétur into the back seat, she couldn't refrain from shouting: 'But if you don't stop inviting teenagers here, I'm going to pull that Suzuki apart with my bare hands, toss the parts in the sea, and scatter them around the fjord.'

She circled around to the driver's side, ignoring Jón's mutterings from his doorway. 'You know what, Beta? Sometimes I'm not sure if we're working for the police or waste management,' she said as she buckled her seatbelt. 'We keep on recycling the same shit over and over. You think you've handled something, but lo and behold, it drops into your lap again during your next shift.'

'I'm sure it's not going to be our last visit to this address,' Beta agreed. 'What do you think: where will Jón move later in the month, when winter comes and the area closes down?'

'That's not very high on the list of things I care about.'

Hildur drove toward the centre of town. Jón would be called in for questioning about the narcotics possession, which would result in nothing but a fine, tops.

'When you question Jón, you can bring along that Finn,' Beta said. 'He's supposed to arrive tomorrow afternoon.'

'What was his name again?' Hildur asked.

'Jakob. He seemed competent. Although I must admit, I don't really understand why anyone would want to come to such a small place on exchange when the same amount of trouble would get you experience in Oslo or Copenhagen.' Then Beta glanced in the back seat. 'And you, young man, first we're going to take you in for drug tests and then back to rehab. Child protection services will handle your transportation south when we're finished.'

She gave Pétur a brisk smile. Pétur replied with an apathetic look and gave Beta the finger.

Statistically, adolescent drug use had decreased in Iceland over the past twenty years. But the kids who did get into trouble were in a class of their own: they ordered whatever they could online and mixed substances. Their problems mounted and multiplied. Meanwhile, the number of treatment slots set aside for juveniles had been radically reduced. Apparently there was no money; cuts had to be made. It was impossible to get a bed in rehab for everyone who needed treatment. And some lucky enough to get a spot were unable to cope with it. The treatment centres didn't have the staff to monitor the residents' movements twenty-four hours a day.

28

'It would be great if you tried to stay in detox this time,' Beta said. 'You might get your life in order. Because the future that's waiting for you if you keep this up isn't a very rosy one.'

'Who gives a shit?' came the answer from the back seat.

Beta sighed and touched the passenger window. It was still raining.

Chapter 4

After work, Hildur carried her bicycle out of her basement and put on her helmet. The residents of Ísafjörður didn't keep bicycles indoors because they were afraid a thief would nick them. No one would dare steal a bicycle in such a small town; they'd be caught by the next day. Keys were left in ignitions and front doors were kept unlocked. Folks seemed to believe that because everyone knew each other and each other's business, nothing sinister could happen. Danger came on a wind from the sea, not from next door.

Bicycles were stored in basements because of the weather. It rained heavily when the storms picked up late in the year. A north wind blowing off the Atlantic would knock the sturdiest mountain bike to the pavement, and a crash like that was liable to break a lot more than the front reflector. The storms dwindled as summer approached, and generally by mid-May, the snow and ice had melted and the winds died. Only then were bicycles and scooters hauled out of basements, and did their owners dare leave them out for the night.

Hildur had a spacious two-bedroom unit with a balcony in the heart of the old town. The unit on the other side of the wooden house was occupied by Freysi Gunnarsson.

Freysi was a thirty-year-old bachelor and the physical education teacher at the local school. He could run a marathon in well under four hours. He also smoked nonstop. Freysi had moved in next door to Hildur a couple of years ago, and over time they'd grown close. First, they'd gone for the occasional run. Eventually, the runs were followed by joint stretching sessions in either living room, and from the living room, it was a short trip to the bedroom.

They saw each other regularly, but it would be a mischaracterisation to call them a couple. Hildur had been relieved when, after their first night together, Freysi had said he wasn't interested in a relationship. That was exactly what she'd been hoping for. Impromptu company with no agreements, joint bank accounts, or obligations to explain.

Despite meeting exclusively at each other's homes, Freysi and Hildur figured the whole town was aware of the casual relationship between the police officer and the PE teacher. *Let them whisper*, Hildur thought as she turned her bicycle around.

She noticed Freysi smoking outside and waved.

'Hi. How's it going?' Freysi said, stubbing out his cigarette and putting the butt in the rubbish.

'Trying to forget a long work day. I'm headed to my aunt's for dinner.'

'I was going to ask if you wanted to go for a run,' Freysi said, his boyish smile bringing out deep dimples in his cheeks. 'But I forgot it was Monday.'

'Yup, it's not Monday without my aunt's sausages. Let's do something fun later this week.' Hildur climbed on her bicycle, and Freysi whistled as she rode away. Hildur looked back, flashed a smile, and pedalled harder.

She started down the pedestrian-and-bicycle lane that followed the fjord's winding shoreline. The new part of Ísafjörður was located a couple of kilometres from the old town, at the butt of the fjord. Hildur's aunt had built herself a big house there with a handsome garden.

The brand-new suburb held no appeal for Hildur; she preferred to live near her work. The homes were smaller and the lots more cramped in the centre, but the village-like ambience created by the old town's wooden houses was pleasant, and all amenities were within walking distance.

Hildur signalled right and turned from the bike path into the residential neighbourhood. Tinna Atladóttir had retired a few years earlier from her profession as a singing teacher. Now she spent most of her time at home, doing handcrafts and listening to audiobooks. Hildur knew her aunt loved living further out, surrounded by large yards.

Hildur didn't ring the doorbell or knock; she just walked in the way she always did. Tinna had heard her arrive and was waiting in the entry hall. She immediately wrapped Hildur in a tight embrace.

'It's so good to see you. Sorry I'm late,' Hildur said apologetically. 'I had to work overtime.'

'Bah. We're not on a timetable,' Tinna said, giving Hildur two kisses on her right cheek. It was the custom in Iceland to greet loved ones with a light kiss on the cheek. But Tinna gave two kisses instead of one, and she didn't settle for quickly grazing the skin: she laid on juicy, wet smooches.

Hildur followed Tinna into the big, bright kitchen and sat at the island. A delicious smell wafted from the sauce simmering on the stove as Tinna stirred it. Hildur shut her eyes and let a satisfying languor spread through her limbs. After a moment, she felt happy.

She enjoyed these weekly visits with her aunt. Hildur had been a minor when her parents died, and her mother's sister had taken her in. Hildur had another aunt, too, but she lived in the Faroe Islands. The two of them weren't close; Tinna and Hildur were. When Hildur was studying in Reykjavík, she and Tinna had stayed in constant contact. Hildur's phone had rung at least once a day. And the bond between them had grown even stronger upon Hildur's return to Ísafjörður ten years ago.

Tinna was the only living relative Hildur felt close to. They were the last of the line.

Tinna had prepared Hildur's favourite dish: *slátur*, a fatty sausage made from sheep's innards. She fried it in butter and served it with white sauce and boiled potatoes. Tinna set the pots and pans down on the table and asked Hildur to dish up a big slice of sausage and plenty of potatoes for each of them, then to top off the deliciousness with some lovely thick white sauce.

The grease squirted as Hildur sank her teeth into the scrumptiously salty greyish-brown sausage. She wiped her lips on a paper towel. 'This is so good,' she said, her mouth half full. The crispy-skinned sausage tasted like childhood, when *slátur* had been ordinary, everyday food. At Hildur's childhood home, dinner had always been served at seven o'clock. When the evening news began, Hildur and her sisters would come inside, cheeks red and hair wind-tousled, and take their seats on the wooden benches at the kitchen table. Mum would set the pot and the rye bread down in the middle of the table and sit across from them, next to Dad. The best sausage had been the kind Dad made, which they always had in the autumn after the slaughter. No one really made sausage nowadays. It was bought vacuum-packed from the cold cuts section of the supermarket.

'You sound a little tired, dear heart,' Tinna said. 'How are you doing, really?'

'Same as ever. Kind of a rough day at work.'

'Sure. But what about generally? I know this is a tough time of year for you. It always has been.' Tinna paused. 'It's been almost twenty-five years since your sisters went missing.' Hildur flinched. Her aunt was right. Late autumn was always a hard time for her. And although she recalled her sisters' disappearance, she didn't care to discuss it. She remembered panicked calls to neighbours, *lummur* gone cold in the brown frying pan, police who came to the house but didn't say anything.

'I don't feel like talking about it right now,' Hildur said. Talking wasn't going to do any good; she knew that from experience. Old events rose vividly to her mind in late autumn. Talking sharpened some of the memories, making them even more painful. But talking had never brought clarity, nor had it helped her remember the details of what happened that autumn. That was why, in this particular instance, talking was useless. It just made her sometimes-heavy mood even heavier.

The heaviness had settled inside Hildur as a child. She could no longer remember what it was like to live without it. Too often she felt like she was in the wrong place at the wrong time. Too often she knew too much and yet not enough. She was often everywhere, but spread thinly about. There was a piece inside her that was the wrong size and threw her off balance.

The day her younger sisters disappeared, Hildur had felt terrible from the moment she woke. She hadn't been able to get out of bed, let alone put on her backpack and board the bus. And so she'd stayed home when her sisters went off to school.

If Hildur had been around, maybe her sisters never would have disappeared. She had grasped this possibility at the age of ten and lived with the burden since. Every year on the cusp of October and November, the heaviness within her swelled.

Hildur swallowed her last bite of sausage, washed it down with a swig of *kvass*, and looked out the window. If it weren't so dark, she'd be able to see the mountain and the avalanche barriers that protected the town at its base. A somehow endearing human attempt to control the uncontrollable.

Tinna laid her hand over Hildur's and turned to face her. 'Hrafntinna's legacy can be hard to bear. It came to you. You didn't choose it.'

Now, this was a subject Hildur truly hated. Tinna meant well but didn't realise her words added to the weight of Hildur's burden. Just now Hildur had no interest in listening to any explanations about her familial inheritance.

'Uh-huh. I just don't feel like talking about it right now.'

Tinna patted her niece's hand and urged her to take a second slice of sausage.

Once upon a time, Tinna's *amma*, her grandmother Hrafntinna, had been Iceland's best-known seer. She saw everything. She spoke to nature, and nature spoke back. Many Icelanders travelled long distances to see Hrafntinna at the Fjord of Swans and seek her advice. Back then, talking to the hidden people had been completely normal. These days, it was considered a sign of mental illness. Instead, analysts in dark suits were consulted regarding forecasts for the upcoming year, and those analysts lived in waterfront homes in Reykjavík, not the Fjord of Swans.

According to old folk tradition, the gift of foresight was passed down, unpredictably so. Tinna said Hrafntinna's gift had skipped a couple of generations and been passed down to Hildur. But the gift had diluted somewhere along the way. Hildur never knew anything specific about the future. She could tell if something awful was about to happen, but she couldn't say what, where, or when. A moment before the misfortune occurred, the heaviness inside her would swell, but because she never knew its source, she could never forestall the imminent misery.

And the wave of heaviness had been exceptionally massive on that snowy winter morning twenty-five years ago.

As Hildur entered adulthood, Tinna had suggested the gift of foresight was the cause of her anxious spells. Hildur wasn't sure what she herself believed, but it didn't involve a virgin birth or the subjugation of women. And so she'd left the church the moment she came of age.

Hildur was still gazing out into the blackness. An interior design programme was blaring from the television in the living room. Tinna began to gather up the dishes and gave Hildur a hug as she walked past.

'Your shoulders feel hard. You're going to look like a starving polar bear before long,' Tinna said. 'You're remembering to eat the rest of the week, aren't you?' she asked, taking the dessert from the fridge and setting it on the table: fruit salad topped with whipped cream and fatty yoghurt.

'Yes, I eat. But I also work out a lot.' Hildur decided to change the subject. 'I get a new colleague tomorrow. A Finnish policeman is coming in on the afternoon flight. We're going to be partners.'

A mischievous smile broke out on Tinna's face. 'Be sure to let him know you see elves who tell you what's going to happen in the future. Foreigners love that stuff.'

'OK, I'll be sure to let him know. I'll also tell him to try rotten shark,' Hildur said, bursting into laughter. 'A traditional delicacy loved by all the locals.'

At the door, Tinna gave her niece a long hug and put a blue plastic box in her hand.

'I packed up the rest of the sausage for you to take home. Heat it up in the microwave for lunch,' Tinna said, lightly pinching her niece's cheek. 'Promise me you'll get out and do something fun too. Go see your neighbour a little more often.'

'Oh, you've heard about that?'

'Everyone knows you two have a thing. My neighbour says Freysi is being constantly pestered in the teachers' staffroom as to when he plans on proposing since he's found such a good catch.'

'Tinna! We're not even dating. We just, well, hang out sometimes.'

'I know, I know. You two just have all the fun you can. Don't worry about what anyone else says.'

Tinna gave her niece a final hug, and Hildur stepped out into the night. She turned on her headlight, strapped on her helmet, and bungee-corded the leftovers to the back of her bike.

Thanks to a tailwind from the south, the ride downtown only lasted ten minutes. Water splattered from the tyres to Hildur's trouser legs, and as she approached her home, the rain turned to snow.

Hildur's house stood between the fire station and the police station. *You couldn't find a safer place to live*, she reflected. The hospital was less than a kilometre from her front door, as was the town's only pub.

Hildur spotted a big, black raven on the illuminated tower of the fire station. Ísafjörður had a sizable population of ravens, so there was nothing unusual about seeing one. But the bird perched on the roof looked unusually large and seemed to be staring right at Hildur.

In northern mythology, ravens delivered messages to the gods and decided which warriors would live, which would die, and which of the dead would enter paradise: the bright halls of Valhalla.

This raven croaked three times. That meant death.

Chapter 5

'Don't worry, this is completely normal,' the flight attendant said, attempting to reassure Jakob. His knuckles were white from gripping the armrest. His face was sheet-white too.

Just then, the prop plane lost a little altitude. The drop felt like a cold, nasty punch in the gut. A groan escaped Jakob's lips. 'Dear God. Are we falling?' he gasped, looking the flight attendant in the eye.

Jakob Johanson was sitting on the aisle, but because the seat next to him was empty, he could see the mountains outside the oval window. Through a gauzy veil of clouds, he spied an uninhabited-looking plateau and narrow strips of sea. The fjord-slashed terrain looked strange from above. The mountains weren't peaked; it was as if the tops had been sliced off with a massive knife.

But he was having a hard time enjoying the view. The aeroplane lurched, and Jakob's grip on the armrest tightened again. The flight attendant sitting in the cabin-crew seat opposite gave him an encouraging smile and shut her eyes. That's what people who were sure of themselves did. *I know all about this. I've been through it before. Trust me.*

'No, we're not falling,' she said, opening her eyes. 'This turbulence is totally normal. It happens every time the plane passes the mountains and turns toward the fjord for the descent.'

Did she say every time? Jakob thought to himself. *The turbulence is this bad every time?* He knew the prop plane was scheduled to fly this route twice a day year-round, and he'd been warned about last-minute delays. Domestic flights between Reykjavík and Ísafjörður often had to be cancelled due to poor visibility or strong winds.

The flight attendant took a deep breath, then told Jakob flight conditions were particularly good today.

Jakob had made a note of the strange custom on the airport bus. When the locals were communicating something they felt was important, they inhaled sharply before they spoke. Perhaps the intake of breath was intended to emphasise their message, but to Jakob's ears it sounded as if the co-conversant were fighting for their life.

Then again, he felt like he was fighting for *his* life, too. The aeroplane started shaking and tilted violently.

Jakob had arrived in Iceland that morning and decided to connect directly to a domestic flight. The drive to the furthest corner of Iceland's western fjords would have taken over six hours, and Jakob hadn't felt like fooling around with rental cars. Especially when evening fell so early.

'We're landing in ten minutes,' the flight attendant said in a soft voice. She nodded at the window. 'You should enjoy the view until then.'

'I don't think I can,' Jakob said, twisting his face up in what he hoped was a friendly smile but felt more like an awkward grimace. 'I'm just waiting for this to be over.'

'Are you going to be staying in Ísafjörður long?' the flight attendant asked. Evidently, she was trying to distract the passenger from his fear of flying.

'At least six months. I'll be working there.'

'Wow, the whole winter! You'll have plenty of chances to fly this route if you have business to tend to in the capital.'

'I think I'd rather ride a bike next time.'

Jakob heard the flight attendant stifle a burst of laughter.

He gave her a longer look. *Quite a vision,* he thought to himself. She appeared to be about his height. Thick blonde hair, dark eyes, and a broad smile that formed tiny dimples under the eyes. Her demeanour radiated confidence and experience, even toughness. That might have been because of her commanding posture. She sat on the crew seat as if it were a throne.

A moment had passed since the plane had last shuddered. Jakob felt a bit more relaxed. 'Where are you going to be working?' the flight attendant asked.

'I'm a police officer. From Finland. I'm here on exchange.'

'In Ísafjörður? Not even all Icelanders know where to place it on a map. How did you end up here?'

Jakob wasn't sure how to answer. They only had a few minutes left before landing. That wasn't enough time to explain everything – not that he wanted to. The divorce. How his Norwegian ex-wife, Lena, was preventing him from seeing his child and disparaging him to anyone she met. The personal crisis that had triggered insomnia, robbed him of his desire to live and made him quiver in fear and rage. How he'd been forced to change professions and then surroundings to keep his head from exploding.

Formerly a biology teacher, Jakob now attended the national Police University College in Finland. He only had a few credits left to complete his degree. At the college, he'd heard about Nordcop, a pan-Nordic exchange programme for officers in training and instructors at police colleges. Jakob had wanted to come to Iceland. He'd seen an interesting television documentary about the country's westernmost region, the Westfjords. The landscape, nature, and quiet had made an impression on him. He'd craved peace, calmer waters. Not even double pay could have lured him to a metropolis like Copenhagen or Stockholm. After all he'd been through, Jakob yearned to be surrounded by silence and space. So he'd emailed the police department in Ísafjörður, the biggest small town in the Westfjords, and enquired about the possibility of an internship. To his delight, he'd quickly received an answer in the affirmative.

Jakob took a deep breath and folded his hands in his lap. Maybe it would be better to talk to the flight attendant about a less fraught topic. He didn't want to lie, but he didn't have to tell everything either. That wasn't avoiding the truth; it was choosing a point of view.

During the most difficult period of the post-divorce crisis and custody battle, Jakob had picked up a new hobby. He'd read an article about the beneficial effects of handcrafts. According to the neuroscientist and psychologist interviewed for the article, handcrafts relaxed the mind, slowed the heart rate, and lowered blood pressure. Jakob had decided to give it a shot. He'd already tried everything else: sleep aids, exercise, meditation, therapy, a support group for victims of narcissists. *It's not like knitting sweaters is going to hurt*, he'd reflected at the time. He'd been living in Tampere back then; that's where the police college was. He'd marched into the first craft store he came across and announced he wanted to buy patterns, yarn, and needles to make a sweater. He'd known a big, bearded man who worked out regularly wasn't exactly the shop's standard clientele, but he'd been given excellent service nonetheless. The saleswoman had helped him pick the right yarn and needles, shown him how to read the pattern, and told him about useful knitting groups on Facebook. Jakob had ordered his yarn from the shop on Ilmarinkatu ever since.

Jakob had fallen in love with Icelandic sweaters in particular. The upper part, for which he'd quickly learned to use the correct term *yoke*, brought just the right amount of challenge to his knitting.

Icelandic *lopi* yarn was pleasant to work with and easy to knit. Knitting helped Jakob regulate his stress and tolerate the inevitable disappointments of life. Naturally, it was frustrating every time he dropped a stitch or made a mistake. But he just unravelled what he'd done, fixed the mistake, and knitted again. The sensation of disappointment turned into one of success.

Ultimately, knitting was a lot like life. Unpredictable. Chaotic, even. It didn't matter if you were the one wielding the needles, choosing the yarn, and following the instructions, the outcome was never guaranteed. Something could always happen. Sometimes it was better to follow the instructions, sometimes not. You could never know if a sweater was going to turn out right until you knitted it and saw the outcome.

These knitting-related observations gave Jakob self-confidence. He never would have known what a hateful person his ex-wife Lena could be if they'd never met. But if they'd never met, he wouldn't have Matias. And in the end, his son was the most important thing in his life, even if the present circumstances prevented them from spending time together. Yes, it hurt. But it didn't make him a loser.

Jakob leaned his head against the headrest and decided to tell the flight attendant about his sweaters.

'I had some room for adventure open up in my life. I knit Icelandic sweaters as a hobby, but I'd never been to this part of the world before. I got an opportunity to mix business with pleasure, so here I am.'

Jakob noticed the flight attendant eyeing the sweater he was wearing. It was one he'd knitted himself, and anyone who'd ever knitted would have recognised the pattern: Riddari, one of the world's most popular Icelandic sweater designs. Jakob had knit this particular Riddari a few years ago. These days, he designed most of the sweaters he made. It brought a fascinating extra challenge to his pastime.

The flight attendant scratched her head and ran her fingers through her hair from the roots to the tips. 'The mysterious sweater-man from Finland.' She leaned toward Jakob and lowered her voice. 'If you find yourself missing the sauna, there's a nice one at the public pool. There's a men's sauna session several times a week.'

Jakob was sure the flight attendant had winked at him. Was she flirting with him? He couldn't tell. He was intrigued, but it had been years since he'd flirted with anyone. He didn't even believe it would be possible again. Maybe he wasn't totally rusty after all.

His face broke out in a boyish smile. 'Aren't there any mixed saunas?'

The flight attendant smiled back and let her gaze slide down from Jakob's eyes. 'You'll have to go somewhere more private for that.'

By now the aeroplane was at an altitude of no more than a few hundred metres. Its path curved toward the butt of the fjord, executed a sharp turn over a residential area, and set course for the narrow runway near the mountain. But it seemed to be arcing too far to the left. All that could be seen out the window now was water. Jakob started to panic again.

'The pilot has to make a U-turn. Because of the wind, we have to land facing north, toward the sea. The turn is what makes it impossible to land here if visibility is poor. The mountains are so close,' the flight attendant said. 'But visibility is excellent today.'

The plane's tyres hit the runway, and the aircraft braked hard. Jakob jerked forward in his seat, and the space was so cramped his knees grazed the legs of the flight attendant sitting across from him.

'Yes, the view certainly seems excellent,' Jakob said, feeling a thrill bubbling up inside him. He'd survived the thirty-five-minute rollercoaster of a flight in one piece.

The flight attendant reached for the microphone. She gave the welcome spiel first in Icelandic and then in English. 'Welcome to Ísafjörður. Please remain in your seats with your seatbelts fastened until the pilot has turned off the seatbelt lights.'

After making this announcement, she opened the door at the front of the plane, and the airstairs lowered to the cold tarmac. The wind blew into the cabin as the passengers put on coats, hats, and gloves and exited the plane one at a time. Jakob had stowed his coat and backpack in the overhead locker. He was finally able to open it once the aisle had emptied of other passengers.

'See you,' the flight attendant said, when it came Jakob's turn to exit the aircraft. Jakob would have bet the yarn for his next sweater that she watched him walk down the airstairs. He could feel a pleasant warmth on his back.

Jakob followed the other passengers across the hundred metres to the tiny terminal cladded in corrugated metal. Two dozen people swarmed by the small baggage carousel to wait for belongings that had been transported in the hold. Eventually, a hatch in the wall opened, and an airport employee began lifting luggage onto the belt. Jakob retrieved his wheeled grey bag with the backpack straps. He'd had it when he Interrailed around Europe and met Lena amid the tourist-office chaos at the Budapest train station. Lena had been travelling alone, too, and the pair of them had immediately struck up a companionship. They'd ended up spending a romantic week together in Budapest. They walked along the Danube, bathed at the spas, ate at the old cellar restaurants on the Pest side of the river, and fell in love. It was like the movie *Before Sunrise*, except they weren't in Vienna and didn't say goodbye on the last day; instead, they headed to Norway together, embarked on a relationship and moved to Finland for Jakob's work.

Jakob scanned the minuscule airport. The waiting area was furnished with a leather corner sofa where a dark-haired, stern-looking woman about his age sat in an ankle-length parka. She was holding a sheet of paper with *Jacob* scrawled on it in marker.

Jakob walked over, extended his hand, and introduced himself in English.

'It looks like you're here to meet me. I'm Jakob. Jakob with a k.' Jakob was born in Germany, where his parents had lived and worked for a few years when he was very young. They'd wanted to give him an international name.

Jakob was caught off guard by the firmness of the woman's handshake. She gripped his hand as if it were a barbell.

'I'm Hildur. Hildur with an h. Nice to meet you. How was the flight?'

'Horrible, but I survived.'

Hildur glanced at the exit, crumpled the piece of paper in her hand, and tossed it in a nearby bin. 'I'll take you to your apartment and show you where the police station is. We'll start work tomorrow.'

No pointless small talk, just right down to it, Jakob thought, as he nodded in agreement.

Hildur took the bag from Jakob and started pulling it behind her. 'Today you're a guest. Starting tomorrow you can carry your own bags.'

The glass doors gave onto a windswept car park with the tall, flat-topped mountains rising beyond. Jakob looked up and reflected it was the mountain range he'd just flown over in a prop plane.

Hildur walked up to a police car, tossed the bag in the boot of the Škoda, and slammed it shut. Jakob climbed in the passenger seat.

'Thanks for picking me up. There probably aren't any taxis in such a small place.'

'We have taxis, at least two of them,' Hildur said, starting up the car. 'But I was happy to pick you up. You and I are going to be partners. I wanted to see what sort of guy they sent us.'

A loud, sudden honk made Jakob jump. He looked out the passenger window and saw a big red Toyota Land Cruiser. The flight attendant he'd just met was smiling cheerfully at him from the wheel. Jakob raised a hand in greeting. Then the flight attendant hit the gas, and the Land Cruiser raced out of the lot and onto the road leading to the village.

Guðrún Davíðsdóttir, fairy godmother of the skies.

Hildur shot Jakob a questioning look.

'We met on the flight. She helped distract me when I was feeling really terrible.'

Hildur's lips curved up in a broad smile. 'Guðrún is good at that! I know her really well; we went to school together. She spends winters working as a flight attendant and filling in at the daycare. During the summer she's a guide for cruise-ship tourists. She can get even the most obnoxious Americans to form a straight line.'

Jakob was surprised. 'That's quite a few jobs.'

'The island life. Everyone does a bit of everything.' Hildur flicked her turn signal. 'Guðrún is pretty, hmm, adventurous. But she has a soft side, too: she owns a yarn shop in the village.'

Now isn't that lucky, Jakob thought to himself, as he leaned his head back against the headrest. Darkness had begun to fall over the fjord. He let his gaze slide beyond the windscreen. The town up ahead looked tiny, and there wasn't much traffic. The orange glow of the streetlamps shimmered on the dark surface of the sea. It was a soothing sight. Jakob felt like he had arrived – if not at home, then at least at a stop on the way there.

Chapter 6

The good book says: the sluggard will not plough by reason of the cold; he will return empty-handed from the harvest.

The cold has come, and I have ploughed. I have ploughed plenty. My hands ache. I sit on a rock and let my gaze rest on the sea. I am weary, but I feel light and energised.

I am finally here. At long last, the time has come to carry out the plan I've been hatching since my loss. The plan is what has kept me going, even in my darkest moments.

It took Solomon seven years to build his temple. It took me seven years to bring my plan to fruition. That's how much time has passed since they departed this world.

I saw a pod of killer whales today. Killer whales so close to shore are a rare sight this late in the year. That's when I knew today was the day I would execute the first phase of my plan.

I smoked a cigarette and calmly watched the whales leap. The black-and-white creatures looked gentle, like the cute, trained performers of aquariums. But their appearance is deceiving. Killer whales are torpedoes who hunt in groups. They're predators who like to play with their victims. Sometimes killer whales attack other whales, and when they do, they dine slowly and at length. The bigger the mammal, the longer it takes for death to come.

Today's victim was big, but death came quickly. Well, I'm not a predator, nor do I hunt in a group.

My good deeds bear witness that I'm on the right track.

Chapter 7

November 2019, Ísafjörður

Beta opened the break-room fridge. There ought to have been one more frozen Dr Oetker tomato and mozzarella pizza she could heat up for lunch. But when she pulled open the door to the freezer compartment, she started. She gawped at the freezer's contents, or rather the tiny sliver that was visible, and slammed the door.

Irritated, Beta walked to her desk and grabbed the phone. In a small town, the tasks of the police chief included not only investigations and administrative duties but routine matters no one else had time to take care of. Her small-town budget wouldn't stretch to hire an assistant. She couldn't even afford jail guards. If someone was causing trouble and needed to be kept overnight in the holding cell, one of her staff had to do overtime.

Beta pulled up Júlíus's number. After two rings, a relaxed male voice answered. Beta introduced herself, although she knew Júlíus recognised the number.

'We have a little problem here. The freezer compartment in our fridge is frozen solid. It ate at least one pizza. The fridge has been making this loud hum for the past few days. It needs looking at.'

Beta grunted a couple of times in agreement with Júlíus' response and ended the call, satisfied. Júlíus was the county's facilities manager and he was over in the next village, bleeding a radiator at the business centre. He would be by at the end of the week to replace the fridge.

There was a decent grill below the police station. The smell of greasy sausages happened to waft up just then, and Beta was hungry. She decided to go down and get two hot dogs with the works. A heavy lunch would help her get through the long shift ahead.

At the entrance to the station, she ran into Hildur with a man at her heels.

Hildur made introductions. Last names are rarely used in Iceland on such occasions; first names are enough. 'Elísabet, this is Jakob from Finland. He arrived yesterday. Jakob, this is Elísabet Baldursdóttir, our boss.'

'Nice to meet you,' Jakob said, extending a hand.

Beta shook it and welcomed her new subordinate: 'Just call me Beta. Everybody calls me by my nickname.'

She eyed Jakob and decided she liked what she saw. He made the same impression in person as he had during the video interview: calm, curious, not so young anymore.

Beta said she was going to get hot dogs from the grill. She offered to bring Hildur and Jakob lunch, too, but they weren't hungry. 'OK. We'll talk more in a minute,' she said, hurrying out the glass door.

Hildur and Jakob stepped inside. Stairs rose from the vestibule to the second floor, where there was a small lobby furnished with two sofas. A stack of old magazines stood on the corner of a coffee table. A picture of the president and a framed map of Iceland hung on the wall.

'So besides Beta, those working in investigations include me, and now you. Seven junior officers handle the patrols. Óliver and Ari graduated from the police academy a couple of years ago, Sigga has been in the field for a few years now, and Tómas will graduate next spring. Then there's Elín, Atli, and Svenni, who haven't had any training, but that's just the way it is.'

Jakob wanted to make sure he heard correctly: 'Haven't had any training?'

'Yup. For the life of us, we can't get trained officers to come work out here. You have to play the cards you're dealt. One partner has to have official police training, but the other one can be a forklift driver who got fired from the cannery.'

Jakob was unable to conceal his bewilderment. 'Wait, how is that even possible?'

Hildur shrugged. 'It always works out somehow.'

They stopped at the large map, where the Westfjords had been outlined in red.

Jakob stroked his beard as he studied the map. 'Lots of valleys and mountains.' He knew he hadn't come to some rapid-growth urban area. The Westfjords was Iceland's most sparsely populated region, and distances were long. In some cases, it looked like there might be several hundred kilometres between villages. 'So the ten of us are responsible for all law enforcement in the area, including traffic?'

Hildur jabbed a forefinger at two names marked with yellow pins. 'These villages have little police stations. Four officers each. If someone gets sick, they borrow a body from another village.'

Jakob looked at the consonant-heavy place names at the ends of the long fjords and decided it might be a while before he learned how to pronounce them correctly.

The lobby gave onto a narrow, windowless corridor with three doors off it. The first led to Beta's office, the second to the break room, and a little conference room lay behind the third. The corridor ended in an open-plan workspace with southern views toward the mountains and the butt of the fjord.

Hildur flicked on the lights. 'This is our area. You can sit there across from me. If you want a cubicle divider, we can get one from storage downstairs.'

The desk came with a rolling filing cabinet and an upholstered office chair that had seen better days.

'Toilets, showers, and locker rooms are downstairs, and so are the cells. There's a smelly fridge and an oven in the break room; there's a little grill downstairs where you can get food from eight in the morning until eleven at night.'

'Sounds good,' Jakob said, sitting on what was to be his desk chair.

Just then, Beta appeared in the doorway with two steaming hot dogs. 'I see you two have got into the spirit already. Should we sit in here? My office is a mess, and you can't really fit three people in it without suffocating.' She grabbed a stool next to the wall as the aroma of warm sausage filled the room.

'We'll go get coffee first,' Hildur said. 'Jakob, I can show you how the coffeemaker works. I assume you drink coffee?'

'Of course. Black with sugar if there is any.'

Hildur pressed the start button on the single-serve coffee machine and let strong coffee drip into two cups. She found the sugar bowl in the cupboard and tipped in a spoonful. Then she added a second spoonful and looked questioningly at Jakob.

'One more,' Jakob said with a big smile. 'It's my only vice.'

Hildur shook her head incredulously and handed the red mug to her new colleague. 'Here's your sugar with coffee. *Samfylkingin.* You get to be a social democrat. You'll find a mug for every political party and football team in Iceland in this cupboard.'

When they returned to their office, Beta started going through practicalities. 'For the duration of your exchange, Hildur will be your partner. I understood you're especially interested in the missing children's unit. You'll have a chance to do some work with them and assist in criminal investigations. Your working language as partners will be English, and Hildur will do all the talking in the field.'

'Got it,' Jakob said. He didn't speak Icelandic but was fluent in Nynorsk, which would help him in picking up the local language.

'Iceland has always had a close relationship with the United States, so almost everyone speaks English. But some people are too shy, so let's be understanding. If you have any questions at all, ask me or Hildur. We have a very small police station here that's responsible for a rather large area. There are no break-ins or car thefts to speak of, and violent crimes are rare in Iceland.'

'Sounds like *Moominvalley*,' Jakob said.

Beta and Hildur smiled. Everyone in Iceland knew the Finnish cartoon characters the Moomins, the Hemulen, and Little My.

'There's an average of about one murder a year,' Hildur said, then quickly clarified: 'But there are plenty of other problems.' She listed drink driving, domestic violence, driving without a licence, and narcotics-related crime – all the things that kept them busy every day. The number of sex crimes had grown markedly in recent years as well.

'Same thing in Finland.' Jakob explained that while sexual assault wasn't necessarily becoming more common in Finland, it was being reported more often, and that was visible in the statistics.

Hildur and Beta recognised the pattern. These days victims were more likely to talk about what they'd suffered and report crimes. In many ways, Iceland had been a model country for equality. After all, the first democratically elected female president in the world had been Icelandic, laws regarding equal pay between genders had been legislated for years, and Iceland's parental leave model had steered fathers into staying home with their children for two decades now. However, sex crimes and – in particular – violence against women had remained in the shadows. Especially if a crime took place within the family or extended family, the tendency was to sweep it under the rug. And the more influential the perpetrator, the higher the chances a crime went unreported. Deals were made to keep things quiet. The victim was pressured into silence. The #MeToo movement had shone a light on the extent of the problem. 'The scum rises to the surface more often these days,' Hildur summarised, draining her coffee.

Beta glanced at her watch. Her next remote meeting was about to begin, and she wanted to pick up the pace. 'We'll provide you with a uniform and all the necessary gear: handcuffs, telescoping baton, pepper spray. Have Hildur take you down to the storage to get what you need.'

'What about a firearm?' Jakob asked.

'Icelandic police don't carry firearms. They're kept in a locked compartment in the patrol car. Special permission is required from your superior to use them. And because you don't have the authority to act as a police officer in Iceland, you're not allowed to use a gun here,' Beta said.

'Oh yes, that's right,' Jakob said.

He didn't appear surprised by the national policy regarding firearms. The police in Norway didn't carry guns either. Police firearms were a regular topic of debate, but no changes had been made to the legislation yet. And Icelanders were in no way anti-gun. There were actually quite a few guns in the country because a lot of people liked to hunt.

Beta didn't miss carrying a gun. In her experience, the average Icelandic police officer rarely needed a firearm in the field. 'If we're dealing with a dangerous situation, we call in a special armed unit from Reykjavík. Over the last ten years, we've needed their help once here in the Westfjords.'

Jakob nodded, opened his leather shoulder bag, and reached in. He pulled out an unfinished sweater and knitting needles and began untangling the yarn. Hildur and Beta fell silent and stared at the pearl-grey start of a wool sweater in Jakob's lap.

'You don't mind if I knit while we talk, do you?'

'Of course not. I was just thinking, so soon? You've only been in Iceland a little over a day, and you already have a sweater half done.' Beta eyed the hem Jakob had knit. The result was surprisingly neat. *Looks like he knows his way around a pair of needles*, she thought to herself. She was frustrated she'd had so little time to knit in recent years.

Jakob glanced at Beta and picked up his needles. 'Knitting isn't considered a very masculine hobby in Finland, so I'm used to raised eyebrows. But knitting helps clear my thoughts. It offers a good counterbalance when life gets hard.'

Hildur observed Jakob's quick-fingered work with the yarn. 'Beta, maybe you and I should start knitting, too.'

'Speak for yourself; I'm totally Zen. I'd knit if I had time, but the kids have been sick lately and my husband is always travelling for work.' Beta stretched her arms. 'I have a video call with Reykjavík starting soon. Administrative planning. The joys of a supervisory position.' She rose from her stool and walked to her office, leaving Hildur and Jakob alone in the room.

Hildur studied her new colleague and decided she was pleased. Jakob seemed like a nice guy she'd find it easy to get along with. Not too stuffy, but not a cocky meathead either. A little stiff, maybe, but that might be because of the language barrier. They compared the differences between police training in Finland and Iceland. Then Jakob started to read bulletins about the activities of the Icelandic police, and Hildur focused on her paperwork. The office filled with the steady tap of fingers against keyboard and the clack of knitting needles.

After a while, Jakob broke the silence.

'Are those your children?' he asked, looking at a postcard-sized photograph of two pigtailed girls in snowsuits tacked to the corkboard by Hildur's desk.

'No.'

Hildur stared at the papers in front of her, hoping Jakob would drop the subject. The photo was one of the few pictures of her sisters she'd found among her parents' belongings. Probably the only one, as a matter of fact. Hildur spent more time at work than at home, so she'd brought it to the office. But she'd forgotten to stash it in a drawer, hide it from her new colleague's prying eyes before his arrival. She cursed her forgetfulness.

'They just look a lot like you,' Jakob said, as one skein of yarn ended and he started in on another.

'They're my sisters,' Hildur said in a quiet voice. 'Or were.' She continued staring at her papers, letting it be understood she had no interest in continuing the conversation.

Jakob's expression abruptly changed. A stiffness fell over his face, and his gaze turned inward. 'I'm sorry; I didn't mean to be nosy.'

Hildur winced. Maybe she'd been too harsh. Jakob hadn't meant any harm by asking about the photo. He wanted to get to know her and saw a picture of children next to her desk. The prominently displayed photograph was an open invitation to discuss the people in it. She was the one who'd forgotten it there.

Hildur drew a couple of breaths and wondered what to say. If it were wholly up to her, she wouldn't say anything. But sooner or later Jakob would hear the story somewhere else, and some of the rumours about her sisters' fate were wholly fabricated. Maybe it would be better if she told him herself, so she wouldn't have to correct any embellishments after the fact. Besides, she and Jakob were partners now, and they needed to be able to trust each other completely. 'I didn't mean to be rude. It's a kind of . . . um, complicated subject.'

Jakob stopped knitting. He didn't say anything; he simply looked at Hildur. He was giving her the opportunity to continue without subjecting her to further probing.

'They're my little sisters, Björk and Rósa.' Hildur explained they had disappeared twenty-five years before. One day they just never came home from school. 'They were six and eight when they vanished. That picture was taken that same winter . . .'

'That's awful. I'm so sorry,' Jakob said and looked as if he truly meant it. The stony face had softened, and the openness had returned to his gaze.

Hildur rubbed her temples. 'A lot of people have guesses as to what happened, mostly about how they somehow went missing in a tunnel, but no one knows. They were at school like any other day, but they never got on the school bus that afternoon.'

Even now, the hardest thing was the uncertainty. No one seemed to know anything. No one had seen the girls after the school day ended. Hildur's parents had searched for them, as had the neighbours and the police and a volunteer search crew, but in vain. No clues were ever found.

'It was like they'd suddenly vanished from this world,' Hildur said, her mouth emitting a sound reminiscent of a deflating balloon. 'Gone. In the blink of an eye.'

Many suspected the girls had drowned in the sea or got lost in the mountains during the snowstorm. But no trace of them was ever found.

'My parents never got over it. They died not long after my sisters went missing,' Hildur said.

In the days following the disappearance, Hildur's mother had spent hours on end at the mirror, furiously brushing her hair. Hildur remembered how her mother's raw skin began to bleed from the brushing. Neither the hair in the bathroom sink nor the blood oozing from her scalp could get her to stop. Eventually, she cut her hair short and took to wearing a scarf. 'They decided to sell the house and move to Reykjavík. I don't think they would have been happy there. But staying would have been hard, too.'

'Yes,' Jakob said, pulling the sweater forward on the circular needles to start a new row. 'Sometimes it's better to leave and get a change of scenery just to stay alive.'

Hildur stared at her hands before continuing: 'They never made the move. They died in a car crash a little over a year after my sisters disappeared. And now I investigate traffic violations and lead the missing children's unit for rural Iceland. Ironic, isn't it?'

Hildur asked if Jakob had any children of his own.

'I have a five-year-old boy. His name is Matias. He's in Norway now.'

'In Norway?'

'It's a long, convoluted story. I'll tell you some other time, if you don't mind.' The look Jakob shot Hildur made it plain it was not the time for further questions.

They chatted for a minute about daily routines at the station, then Hildur went over the most pressing cases. The owner of a nearby fish-processing plant was suspected of paying work-ers under the counter. They would have to search the place and talk to the managers and employees. Jón from Fjallavegur would be interrogated soon, and she had a presentation to prepare for next week's meeting of the Association of Women's and Chil-dren's Shelters.

At the end of the day, Hildur told Jakob where the heated public pool was, showed him a few jogging routes on the map, and reminded him the grocery store in the centre of town closed its doors at 7 p.m.

Hildur was the last to leave the office. She turned off the cof-feemaker and killed the lights. By five, it was already pitch-black outside. She went down to the grill and picked up a couple of pepperoni pizzas. As she waited for her order, she typed out a message to Freysi. He invited her over.

Hildur walked home, but she didn't climb her own stairs; she went around to the back, where the entrance to Freysi's flat was. She reached for the handle, opened the door, and stepped inside. The floor squeaked cosily, as was only fitting in an old wooden house.

Freysi was standing there in a thin white T-shirt and tight tracksuit bottoms. He took the pizzas from Hildur and smiled as he watched her remove her fur-trimmed parka and try to find a place for it on the coat-rack.

'The highly anticipated yet unexpected visit from the detec-tive. I just got back from a jog, so I have no reason to go out again tonight.'

The entryways in old houses were small. Freysi only had to store one person's outerwear, but even so the tiny room was over-flowing. The coat-rack creaked ominously under the mountain of coats as Hildur draped hers over the top. The shelves from a Swedish home furnishings company were stuffed with mittens, beanies, and running gear. When it looked like the coat would stay put, Hildur carefully backed away from the rack.

'I just might need to perform a thorough search of the premises,' she said, squeezing Freysi's arm.

He pressed his lips to Hildur's neck. 'Only if I get to use my baton on Ms Detective first.'

'Listen, before we do anything else, we're going to eat some pizza,' Hildur said, pulling the door between the entryway and the living room shut behind her.

The snowfall that night was exceptionally heavy. The next morning, winter had arrived.

Chapter 8

July 2019, Hornstrandir

The sun shone from a cloudless sky. The rippling sea looked like a slinky sequined skirt. There were no waves, no wind; the only sound was the twitter of birds. It was still morning, but the temperature had already climbed to 15°C. Lísa decided to take a break. She took off her windbreaker and slipped it through the side straps of her backpack. She filled her water bottle at a small, swift-moving stream and took a sip from the bottle's mouth. The fresh, ice-cold water slid slowly to her stomach.

The day was exceptionally beautiful. Lísa inhaled the scent of grass. She listened to the songbirds warble. There was a reason Icelanders called weather like this 'creamy'; it was almost too good to be true.

And it was going to be the most important summer of her life. The week before, Lísa had learned her prep-school grades had earned her a spot at the University of Iceland Medical School. She was going to become a doctor! If everything went well and she applied herself, she could eventually become a heart surgeon. It was a thrilling thought. She'd read and reread the letter of acceptance until she knew it by heart.

She could be anything anyone else was. She could dream of having the things others her age dreamed of: a good career, a home of her own, maybe even children. Above all, she could be just as good as everyone else.

The road to this point had been far from smooth. Lísa had spent sixteen years living with a foster family on a farm in north-eastern Iceland. Her foster parents had been the only parents she'd ever known. She'd been taken into custody as a newborn and had never met her biological father or mother.

Lísa had grown up in a safe home with two other children. Her parents had treated her as well as their birth children, but even so, Lísa had sometimes felt like an outsider in the family. The older she got, the stronger the feeling grew. No one enquired as to her preferences regarding which television programme to watch or their plans for the Easter holidays. She was always welcome to participate in the family's activities, but no one cared how she felt about them.

And so she'd gradually started distancing herself from the rest of the family. She had fewer and fewer things in common with her foster siblings. She had a different disposition; she was interested in different things. She didn't want to live in the countryside and look after cows and horses anymore. She wanted to do something else.

After finishing her mandatory schooling, Lísa had hoped to attend prep school in the capital. The prep school in downtown Reykjavík was one of the best in the country. Many students in the natural sciences programme went on to medical school, and that was what Lísa had wanted to do too. Luckily, her parents hadn't opposed her move. Just the opposite: once she'd been accepted, they'd done everything in their power to help her find and furnish a sublet. They'd even given her a couple of million krónur for living expenses so she wouldn't have to take student loans for her studies.

Even though her parents had generously supported Lísa as she strived for her dreams, she couldn't help but notice they hadn't seemed the least bit disappointed by her departure. It was almost as if they'd been relieved she'd decided to move out of the house so young. During her first year at prep school, she'd gone home for Christmas and Easter, but since then her visits had grown less frequent. Her parents had put spending money in her account until she turned eighteen and checked in on her now and again. She'd last called them at Christmas and hadn't heard from them since. Lísa couldn't explain why things had gone the way they had. Relations had gradually cooled, and eventually, contact had simply stopped.

Lísa shook the sad thoughts from her mind. After all, she'd just got what she wanted: acceptance to medical school. Besides, she'd grown close to her lovely landlords in Reykjavík: the retired couple Pétur and Margrét had become like family to her. Margrét, a former teacher, had helped Lísa prepare for her chemistry and mathematics exams, and Pétur had encouraged her to maintain her interest in outdoor activities. Pétur was the one who'd organised this trek for her. Bought her bus and boat tickets to the nature reserve, booked her lodgings along the route, and made sure she'd packed enough clothes and food for the three-day hike.

She'd dreamed of visiting the Hornstrandir Nature Reserve for ages. The social media posts of her hiking club friends had included stunning photographs of sheer mountains dropping into the sea, the Arctic foxes that lived on the shore, and meadows that went on as far as the eye could see. After receiving her acceptance letter, she'd decided this was the landscape where she wanted to celebrate her initiation into medical school.

She took a small bag of dried catfish from the pocket of her hiking trousers and tore off a piece. The fish jerky was a filling, protein-rich trail snack and tasted good.

Today's route had taken her from the beach at Aðalvík over the plateau to the valley of Reyðardalur and from there to Hesteyri. Technically it had been an easy hike; Lísa had circled the highest mountains, and there had only been three hundred metres of altitude gain. That had made the trip longer but safer. When you were hiking alone, it was smartest to take as few risks as possible. Pétur had taught her that, too.

After five hours of walking and a couple of short snack breaks, Lísa saw a cabin that corresponded to the description Pétur had given her. It was a little black cottage that offered lodging for a few trekkers at a time.

Before entering, Lísa took off her hiking boots. She left her insoles outside to air. She would let her boots air for a while, too.

Lísa took hold of the wooden handle and pulled the door open. 'Hello,' she called out in a cheerful voice, then listened for a response. None came.

She looked around the compact entryway and noticed a handwritten note on a yellow stool: *I'm out collecting herbs in the highlands. The bunks are at the back of the house, through the door to your right. Make yourself at home. I'll be back by evening. Cash only. There's fish soup on the stove.*

Lísa walked down the hall to the bunk room. She took her sleeping bag out of her backpack and unrolled it on the lower bunk on the left-hand side. The mattresses were covered with flowered sheets. Lísa was delighted when she saw there were pillows – they were a luxury you didn't find at every guesthouse. Lísa tried not to spread her belongings around more than necessary. There would no doubt be others who showed up to spend the night, as there were only a handful of these cabins in the area.

The floors of the old house creaked cosily underfoot. The rich aroma of fish soup filled the little kitchen. Lísa's mouth began watering. Bowls and spoons had been set out next to the stove.

Lísa sat down at the kitchen table with a steaming serving of soup. She reached for the dolphin-shaped shaker and added pepper. A little fly buzzed furiously at the windowpane, no doubt trying to escape. Lísa stood to open the window and shooed it out. Seeing it fly off warmed her heart.

Lísa's gaze paused on the view outside the window. Low waves rolled into a beach of black sand. Flat-topped mountains towered against the deep blue sky. The fatigue from the hike weighed on her limbs, but her mind was clear and alert. And she was starving.

Lísa ate with a healthy appetite. Whoever made the soup hadn't stinted on ingredients. There were big chunks of fish, and the carrots and onions were cooked to perfection. They had a nice, firm texture, and didn't turn to mush in her mouth. The soup was seasoned with bay leaves, tomatoes, and salt. She would have to remember to give her special thanks for the meal. It was the most delicious soup she'd ever tasted.

And the last meal she ever ate.

Chapter 9

Two medium-sized cod lie twitching in the bottom of the boat. I raise the oar and brain the bigger one first. Then I look at the smaller fish. Its gills move as the poor thing tries to keep itself alive. I give it a firm whack behind the head. You can't let a fish wait too long to die. Suffering decreases the quality of the flesh. Evidently, it's because of the lactic acids.

I steer the boat back to shore. An incredible sense of accomplishment flows through my body. Two cod. They're easy to gut, and cod makes for a good fish hash. Or maybe I'll make a big pot of soup instead.

I cut the engine and lift it out of the water. The swells rock the boat as it slides toward the shore. Luckily the tide is rising, so I don't have to wade far. I pull the boat onto the beach and tie it up. Once on land, I slash the fish's throats, sever the gill arteries, and watch the blood drain away.

After all, a fisherman is a predator only when he brings home something to eat.

I watch the soup simmering on the stove. I set out a bowl, a big spoon, and a thick slice of bread. I sit at the table. Focus on my meal.

I know I'm doing the right thing. I received final confirmation when the sun was at its highest. I'd set aside the entire autumn to execute my plan. Everything was supposed to happen now, seven years after their passing, but a higher power intervened and unexpectedly drove one of the catches into my nets. She was such a sweet girl. But I couldn't spare her. There was no way.

65

The tastiest fish are those you kill yourself. These days I have time to concentrate and eat at my own pace.

At the house with the red roof, I was ordered around. That's one place I'm never going back.

It says in the good book that the hand of the diligent shall bear rule: but the slothful shall be under tribute.

No one is going to order me around. Not anymore.

Chapter 10

November 2019, Ísafjörður

Hildur woke before the alarm, at six. Once again, a pressure weighed on her chest like a heavy blanket she couldn't shift aside.

She was tired, but she knew she wouldn't be able to fall asleep again. Her head was thick from sleep, and an iron taste lingered in her mouth. She knew from experience the only way to win the coming day was to get out of bed immediately and challenge her body.

She tied her thick, dark hair into a bun and started a bodyweight workout on the living room rug. Five minutes of short, gentle stretches to wake up her muscles, followed by circuits: twenty push-ups, twenty squats, twenty crunches, and five pull-ups on the bar installed in the doorframe in Freysi's living room. Her breathing intensified; her pulse rose. After the fourth circuit, she lay on the floor, sweating and catching her breath.

The heavy blanket had lifted, at least for now.

She rose from the floor, shook out her limbs, and walked into the kitchen to turn on the lights. A touch of the volume button and the radio on the windowsill came to life. Icelandic public radio was broadcasting the weather report from the national meteorological agency. The calm reading of the wind, precipitation, and temperature forecasts imbued the day with a sense of manageability. It was as if the anchor were stating the day's framework in a neutral tone and encouraging listeners to do what they wanted and were able to within those bounds.

Well, it's winter now, Hildur thought as she cracked open Freysi's kitchen curtains. Last night's snowstorm had left a frosty film on the window, making it almost impossible to see out. Hildur brought her face close to the glass and peered through the crystals. A white blanket nearly half a metre thick had fallen over the cars parked on the street.

Hildur knew it would be a busy morning. Every winter began the same way. The first day it snowed, people forgot to slow to speeds appropriate to the new conditions. The town's lone roundabout was the site of constant fender-benders, as drivers rushing to work tried to exit it at summer speeds. Others overshot tight turns in car parks.

Hildur measured the coffee into the filter, filled the reservoir with the water jug, and turned on the coffee machine. She heard Freysi knocking about in the bedroom wardrobe. A moment later, he stepped into the kitchen wrapped in the striped black-and-white bathrobe Hildur had given him a few weeks earlier for his birthday.

He likes the present I picked out for him, Hildur thought as she poured coffee into two mugs.

'Have you been awake long?'

Hildur handed one of the mugs to Freysi and ran the back of her hand over her eyebrow to wipe away a bead of sweat caught there. 'I woke up early. I've been doing all sorts of stuff.'

Hildur didn't tell anyone about her insomnia or the heaviness that occasionally settled in her chest. She enjoyed Freysi's company, but she didn't want to get into her problems with him. It wasn't as if talking made the problems go away.

That therapist in the ankle-length cardigan hadn't been any use. She'd asked Hildur to talk about her childhood and pressured her to dig into her memories. Going over old events had felt pointless, and Hildur's anxiety hadn't diminished, just the opposite. The cardigan lady had suggested medication to help with the anxiety and a visit to a nutritionist because in her view there was an obsessive dimension to Hildur's exercise. Upon hearing this, Hildur had stood up in the middle of the session and announced she wouldn't be coming back. With the money she saved, she'd bought herself a couple of new surfboards.

Freysi took his coffee and stepped out for his morning cigarette. Hildur didn't understand how he could be so athletic while living such an unhealthy lifestyle. He puffed like a Norwegian chimney and still maintained an astonishingly low heart rate while running dozens of kilometres. He was offbeat in a different way than she was, but offbeat enough. Familiar. The type that refused to fit into any sort of predetermined mould.

Hildur took brown sugar and chocolate granola from the cupboard, sour milk and a yellow-capped bottle of fish liver oil from the fridge and sat down at the kitchen table to enjoy her breakfast. She mixed granola into the sour milk and sprinkled sugar on top to soften the milk's yoghurty tang. When her bowl was empty, Hildur poured herself a tablespoon of Lýsi oil. It was made from the livers of Icelandic fish and consumed for its vitamin D and fatty acids in nearly every Icelandic home, especially in the winter, when the sun didn't show itself for months. Today's fish liver oil was much better than the variety from her childhood. Back then, the daily dose of cod liver oil had tasted rancid and made the stomach acid rise to her throat.

Hildur moved aside a stack of papers she assumed were Freysi's workout routines. She glanced at the printouts out of curiosity but understood nothing of what she read there. She saw some strange words, and the margins were filled with notes in ballpoint pen. She took a closer look, trying to decipher the tiny script.

Suddenly, she sensed an air current run through her hair and felt a powerful hand grab her shoulder. She instinctively stepped to the side, knocking her cereal bowl to the floor.

'Holy hell!' she cried. She heard laughing behind her.

'I was trying to scare you. I guess I succeeded.' Freysi had come back in from his morning cigarette so quietly she hadn't heard him enter. 'You were so focused on reading those papers and sticking your butt out that I couldn't resist the temptation.'

Hildur frowned and tried to pretend she was offended, but her acting skills were negligible. 'Someday you're going to give me a heart attack,' she said, retrieving the bowl from the floor. Luckily it was still in one piece.

Freysi wet a dish rag at the sink and started wiping the milk splatters from the laminate. When he finished, he stood, rinsed the rag under running water, turned off the tap, and folded the rag over the edge of the sink.

'There's something I wanted to talk to you about. It involves those papers.'

Hildur grunted as she filled the dishwasher but encouraged Freysi to go on.

'I've been looking into my family tree lately. I found some interesting things and wanted to share them with you.'

Hildur was about to drop a dirty spoon into the cutlery basket when she stopped short in surprise. Genealogy sounded pretty personal. Their relationship wasn't even at the point where they talked about friends or parents, let alone distant relations.

'I hate to tell you, but doing genealogy is a sure sign of middle age. I don't think I'm quite there yet.'

'But this story is pretty interesting.' Freysi leaned against the counter with his arms folded across his chest as if he were ready to discuss the topic at length.

70

At that instant, Hildur's work phone rang. She fished it out of the pocket of the sweater hanging from the chair. An agitated voice could be heard speaking on the line. Although the information Beta was communicating outraged Hildur, her demeanour grew calmer. Hiding behind the cucumber-cool mask of a public servant came naturally to her. She walked into the entryway and started putting on her shoes.

'I'll see you at the station in ten minutes,' she said, then hung up. Freysi looked at Hildur inquisitively.

'I have to go. It's urgent. I'll see you later.'

Freysi rinsed the coffee pot in the sink and hung it to dry over a dish towel he'd laid on the counter. Hildur pulled on her coat, slipped on her hood, and waved. Freysi didn't have time to respond before she was gone.

Chapter 11

Hildur sped from Ísafjörður's lone roundabout onto the shoreline road. The locals called the road the highway because it led south from the centre, toward Reykjavík. This stretch of the highway ran through town, so Hildur had to maintain a speed of under fifty. The maximum speed on Iceland's roads was ninety kilometres per hour, but locals would exceed the limit on routes where there was no monitoring.

By now the speedometer in the police car read 110. Hildur turned on the siren and the emergency lights. She loved driving in difficult conditions; it made steering feel like surfing. The important thing was to react quickly. If you hesitated too long, the wave would swallow you up, the slippery curve hurl you from the road.

'Do you want to tell me what's going on?' Jakob asked, his elbow leaning casually against the passenger window. 'I came to the station this morning like we agreed, and before I could take off my coat, you told me we were going someplace that starts with a U.'

Jakob looked out the window at the snow piled at the side of the road. He was wearing a thick down coat and had pulled his brown beanie with white stripes over his ears. To Hildur, he looked more like an enthusiastic glacier tourist than a police intern.

Hildur liked Jakob's easy attitude. He was fitting in well already. He hadn't seemed perplexed by local customs or his new surroundings, nor did he suffer from tourist syndrome – in other words, go on and on about his supposedly interesting observations about Iceland. Hildur remembered the Danish police intern who'd been her partner a few years back. The guy had been aggravation personified. He had perpetually marvelled at how small the town was, been shocked by the long distances, and complained all winter about not getting Beaujolais Nouveau from the local wine shop in November. Jakob seemed different. He had just shown up with his yarn, pulled on his parka, and been eager to get down to work. He exuded self-confidence.

Hildur shot Jakob a quick look and smiled. 'Not someplace that starts with a U; Súðavík.'

Jakob replied with silence.

'We're going to Súðavík. It's a village of about two hundred people on the next fjord over. It takes about fifteen minutes to get there. Or ten, to be exact.' Hildur gave it more gas. The road before them was straight and recently ploughed.

'A call came in this morning from northern Iceland, from the Akureyri police. About a custody battle.' Hildur repeated that morning's brief for Jakob's benefit. The boy was five; his mother and father lived in Akureyri. They had divorced several years before. The mother had custody, and the father had visitation rights. The boy's visits with the father, Örn, hadn't gone so well. Apparently, Örn didn't show up to pick up the boy at the scheduled times, or when he did, he prolonged the visits at whim. Sometimes he'd threatened to not return the boy at all.

Jakob sat there at Hildur's side, listening intently.

Last week, Örn had made good on his threat. He hadn't brought the boy back to the mother after a scheduled visit. He'd turned off his phone. None of his acquaintances had seen him for days. Naturally, the mother was beside herself with worry.

'That's awful.' A couple of beads of sweat had formed on Jakob's brow, and he wiped them away. It was hot in the car. Jakob turned off his seat warmer.

The Akureyri police had got a call that morning from Örn's aunt, who lived alone in a big house in Súðavík. The elderly woman had woken to the sound of a car in the middle of the night and tiptoed over to see who'd driven up at such an unusual hour. Her nephew Örn had appeared at her front door and said he was taking his son on a little vacation. Örn had carried the sleeping child, wrapped in a wool blanket, to the couch inside. He suggested he and the boy stay with the aunt until the snowstorm passed, then they could be on their way again.

The aunt had been aware of her nephew's unfortunate circumstances and problems but had set up a bed in the living room and offered him tea without asking any questions. After Örn fell asleep, she'd snuck downstairs to call her sister, who'd confirmed the aunt's suspicions. Örn wasn't on vacation; he'd taken the child from his mother without permission.

Örn's mother had called the police right away and given them the location of the child and his father.

'Is it just the two of us going there?' Jakob asked.

'Yup. At least for now. The traffic police usually accompany us on cases like these, but they're dealing with a head-on collision across the fjord and can't come right away. When we arrive, you and I will go in.'

On a rural police force, everyone did a little of everything. Hildur investigated crimes, handled interrogations, combed through evidence, and occasionally answered emergency calls – especially if the emergency involved children in any way. She'd worked so closely with child protection services in Reykjavík that she was better equipped than many of her colleagues to consider child protection perspectives.

Iceland was a small, peaceful country that had suddenly prospered after the Second World War. The standard of living was high. Vacations to sunny locations, four-wheel drives, and big home theatre systems were everyday luxuries for many. But a scratch of the surface revealed all kinds of problems. The parents of more and more children were divorcing, and in some of those divorces, the children ended up in fraught situations. Domestic violence still wasn't dealt with firmly enough. More often than not, alcohol played a role in child neglect, and such problems weren't exclusive to any social class. Some high-flying corporate types would ease the pressures of the job with an expensive bottle of French wine. Or there were those who didn't work and tried to relieve the stresses of their financial predicament with alcohol. Instead of outrageously expensive red wines, they would pick up the cheapest Caraway vodka they could find at the liquor store. And almost without exception, those who carried the biggest burden in these maelstroms of misery were the children.

'What kind of guy is this Örn?' Jakob asked.

Hildur had quickly checked Örn's details that morning from LÖKE, the Icelandic police database. He had a few convictions for assault and selling narcotics.

'He might boil over, so it's better if we get there before he wakes up. Custody fights can get really ugly sometimes.'

'Unfortunately, I know all about it,' Jakob said. He took off his beanie; the Škoda's heater was powerful.

Hildur turned right from the winding highway into the centre of Súðavík, which stood at the foot of a snow-covered mountain. Icelandic mountains were squat in the eyes of those accustomed to more alpine views. The flattened shapes were the result of the heavy masses of ice under which they'd formed millennia ago. It was at the foot of one such squashed formation that this tiny village stood.

'Now, this is unique town planning. Why are the houses in a line like this?' Jakob took in the two-kilometre file of streetlamps illuminating the façades of the houses. It looked like the houses had been sprinkled one after the other along the shoreline, skipping over a big black spot in the middle.

'An avalanche swept some of the houses away.' Hildur explained how the fishing village wedged between the mountain and the sea had experienced a massive avalanche in the 1990s. It had claimed twenty or so lives and destroyed dozens of houses, and new ones had never been built in their place. The empty space still divided the village into two halves: the new and the old. Örn's aunt lived behind a playground named Raggagarður at the northern end of the village.

She pointed out the driver's window. 'A local mother built that playground about twenty years ago.'

Jakob looked at the park, where the deep layer of snow buried jungle gyms, swings, and merry-go-rounds.

'One of the boys from the village died in a traffic accident at the age of seventeen. He'd just got his driver's licence. The boy's mother built this place in memory of her son.'

Hildur pulled up behind the playground and killed the engine. The plough hadn't made it to this side of the village yet, so they couldn't drive right up to the house. They would have to trudge the rest of the way through the snow.

Hildur stepped out of the car and scanned the surroundings. Örn must have parked even further away, but his footprints were no longer visible in the snow. The constant snowfall made the place look like some abandoned outpost. Most of the houses were still dark, but the orange lights of the plough were flashing in the old part of the village.

The steam from Hildur's and Jakob's breath dissipated in the cold air as they strode through the snow toward the house.

'I want you to come in and back me up, but don't say anything,' Hildur said. 'The patrol should be here within fifteen minutes.'

'Got it,' Jakob replied. 'I'll be the policeman who doesn't know how to speak or write.'

Hildur looked at him in confusion.

'It's from this one Finnish comedy sketch,' he explained. 'I'll tell you someday.'

They approached a house clad in green corrugated metal. A metal façade protected old stone and wooden buildings from strong winds and constant precipitation. Örn's aunt's home stood on the slope and had an expansive view in all directions. As it was the last house in the village, there was nothing stopping the wind from buffeting its walls from every angle. A grey, waist-high lion stood in front of the weather-beaten dwelling, its head poking through the snow. 'That's an unusual yard ornament,' Hildur remarked, stepping past and up to the house.

She tapped her forefinger against the pane of glass in the door.

Apparently, Örn's aunt had been waiting, because it opened immediately. A tired-looking old woman in a yellow floral-patterned robe, she let Hildur and Jakob in and pointed upstairs. 'They're asleep in the living room. It's the left-hand door.'

Hildur nodded.

'For the life of me I cannot understand how Örn turned into such a difficult person,' the aunt whispered as she slipped her hands into the pockets of her robe. She clearly wanted to continue talking, but Hildur cut her off:

'Is there anyone else in the house?'

'No. Just me and Markús, my cat, but he sleeps on the heated bathroom floor until noon.'

'I want you to wait down here. Go into the bathroom and lock the door. My colleague and I will go up, and I'll let you know when you can come out,' Hildur said. 'Thank you for calling and reporting Örn's location,' she added as she started up the stairs. She took her radio and informed the backup patrol that she and Jakob had entered the house and the suspect and child were on the second floor.

The stairwell carpeting had seen better days; it was thread-bare, and there were big holes on every tread. The stairs rose to a hall with three doorways. Hildur gave each room a quick glance. One door led to a kitchen with brown cupboards and appliances and an old-fashioned electric stove. There was a bag of mandarins on the table. The second door led to the study, and the door to the left opened onto a large living room. Two leather easy chairs were parked in front of a big flatscreen television, and an aquarium stood along the longest wall.

In the far corner there was a sofa bed with two figures sleeping on it. The bigger one was fully dressed and lying on his back. Örn's straw-coloured hair was a mess, and the chapped lips visible under the untidy beard quivered in time to his snoring. The smaller figure was curled up in a light-brown blanket next to the wall.

Hildur estimated the distance to the sofa bed as a few strides. She wondered whether she could retrieve the boy without waking Örn. The patrol should be arriving any minute, too. Just as she was stepping closer to the bed, the snoring stopped as if severed by a knife.

Örn leaped to his feet.

'Police. I'm Hildur Rúnarsdóttir with the Ísafjörður police. This is my colleague Jakob Johanson.' Hildur spoke calmly, try-ing to establish eye contact with Örn. 'We're here because we need to get your son home. His mother is worried.'

Caught off guard and groggy, Örn looked around in alarm. But he quickly pulled himself together. He seemed to grasp what had happened: his aunt had called the police.

'Lilja! We're supposed to be family,' he roared. 'My son and I came here to visit you, and you call the police, you damn whore.' Rage had kindled in his eyes. He assumed a forward-leaning stance as if readying for a fight. Spittle flew from gritted teeth as he cursed the old woman huddling in the bathroom downstairs. His hair was matted from the night; his shirt was wrinkled. He smelled of sweat.

'Get the hell out of here, both of you!' he shouted, raising his fists at Hildur. Things had taken an unpleasant turn.

Hildur tried to engage Örn. Jakob stood back, quietly covering her as agreed.

The head of a frightened-looking boy popped out of the wool blanket. His blond bangs had pressed against his pillow and were now standing on end. He looked like a tufted bird. He frowned at his father and then at Hildur. Hildur noticed how he tried to curl into as small a ball as possible.

'Örn, take it easy. The boy's mother is worried because you didn't tell her where you went,' Hildur said. 'Let's take the boy back home together.'

'I'm not giving my son to you.'

Hildur nodded at one of the black leather chairs. 'Örn, could you step aside and sit in that armchair?' Her hand instinctively moved to the pepper spray hanging from her belt.

'Not a chance. My son isn't going anywhere. He's with me now, because we're taking a little vacation, and once you start a vacation you finish it.' Örn grabbed the boy and held him tight. 'I'm never giving up my son!' he shouted as he backed up to the wall, son in his arms.

A vase on the coffee table rolled to the wooden floor and shattered. Shards scattered everywhere, and the water from the vase soaked into a folded newspaper next to the couch. The boy began to cry.

'Let the boy go,' Hildur said more forcefully.

Örn shook his head and squeezed his son harder. The boy's wails had turned to panicked sobs.

'Let the child go, so you don't cause yourself any more problems,' Hildur said, taking a step toward Örn.

'No. Come any closer and I jump from the window with the kid in my arms,' Örn replied. 'I'll cause *you* some goddamn problems.'

Hildur retreated a couple of steps.

'If I can't be with my son, no one can,' Örn hissed. He was short of breath, and his eyes were bouncing off the picture windows. The situation was getting dangerous.

Hildur knew she could take Örn down, but she didn't know if he was armed. Above all, she had to protect the little boy.

She silently cursed the patrol's delay. They needed backup now.

Jakob, who'd been standing behind Hildur this whole time, cleared his throat and directed his words at Örn. 'Excuse me, can I tell you something?' he asked in English.

Örn whinnied in amusement. 'What the hell kind of foreign bastard is this? Can't this country afford its own police anymore?'

Jakob looked at Örn and spoke slowly: 'I'm not a real police officer. I'm only interning here. I just wanted to tell you I know what it's like to be in your shoes.'

'Yeah, right,' Örn said with a snort. But he also paused to listen. 'How's that?'

'I have a boy the same age as yours, five, who likes to play fireman and hunt Pokémon. I haven't seen him for a long time

80

because his mother took him away from me. I'm here in Iceland now because I couldn't stand to be at home anymore.'

Örn stared at Jakob. Then: 'You're lying!'

'I wish I were. I wish it weren't true. But it is,' Jakob said. 'She took my child from me. Do you think I chose a place like this to work for fun?'

Örn looked thoughtful, then gruffly replied: 'That's the way bitches are. First, they pretend to be so nice and in love. They make you coffee in the morning and pack you lunch and leave it in the fridge. Then they jet and take the kid with them.'

'Exactly. Threaten you and take you to court,' Jakob added.

Hildur listened quietly to Jakob and Örn's conversation, kept her eyes on the boy Örn was clutching, and noticed the father's grip on the boy had relaxed.

'Then they tell the daycare director not to let me have my son, to call the police if they see me anywhere near the daycare.'

Jakob nodded slowly in acknowledgement. 'My ex-wife took my son from daycare one afternoon in the middle of a football game.'

Hildur understood Jakob was trying to draw out the conversation. And he seemed to be succeeding. Örn's attention was now focused on Jakob, not on her or the boy sobbing in Örn's arms.

'They moved away,' Jakob said. 'I haven't seen him since.'

Örn huffed. 'I still have the video of the police coming for me even though I was just picking up my son from daycare.'

He started searching his hoodie pockets for his phone and momentarily forgot about the child in his arms. The boy dropped feet first to the floor and ran behind a nearby armchair for safety. Once there, he curled up in a foetal position, terrified.

Jakob moved to protect the boy.

Örn rushed after his son, but Hildur reacted first. She already had the pepper spray in her hand; she raised it at the lunging Örn and pressed. There was a faint hiss as the capsaicin foam squirted in his face. Örn howled in pain, dropped to the floor, and lay there, hands rubbing his eyes. The spray stung badly. Hildur knew Örn had lost his sight for at least ten minutes. She strode over and clicked the handcuffs around his wrists. 'This might hurt a little, you miserable bastard,' she whispered in his ear. Then she sat on his leg with all her weight.

Örn howled in pain again.

'I'm so sorry. Try to keep still so our legs don't get tangled,' Hildur said audibly and stood, leaving Örn there on the floor. She turned to Jakob, who had the little boy in his lap in one of the easy chairs. She looked her partner in the eye and mouthed *Thank you*.

As Hildur hoisted the cuffed Örn to his feet, she felt relief. They'd successfully navigated a situation that had started spinning dangerously out of control. Apparently, Jakob knew how to talk to people. That was a critical skill for a police officer. Hildur remembered how the fieldwork instructor she'd respected so highly at the academy had emphasised the importance of social skills. *Icelandic police officers aren't allowed to carry firearms, so they have to use their silver tongues*, the instructor had joked. Jakob had handled today's situation beautifully. Hildur herself wouldn't have been capable of a similarly spontaneous performance, and in a foreign language to boot.

But the story Jakob had told Örn kept going through Hildur's mind. What had Jakob been forced to endure before his arrival in Iceland?

Her thoughts were interrupted by the sound of a siren outside.

'The suspect has been detained,' she said into her radio. 'Come upstairs. You get to escort him back to the station.'

Once Örn had been taken away, Hildur squatted in front of the boy in Jakob's lap. She pulled a package of dried mango from her pocket and offered him a slice. Hildur loved the sweet-tart flavour of mango and snacked on it during long shifts. The boy reached into the bag for a piece of mango and put it in his mouth.

'We'll take you home to your mum soon. She misses you a lot. First, we're going to go to the police station, and right after that you can talk to your mum. OK?' Hildur said. 'If you want, I can put on the flashing blue lights while we're driving.'

The boy nodded and gave a little smile. Then he curled into an even tighter ball in Jakob's lap.

The station was quiet. The snow muffled the sounds of the sparse traffic and there was no rampaging wind knocking things about. The storm had subsided. The tranquillity was augmented by the obituary programme on the radio. Obituaries and memorial announcements were read on Icelandic public radio afternoons and evenings on weekdays, afternoons on weekends and holidays. The low voice remained perfectly steady as it read all the announcements. Hildur loved the show. An entire human life captured in a few sentences.

'*Ingibjörg Atladóttir, housewife and handcrafts teacher, died at home in Vík on October 20th. She is mourned by her children, grandchildren, and great-grandchildren. The funeral will be held at the Vík church on Saturday, November 2nd. The family politely declines flowers . . .*'

'*Psychologist Eiríkur Hermansson, BBA, of Reykjavík, died surrounded by his loved ones at the hospital after a brief illness. The funeral date will be announced at a later time. Partner, children, and relations . . .*'

Hildur handed Jakob a cup of coffee and sat at her desk, eyeing the lunch in front of her. She had heated up a piece of the greasy *slátur* in the microwave. She showed Jakob the slice of greyish-brown sausage on her plate.

'You want a taste? There's enough for two.'

Jakob waved his half-eaten granola bar in the air and declined with a shake of his head. 'It smells funny.'

'You get used to it.' Hildur jabbed her fork into the hunk of meat and took a big bite.

A satisfied-looking Beta appeared in the doorway. She glanced at Hildur and Jakob in turn and thanked them for the successful operation. Örn was in the holding cell, waiting for a patrol car from Akureyri to pick him up. The case would, in all likelihood, be investigated as illegal restraint.

'And the Akureyri police are handling the investigation because that's where the abduction took place?' Jakob asked.

Beta nodded, 'They have more resources than we do. Prison guards and everything.'

'What about the boy?' Hildur asked. She sensed Jakob wanted to ask about him, but he seemed wary. So she asked herself.

'He'll be with local child protection services until the mother gets here. Hildur, you could talk to the social workers and confirm whether they need anything else from us. If you finish the paperwork today, tomorrow you and Jakob can spend some time driving around and get to know the area.'

Hildur wiped her mouth on her sleeve and nodded. 'I'll go over now.' She pulled on her parka, lifted her hood, and stepped out. Luckily she didn't have far to walk.

The social services office was in the building next door, on the same premises as an insurance company branch and the bank. That morning's assignment had been heavy, but in no way terribly unusual. Visitation conflicts in instances of divorced couples appeared regularly on Hildur's desk. It was typical for one parent to move to the capital after a divorce, and children travelled long distances between homes. The majority of visitation conflicts that reached the police involved the child not being returned as agreed at the end of a visit.

Another problem that demanded significant police and child protection resources was adolescent drug use. When young people battling addiction ran away from home, a foster family, or rehab facility, they had to be recovered and returned to their starting point. Almost always the fugitives were found and brought to safety.

Each instance of helping a child or troubled adolescent was a personal and professional win for Hildur. The most disheartening cases were those in which no one noticed the child was gone. It happened from time to time. If the mother and father drank from dawn to dusk and headed who knows where with their drinking buddies at night, there was no one at home to care. The kids had to make do on their own. Often the problem only became evident when the school reached out. The teachers were generally the first to notice if a student regularly showed up at school without warm clothes, was frequently absent or showed signs of neglect. In some families, an older sibling – who was barely a teenager – cared for the younger siblings and didn't have time to focus on their schoolwork themselves.

Hildur looked at the snow-covered houses in the vicinity and reflected how, even in this tiny town, two parallel realities existed. One where people had everything imaginable. And the other, where they had nothing.

Chapter 12

At seven thirty the next morning, Jakob woke to his phone's cheery melody. He glanced out the window of his tiny bedroom: not so much as a promise of light. The slight headache at his temples was a sign of exhaustion. He swiped the green icon and lifted the phone to his ear.

'What are you doing, Jakob?'

It was Hildur. Considering it wasn't even eight o'clock on a morning off, she sounded far too perky.

'I was asleep,' Jakob replied groggily. 'I thought we weren't supposed to meet until noon.'

'I know, I know, but that was yesterday.' Hildur's voice was quivering with enthusiasm. Jakob could hear a coffeemaker burbling in the background.

'You want to go surfing?'

Jakob hauled himself half-upright in his bed and groped at his nightstand, found the switch, and turned on the lamp. *Surfing? What is she talking about? Swimming in the sea? It's winter, dark as a troll's ass outside and way below freezing.*

'I thought you were going to show me around today. Are you proposing extreme sports instead of the usual tourist itinerary?'

'Yes. That's exactly what I'm proposing. The sea is at its best during the winter, and right now the weather is perfect.'

The weather is perfect? Jakob shook his head and laughed. Of course he would go. Hildur didn't sound like she meant to deny herself this wintry expedition into the waves, and he had no interest in sitting at home alone all morning.

But before he could answer, Hildur continued her campaign: 'The wind is blowing from the right direction. The waves are only a metre high, but the gap between crests is over ten seconds. Trust me, this isn't the kind of ride you see every day! Besides, I have an extra board – a soft one for beginners – and a large wetsuit. You can use them.'

Jakob tossed aside the covers and sat up properly. Hildur was clearly determined to get her way. 'I'll come. I'd been thinking I'd drop by Guðrún's yarn shop, but I can go later.'

'How's the sweater coming?'

Jakob could hear Hildur was talking with her mouth full. For some reason, it didn't bother him. Just the opposite: it felt pleasantly familiar.

'I got the sleeve attached to the body yesterday. I'm going to have to adjust the pattern slightly; it's a little asymmetrical.'

'That means nothing to me, but thanks for sharing.'

Jakob chuckled. A Finn teaching an Icelander the mysteries of Icelandic sweaters. And then a fantastic idea occurred to him: he would knit a sweater for Hildur as a present. Every Icelander's wardrobe was piled high with warm, heavy sweaters, or at least he imagined so. He'd seen Hildur wearing a long cardigan and had immediately recognised the pattern: Fleygur, an ankle-length model made from heavy Álafosslopi yarn and designed by the Icelandic textile company Ístex. Jakob was currently knitting a traditional pullover from the lightest Léttlopi yarn. Once it was finished, it would be staying in its homeland.

'I promise we'll be back before the shops close,' Hildur said. 'I'll have a second breakfast and be there with Brenda to pick you up in an hour.'

*

An hour later, Jakob was standing outside his apartment in his heavy parka, warm leather gloves, and tall winter boots. As he waited for Hildur, he gazed up at the mountains. Ísafjörður was hemmed in on both sides by steep, gleaming slopes. Jakob was glad for the snow; the place would be really dark without it. Not that he found darkness problematic. But there was something reassuring about being surrounded by high mountains and the icy sea. He was comfortably penned in, and there was no need to think what lay beyond. This was his place now.

Before long, a grey Toyota Land Cruiser appeared around the corner. With its massive tyres, the four-wheel drive made for an impressive sight, but its best years were clearly behind it: a few rust spots had crept onto the bonnet, and there were two visible dents below the taillights. Jakob opened the door and climbed in. This was not a vehicle you lowered yourself into. Despite being well over six feet tall, Jakob had to push himself off to reach the seat. *Nice ride,* Jakob thought as he fastened his seatbelt. He noted the Land Cruiser already had over 300,000 kilometres on the clock. But it navigated the snowy road steadily, and the view was totally different than when sitting low in a passenger car. He wouldn't mind having a high-riding SUV like this in Finland.

'I've never felt the need to exchange it for something newer,' Hildur said as if reading Jakob's thoughts. 'I've never got stuck anywhere in this car. Ever.' She knocked on the central console. 'Seven, nine, thirteen.'

Jakob shot her a questioning glance and unzipped his parka.

'Seven, nine, thirteen. It's a good luck thing. You have to knock three times while you say: "Seven, nine, thirteen." That's how you protect yourself against bad luck.'

Jakob nodded and reflected that in Finland, the custom was knocking on wood. Iceland had almost no trees, so maybe that was why Icelanders relied on numbers instead.

When they reached the supermarket, Hildur turned onto the mountain road leading to the next fjord.

'Weren't we supposed to pick up Brenda?' Jakob said.

Hildur guffawed and slapped the steering wheel. 'This is Brenda. Brenda's my car.'

It was Jakob's turn to laugh. 'Why Brenda? Did they show that Beverly Hills show from the '90s on TV here, too?'

'Of course, but I didn't watch it,' Hildur said. She pointed at the little mascot swinging its hips on the dash. 'I picked up a hitchhiker one day. In return, he left me that doll with the grass skirt. Its name is Brenda.'

The doll whipped its yellow skirt from side to side on the bumpy, snow-covered road as Hildur steered toward the gaping black hole in the mountain. Brenda slid into the tunnel, and Hildur shut the AC flaps.

A sign at the side of the road indicated the tunnel was six kilometres long. After two kilometres, it forked. One road led to a fishing village in the west, the other to one in the south. After the fork, the tunnel narrowed to half its original width, forming a single lane.

'Those headed south yield. When you see headlights approaching, you have to pull over at a spot like that and wait,' Hildur said, pointing at a turn-out through the passenger window. In winter there wasn't much traffic, but during the summer the tunnel grew crowded, as the stretch of road filled with buses hauling cruise-boat tourists.

The tunnel's dark walls rose up alongside the driving lane. Lights had been installed in the relatively low ceiling, and their warm orange glow offered a little visibility in the otherwise black passage.

Two points of light in the distance were heading their way. Hildur pulled over at the next turn-out and waited. They heard an approaching rumble, and eventually, bright headlights filled the tunnel. Jakob could feel the ground beneath Brenda shake as the Eimskip transport-company semi passed by. Once it was gone, the darkness returned. Hildur pulled Brenda back onto the road, and their journey continued.

Jakob gazed at the forbidding walls and gauged the tunnel's width. Some small spaces created a sense of safety, but this wasn't one of them. The dim, narrow tunnel felt eerie somehow. Sheer black rock flashed past as Brenda raced through the mountain.

Jakob wondered if this was the tunnel Hildur had mentioned a few days before – the tunnel where her sisters had gone missing years ago. Would it be rude to ask? Hildur seemed like the type who appreciated frankness and tackling tough topics head-on. If she found his question offensive, she would probably just refuse to answer. On top of which, Jakob didn't see the point in wondering what others thought of him. Directness culled extraneous acquaintances.

He shot Hildur a discreet glance. 'Is this the tunnel where they—' Jakob saw Hildur's profile grow stony, and her eyes close briefly.

'Yes. This is it.' And that was all Hildur had to say on the subject.

A few minutes later, Brenda sped out of the other side of the mountain like a lottery ball popping out of a plastic tube. The fjord they'd arrived at was oriented east-west, and the mountains rising from its shores were lower than the ones surrounding Ísafjörður. The rays of the breaking winter sun just grazed their tops, setting the snowy terrain alight. Jakob lowered his sun visor and squinted.

'Beautiful,' he said, scanning the valley opening up around them. From absolute darkness into bright light. The contrast was striking.

'It's about to get even more gorgeous,' Hildur said as she turned onto a smaller road.

Hildur and Jakob were floating a few hundred metres out to sea. They drifted back and forth with the movement of the water and waited.

When the next big wave arrived, one of them would climb onto their board and start riding.

'Here it comes! On your stomach and paddle!' Hildur shouted. She glanced at Jakob, whose right hand gripped his white surfboard as he bobbed in the icy sea.

Jakob pulled himself onto on his board and started paddling shoreward with both hands. His wave-propelled board moved swiftly. As it climbed the crest, Jakob tried to stand the way Hildur had taught him on shore. He managed to get up on his right knee before the saltwater washed over him.

He toppled, and the wave pushed him into the frigid sea's embrace. Jakob held his breath and pulled himself back to the surface with a few brisk breast strokes. He saw his board floating nearby, grabbed it, and looked around for Hildur. She had caught the next wave and was off in the distance, gliding parallel to the waterline as she smoothly headed landward.

'How's it going?' Hildur shouted from the shore.

'I'm alive. But this isn't exactly like snowboarding, I have to say.'

'Come on. Let's go again.' Hildur walked deeper into the water, her surfboard under her arm. She lay down on it on her stomach and paddled toward Jakob. 'Let's go out a little further. I'll tell you when to get on the board. Don't try to stand; just kneel and go from there. You'll gradually grow familiar with the movement of the water.'

*

Four hours and one snack break later, Hildur and Jakob were warming up inside Brenda. The wetsuits had been stowed in the back; Hildur would hang them in the shower to dry after she got home. There was hot coffee in their Thermos mugs and an open bag of deliciously greasy *kleinur* donuts on the dash.

'How long have you been surfing?' Jakob asked, taking a bite of his donut.

'Since university. I love surfing. When you're in the sea, you don't have time to worry about anything else. You have to dedicate your full attention to staying on the board.'

Jakob could relate to the phenomenon Hildur was describing. Escapism. Some people watched movies; others splashed around in freezing water. He'd spent the last few years knitting sweaters to keep his thoughts together.

'What do you do if you can't go surfing?'

'Go to the gym or for a run.' Hildur reached into the back seat for the Thermos and poured them more coffee. 'How do you feel about yesterday?'

Jakob sensed she wanted to discuss the previous day's emergency call. He stared out the window. It was starting to snow. As it came down, the boundary between sea and sky blurred, and the horizon was impossible to make out. The grey SUV melted into the soft landscape. The world's contours gradually faded into non-existence.

'I'd like to talk about what happened at that old woman's place yesterday. It went really well. Is it OK if we talk about it?'

'What about it?' Jakob asked. He figured Hildur would keep asking until she got an answer that satisfied her. He could also tell she knew he was playing for time.

'Is it true about your son? Or did you make that up on the spot?'

Jakob sighed and turned to the window, even though there was nothing to see out there. A grey curtain had fallen over Brenda. 'I wish.'

'I feel you. Usually the most horrible things are true.'

Jakob hesitated. He wasn't sure he was prepared to delve into this with an outsider. On the other hand, Hildur knew almost nothing about him, so she might be able to see things at a remove and without feeling sorry for him. Pity was the one thing Jakob couldn't take. Pity cut too deep. Hildur felt like an ordinary person, in a good way. Besides, they were partners now. There had been a lot of talk at the police college about the importance of trust between partners. And Hildur had told him about her sisters, even though it was clearly a sensitive subject.

'I met Lena seven years ago when I was backpacking around Europe. We met in Budapest. She was . . . She was one of those people who when you see them, it's impossible to turn away.'

'One of those people who fills the room and seems to suck up all the oxygen.'

Jakob shot Hildur a grateful glance and nodded. She'd immediately understood.

He continued telling Hildur about Lena. When he and Lena moved to Norway, Lena had captivated him with her fishing skills and homemade fish soup. Dating had been followed by moving in together outside Oslo. Jakob started his dissertation in biology at the University of Oslo and worked as a teacher; Lena had a demanding position at an insurance company. The first years had gone pretty smoothly. Jakob had learned Norwegian and made friends.

But a year after Matias's birth, Lena started to change. She'd always had jealous tendencies, which Jakob had put down to her need to control to her fiery nature. But now she was claiming

93

more space in general: she decided when they'd take time off, criticised Jakob about minor childcare issues. She always wanted to know where he was at any given time, down to the minute. And he was increasingly hearing how strange his views were, how childish his thoughts.

'Sometimes she'd drive me to the brink of rage. One day she spent over an hour tearing strips off me and my family. Eventually, I grabbed a half-eaten apple from the table and threw it at her,' Jakob said, shaking his head. 'She recorded the incident on her phone and used the video against me in court.'

Hildur huffed in outrage. 'She must have planned the whole thing! There's no other way she would have been able to record a spontaneous reaction.'

'I know. I eventually figured that out. But it was too late.'

Not long after the apple incident, the little family had travelled to Finland on holiday. Lena had wanted to cut the vacation short by a week and take Matias back to Norway. 'We fought that entire summer. Lena suggested I spend a few days with my friends in Finland while she went back to Oslo to get Matias ready to start daycare.'

Hildur's thirst for information wasn't slaked yet. She could already sense what was to come, but she wanted to hear the story from Jakob. 'So what happened?'

'When I got back to our place in Oslo, it was empty. Lena had taken Matias and moved out. I had no clue where. She left me the couch and a broken floor lamp. Five days later, she emailed me that she had a lawyer and I wasn't going to get Matias.'

Hildur let her hands fall into her lap and faced Jakob, who was still staring out into the deepening gloom. 'That's awful. I'm so sorry.' She lowered her right hand to his shoulder. It was a clumsy attempt at consolation, but she didn't know what else to do.

Jakob turned toward Hildur and nodded almost impercep-tibly. For a moment, the silence was absolute. They hadn't said much, but they appeared to understand each other.

'I lost my faith in everything. The catastrophe was too much for my body to handle, and it gave out. My legs refused to carry me. I fainted in the stairwell.' Jakob was startled by the words that emerged from his mouth. He'd just shared details he'd never shared before with someone who was little more than a stranger.

Hildur registered Jakob's distress and led the conversation in a more practical direction. Besides, she wanted to hear what happened next. Was there any escape from such a tangled situa-tion? 'Did you get a lawyer?'

'Yes, but as you can imagine, they don't come cheap. I took all the teaching I was offered, and on weekends I worked as a bartender. Even so, I was drowning in legal fees.'

'Goddammit,' Hildur snorted. She'd heard about comparable situations in her line of work. You had to be either completely penniless to get free legal representation or truly wealthy to pay for a lawyer out of your own pocket. The fees could run into tens of thousands of euros. Not many home insurance policies covered court costs incurred by custody cases. International custody battles were even more expensive, since you had to pay for the translation costs of documents and find expertise in international law.

Jakob dropped his head against his headrest and let his gaze linger on the upholstery overhead. 'What was most unfair was Lena used my night classes against me in court.'

Lena had claimed Jakob wouldn't be able to care for the child, because he spent every night, even his nights off, at work. Child protection services had sided with Lena, bought her story about her Finnish husband being violent. Jakob had lost custody, and since then, he'd only been able to see his son on rare occasions in the presence of child protection services.

This wasn't the first time Hildur had questioned decisions made by the lower courts. She recalled a specific case from her Reykjavík years. Thinking about it still made her blood boil. Hildur had been investigating a suspected rape, conducting interrogations and collecting evidence. The suspect had been charged and found guilty. But the lower courts had given him an incredibly light sentence. The reasoning was that he was married and had underage children and a permanent job. Ironically, he was arrested again a couple of years later for a similar crime.

'I assume you appealed the decision?'

Jakob shook his head. 'I couldn't afford to continue fighting it in court.'

Hildur and Jakob sat there side by side, watching fat snowflakes fall from the sky. They stood out distinctly in the dusk as they drifted down. Those whose journey came to an end on the windscreen melted and trickled down the cold metal surface in liquid form.

'A lot of friends judged me, said I'd abandoned my child,' Jakob said, turning toward the sea. 'My head couldn't take it. I moved away. I went back to Finland and got a new profession. I started at the police college. I travelled to Norway whenever I was scheduled to see Matias, but most of the time Lena came up with some excuse for why I couldn't.'

'When did you see him last?'

'Almost a year ago. Christmas Day last year. I try to stay in touch through video calls. We Skyped for a little while last week.' Jakob's voice dropped to a whisper, then cracked: 'But Matias is still so young. I'm afraid he's going to forget I exist.'

Hildur felt herself growing furious. The situation was unfair to Jakob. Incredibly unfair. She wasn't in the habit of holding back, and she had no intention of keeping her views to herself now. She slammed her fist into the steering wheel. 'What an asshole!'

Jakob turned to Hildur. Her gaze was hard. It conveyed frustration and maybe even a little anger, but not a drop of pity. That felt good.

After a brief pause, he continued. 'You know, it's a weird thing, but I got this really nice feeling when we drove past that playground yesterday. There's something beautiful about a mother who lost her child building a playground for the other kids from the neighbourhood.'

'I think so too. Some parents hide their children from each other, while others do everything in their power to make sure their children won't be forgotten.'

They sat in silence, drinking their coffee and gazing out at the falling darkness: two strangers sharing the same space, the same view, the same thoughts for a brief moment.

Then the phone in the glove compartment started ringing. Hildur reached in and pulled it out. The flashing number on the screen told her who was calling. Beta sounded agitated.

'Hildur, where are you?'

'Surfing at Önundarfjörður.'

'I thought you were going to show Jakob around.'

'Jakob's here with me. We're just sipping coffee and having deep conversations.'

'You two need to get back here right away. I guess you haven't heard yet.'

A cold weight slid over Hildur's limbs. She'd been troubled by an unpleasant feeling all day: the familiar angst had risen into her chest that morning, growing heavier and heavier as the hours passed. Hildur had put it down to late-year melancholy, but her boss's urgent tone told her something was badly awry again.

'There's been an avalanche at Seljalandshlíð. The cottages are buried in snow, and we have a strong suspicion the resident of one cottage is trapped inside.'

As she started up Brenda, Hildur thought there was no way there could have been an avalanche. It had only been snowing for a few days.

Apparently, the search-and-rescue team was at the scene. They had already started digging, but all hands were needed at the site. Hildur calculated they would be there in half an hour or less.

'I'll bring the coveralls and gear,' Beta said.

Hildur knew how bad an avalanche could be. The falling darkness had snatched the last ray of afternoon light. As they flew down the winding road, Brenda's high beams were like fast-moving lightsabers slicing through the mass condensing around them. The flurries intensified as Brenda whipped down the road toward the avalanche zone.

Chapter 13

The web of yellow streetlights covers the village like a fisherman's net. They thin at the fringes, then die out altogether. The blue hearts of the emergency vehicles are beating at the seam between light and darkness.

I drove straight here when I heard about the avalanche. First one car arrived carrying two people. It was soon joined by the next, then the one after.

The flock of people move about, corralled by snowbanks. There they scamper, back and forth, legs shaking, like lambs separated from their mothers. Blowing into their hands as if it made any difference! They should be in a hurry to start digging.

Go to the ant, thou sluggard; Consider her ways, and be wise. So says the Old Testament.

My work is not done, but so far all has gone according to plan. The avalanche accelerated my schedule, but that's fine. So it is for all those at nature's mercy. I will continue my mission.

I exhale the last curl of smoke and watch it disappear in the falling snow.

Things are moving in the right direction. Joy fills my heart; I almost feel like breaking into some lively folk song. I press on the gas, tap out the beat on the leather steering wheel, and sing:

Hey, hey, hey! The fox ran through the tall grass.

It yearns to wet its whistle with blood.

And somewhere a curiously deep male voice cried.

The outlaws of Ódáðahraun must be driving their sheep down on the sly.

I move on the sly, too. Soundlessly and surreptitiously. I'm not going to take the whole flock, only one. When one wanders away from the flock, that's when I'll snatch it.

Chapter 14

November 2019, Ísafjörður

Hildur's phone beeped incessantly the entire drive. Messages from friends, calls from neighbours. She glanced out the corner of her eye at the phone in its stand and noticed the next incoming call was from Tinna. Hildur always had time to talk to her aunt. Tinna sounded out of breath.

'Dear God, did you hear about the avalanche?'

'I'm just on my way there with a colleague.'

'I can't believe it. Last week the slopes had only a dusting of snow, and now this.'

'There have been a lot of flurries over the past few days. Luckily the cottages where the avalanche came down are empty.'

'Empty? I've heard from several people that one of the houses was occupied.'

How could word of people buried in the snow already be making the rounds? Hildur thought to herself. Suddenly, she was in a hurry to get off the phone.

The road was full of parked cars. Hildur slowed to a crawl when she noticed the pavement coming to an end. The snow that had crashed down the mountain had swallowed up the end of Fjallavegur. The plough markers that usually stood on either side of the road must have been knocked over by the force of the slide because there was no sign of them.

Hildur backed up behind the chain of cars and parked Brenda behind the other vehicles, training her headlights on the avalanche zone. It wasn't even five o'clock, but it was already dark. The powerful surge of snow had destroyed some of the streetlamps and knocked out the electricity. Headlights were needed to illuminate the accident scene.

She left a couple of metres between Brenda and the car in front of it: a four-wheel-drive search-and-rescue vehicle that might need to pull out quickly. With its oversized tyres, the search-and-rescue SUV was a real mountain monster. It could even navigate glaciers. If air were let out of its tyres, it would have no trouble driving through snow and could be pulled up closer to the avalanche zone. The decision had been made not to do that, however, because it was important to keep the area where they'd be digging clear of everything extraneous.

As Jakob and Hildur stepped out of Brenda, the back door of the SUV opened, and Beta peered out. 'Come get changed into your gear. Jónas, the head of the search-and-rescue team, is in charge. We'll lend a hand wherever it's needed.'

'What's the situation?' Hildur asked, following Jakob into the SUV.

Hildur and Jakob pulled on yellow safety coveralls. She told him to tuck the police ID hanging from his neck inside his bib; it would be easier to shovel if he didn't have anything swinging in front of his face.

Beta told them what she knew. The avalanche had come down a little over an hour ago. Five cottages and a few sheds had been caught under the mass of snow. Experts from the Icelandic Meteorological Office were on site, working up projections about possible secondary avalanches.

Hildur looked out the windows of the SUV. The headlight-illuminated snowbanks looked unnaturally large. Earlier today, buildings had stood here; now all that remained were towering mounds of snow and tons of debris.

Once Hildur had tightened her coveralls' leg straps, the trio was ready to exit the vehicle. As they strode toward the scene, they were surrounded by the loud voices of rescue workers clearing snow. Someone behind them called Hildur by name.

It was Hlín, the regional reporter for the Icelandic national broadcasting service. Hlín was an active member of the Icelandic horse community. She kept her horses in a stable at the base of the fjord. In the wintertime, she trained them at an indoor arena; in the warm months, she took them on long treks into the highlands. Hildur and Hlín rode together a few times every summer. But Ísafjörður was such a small place they also saw each other frequently on the job. Hlín was the only journalist in the Westfjords and wrote all regional news stories, from accidents to search-and-rescue operations for lost sheep and launches of new businesses.

'I already talked to search-and-rescue. There was likely someone in one of the houses. Would the police care to comment?'

Hildur cut Hlín off; Beta usually handled all media communications. 'Have you already spoken to Beta?'

Hlín glanced at Hildur from under her brows. 'Come on, you know Beta. She never gives any answers in situations like these.'

Well, you're not getting any answers from me either, Hildur thought to herself. She wasn't going to confirm any rumours yet, but she didn't want to deny the suspicion that had formed either. She'd be lying if she did, and she didn't want to lie. Besides, she knew Hlín personally. 'Wintertime occupancy of these cottages is forbidden due to the risk of avalanche. At this point we can't elaborate on any material damage or whether anyone may have been trapped under the snow.'

Hlín gave Hildur a crooked smile. 'Now, that was a diplomatic answer.'

'I'm sorry I can't tell you any more than that now. I'll let you know right away if there's anything else to report,' Hildur said, pulling her hood over her head. 'I promise.'

Hlín appeared to accept Hildur's response and began scanning the crowd, looking for other potential interviewees.

Beta continued telling Hildur and Jakob what she knew. She gestured a couple of hundred metres up the road, where they could see a group of rescuers wearing headlamps digging. 'The house they suspect was still occupied was a little green cottage.'

Hildur instantly knew the cottage Beta was talking about. 'Jón's place.'

Beta nodded. She lived lower down the same street and knew the area like the back of her hand, including who owned every cottage. And not many days had passed since she and Hildur had last been by Jón's place.

There'd been no sign of the old man when he'd been scheduled to show up for questioning. Hildur had meant to go to his house and bring him in, but as the more urgent matter the Súðavík kidnapping had taken precedence.

Jakob appeared at ease in the deep snow. He surveyed the surrounding destruction and tried to deduce the location of Jón's house. 'Why do you think he was inside?'

Hildur pulled Jakob aside and pointed a few dozen metres ahead, where a large snowbank was littered with debris carried off by the avalanche. A car bumper was sticking out of the snow. 'Jón never went anywhere without his car.'

The back of the old Suzuki was all that was visible, but Jakob was sure: it was Jón's.

Their surroundings were chaos, as if the world had abruptly lurched out of place. Some structures were only half buried under the snow. Windows had shattered and walls had collapsed. For a stretch of about a hundred metres, all that remained were snowbanks studded with shards of lumber, lamppost parts, and warped sheet metal.

The nearby slopes were about thirty degrees steep, and the area had long been classified as a risk zone in avalanche calculations. That was why the cottages could only be occupied in the summer and anyone who violated the rule received a hefty fine. Winter snows were frequent in the Westfjords, and the mountainous terrain was rich with ideal avalanche sites. Major avalanches frequently took place on slopes of this exact type.

'I've never seen anything like this,' Jakob said in awe. 'It looks like a war zone.'

They started trudging toward Jón's house, where digging was well underway: a path half a metre wide had already been cleared through the snow so search-and-rescue personnel could access the site.

Jónas, commander of the local search-and-rescue team, stood approximately where the entrance to Jón's house had once been. He was a big man with a resonant voice. 'The dog marked this spot. The mark was pretty faint, so it's possible the person we're looking for is already dead.'

Then he gestured up the slope at an angle: 'We strongly suspect the sleeping areas were located about there.' Jónas's voice echoed with certainty brought by experience. He'd been involved in numerous similar operations following natural catastrophes.

When the volcano at Eyjafjallajökull erupted ten years ago, he'd rented every unused truck in the area and travelled to the southern shore of Iceland to help evacuate livestock.

'We started digging along the eastern wall, where the least snow had accumulated. We're cautiously proceeding from there. We've focused all digging efforts on the cottage. We'll expand tomorrow in the daylight. We're pretty sure the other houses that were damaged in the avalanche were empty. We'll call the owners to confirm.'

Hildur translated Jónas's words for Jakob. Then they grabbed shovels and, along with Beta, started digging at the spot indicated by Jónas. Luckily the snowstorm had eased, at least temporarily. Heavy snowfall would have interfered with visibility.

Hildur thought back to the avalanches from her childhood. A couple of decades had passed since any had proved fatal. The Westfjords had seen two serious avalanches in 1995; both took place at night when everyone was sleeping. A total of almost forty people had died. Hildur's family had been spared, but as a resident of a sparsely populated area, she'd known many of the victims and their families.

Even so, the avalanches hadn't made a particularly vivid impression on Hildur, as at the time her family had been struggling with the disappearance of her sisters. Only a year had passed since they had gone missing, and the agony of that fear and uncertainty had muffled the trauma of the avalanches. The pain she felt was ruthlessly personal.

Jakob grimaced as he shovelled the heavy snow aside: 'This is like cement.'

Hildur panted, out of breath, and wiped the sweat from her brow. 'The snow condenses like this when it comes down the hill fast and hard.' The fast-moving slide first generated a pres-

106

sure wave that shattered windows and often blew doors off their hinges. The heavy mass of packed snow followed.

Hildur noticed a dog with pale markings and a black coat nosing its way across the snow. It was Molli, the village search-and-rescue dog. She was trained first and foremost to smell for any living bodies trapped under the snow, but apparently, she could smell the dead, too. Hildur had been running into Molli and Molli's handler lately when jogging near the village.

Molli found those buried in the snow based on the smell of their skin. The avalanche could carry someone long distances from a house, and Molli's assistance made it faster to find the right spot to dig. Without a dog, those buried under the snow wouldn't necessarily be found in time. That was why just about every mountain village in Iceland had at least one dog trained to locate people trapped under snow.

A search-and-rescue dog had been used in Hildur's sisters' case. The dog had picked up their scent; Hildur had heard her mother discussing it with the unusually stiff police officers at the kitchen table. Hildur had been hiding in the next room, listening to the grown-ups' conversation through the cracked door. Apparently, the dog had trotted unwaveringly from the centre of town to the mouth of the tunnel. But once she made it into the tunnel, the dog had got confused. It was as if the scent had hit an invisible wall.

Hildur remembered lying under her Snow White duvet and listening from her dark room. Before that, she had loved animals, dogs most of all. But in that moment, her mind had done a U-turn. For some time, she'd been afraid of dogs, hated them. Especially the dog that hadn't found her sisters.

'Pretty harsh that something like this can happen all of a sudden,' Jakob said.

Hildur emerged from her reverie and watched her colleague toil away at his shovel-handle. 'Tell me about it. We'll never be able to control this land, no matter how many technical gadgets and barriers we have.'

Hildur, Jakob, and Beta had been shovelling for almost forty-five minutes without a break, and all they'd dug up were dishes, random articles of clothing, and snow. Their exertions had caused a nasty ache in their right ribs. Hildur switched her shovel back to her other hand to change the direction her body was twisting.

A constant stream of helpers was flowing into the area. The rescue team from the neighbouring fjord arrived with a second canine. There had even been an offer of help from Reykjavík. Iceland's network of volunteers meant over three thousand rescuers who'd completed gruelling physical training were on the alert at any given moment. Without the teams of volunteers, quickly organising a major dig would have been impossible.

The snow covering Jón's house gradually receded. A bit of gutter from the front porch came into view, then a sliver of roof. Hildur, Jakob, and many others set to moving away the snow cleared by the rescuers digging at the house. One of the external walls had collapsed, and the house had partially fallen in on itself.

'The southern wall is standing, and the bedroom window is visible. We'll enter there,' said a voice from the middle of the dig.

The mood turned electric. Soon the first rescuer was more or less inside the house. The digging continued. Heavy, condensed snow flew out the window one shovelful at a time. Gradually space formed in the snow-filled room. Before long, a second person fitted inside, too, then a third. Now there was so much space that it was possible to stand inside the room – or what was left of it. The diggers' faces were sweating, and they were panting loudly. Every second mattered. If Jón had been caught in an air pocket, he might still make it. The faster a body was rescued from the snow, the more likely the victim was to survive.

Jakob and Hildur approached the window that had been halfway excavated from the snow. Three diggers were labouring in the bedroom, where the rescuer with the broadest shoulders was poking at the snow with a long stick. The stick was used to locate people so the rescuers would know exactly where to dig. Hildur noted the mismatch between the brawny rescuer's bright-red, tasselled beanie and the rest of his gear. The lip of the beanie was emblazoned with the logo of the Reykjavík women's ice-skating team.

'I feel something about a metre down. Could be a mattress, could be a person,' he said.

The diggers who had crammed into the bedroom began clearing snow at the spot indicated by the beanie man. First by shovel, then by hand. Eventually, two grey socks poked out of the snow.

'Clear his face, fast, clear his face,' one of the diggers shouted.

The snow flew faster and faster, but the body didn't move. Whoever was lying there was either dead or unconscious.

Hildur had been watching these developments from her spot outside the window. She shouted for the medics to come in with a stretcher.

The man in the skating club beanie brushed the last of the snow from the man's face and bent down to feel for a pulse. He took off his glove and was just pressing his fore-and middle fingers to the man's jugular when he flinched and froze.

An agonised roar filled the demolished room. Everyone nearby fell silent. 'What is it?' Hildur asked.

The beanie man's lips mumbled something unintelligible.

'What is it?' Hildur repeated. She stepped through the window and into the room, then took a look over the beanie man's head at the body on the bed. She gasped in shock.

The scarred forehead confirmed the corpse lying there was Jón's. 'Doesn't look like he needs resuscitating,' she said.

Jón's throat had been slit from ear to ear.

Chapter 15

The mood in the avalanche zone had done a 180 since the body was found. Adrenaline-spiked enthusiasm for the task at hand was replaced by a baffled paralysis. The accident scene had turned into a crime scene.

The searchers working the avalanche site had returned to their homes to rest. Molli had whimpered for more action and been rewarded for a job well done with fifteen minutes of hide and seek in the snow with her handler.

Beta had called for a doctor to come in and declare the victim dead.

After that, Hildur had performed a quick, superficial examination of the body, making sure not to needlessly disturb any evidence. She hadn't found any signs of livor mortis. She, Beta, and Jakob were in unanimous agreement that the lack of coloured splotches on the skin was due to significant bleeding. The snow had destroyed most traces of blood, carrying them off as it came down with explosive force. But the victim's clothes and bed linen were so stained with red that it had been easy to deduce the severed jugular was the cause of death. Jakob had watched Hildur probe the victim's limbs. He and his fellow students at the police college had been taught the same procedure: a corpse needed to be tested for rigor mortis, as that could help determine the time of death. In this instance, the body showed no signs of stiffness, which meant several days must have passed since Jón's death. But there were no signs of decomposition either, so Hildur said the killing must have taken place about three days before.

It seemed clear, then, that Jón had bled out and that someone had killed him. There was no way he could have inflicted such a wound himself. Even so, the three police officers knew final confirmation of the cause of death would have to wait for the post-mortem.

In Iceland, all autopsies were performed in Reykjavík. The Westfjords Police didn't even have their own forensic investigators.

But the body couldn't be left unattended until the forensic team showed up. Hildur and Beta had returned to the station to initiate the investigation. Hildur intended to call Hlín and tell her about the body found in the snow. The criminal aspect would not be announced publicly yet; that information could be revealed later. Jakob had promised to stay behind and keep an eye on the crime scene, which had been cordoned off with a wide plastic ribbon.

Jakob leaned against the one wall of Jón's house that remained standing. He had a direct line of sight to the body on the bed. The wound at the throat looked nasty. Drawing the blade had demanded nerves of steel. What had been the killer's MO?

Jakob pondered the body's position on the bed. There was a tranquillity to the way it was laid out. The victim was on his back, legs straight and arms relaxed at his sides. As if he'd died in his sleep. But there was no way that could have happened because the incision was huge and there was so much blood. Besides, such acts of violence were almost always preceded by a struggle, and Jón wasn't exactly a small guy. The killer must have been strong. *I guess we'll find out more from the autopsy and the forensic investigation*, Jakob reflected before turning away.

Not so long ago he'd been a biology teacher in Norway. Now he was in a remote Icelandic fjord, standing watch over a corpse. Evidently life was full of surprises.

The rescue workers had left Jakob a lightweight panel to stand on, for which he was grateful. With its aluminium membrane, the thin layer of cellular plastic insulated him from the cold and made for a comfortable perch. Even though he was standing almost still in temperatures well below freezing and buffeted by a brisk north wind, he didn't feel cold.

Jakob's eyes swept across the terrain. The electricity was still out. He'd been left with a couple of portable, battery-powered work lamps to turn on. But he didn't want to use them. He wanted to be in the darkness. Somehow it felt a lot more pleasant than the harsh artificial light.

The brightness of the stars caught him off guard, but maybe their beauty was something you just didn't normally notice with all the light pollution. Jakob could spot the North Star, the Big Dipper, and Orion's belt. Three bright stars side by side in a straight line: Mintaka, Alnilam, and Alnitak. He'd always been fascinated by the night sky. As a child, he'd memorised the names of dozens of stars and written them down in a big blue notebook he had named the Star Treasure Map. Jakob smiled at the memory.

He and Lena had spent a lot of time camping his first year in Norway. The first night they went, Lena had led him from their tent to a nearby seashore and laid down on her back. Jakob had lowered himself at her side. Lena had told him to search for shooting stars. He'd be sure to see them if he just had the patience to look long enough. And so Jakob had stared at the infinite black firmament studded with bright dots. And then he'd seen it: a speck of light moving among the constellations. It had felt like a life-changing observation. How miraculous it had been to see something for the first time. Something that had always been there but that he hadn't seen until Lena showed it to him. *A meteor, that's incredible*, he'd sighed. Then Lena had burst out laughing and told him they were satellites. For a moment, he'd felt simple. Why hadn't it ever occurred to him that it was possible to see satellites on a dark, cloudless night? And then Lena had rolled over on top of him, and any thoughts of satellites had been thrust from his mind.

Jakob swung his arms briefly and raised his face to the sky, scanning it for satellites.

Suddenly, he remembered. Jakob reached into the lined breast pocket of his coveralls and glanced at the time. A few minutes to eight. He and Lena had agreed he could speak with Matias tonight at eight o'clock.

The courts had decided that Jakob could meet Matias face to face in the presence of child protection services and have weekly Skype calls with him. Jakob tried to call at this same time every week. The last time, Matias had been so shy nothing had come of their chat. Jakob couldn't say for sure what was going on. Was Matias really shy of him, or had Lena done something to provoke the upsetting situation?

Jakob brought up Skype and selected Lena's user ID. The temperature had dropped, and the stronger breeze made it feel even colder. As the phone rang, Jakob pulled his gloves back on and turned on one of the worksite lamps. He positioned himself and his phone behind the lamp so the light would illuminate his face but not blind him.

Lena answered. She appeared to be in her living room. Jakob had never been there, but he'd seen the Ikea print of an urban silhouette during previous video calls.

'Hey, how's it going?' he asked.

Lena greeted him in return. She didn't smile, but she did look at him and seemed cooperative. That made Jakob feel good. Maybe this call would go better than the last one.

'I'm tired. Things are always busy at work at the end of the year, and Matias has been a little under the weather. Other than that, things are fine.'

'I'm sorry to hear it. How's Matias?'

'I just said he's been under the weather,' Lena said in a harder voice.

Jakob decided to back off. He wouldn't let himself get caught up in Lena's provocations; he would be the bigger man and ignore them. He calmly drew a breath and tried to continue the conversation as normally as possible.

'It's probably just an ordinary autumn flu. But what do you think?'

'What do you think? What do you think?' Lena mimicked in a mocking tone.

Jakob felt the small electric shock run through his body again. The conversation had got off on the wrong foot once more. He'd tried to keep the call civil, but Lena had brought in the power drill. He was losing his temper, but he decided he wouldn't let Lena get to him. Because that was what she was trying to do. Force him to snap at her in a way she could use to hang up.

'Kids get little colds in the autumn all the time. I was just wondering if that's what it was or something more serious.'

'Well, you're no childcare expert, so there's no point you diagnosing him long distance.'

Jakob didn't immediately reply. He could tell where this was headed. So he went straight to the point, keeping his voice as friendly as he could. 'Could I please speak with Matias?'

'I just told you he's sick.'

'Can I just see him, then?'

'He's sick!' Lena's voice had risen a couple of octaves. 'It's not a good idea.'

She shifted away from the phone, and Jakob saw his son sitting on the couch with a friend his age. They were watching television together. Matias looked relatively happy. He was laughing at something he was watching and pointing at the television. His hair was lovably mussed. A big dimple formed on his left cheek. It was still as prominent as it had been as a baby. Amazing how the skin could dimple like that.

Jakob remembered how a broad smile of boundless joy broke out on the boy's face every morning when he'd rushed into his parents' bed to wake them. Matias had giggled and smelled of morning.

Jakob's yearning for those moments was acute. He missed his son. His chest and arms ached with longing.

'You have visitors?' Jakob asked, his voice tense but steady. 'So is he sick or not?'

'Now you're accusing me of lying?' Lena said, launching into one of her lectures: 'We need to be teaching our son about trust, but you're just sowing suspicion and accusing his mother of being a liar!'

'I never said that,' Jakob said, despite knowing arguing was pointless.

'Where are you, anyway? Skiing somewhere?'

Jakob felt bad that Lena didn't remember where he was. He'd informed her about his move to Iceland in good time before his departure. Or who knew, maybe she remembered but wanted to pretend otherwise. Pretend Jakob played such a small role in her life that she didn't even need to remember where lived.

'I'm at work. On exchange in Iceland. I told you I'd be spending a few months here.'

Lena's face broke out in a knowing smirk. Her voice grew honey-soft. As if wrapping a cruel message in a sweet package, her malice poking through more sharply than ever. 'See that? There you go again. You're accusing me of having a bad memory. Somehow you always manage to pin everything on me. That sort of behaviour isn't good for a child. You're a bad male role model for Matias. A toxic person. Very toxic.'

After uttering these last words, Lena broke into an aggravatingly tender smile and ended the call.

Jakob stood there in the snowfield, phone in hand, staring at the black screen.

What was he supposed to do? Nothing he said helped. Nearly every conversation with Lena ended up here. It made no difference what he said; she heard what she wanted to hear and twisted it to serve her own purposes. He'd tried to talk less, talk more, stay calm, shout back. The result was almost inevitably the same: Lena would accuse him of something and claim his attempts at contact were bad for Matias.

Jakob walked back to Jón's house, assumed his spot on the insulating panel, and leaned against the wall. He felt hopeless. As powerless as the dead man lying in the ruins of his demolished home.

Chapter 16

November 2019, Reykjavík

Heiðar Arason used his left hand to sweep back a rogue curl at his temple before glancing at his wrist. The gold Rolex there was a source of immense delight, an off-catalogue model few could afford. *This thing cost as much as half a year's gross salary for a nurse,* he reflected. He smiled at himself and stepped into the elevator.

Heiðar was a success. His workdays weren't spent surrounded by the sweaty stench of the diseased. Just the opposite! He was the guy who made others sweat.

It's 1.30 a.m., but who cares, he thought. He'd do a little line in the morning to wake up, and a new day of victories at the law firm could begin. Five hours of sleep would be plenty. If his wife woke to his middle-of-the-night arrival and asked about the lateness of the hour, he could always make the excuse of working overtime for an important client. Heiðar lived according to a simple principle: the one with the money called the shots. And because he was the one bringing home the bacon, he would decide what time he'd be coming home.

He shook his head at the thought of Kolfinna, his wife. She did nothing but sit at home in their waterfront house all day. Occasionally she would paint astonishingly ugly pieces in oil and hawk them through her socialite friends' galleries. She had managed to sell two floral still lifes last year and now she called herself an artist. Heiðar found the whole thing idiotic, but he didn't want to poke at his wife and rock the boat. He occasionally bestowed a few words of praise on her paintings and otherwise kept her satisfied with little gifts and acknowledgements.

A wife was supposed to be cheerful at all times and look gorgeous on his arm at important social functions. Kolfinna's father owned one of the country's most successful fishing businesses, which would one day be theirs. In other words, his.

That meant divorce was not an option. Not to mention Kolfinna looked like Penelope Cruz. Or at least she had. When Almodóvar's *All About My Mother* was released twenty years before, Heiðar and Kolfinna had gone to see it together. At the time, the resemblance between the lead actress and his date had been apparent. But Kolfinna was over forty now. *She's still pretty hot, but a forty-year-old has a forty-year-old's ass*, Heiðar thought to himself.

And then a blissful smile spread across his face. *Nothing beats a woman in her twenties.* Lára, the current intern at Heiðar's law firm, was any straight man's dream. Flowing blonde hair, big eyes, and firm tits that jiggled softly as she stalked the company's corridors in a sheath skirt and black open-toe heels. When the twenty-five-year-old law student strode through the doors of Heiðar's law firm for an interview the previous summer, the partners had been unanimously in favour of recruitment.

Meanwhile, the men had placed wagers: the first to sample the pleasures of the new blonde would get a 5 per cent productivity bonus at the end of the following quarter. The firm's sole female partner hadn't been cc'd on the email laying out the bonus plan, but she had let the unanimous recruitment slide.

Heiðar had won the bet. Of course. Heiðar won anything he set his sights on.

The preparations had required meticulous attention to detail: he'd hidden his wedding band in his desk drawer and tightened up the privacy settings on his Facebook profile. His address wasn't listed in the public register, nor did he keep a photograph of his wife prominently displayed in his office. He never gave the gossip rags permission to photograph him at social events. He was able to pose as a single man because a Google search wouldn't reveal any information to the contrary.

First, he'd taken Lára for a coffee during lunch to hear about her career plans and advise her on her choice of a thesis topic. They'd had a nice time. The next week, there'd been a couple of lunches and a drink after a successful workday. Heiðar had flirted with Lára, and she had returned his attentions eagerly. The law student must have found it flattering getting to know one of the best-known – and wealthiest – corporate lawyers in Iceland.

Heiðar couldn't take Lára on dates in public places, so he'd had to make an impression on her during the work day. He'd ended emails with emojis and queries about her evening plans.

One time they'd attended the premiere of a play because Heiðar's guest had supposedly cancelled at the last minute. There had never been a guest, of course. Heiðar had made the whole thing up to get Lára into the firm's box, occasionally used for entertaining clients. In the theatre's soft lighting, Heiðar had plied Lára with gin and tonics and praised her contributions at work. He'd promised her a permanent position once she finished her thesis. After that, all inhibitions had flown out the window. When the play ended, the two of them had walked the few blocks between the National Theatre and the firm's offices to continue their evening.

They'd screwed in the bathroom then and there. Lára had perched on the sink and spread her legs on command. Heiðar had lowered his trousers, entered Lára, and snapped a shot of himself winking in the mirror. Lára hadn't noticed that he'd taken a picture, obviously, or that he'd sent it to the partners' WhatsApp group. The chat had immediately filled with emojis: high fives, winks, trophies, stacks of cash.

Heiðar emerged from his reverie. The chime told him he'd arrived. He stepped out of the elevator at the basement level of his office building, where his car was parked.

Today had been a particularly good day as well. He'd crushed his opponent in court, an entrepreneur in his fifties whose metals business had gone belly-up. The poor bastard had such lousy representation that Heiðar almost wanted to laugh. He'd clobbered the old beer belly six-nil and would soon be sending the former entrepreneur a fat invoice.

A successful day at district court always made Heiðar horny, and so right after the trial he'd texted Lára from outside the courthouse and proposed they meet. She had promised to come. Of course. Lára always came when he asked.

They'd eaten dinner in a suite at a nearby hotel and washed it down with the most expensive red wine on the menu. After the meal, they'd got down to business: snorted some lines from the glass table while Lára undressed. Heiðar had seated himself in the leather armchair, pulled Lára over in front of him, and told her to hop in place. He still grew weak at the image of her big tits softly jiggling overhead. Then he'd taken Lára from behind on the hotel's big bed. Because he always got what he wanted. After a few hours of play, Lára had fallen asleep. And Heiðar had decided to leave her there and drive home.

Heiðar walked to his car, satisfied. The white Range Rover gleamed in the furthest corner of the garage. His head and balls ached after the night of hard-core partying, but he had no regrets. Of course not. *Losers have regrets, winners have fun*, he thought to himself as he pulled his keys from the pocket of his Boss coat. Suddenly, he felt a pang of sadness. He knew the fun with Lára would come to an end the following spring. She would be graduating then, and his promise would obligate him to hire her permanently. Not that he would. They'd just take on a new intern at minimum wage to handle routine cases. Besides, Heiðar knew from experience the longer an affair went on, the more difficult the woman would get.

Where the hell are my car keys, Heiðar wondered in frustration. He patted the other pocket of his wool coat. The car keys weren't there either. *Maybe I left them at the hotel.*

He was just turning back to the elevators when he saw his Range Rover start up. The SUV's headlights came on, and the engine emitted its familiar growl.

Heiðar couldn't believe his eyes. His car nudged into motion.

Had he left the keys in the car? What was going on? Was someone else driving it, or was he hallucinating? He closed his eyes and shook his head. When he opened them, the Range Rover was still running. Now it was moving, accelerating right at him. The headlights were blinding. A cold terror washed over Heiðar. The Range Rover continued to pick up speed.

And then it struck. Heiðar fell to the ground and roared in pain.

The car had hit his leg. He felt an intense, pulsating pain. He lay there and looked down at the limb, which had twisted into an unnatural position. His trousers were torn, and the leg bone was protruding.

Heiðar tried to scramble to his feet. He'd just managed to rise to one knee when he heard the purr of the engine once more. He glanced back and saw the car reverse, turn lightly, and come straight at him again. Thanks to its first-class shock absorbers, the Range Rover glided over the black-and-yellow-striped speed bump in the garage floor as if it were gauze.

Heiðar tried to crawl behind a nearby pillar to hide, but he couldn't get himself out of the way fast enough. He tried to shout, but all that emerged from his lips was a feeble rattle.

And then the world went black.

Chapter 17

November 2019, Ísafjörður

The shrill, loud bark penetrated the front door. Hildur peered through the pane of glass and saw a small golden-brown dog sitting at the threshold, yapping at her. *Probably an Australian terrier*, she guessed. A watchdog whose bark was bigger than the pooch itself. Hildur knocked on the red door a second time. The dog would make sure her arrival was noticed.

Before long, a man approaching retirement age came into view, garbage bag in hand.

The door opened.

'Well. Hello,' he drawled, eyeing Hildur questioningly.

'Hildur Rúnarsdóttir, Westfjords Police.' Hildur showed her badge. 'We're investigating the death of Jón Jónsson, who lived over in the Fjallavegur cottages. We found him yesterday in a house destroyed by the avalanche and have cause to believe he was the victim of a homicide. Did you happen to see Jón this past week? Or anyone moving around Jón's place?' The words came as if from a conveyer belt. Hildur had already been to dozens of homes near the avalanche zone, asking the same questions. Almost all those who'd known Jón said the same thing: they hadn't seen him in weeks. Many had speculated that he preferred solitude. In this they were right. Jón had no friends. Surprisingly many hadn't recognised his name at all. A few had said they'd seen a police vehicle and two police officers at Jón's house – that had been Hildur and Beta picking up the adolescent runaway Pétur.

But Hildur had kept asking. She hoped she'd come across someone who'd seen Jón or otherwise knew something about him. Even a tiny, trivial-seeming observation might be relevant. The results of the forensic investigation hadn't come in yet, and it would be a while before the autopsy was completed.

Forensics didn't spark much passion in Hildur. Of course, she understood the field was critical to contemporary criminal investigations. Technicians photographed, took fingerprints, collected samples, and produced sketches of the crime scene, while the analysts in Reykjavík handled more demanding forensic examinations. Fingerprints, fibres, and DNA samples could produce near-incontestable investigative evidence. And advanced methods were making it possible to glean results from ever-smaller samples.

So Hildur accepted the importance of forensic investigations and viewed them as an inherent element of police work. They were based on science. Mundane, indisputable. But indisputable mundanity didn't imbue the field with any appeal for her.

What she found more meaningful was digging into people's pasts. Finding out what had happened to them and why. How life had pushed people into abuse, fraud, or heavy debt. She was interested in the stories of those wrapped up in a crime. A DNA sample might reveal the perpetrator, but it couldn't reveal a motive. A forensic investigation produced evidence that might suffice for a guilty verdict. But if the motive remained undiscovered, the crime remained partially unsolved. For Hildur, the most important word in her work was *why*. On some occasions – extremely rare ones – pure happenstance had played a role. But there was always a reason behind a crime. Hildur knew her way of thinking set her apart in her profession, and so she didn't usually discuss her views. She performed all tasks related to her work as well as she could, but delving into people's lives was what she enjoyed most.

The man stared across the threshold at Hildur, garbage bag still dangling from his hand.

'Well?' Hildur asked, shifting her weight to her other foot.

'Thanks for the good news,' the man said. 'I'm glad he's dead.' A ghastly, fishy stench was rising from the garbage bag. Hildur breathed through her mouth.

'Did you happen to see him recently?'

'I don't know anything about that paedophile's movements. I haven't seen anything, I haven't heard anything, and that's just the way I like it.'

'If you happen to remember anything, anything at all, would you please give me a call?' Hildur said, handing the man her business card.

He eyed the card sceptically before accepting it and jamming it into his back pocket. 'Sure.' He held out the smelly bag. 'Do you mind taking this rubbish for me?'

At the previous house, a bag of donut holes had been pushed on Hildur instead of refuse. Apparently the police officer trudging alone through the cold had prompted feelings of pity in the old woman who lived there, and she'd wanted to brighten the officer's day. The sweet gesture had warmed Hildur's heart, and the miniature donuts had been delicious. She had devoured two right away and left the rest on the passenger seat.

'My legs are bad,' he cajoled, still extending the bag toward Hildur. 'There's ice under the snow, and if I slip it will mean a long stay in the hospital.'

Hildur took the bag, said goodbye and dumped the rubbish in the bin on the other side of the fence.

It was 2.30 p.m. Hildur would have time to make the rounds of all the remaining houses before dark. Any eyewitness observations would be a big help. She and her colleagues didn't really have anything else to go by. The forensics team had finally made it from Reykjavík the evening before. They'd combed through the crime scene, but the results had been minimal. The avalanche had fouled most of the tracks.

Aside from the neat, sizeable incision, no visible traces had been found on the body. The weapon had presumably been a very sharp blade. One of the forensic investigators had wagered a filleting knife, but there had been no sign of the weapon itself. Either the perp had taken it, or it had been carried out of the house by the avalanche.

Late that night, the forensic team had packed and loaded up the body and shipped it to Reykjavík to await autopsy.

Hildur walked down the snowy road to the next house and pondered the positioning of the body. Jón had been lying serenely in bed. Might he have died elsewhere, with the killer laying him out on his mattress after the fact? Jón's phone records hadn't been recovered yet. Hopefully they would arrive tomorrow and reveal something.

Hildur knocked on the next door. A woman slightly younger than Hildur, about thirty, came to open it.

'Hildur Rúnarsdóttir, Westfjords Police.'

A fearful look spread across the woman's face. 'Did something happen to Mum?' she asked in a panic, quickly continuing: 'I knew this would happen! I've been telling her for ages to move out of that big old house and into assisted living.' Her voice began to crack. 'But she's so stubborn.'

Hildur corrected the misunderstanding and assured the woman she wasn't there about anyone's mother. She explained about Jón and the avalanche and asked if the woman had seen anything.

The woman's face instantly relaxed. Yes, something tragic had happened, but not to her. Looking relieved, she let out a deep sigh and leaned against the doorjamb. 'This is what it's like when your parents get old. You're always worried about them.'

Hildur nodded empathetically. 'Do you remember having seen Jón or any activity involving him lately?' Hildur nodded in the direction of the cottages. 'It was against regulations, but he was still staying in his place nearby.'

The woman looked thoughtful. 'Well, now that you mention it, there was one thing . . .' Hildur pricked up her ears. 'All that snow came down last week. I was out here every night, shovelling the stairs and the walk,' the woman said. The shovelling had been done today, too, Hildur noticed; the snow had been pushed into a tidy pile at the eastern edge of the property.

The woman tucked a strand of loose hair behind her ear and glanced in the direction of the road. 'The pizza delivery car drove past a little before seven on Tuesday. I'd just come from football practice, and I know I shovelled the walk before the seven o'clock news.'

'Pizza delivery?'

'Yeah. It struck me as odd to see the delivery driver driving into the cottages, where no one should be staying in the winter.'

The woman continued chatting amiably. She said during the winter she tended to notice cars driving past because there was so little traffic. Her house was the second to last on the road, and only the cottages stood beyond.

Hildur thanked the woman and wished her a pleasant day.

*

The pizzeria's automatic doors amused Hildur. Entering the small-town grill was like stepping into a big-city shopping mall. The restaurant was quiet. A couple of old timers sat at one table, slurping coffee. Hildur greeted them with a wave as she walked over to the counter.

A kid in a red uniform, maybe sixteen, was refilling the coffee machine. A couple of fistfuls of beans accidentally spilled from the mouth of the bag to the floor.

'Motherfrick,' the boy said, grabbing a broom and scooping the beans into a dustpan. His spontaneous reaction put a smile on Hildur's face. She stepped in front of the counter and coughed to let him know he wasn't alone.

'What can I get you?' The boy's voice was exaggeratedly calm. After tipping the coffee beans that had rolled across the floor into the trash, the boy returned the dustpan and broom to the cupboard.

Hildur hadn't meant to buy anything, but when enveloped in the alluring smell of grease, she realised she was starving after all the walking she'd done. On top of that, she'd missed lunch. Two pizza slices and a half-litre bottle of orange soda would fix things.

The boy indicated the case: 'All we have ready is pepperoni.' He washed his hands in the sink next to the counter, carefully dried them on a paper towel, slowly packed the pizza into cardboard boxes, and slid the purchases into a paper bag bearing the pizzeria's logo.

There were no customers aside from the two scruffy men, and they were sitting too far away to hear Hildur and the boy. Hildur decided there was no need to pull him aside; she might as well ask the questions here.

She introduced herself and explained about the avalanche and the man found in the house. Hildur noticed the boy stiffen at the mention of the house buried in the snow.

'Do you know who did the deliveries on Tuesday? I need to talk to whoever it was.'

Pink splotches formed on the boy's throat. He shifted his weight to his other foot and fidgeted with his glasses. 'I always handle the deliveries at the beginning of the week,' he said, closing the register drawer too hard. The bell on top of the cash register tinkled. The boy set the receipt down on the counter in front of Hildur.

'And your name is?'

'Siggi. Sigurður Pétursson.'

'Listen, Siggi. I'm investigating the death of Jón Jónsson, who lived on Fjallavegur. His body was found buried in the snow.'

Despite Hildur's informal tone, the boy didn't relax. There was nothing unusual about this. Most ordinary people avoided the police and grew flustered when they came around asking questions.

But something about Siggi's demeanour struck Hildur as off. He wasn't shy; he seemed tense. Suspicious. His eyes had narrowed, and his jaw had dropped. He hadn't been able to conceal his emotional reaction. Hildur was sure he knew Jón. As did many others, of course. The majority of Ísafjörður's residents knew each other at least by name, and those who stood out from the crowd always made a bigger impression. There wasn't a soul who had lived in town for a few years who didn't know who Jón Jónsson was.

'Pizza was delivered to him on Tuesday in a car marked with this restaurant's logo.'

The corner of Siggi's mouth began to twitch. To keep his hands occupied, he began organising the hundred-króna lottery tickets in their stand.

Hildur was patient. She didn't say anything; just waited for him to respond. The front of the restaurant was practically silent.

The clatter of dishes carried from the kitchen. The creak of the rotating pizza rack, the faint hum of the ice cream machine. After arranging the lottery tickets to his satisfaction, Siggi stood up straight, as if seeking strength for his words.

'That guy ordered pizza every Tuesday. On Tuesdays, you get a pizza with three toppings for a thousand krónur. He would call in his order around six and pay with a credit card over the phone. The order was always the same: shrimp, chicken, and pineapple.'

The thought of chicken and shrimp on the same pizza made Hildur shudder. No wonder the kid remembered the toppings by heart. There was no way you could forget a combination like that, even if several hundred pizzas were sold on Tuesdays. Many locals came and picked up a pizza for dinner after work on Tuesdays, including Hildur.

Hildur wanted to know how Jón had seemed on Tuesday. 'Did you happen to see if he had visitors when you dropped off the pizza?'

Siggi shook his head and reached for the lottery ticket shelf again. The flush on his neck rose to his face. 'Well, actually. That's not exactly what happened.'

Hildur asked Siggi once again if he'd been the delivery driver. Siggi nodded, but something about his body language said otherwise. He folded his arms across his chest, shut his eyes, then snorted a slightly louder voice: 'I hated delivering to him. He was a dirty old man. He was always asking me to bring the pizza all the way inside.'

Hildur had already guessed: Jón had tried to lure Siggi into the house.

'I never did,' Siggi quickly clarified, then added in concern: 'Do you have to tell my boss? Because we're always supposed to hand over our deliveries in person.'

131

Hildur gave a little smile, encouraging Siggi to continue. She didn't want to rush him; it wouldn't do any good.

Siggi slid both his palms to the counter, leaned in, and lowered his voice. 'So this weird thing happened outside Jón's house. This creep came out to the car.'

Hildur was instantly on the alert. Who was this creep? What were they doing there? This was important information.

Siggi hadn't recognised the person. He said the stranger approached him the second he stepped out of the car, claimed to be visiting Jón, and offered to bring the pizza in. 'So I took the pizza from the carry bag, handed it over, and drove to the next address.'

Visiting? Jón didn't have any friends. He didn't even have a crowd he hung out with. He spent almost all his time alone.

Hildur asked Siggi to describe the stranger's appearance. Man, woman, old, young? Big or small, what did the face look like?

'I couldn't really see. They had this thick scarf wrapped around their head. A pretty big person. The voice was kind of weird and nasal. Like they had a cold or something.'

'Do you remember seeing a car? Jón had an old Suzuki. It was always parked outside his house. But did you see any other cars?'

Siggi thought some more, then shook his head. 'I know I should have taken the pizza to the door, but I was happy I didn't have to walk up and see that gross dude.' He was still speaking in a low voice, and Hildur had a hard time making out his mumbling. 'I never went inside,' he repeated, eyes on the floor.

Hildur left her card next to the register and asked Siggi to call if he remembered anything else about the incident. Anything at all. Pizza in hand, Hildur strode out of the grill and into the dusky afternoon. Siggi seemed like a stable, conscientious kid.

But even so, Hildur got the strong sense he was hiding something.

Chapter 18

Hildur stood in her unlit kitchen, filling a glass at the sink and tapping out a text message.

Quick run before work?

Freysi's reply came instantly:

Yup! Ready in 15. Meet you outside

It was a few minutes to seven. Hildur had remembered correctly. Freysi's workday wouldn't begin until nine today.

The cold water felt wonderful as it slid down her throat. She followed it with her morning vitamins and half a banana. She was ready to go. The kitchen and bedroom windows could stay open while she was running. Her place could stand an airing after the night.

Her spiked traction cleats slipped smoothly over her running shoes. She pulled her headlamp over her thin beanie and wrapped reflector bands around her right arm and leg. Crisp winter air surged into her at the front door. The sky looked cloudless, and there was only the tiniest breath of wind.

Hildur did a few quick stretches outside her house to warm up her main muscle groups. A ten-second stretch of her quads, the same for her hamstrings and calves. Making big circles with her arms forwards and then backwards got some movement into her shoulders. Runners often forgot to warm up their upper body before starting off. Having one's circulation flowing throughout the entire body made running easier.

The lights were on in Freysi's kitchen. Hildur scooped up a fistful of snow, patted it into a solid ball, and aimed at the kitchen window. A moment later, the front door opened, and a man in a beanie and impressively snug running trousers stepped out.

'I see you already noticed my new running pants,' Freysi said. Hildur looked up from his midsection. Freysi was a very nicely built man. 'See? There's more to me than a sculpted butt.'

'Yes, I can see there's not much to complain about in front either,' Hildur said, turning on her headlamp.

She got a kick out of sparring with Freysi. It was just friendly, flirtation-spiced banter, but it cheered her up and put her in a good mood. She still didn't get how he could be in such good physical condition, considering how much he smoked and how often he reached for a cold beer instead of a protein shake after a workout.

They headed out on their usual hour-long run, jogging side by side. Their route circled the harbour and the reclaimed land south of it, which over the years had turned into the locals' unofficial dump. After passing the old fishing nets, piles of tyres, and empty oil barrels, they followed the shoreline up to a small patch of forest and the recreational path that ran across the slope above the village.

'How's work?' Freysi asked.

'It's work. The avalanche is a pretty big deal.'

'One of my fellow teachers has a cottage in the avalanche zone. Or had. She's eager to get in there and start looking for her stuff.'

'The weather's good today. They'll be able to continue clearing the area.'

They ran in silence for a moment. The snow squeaked underfoot, and now and again there was a tiny screech as shoe-spike met rock. The path on the avalanche barrier entered a steep rise. There was a lot of snow, so even a slow pace brought them out in a sweat.

Freysi wiped the beads of perspiration from his upper lip and shot a questioning glance up the hill.

'Ugh, maybe there's too much snow,' Hildur said. They could do their hill training some other time. 'Let's take the lower route.'

'I read about that killing in Reykjavík yesterday. He was found dead in an empty parking garage. What the heck happened there?'

Hildur had heard about the case from her colleagues in the capital. She had a lot of solid acquaintances from her years on the force in Reykjavík; it was unusual for a week to pass without her speaking to someone there. And homicides were such a rare occurrence in Iceland that they never escaped notice. So when Hildur saw the news about the parking-garage killing, she'd immediately called her former colleagues and asked about the case off the record.

The whole affair had sounded truly bizarre. As far as she could recall, nothing like it had ever happened in Iceland before. People died in traffic accidents every year, but this man hadn't been knocked down by a random car speeding past. He'd been killed with his *own* vehicle – and a preliminary examination of the mangled body indicated it had been run over multiple times. A horrific fate. But as the information about the method of killing wasn't public yet, she couldn't share it with Freysi.

Hildur was panting. She glanced at her sports watch: her heart rate was grazing 165. Running in the snow was surprisingly laborious. She could barely form complete sentences between breaths. 'I don't know much about it. It seemed like a pretty unusual case.'

Luckily the end of their route led downhill on its way back to the heart of town. Hildur's breathing steadied, and her legs felt lighter. She and Freysi jogged cheerfully side by side like an old couple. The steam from their breaths mingled and rose like smoke signals before dissipating in the dark-blue morning.

When they reached the grill, Freysi stopped. 'Have coffee with me?'

'I wish I could, but I don't have time. I'm actually going straight to work. I'm going to change there.'

'OK, cupcake,' Freysi said, brushing a quick kiss across Hildur's lips. 'We'll have coffee later.'

Hildur stood there, watching his receding back. Then she turned and, invigorated by the run, continued to the station.

A piece of paper taped up in the window of the hair salon across the street advertised scalp-treatment shampoo products for 50 per cent off. The handwritten ad looked cheap, but so was the price. The old building housing the salon had seen better days. A curving concrete wall had been poured in front of the entrance to shield it from the rain and the wind. These protective structures were common features on the town's oldest buildings.

A figure in dark clothes was standing out of sight, behind the wind barrier. Once the joggers had gone their separate ways, the figure emerged from the recess and stalked off briskly in the opposite direction. No one noticed the stealthy shape slinking through the shadows.

Chapter 19

The wind had died, and the sky was clear. Hildur and Jakob had parked on lower Fjallavegur and were walking toward the avalanche zone. Bulldozers had excavated most belongings from the snow. Some had been crushed, while some seemed to have survived nearly intact. There were numerous piles, and they all had to be picked through. That meant the flipping over of broken and undamaged objects, the clustering of matching parts, the collating of wholes – finding anything at all that could give them a clue as to what had happened. Anything that would reveal something about Jón's life, but especially his death.

They'd prepared to work a full day outside and were wearing winter coveralls, warm shoes, and hats with earflaps.

Jakob pulled on a pair of thick gloves and readied himself for the upcoming exertions by stretching his neck from side to side. 'Tell me where to begin, and I'll start shovelling.'

He'd spent the past couple of days working inside. As he didn't speak Icelandic, he wasn't able to question anyone or dig up any possible eyewitnesses. He'd tried to make himself useful by organising the station archives and maintaining the printers. He was happy to be able to do something physical today.

Hildur scanned the area. 'We'll start below Jón's house, then branch out to the sides. Let's go through the junk excavated from the snow first.'

It was only then that Jakob grasped the hopelessly monumental task before them. 'This is going to take days,' he sputtered, eyeing the heaps of debris in disbelief.

'A little bit at a time. Let's not stress out over it.'

'There's enough work here for ten big guys,' Jakob said.

The forensic investigators from Reykjavík hadn't come across anything worth taking from the site, despite having combed the area for hours and having the findings examined in the forensic laboratory. They had flipped over every object in the bedroom in a vain search for the murder weapon or any clue about the perpetrator. No evidence had been found. No fingerprints, no relevant fibres, nothing.

Jón's bed had stood next to a solidly built wall, so the body had made it through the avalanche more or less undisturbed. The rest of Jón's house had been almost wholly destroyed. The heavy snow had turned the partially collapsed bedroom into such a state of chaos that the forensics team hadn't been able to take any fibre samples, footprints, or fingerprints. Belongings had been scattered at a distance from the house. Nature had barrelled in through the wall and carried everything off. If the perpetrator had left any clues at the scene of the crime, the avalanche had swept them away.

On Tuesday, Jón had still been alive and ordered a pizza. Then the avalanche had come, and at some point between the shrimp-and-chicken pizza and the snow slide, he had died.

Perhaps something would turn up that would illuminate Jón's life and death? *Maybe we'll even find the murder weapon*, Jakob reflected.

He inhaled the brisk winter air and got down to work, picking through the first pile of detritus: two pots without handles, a box of little old spoons, splinters of wood that appeared to be from a window frame. Scarves with snow clinging to them. A lot of unidentifiable plastic rubbish, its original purpose a mystery.

Then Jakob's gloved hand struck something soft that squeaked. Jakob flinched. He instinctively moved closer to the squeaking sound and started clearing the snow from a heap of junk by hand. He heard the squeak grow louder. Half of a broken camping plate seemed to be covering the sound; Jakob removed it and set it aside.

Big eyes stared back at him from the snow.

A yellow bath toy with a big head was playing a cheery children's tune. Apparently, Jakob's assault on the junk heap had turned it on. He sighed, put the toy to the side, and kept digging.

A couple of hours later, he and Hildur climbed into the car for a coffee break. Hildur poured coffee from the Thermos into plastic cups, then reached into her pocket and pulled out a baggie of sugar.

She had remembered the sugar. *What a good pal*, Jakob thought, pleased.

After the open-air exertions, the coffee tasted heavenly, but both Hildur and Jakob seemed a little down. The take from a full morning of scouring had been negligible.

'Jón had a red mailbox in front of the house. I couldn't find any sign of it. Either the box or the mail,' Hildur said, fingering patterns on the fogged car window. The contents of the mail might have given them some information on Jón.

'But we'll keep going until it gets dark, right?' Jakob said, impatiently draining his coffee.

They put their coffee mugs in a canvas bag on the floor. Jakob slipped the baggie of sugar cubes into his coveralls.

The freeze seemed to have deepened. There was no wind, and the still weather gave the sea a velvety sheen. The blue light of winter imparted a serene cast to the mountainous terrain. It was an unusually gorgeous, windless winter day. Generally, the cusp of autumn and winter was a stormy period. The south wind brought substantial precipitation, which the north wind froze where it fell. Sometimes the wind came from the north-west, and that was the worst, as it blew straight from the open sea to the butt of the fjord. Clear, beautiful days were a rarity in early winter. It was best to enjoy them when you could.

Jakob got out of the car and returned to Jón's house to dig. The bulldozer had heaped the remnants of the entryway walls into a pile. Boxes and bits of shelves poked through the snow. Jakob started rummaging through them. Hildur was toiling at a bookcase further away.

From one of the snow-filled boxes, Jakob pulled mismatched men's running shoes. There was nothing interesting in a pile of used shoes. Old winter coats, a warped shoehorn, the welcome mat, a stack of empty yoghurt containers. Then he heard Hildur call out sharply.

'Come here! I think I found something.'

Jakob strode briskly toward the south side of the house. He took a shortcut, stepping off the cleared path into the snow. He sank in up to his thighs. Moving was so onerously slow that taking the shortcut hadn't saved any time, just the opposite. Once he made it out and back onto the path, he saw Hildur. She was around the corner of the demolished house, bending over the partially crushed bookcase. She held a little metal box in her hands.

'Look at these,' she said, handing Jakob a stack of photos she'd removed from the box.

Jakob flipped through the Polaroids without pausing to take in the details. He didn't want to see them. The pictures were of scantily dressed teenage boys in various poses. The backdrop seemed to be the same in nearly all cases; only the subject changed.

'Jón's photo collection. Most were taken in Jón's living room,' Hildur said, pointing at the furniture in one of the photos. 'I remember that couch.'

Sick, Jakob thought, handing the photos back to Hildur. 'Do you know who they are?'

'I don't recognise all of them off the bat. But this boy I know. It's the kid from the pizzeria.'

Chapter 20

Beta twirled the Centre Party mug in her hands. She found the pastel unicorn on its side distasteful. She placed it under the single-serve coffee machine and pressed the mug icon. The device rattled for a second, then a dark-brown brew began to drip into the cup.

A pastel unicorn was a strange logo for a political party, but then again, the entire party was strange. The chair had once led another party and served as prime minister. When his name had appeared in the Panama Papers, suspicions of tax evasion arose. He resigned as prime minister and founded a new party, the Centre Party. Some of the party's members used language that was too colourful for Beta's tastes. One night not long ago, a few of its most prominent figures had got drunk at a bar next to the Houses of Parliament and loudly repeated off-colour jokes about women, the disabled, and the poor. A journalist had heard the conversation and written a big newspaper article on it. The party seemed to float from crisis to crisis while maintaining a few percentage points of support. Although most Icelanders couldn't stand it, the party had managed to scrape together a small, loyal band of supporters.

Beta had no interest in party politics, which was surprising because both her parents and her husband were passionate supporters of the right-leaning Independence Party. The party was founded in the 1920s when it advocated for Iceland's independence from Denmark. At every family event and reunion, talk inevitably turned to politics. Beta usually excused herself at that point to do something in the kitchen or start up a football match with the kids. In her view, party politics was a game people played to gain power, and she wanted nothing to do with it. She never publicly supported any electoral candidates, posted views on nominees on social media, or attended a single meeting of the local business leaders, despite having received several invitations to speak at their events as police chief. She fulfilled her duties as an officer of the law, and that was enough.

Beta sipped her coffee and glanced at her phone again.

She was waiting for the results of the forensic autopsy. Jón's post-mortem had been completed, and the report was being finalised. Axlar-Hákon, the pathologist in Reykjavík, had promised to call today.

Axlar-Hákon, or Hákon the Axe, was Beta's old fling from her university days. They'd got to know each other as twentysomething law students and dated for a couple of years. Hákon had got his nickname at the spring play put on by the department's students. The head of his class, he'd done a credible job of acting the lead, Axlar-Björn, the most infamous serial killer in Icelandic history. It had been a memorable performance, fake blood and all.

After earning her degree, Beta had applied to the police academy, and Hákon had continued on into medical school. Nowadays, Axlar-Hákon worked as Iceland's only pathologist at the National University Hospital of Iceland, which had the only facility in Iceland where autopsies were performed.

As she waited for the call, Beta opened a news site and took a couple of chocolate cookies from her desk. She always kept a small supply in her top drawer. She noted the package of oatmeal cookies was over halfway gone. She'd have to remember to stock up on replenishments when she went to the store tomorrow. But for now, the oatmeal cookies dipped in chocolate were divine.

The news headlines reported that Prince Harry and his wife did not intend to spend Christmas with the royal family. Beta wasn't interested enough to click on the link. But the delicious-looking recipe for a gluten-free chocolate cake did catch her attention. Just as the inkjet printer started spitting it out, her phone rang. It was Hákon's number.

As usual, Beta and Hákon began by exchanging the latest news about themselves and their families. The two of them had parted on good terms and continued to enjoy a good relationship. They weren't best friends, but they caught up with each other whenever they were in touch. Hákon was a workaholic, which was no wonder: he didn't really have a choice. Hákon lived with his family in a big waterfront home in Reykjavík. As a medical student, he'd fallen head over heels in love with his professor of public health. Hákon and his professor had had a shotgun wedding, and Hákon had become a stepfather to his wife's school-aged children. As Beta recalled, the kids were well over twenty now.

'My wife is at a conference in Denmark, and both kids are studying in London these days. I've been able to put in long hours without any pangs of conscience. How are things out west?'

'The family are fine, winter came early, and a man was found in an avalanche with his throat slit. I wouldn't mind at all if Christmas came early this year.'

Hákon held a pause before slowly articulating a *jæjja*. I see. That was the signal he was about to get down to business. 'I finished the file. I'll email you the full report, but I wanted to call you because this is something I have to tell you over the phone.'

Beta shivered. She always felt a wing brush across her lower back when something consequential was about to happen. She asked Hákon to continue.

'In the first place, about this Jón. It's plain he died from the sharp force injury at the throat. But it isn't that simple.'

Beta had the impulse to immediately prod for details, but she kept her mouth shut and let Hákon speak in his own time. He was a precise, pedantic man who didn't care to be interrupted.

'The thing that makes our dead man interesting turned up in the more nuanced blood tests. Significant amounts of benzodiazepines were found in his blood.'

Beta immediately understood the ramifications: sleeping pills.

'He'd taken so many, he must have been completely out of it,' Hákon said, then held a pause.

Beta remembered her former boyfriend's ways well enough to know now was a good moment to ask, 'Can you say whether he died of an overdose?'

'He did not die of an overdose. All signs indicate his heart was still beating at the time his throat was slit. Besides, the good thing about benzodiazepines is they're pretty safe when it comes to overdoses. They usually result in unconsciousness, rarely death.'

Beta took a moment to think. She and Hildur had spoken that morning about the mysterious person the pizza delivery driver said he'd seen outside Jón's house the Tuesday before the avalanche. Could the sleeping pills have ended up in Jón's system through the pizza toppings? It sounded strange, but perhaps it was possible.

'The sleeping pills would explain his peaceful position in bed. He didn't wake up when his throat was slit,' she pondered out loud.

'I consider that very likely.'

'And you're positive there weren't enough drugs in his system for an overdose?'

Beta instantly regretted her words. Hákon never said anything he wasn't completely sure of. She remembered a time the two of them had gone to the movies together as students. When she'd asked him what the movie they were going to see was about, Hákon hadn't replied; he'd just given her this strange look and mused there was no way he could know because he hadn't seen it yet. The old memory made her smile.

There had been so much benzodiazepine in Jón's blood there was no way it could have been from one or two tablets. Besides, Hákon had looked into it. Jón had never been prescribed benzodiazepines. Someone must have administered them to him.

First poison, then the knife, Beta reflected. *Someone out there really wanted him dead.*

'But that's not everything,' Hákon continued enigmatically. 'The forensic investigators didn't find any foreign fibres at the site where Jón's body was discovered, did they?'

Beta confirmed this was correct: the technical team had recovered no evidence from the scene. The avalanche had spoiled all tracks.

'Well, I did,' Hákon said, almost jubilantly. This was the Hákon Beta knew: the role of rigid expert was swept aside every time he made an interesting find or solved a problem at work. In such instances, he might even be inspired to use rather coarse language.

'As you know, it's my job to have a look inside any and all orifices. I could barely believe my Lasik-corrected eyes when I pulled this discovery from his mouth.'

His mouth? Beta twirled the mug as she waited to hear what Hákon would say next. 'I found fine blond hairs under his tongue.'

Beta wanted to confirm she'd heard correctly: 'You found hairs under his tongue?'

Hákon grunted in the affirmative. 'A tiny tress of blond hair. Very neatly cut. It's impossible to say much about it at this point, but my guess is it's the hair of a child. Or maybe of an adult with very fine hair.'

Beta fell silent. This case was getting increasingly bizarre. She gulped down the rest of her coffee and instantly regretted it. The liquid that had been standing at the bottom of the mug had turned into lukewarm sludge.

'But wait. It gets even better. Soon you're going to understand why I wanted to call you. Remember that parking-garage murder that happened here in Reykjavík a couple of days ago?' Beta muttered that she remembered. As a matter of fact, she and Hildur had just been discussing it. The victim was not some homeless person who'd been sheltering in the garage or a hoodlum stumbling around in a methamphetamine-induced high, but one of Reykjavík's best-known lawyers.

'So anyway, I performed the autopsy on that body, too. Guess what I found in the mouth?'

Beta closed her eyes. 'Blond hair.'

'Exactly. Blond hair. We did a quick comparison of the strands, and they appear to be from the same head. It's too bad the hair was cut and not pulled out by the root.'

Beta shared this sentiment. 'Which makes DNA analysis more challenging.'

She was no chemist, but she found the work of the forensics laboratory fascinating. She knew determining DNA from severed hairs was laborious at best and often impossible. Even if DNA were successfully isolated, it might be from the person who cut the hair, not the person whose hair it was.

'I'll email you the full report in just a minute. Take care.'

Hákon hung up, and Beta sat there, coffee mug in hand, pondering what she'd just heard. The murders of Jón and the lawyer were linked by a tress of hair. What could the two men have had in common?

Chapter 21

Hildur's shoulders and arms ached deliciously. She felt calmer again. The skin at the base of her middle finger and ring finger was red and raw from the chin-ups. She was sitting on an angled bench at the gym, drinking her post-workout chocolate drink. She'd wanted to go surfing, but her schedule hadn't allowed it: she'd only had an hour. In that time, she'd knocked out a quick upper body workout. Hildur was particularly pleased about the chin-ups. She'd been able to finish them while wearing fifteen-kilogram leg weights.

Half an hour later, a police vehicle turned into the car park outside a small apartment building on the outskirts of the village. The municipality had built this student housing a good ten years ago, when a branch of the University of Akureyri, the School of Marine Sciences, had been established at Ísafjörður. Every year, exchange students and Icelanders interested in the economics of the fishing industry moved here to learn about fishing quotas, healthy seas, and innovations in the seafood industry. In addition to those students, high-school students from rural areas who wanted to spend their weeks closer to school lived in these dorms.

Siggi was seventeen years old and in high school. Hildur had called him right after she found the photographs and told him she needed to have another chat with him. Siggi had promised to be at home after three.

Hildur parked in front of the building and scanned the entrances until she spotted the right one. There was a buzzer next to the street-level door, but its purpose remained obscure because the front door was always open anyway. The stairwell had seen plenty of furniture and people move in and out: the walls were nicked and grimy. A couple of doors had cracks in them, presumably from swift kicks.

Storing bicycles in the stairwells was forbidden, but a quick count revealed at least five leaning against the walls. On the other hand, where else were residents supposed to park their bikes? There didn't seem to be a basement or a bike rack outside.

Hildur climbed to the second floor, found the correct door, and knocked. Apparently, she was expected, because the door was instantly opened by a pale teenager in black sweats and a Metallica T-shirt.

Siggi lived in a small studio apartment. The entryway was furnished with a rickety-looking coat-rack and a mirror, turning left brought you into the kitchen, and turning right took you into a sparsely furnished living room-cum-bedroom. The bed was unmade, and the cardboard box that served as a coffee table was littered with remote controls, coins, and cigarette-rolling supplies. The place was fuggy; it clearly hadn't been aired in some time.

Hildur suggested they talk in the living room. The dejected-looking Siggi took a seat on a couch that had seen better days and sat there, staring helplessly. The couch was the only place to sit, so Hildur took the far end.

'I need to ask a few more questions about Jón,' she said.

When Siggi heard the name, he curled in on himself. His shoulders turned inward, and he hung his head.

Hildur wanted to know how Siggi had met Jón.

'I already told you. I usually did the deliveries on Tuesdays.'

'But how well did the two of you know each other?' Hildur rubbed her hands together. The chafing from the chin-up bar had started to set in.

149

Siggi didn't immediately reply. He stared at the living room floor, paralysed, before eventually saying in a soft voice: 'We didn't know each other.'

'You told me Jón asked you inside once. Did you go in?'

'I just brought him his pizzas,' Siggi insisted.

Hildur sighed. She felt sorry for the kid, but she had to get him to talk. 'Listen. I'm sure this is really hard for you. I know Jón was a real asshole.'

Siggi flinched, but Hildur kept going. She stressed how important it was for Siggi to answer the questions she was asking. Jón's death was being investigated as a homicide. Siggi wasn't suspected of having done anything, but if he refused to tell what he knew about Jón, that might change. Someone had murdered Jón, and it was starting to be plain that Siggi was one of the last people to have had contact with him.

Siggi still didn't say a word. He took the rolling device, pulled a pouch of tobacco from his pocket, and, hands shaking, started to roll. Hildur watched the cigarette form and decided she'd have to nudge the conversation on. 'Siggi, I've seen the pictures. That's why I'm here.'

The radiator in the living room burbled faintly. It needed bleeding.

The silence between Hildur and Siggi had condensed into something so heavy and oppressive you could sink a spoon into it. It wouldn't be long before the kid caved.

Siggi groaned, covered his face with his hands, and doubled over. The cigarette fell to the floor. Hildur felt guilty about putting more pressure on someone already in such a fragile state, but she had to see the boy's reaction to the next question she was going to ask.

'Was it because of those pictures that you killed him?'

The hunched Siggi straightened his back enough to be able to establish eye contact with Hildur. His cheeks were splotched from crying. He looked Hildur dead in the eye. His gaze was filled with the powerless fright of the misunderstood.

In that instant, Hildur knew her initial reaction when she saw the photos had been right.

'No. I didn't kill him.' Siggi leaned into his palms again and sobbed: 'I don't have any money. I've never had any money.'

Siggi told Hildur he earned a normal hourly wage at the pizzeria and got free food during his shifts, but there was no way the money would stretch to cover all his costs. He couldn't take on any more shifts because of school. If he didn't attend class, he didn't pass his courses.

Hildur felt bad for the kid. He was so young. 'Don't you have parents who could help?'

Siggi looked up at Hildur and chuckled mockingly. 'My parents? They never have any money! They're shell lickers.'

The expression was so old-fashioned that Hildur had never heard a young person use it before. In olden times, people had been so poor they'd licked the shells of shellfish they gathered at the shore if there'd been nothing else to eat.

'That asshole gave me money for those pictures. The first time happened a couple of years ago.' Siggi's voice rose; by now he was almost shouting. 'He paid a hundred thousand krónur for one picture and promised he'd never show it to anyone.'

That's quite a chunk of change, Hildur reflected. The stack of photos hadn't been small, and if Jón had paid each subject 600-plus euros per shot, he must have had some money.

She told Siggi the photos had been found in Jón's home. 'They were taken with a non-digital camera; they can't be posted online.'

'Who has them now? Has anyone else seen them?' Siggi raked up the cigarette from the floor and lit it with fumbling fingers. His agitation was understandable. It would be terrible for him if the photos got around.

Hildur reassured Siggi the pictures were at the police station for safekeeping. The police would need them for the investigation into the causes of Jón's death. No one else would be able to see them.

The two of them sat there in silence. The sound of a washing machine in its spin cycle carried from next door; a group of children were having a raucous snowball fight outside. In this home, inside these walls, something unpleasant was taking place. Meanwhile, the lives of those around them seemed to go on as usual. When the cigarette had burned down to its butt, Hildur decided to break the silence.

'Did you stay at his place long that Tuesday?'

'No. Some creep wanted to take the pizza and bring it to him. I didn't go inside that night.'

'Can anyone prove it?'

Siggi thought for a moment, then shook his head lightly. 'I don't know. The creep outside the house. But I don't know who it was.'

Hildur had been convinced by Siggi's eyes and account that he hadn't killed Jón. 'What happened after you delivered the pizza?'

'I had another delivery. I drove straight down the fjord to the next address.'

Hildur concealed her relief and settled for a nod. She'd already confirmed this part of Siggi's story with the pizzeria. Siggi had driven from Jón's house to the other side of town in ten minutes and gone straight back to the restaurant to pick up the next nightly specials for delivery. He'd spent the entire evening, from five to eleven, driving back and forth across Ísafjörður.

'Did you go to Jón's after Tuesday?'

Siggi froze. A stony mask fell over his face, and his eyes glazed over. He seemed to have registered for the first time that he might be a suspect in Jón's death.

And then, with surprising speed, he pulled himself together. He seemed to gather his courage instantly and answered without the tiniest tremor in his voice: 'No way. I didn't want to go anywhere near that place. I spend my evenings at work, my days at school. And I have ever since I moved here and started high school.'

In spite of his age, the boy had been forced to navigate difficult situations on his own. For a couple of years now, he'd had to fight for things many high school students took for granted. He'd got himself a home, warm food, and schoolbooks. It hadn't been easy going. It had been downright horrific, to be honest. No one should have to sell themselves to go to high school. In moments like this, Hildur was disgusted by Icelandic society. Too often it failed miserably when it came to helping people.

The combination living room/bedroom was tiny. The curtain rod over the window was crooked, and there were no curtains. The two transparent rubbish bags at the balcony door appeared to be full of empty bottles and flattened cans.

So Siggi recycled empties. The recycling bins at student housing were probably overflowing with empty beer cans. In Iceland you couldn't return empty bottles to the store; you had to take them to a recycling station.

Hildur looked at the plastic bags. 'It's a pretty long way to the recycling station, isn't it?'

Siggi nodded. 'It's been a while since I've had time to go. I'm always at work or school when it's open.'

Hildur pulled a five-thousand-króna bill from her pocket, smoothed it out, and set it down next to the rolling papers. 'I'll take those bottles. Here's some money for them.'

Hildur knew the amount was almost twice what the bottles were worth. But she wanted to help Siggi somehow and couldn't think of anything else in the circumstances. The price of two movie tickets wouldn't get Siggi far, but at least he wouldn't have to spend hours sorting through empties and taking the bus to the recycling station.

Hildur stood, patted Siggi on the shoulder, and told him to call if anything else came to him.

Carrying the two big bags of bottles, Hildur exited the building. As she crammed the bags into her boot, she reflected Jón's killer might well turn up among his victims. But Siggi wasn't the killer. She was sure of it. The boy's demeanour had told her.

The other thing that spoke on behalf of the boy's innocence was more pragmatic, and Hildur could never speak publicly about it.

Jón had committed a crime. Presumably multiple, as Siggi wasn't the only one Jón had lured into his home to be photographed for money. And at least according to Siggi's account, Jón hadn't touched him. The photos were solo shots of Siggi and hadn't been violent or, from a criminal investigator's perspective, horrifically offensive in content. But a hundred thousand krónur for one picture of a sixteen-year-old in his underwear was so much cash that it was unlikely Siggi would have wanted to turn off this money tap. Of course, Hildur couldn't say this to Siggi, because it might sound as if she were dismissing Jón's actions. The opposite was true. Jón's actions disgusted her more than ever.

Hildur turned from the car park onto the road leading to the recycling station. She would take the empties right away. She was determined to see at least one thing through today.

Chapter 22

After dropping off the empties, Hildur returned to the police station. Beta had scheduled a meeting for four thirty.

Hildur took off her coat and seated herself at the conference table. Jakob came in, carrying three full cups of coffee. He also had a couple of packets of chocolate cookies under his arms. He set them down on the table before glancing at his boss.

'These are the right kind, aren't they?'

The visibly delighted Beta selected the package with the wrapper that promised triple chocolate crème. 'You read my mind. We were running low.'

Jakob took a seat at the table and pulled his knitting needles from his bag. He'd spent the day rummaging through the ruins of Jón's house and stopped by the store on his way back to the station. 'An intern has to try to find ways of being useful. Since there's nothing new to report from Jón's house.'

Jakob had gone through the rest of the stuff recovered from the snow but hadn't come up with anything relevant to the murder. The most interesting item had been a red Moomintroll mug that was chipped at the rim: the mug featuring an aproned Moominmamma cleaning berries had been an unexpected find. Jakob hadn't known that Icelanders, like Finns, were enthusiastic collectors of Moomintroll mugs. Maybe it had belonged to Jón, or else it had made its way into the pile along with the items from some other cottage.

Beta, in contrast, had much to report on the autopsy results.

As she listened, Hildur fished cookie crumbs from the tabletop with her forefinger. The events of the past few days felt
surreal. It was unheard of to have two interrelated murders
presumably committed by the same perpetrator. She couldn't
remember anything of the sort ever having happened in Iceland
before. Not since Axlar-Björn axed and drowned almost twenty
Icelanders to death in the 1500s.

At the same time, Hildur was relieved. It was extremely unlikely
Siggi would have been in any way involved in Jón's death. She
reported on the photographs she and Jakob had found and the
chat she'd just had with the young pizza delivery driver.

'But if there's a connection between the death of a rich lawyer in Reykjavík and Jón's death, I don't see the "Jon's victim"
theory as particularly likely anymore. Unless this lawyer who
was killed in the parking garage defended Jón in court at one
point and some disgruntled character took both of them out.'

'Heiðar didn't take cases like this,' Beta said. 'He was mostly
involved in corporate law.' She added that she'd spoken with the
detective investigating the lawyer's death. The similar hair-tufts
found in the mouths of both victims suggested a single perpetrator. Even so, the decision had been made to investigate the cases
separately, at least for now. Jón's murder would be investigated
in Ísafjörður and Heiðar's murder by the police in Reykjavík.
'But we agreed to cooperate closely and keep each other up to
date. If there is a link between the victims, we'll find it.'

'Who's handling the investigation in Reykjavík?' Hildur asked.

'Jónas Ingimarsson.'

'Are you serious? That prick?'

Hildur knew Jónas. Unfortunately. After graduating from the
police academy, he and Hildur had worked in the same unit for
some time. On the very first day, she'd realised she wouldn't be

156

able to stand the things that came out of his musclebound chauvinist mouth. Jónas looked down on women and didn't try very hard to hide his views.

Hildur's revulsion for her colleague had only grown after she'd heard the stories from other police officers. Everyone on the force knew multiple domestics had been reported from Jónas's home. The violence had been impossible to prove because the wife never said a word to anyone about the abuse. It was always the same story: the bruise on her face was from falling during a hike or tripping on the stairs; the noise the neighbours heard had been coming from the television.

'Jónas is one of the most experienced criminal investigators in Reykjavík, but he beats his wife in his free time,' Hildur explained before Jakob could ask. Beta shot Hildur a look from under her brows that conveyed this wasn't a topic to delve into right now.

Hildur raised her chin in protest but nevertheless agreed to steer the conversation back to the topic at hand. 'I've received Jón's phone records and bank statements. There's nothing we didn't already know in the calls and text messages. He did order a pizza every Tuesday. The bank account info, on the other hand, hit like a blizzard from the north. Jón was really damn wealthy.'

Beta was raking her curls up into a bun on top of her head but stopped mid-movement. The half-made ponytail fell apart as she lowered her hands to the table. This was unexpected news: the man who went around looking like a bum had money.

'How much are we talking about?'

'At the time of his death, he had twenty million krónur in his bank account. And had had for years. He made big cash withdrawals a couple of times a month.'

The wool slipped quickly through Jakob's powerful fingers as he shifted the loops from the finished sleeve to the secondary needles. He'd been listening without interrupting. Now he said: 'There won't be any trace of the cash. He spent it on marijuana and photos.'

'We need to take a closer look at the source of the money. Maybe something will turn up there,' Hildur said, then reported how little she'd discovered from questioning the neighbours. Siggi's description of the mysterious visitor wasn't much use either.

'I think that describes just about everyone in Iceland during the winter,' Jakob said.

Hildur agreed. In practice, they had no useful identifiers for the mysterious individual.

She let her thoughts roll through her head. Presumably the sleeping pills had been mixed in with the pizza, and after Jón passed out, the murderer had finished the job with a knife.

'Jón was murdered by someone who knew he always ordered pizza on Tuesday. Someone familiar with his habits.'

Chapter 23

November 2019, Reykjavík

Lian was holding a small but incredibly sharp knife in her hand. She touched the tip to the taut, swollen skin and pressed. The blade sank in effortlessly and sliced through the soft mass. It was a smooth, beautiful incision.

Lian rinsed the knife under running water, shook off the largest drops in the sink, and put the steel weapon on a dish towel to dry. She took a white plate from the cupboard and squeezed out the contents of the frozen meal she'd just opened. She used a fork to mash the fish-and-potato mix flat on the plate and set it in the microwave to heat through. *Two minutes on high should be enough.*

Lian glanced at her watch. She was tired. She'd meant to take a long nap before her shift, but nothing had come of it. Her spouse, who worked as an IT specialist, had had to go in to work due to some urgent security issue. And that had meant taking the girls to gymnastics had fallen to Lian.

The girls had back-to-back gymnastics classes on the far side of town. There was no direct bus from school, so responsibility for getting them there lay on their parents' shoulders. *Not usually mine, thank God*, Lian thought to herself, rubbing her stiff neck. But the thought of her children put a smile on her face. The younger daughter, in particular, had proven gifted at gymnastics, and practice never felt like an obligation to her. The girls also played football. Fortunately, there was no need to drive them to football practice; the club bus fetched the kids at the end of the school day and drove them straight to practice.

Lian had stood in the bleachers at the gymnastics arena for a couple of hours, drinking a Pepsi Max to stay awake during the long afternoon hours. After practice, she'd made dinner and taken a fifteen-minute catnap on the couch only to realise it was almost time to leave for work. She'd grabbed a package of Grímur-brand *plokkfiskur* from the fridge. One meal before her shift began, and a second a little before midnight, once the patients were presumably – or at least hopefully – asleep.

Nights at the psychiatric hospital varied. Sometimes things were quiet; sometimes not. As a psychiatric nurse, Lian was used to seeing the full range of human existence, which many healthy people had no conception of. Nor was there any need for them to.

Lian liked her work. She found it motivating to help others and provide caregiving services according to each patient's needs. She'd been with Kleppur since moving to her husband's homeland from the Philippines. With the exception of two brief maternity leaves, she'd worked at the same hospital. She was happy there. The ambience was relaxed, her bosses were nice, and the work, although demanding, was interesting. She and her fellow nurses weren't as overworked as the caregiving staff at non-psychiatric hospitals and nursing homes. The psychiatric hospital had continued to be resourced appropriately, at least for now.

The microwave timer chimed loudly. Her fish-and-potato hash was ready. Lian set the plate down on the break room table, seasoned her food with black pepper, and dropped a couple of teaspoons of fresh butter on top. She tasted. Delicious. You couldn't beat a meal cooked by someone else.

As she forked her dinner into her mouth, she used her free hand to tidy the newspapers strewn across the table, then opened yesterday's paper.

She ate and browsed the news. The unemployment rate had risen 0.3 percentage points, to 3.8 per cent. Lian laughed. That was nothing. Finding work in Iceland was no problem; even when she was a recently arrived foreigner who didn't speak the language, she'd got a job right away. Now she spoke Icelandic fluently, and her pay had risen as she'd taken on more responsibilities at work. She'd started by cleaning hospitals and nursing homes. As her language skills improved, she'd studied to be a psychiatric nurse.

The main page reported on a case of suspected corruption involving a large Icelandic fishing company with operations in Namibia. Lian huffed. She couldn't be bothered to read the article, because she knew how these things went. Corporate bigwigs were caught committing fraud. The CEO would briefly step down. A mudslinging campaign would be launched against those who had exposed the wrongdoings. The public would grow tired of following the topic. The CEO would return to his position, and the case would collect dust on the desks of the prosecutor and the lawyers. To Lian, corruption existed everywhere. There had been corruption in the Philippines, and there was corruption here in Iceland, too.

When she made it to the next page, Lian almost choked on her food. She started hacking violently. The fourth furious cough brought up a bit of fish into her mouth.

The blurb in the lower right corner of the national news page had caught her off guard, and she'd forgotten to chew. Lian tried again. This time she ate more carefully and washed down the mouthful with a swig of water. When she was done, she reread the article. Lian spoke Icelandic fluently, but understanding the formal language used in newspapers was more challenging and took longer. She had to read a few words multiple times to grasp the meaning of the article.

Forty-five-year-old lawyer Heiðar Arason died in Reykjavík last week. The police suspect homicide but, for investigative reasons, cannot reveal the cause of death or other details.

Heiðar, Heiðar, Heiðar. An abrupt, heavy coolness washed over Lian. She'd just been shivering from exhaustion, but this was a different chill. She'd suddenly felt an oppressive cold. As if a large chunk of ice had slid to her stomach and started to melt.

Lian had to check right away. She pulled out an older newspaper from the bottom of the stack and unfolded it on the table. The other article had been in the national news, too, just like the story about Heiðar's murder. It had been brief and short on details, and she no longer remembered exactly what it had been about. But she had spotted a familiar name in it.

An avalanche in the village of Ísafjörður, Westfjords, destroyed several summer cottages.

Lian kept reading . . . There it was. Her memory had served her right.

The avalanche also claimed a life. In violation of regulations, Jón Jónsson, 68, had been staying in his house within the avalanche zone and was trapped in the snow. He was found dead and beyond resuscitation. No further details are available from law enforcement at this time. The police thank all volunteers who participated in the search-and-rescue and site-clearing efforts.

Found dead? Why did the news say he'd been *found dead* instead of saying he died in the avalanche? Lian wondered if the police had left something unsaid.

Jón. And then Heiðar. It couldn't be a coincidence, Lian mused. She would have to call the police after her shift. No, she needed to call right now.

But just then, Klaudia, who would be working the night shift with Lian, appeared in the doorway. She seemed to be in a hurry. 'There's a problem in room five. I'd rather not go in there by myself.'

Lian quickly folded up the newspaper and followed after Klaudia. The patient in room five, a recent arrival, behaved aggressively in the evenings. The nurses had agreed no one would enter the room alone.

The patient took precedence over any other concerns right now. But Lian didn't forget what she'd read in the paper. Heiðar and Jón. She'd call the police first thing in the morning, as soon as she got off work.

Chapter 24

November 2019, Ísafjörður

Jakob grabbed the metal handle and pressed down, but the wooden door wouldn't budge. He checked the hours on the sign taped to the door and glanced at his black sports watch. He had rushed straight here from the meeting. The knitting shop was supposed to be open for another fifteen minutes, and the lights appeared to be on. Then he saw a familiar-looking woman carrying a big cardboard box at the back of the shop.

Guðrún noticed Jakob rattling the door.

'Push hard!' she shouted loudly enough for her voice to carry outside.

Jakob pressed the handle down again and pushed firmly against the door with his right shoulder. There was a clunk as the door opened.

'It always swells in the winter and gets stuck. I should replace it,' Guðrún said, setting the box down on a nearby chair.

The box read ÍSTEX in big black letters, which Jakob recognised as the name of Iceland's largest and oldest woollen mill. Ístex was owned by sheep farmers, and most wool from the autumn and spring shearings was sold to the mill and turned into yarn of various qualities. Wool from Icelandic sheep had made a name for itself among knitting communities around the world, and the most popular colours were hard to find outside Iceland. Maybe Jakob would find them here.

He let his gaze scan the shop. Metres and metres of Léttlopi yarn in dozens of colours. Only the back wall had the heavier Álafosslopi. There was a range of colours available of fine Einband yarn and even of unspun Plötulopi. Sweaters and beanies in puffin patterns hung from racks. There were ads for sheep-herding vacations for dogs. A round clock ticked on the wall.

Jakob was surprised to find such a wide selection of yarn in such a small town. He was so lost in thought he didn't hear it the first time the question was posed to him.

'I was just wondering how I could help you, friend,' Guðrún said cheerfully, slipping a stray tress behind her ear.

Jakob coughed and took a moment to choose his words: 'Um, we met on the aeroplane not too long ago. You were working.'

Guðrún stood up straight and put her hands on her hips. 'I remember you! The mysterious knitter from Finland. Have you recovered yet?'

Jakob smiled. He'd been terrified in the small, swaying aircraft. 'I need more yarn. I've been looking for this *ryygbruunn* for a while and haven't found it anywhere. I need one skein.'

Guðrún pursed her lips. '*Ryygd . . .* what?'

Jakob pulled out his mobile phone and activated it using the facial recognition feature, then browsed through his notes to the right colour code. *9427.* It was yarn he needed to complete the pattern of a sweater he was working on.

Guðrún's face brightened immediately.

'*Ryðbrúnn!* You should have said so from the start. It's a rusty brown.'

Jakob knew Guðrún was teasing him about his pronunciation. The only response was to spread his arms in surrender.

'Your timing is perfect. A new shipment just came in from the mills. Come have a look,' Guðrún said, smiling seductively as she hooked a finger, inviting him over.

The frank flirtation caught Jakob off guard.

Guðrún grabbed a boxcutter and sliced through the tape sealing the box. She returned the knife to the pocket of her work smock and raised the box's four flaps one at a time. Then she reached in, pulled out the first packages of yarn, and handed them to Jakob.

'These colours are rich and earthy . . .' she said, dipping her hand back into the box. An expression of exaggerated surprise appeared on her face as she pulled out bright orange and yellow yarns.

'. . . and the delivery is spiced with a few bright colours. Something surprising in the middle of the dark winter,' she cooed, staring at Jakob dead in the eye. 'Do you like what you see?'

Guðrún's high, blonde bun, broad shoulders, and toothy smile made her look like a woman warrior from an action movie or something out of a tourism advertisement for Iceland. Or both at the same time. Jakob was fascinated by her direct advances and her guileless way of expressing interest. She didn't seem aggressive, but she didn't leave anything to guesswork either. She put it out there. Take it or leave it.

Jakob found the situation incredibly strange yet pleasant. This woman was really throwing him off.

'And then I have what you're looking for right here.' Guðrún bent over the shelf at her side, plucked a skein of rust-brown yarn between her thumb and forefinger, and tossed it to Jakob.

Jakob caught the skein and looked at it approvingly. It was just the right colour. 'Yes, that's perfect. I also want to take a look at those new ones, find something nice. I could buy some yarn for a new sweater. I'll have time to knit while I'm here.'

'Yes, let's take a look. The shipment included the latest sweater patterns. I got an advance copy from the designer last week and have had time to have a look. There's one that could really be nice on you; it has a dark blue base with a contrasting pattern in lighter tones.'

Guðrún started removing the plastic covers from the knitting patterns that had come with the yarn shipment. She took the topmost booklet and flipped through it. She found the right pattern, opened the spread flat, and sidled up next to Jakob with it.

She came so close that her bun accidentally grazed Jakob's beard, and a couple of strands of her hair caught in it. She looked at him apologetically, plucked her hair out of his beard with her free hand, and tucked it behind her ear. Jakob was sure she'd done it on purpose. Then he noticed the scent of a spicy perfume: a hint of cinnamon in her fragrance.

It had been a long time since Jakob had been on a date, and he wasn't sure of the best way to go about navigating a situation like this. But maybe it wasn't time to think. Maybe it was just time to go for it.

As Guðrún held out the pattern so Jakob had a better view, she pressed into his body the tiniest bit. He was going to have to jump in with both feet or miss out. It wasn't as if he had anything to lose. It had been so long since the last time he didn't even want to think about it.

He took a deep breath, leaned over the book, and grazed the hand Guðrún was using to hold the book. He placed his forefinger on the dark blue sweater and studied it.

'You're right. I'd like to try this one.'

Guðrún shot him a quick look, and an enigmatic smile spread across her face. 'The instructions are in Icelandic, but I can help translate them for you.'

'That sounds great. I'll take everything I need to make this sweater.'

'The translation service, too?' Guðrún asked as she deposited the relevant skeins in a paper bag.

'That most of all.'

Jakob paid for his purchases and watched Guðrún's movements at the register. Her light-green nails tapped quickly at the terminal. After the payment went through, the device spat out a narrow receipt, and Guðrún slipped it into the bag. She bit her bottom lip and handed the bag across the counter to Jakob.

She suggested they leave right away. Jakob thought it was a splendid idea.

Guðrún hung her work smock over the back of her chair, powered down the register, and turned off the lights. She locked the door and slipped her hand through Jakob's arm.

The snow squeaked under their shoes, and the paper bag in Jakob's hand rustled as it hit the leg of his trousers. Suddenly he was overcome by a powerful sense of joy. He felt sure of himself and buoyant, almost boisterous.

Maybe, at least for a moment, he was happy.

Chapter 25

I inhale the winter air. The petrol smells invigorating. The black hose pulses as the fuel flows. I turn from the north wind and pull my neck in, so the wind hits my collar instead of making its way into my coat. This wind isn't whispering; it's shouting.

Soon all my plans will have come to fruition. Soon all will be ready, and this will end.

I start up the car. It hums faster beneath me at command. I cautiously drive away from the remote self-service station with my headlights off. I don't think anyone has seen me. Even if they had, it wouldn't make much difference anymore.

I'm surrounded by darkness. I drive from darkness into light. The word is light. And I take strength from the light – and the word.

Paul wrote to his colleague, the apostle Timothy: If any provide not for his own, and specially for those of his own house, he hath denied the faith, and is worse than an infidel.

I have provided. I've done nothing but provide! And so far everything has felt right. I've excised evil and made room for good. I've removed the corruption in the face of which all others have been powerless.

The next task is unpleasant, but it must be done. I am doing it for those I love. I must consider the whole.

I'm sorry, Hildur. I don't want to do this to you, as you have suffered so deeply. I'm sorry, but there's nothing to be done for it.

I must do this.

Chapter 26

November 2019, Ísafjörður

The rhythmic whistle of a jump rope filled the gym. The place was dim, but even so, the lights hadn't been turned on.

After warming up, Hildur undid her bun and let her ponytail slide down her back. Her palms grabbed the barbell at each end. A set of deadlifts: legs straight, feet side by side, wide stance, underhanded grip, overhanded grip, mixed grip. After each series of reps, there was a soft thud as the barbell fell to the black rubber mat.

As she went through the reps, Hildur's breathing intensified and her pulse rose. More weights onto the bar. Hildur reached for the metal pail standing on the floor. She rubbed the chalk onto her hands. Sunbeams striving to enter the dark illuminated the puff of white dust floating in the air. Hildur moved back into the shade and took hold of the bar.

She focused. Back straight, muscles tensed, core solid as stone.

First rep, second rep, grimace. The bar was too heavy, but today she had to lift. If she didn't, she wouldn't feel anything anywhere. Except that damned heavy coldness that had snuck up on her again. She had sensed the familiar pressure growing inside her, but today she felt extraordinarily bad. She added two five-kilo weights to the bar. When 120 kilos of iron clanked to the floor after the fifth rep, the sounds of strength reverberated from the walls of the empty gym. The bar was heavy, and she was supposed to feel light.

But she didn't.

Later that evening, the reflective band popped as it tightened around Hildur's right arm. The sleeve of her lightweight yellow parka bunched up at the cuff. She pulled on her beanie and headlamp, slipped on her traction cleats, closed the door behind her, and started off.

Today was Monday, in other words, her day to have dinner at her Aunt Tinna's. Travel or illness were the only two things that kept her from going. She'd felt better after her workout, but she still couldn't claim she felt good. Even so, she wanted to see her aunt. Maybe she ought to go on foot; the walk would relax her and help her clear her thoughts.

Tinna had been a bit lonely since she retired. But Hildur didn't pay these visits purely out of a sense of obligation; she liked seeing her aunt. Aside from the fact that Tinna was Hildur's sole remaining relative, the two of them had always been close.

Hildur drew fresh air into her lungs and shook her shoulders as she exhaled. Hopefully this oppressive feeling would go away. The walk to Tinna's house was under thirty minutes. She turned left at the corner and headed toward the pedestrian-cum-bike path that followed the shoreline. She had to climb a couple of snow piles to reach the path, which to her relief been ploughed.

There was no one else in sight. Not that that was a surprise: walking was pretty un-Icelandic. Especially in rural areas, all journeys, even the shortest ones, were made by car. It was also the custom to leave cars running when the driver popped into the shops. Hildur had never understood her compatriots' attitude toward cars. Cars were the norm; cyclists were poor, hippies, or otherwise suspect.

The icy air felt wonderful in her lungs. Hildur loved exercise; somehow expending energy gave her energy. Calm, repetitive movement was the best medicine for clearing the cobwebs out of one's mind.

She picked up the pace and reflected on the case she was presently working on. Earlier that day, she'd spoken on the phone with Jónas, who was investigating the parking-garage murder in Reykjavík. Jónas had been as unpleasantly arrogant as she'd remembered, but he'd also given her a lot of interesting information.

The victim, Heiðar, had had plenty of enemies, and few people had had anything positive to say about him. He'd been described as arrogant, self-centred, even a liar. What made the case particularly interesting was the fact that the widow didn't seem particularly upset when she learned about her husband's death. Of course, this had immediately piqued the investigators' interest. Usually, the perpetrator of a homicide was found among those closest to the victim. But the widow had an alibi for the night of the murder. She'd been at home and, at the time Heiðar died, on a two-hour WhatsApp video call with a friend who lived in the United States.

The surveillance cameras in the downtown Reykjavík parking garage hadn't been working that evening. Dark wool fibres that hadn't come from Heiðar were found in the SUV, but similar fibres appeared in just about every black wool sweater or wool scarf, garments worn by half of Iceland in the winter. No fingerprints other than Heiðar's were found in the car. The killer who had crushed Heiðar with his own Range Rover had been careful indeed.

At the moment, the Reykjavík police were questioning Heiðar's former clients, opponents in court, and colleagues. Maybe something would turn up there. Jónas had promised to keep Hildur updated on the investigation. In return, Hildur had promised to apprise Jónas of any developments in their search for Jón's killer. She'd shared her theory that the murderer had probably taken the pizza from the driver, topped it with a generous pinch of benzos, and slit Jón's throat after he passed out in his bed. Jónas had chuckled at the pizza robbery and praised Hildur's storytelling skills. But he'd grown serious when he heard they had an eyewitness sighting of the potential killer: a large individual wearing dark clothes and a scarf.

The two cases felt like irrational outbursts on the one hand and well-planned crimes on the other.

It was just below freezing, but the wind from the north made the air feel colder. Hildur started walking faster again. At the former fishing net factory, a winding dirt road turned up into the cross-country skiing area in the mountains. So much snow had fallen that it wouldn't be long before the trails were opened. Freysi was teaching cross-country technique over the Christmas break, and Hildur had immediately signed up for the course to be held over several days.

The shortcut across the factory lot didn't actually shorten the trip at all; off the path, the snow reached halfway up Hildur's legs. But for some reason, trudging through it felt good. Why do things the easy way, if you can sweat your tits off instead? Hildur didn't know the answer. The snowy factory grounds were bounded by a deep ditch, so eventually she had to climb back to the ploughed footpath and walk the last couple of hundred metres like the average person would. She could already make out the lights of her aunt's house.

It aggravated Hildur that nothing new had turned up in Jón's case since Siggi's admissions. She'd been in contact with the juvenile rehab centre where Pétur, the boy they'd found at Jón's house a few weeks ago, was living again. The drug abuse counsellor told her that since his return, Pétur had followed the rules and hadn't left the grounds without permission.

Hildur had spoken with a few people from child protection services, where Jón's was a distressingly familiar name. Everyone knew Jón from the Westfjords, who maintained contact with troubled youth and lured them to him. Hildur had reached the head of child protection services in Akureyri, someone who'd known twin brothers who'd spent a little over a week at Jón's the year before and got hashish from him. In her view, something had happened, but the twins denied everything. Nowadays they lived with their mother in Sweden.

Hildur had also called the *Barnahús* in Reykjavík. The psychologists at the 'children's house' specialised in helping the police investigate crimes where the victims, witnesses, or perpetrators were under the age of eighteen. Jón's name hadn't come up in any investigations over the past couple years.

Jón was like grey matter whose existence was known to all but about whom no one really seemed to know much in the end. He'd lived like a rat in a sewer system he'd dug himself.

Hildur inhaled deeply at the front door, then opened it. She was determined to take a break from her work now and concentrate on spending the evening with her aunt.

As always, Tinna's place was cosy and calm. The clock ticked loudly on the wall, and the glare of the television glowed from the living room. Hildur was sitting in her usual spot, with a big bowl of fatty meat soup steaming in front of her. Tinna sat on the other side of the kitchen table and asked Hildur to pour them pineapple juice.

Tinna nodded at the three-litre pot. 'I made it with lamb from Súgandafjörður. I sang at the celebration after the sheep round-up in September. Hörður from next door brought me a few kilos of soup meat as thanks.'

Tinna made soup in the traditional style, using large chunks of meat with the bone in and fat still attached. Hildur blew on her spoon and tasted. Scrumptious. Her aunt liked to simmer her soups for hours. The bones had given the broth a rich taste, and the meat was deliciously fatty.

They ate without speaking. The theme music for the evening news carried into the kitchen from the living room. Soon they would hear about the state of the world. After the anchor moved on from the international news to the sports, Hildur broke the silence.

'Tell me everything you remember about my sisters' disappearance.'

The spoon that was on its way to Tinna's mouth stopped mid-air, and Tinna turned toward Hildur. She looked flustered, helpless somehow. 'I don't think there's anything I haven't told you already.'

'Tell me again. I want to hear everything again.'

Hildur had been thinking about her sisters a lot lately. The fate of the unlucky but resourceful Siggi had roused memories of her sisters. She set her spoon down on the rim of her bowl and laced her fingers under her chin. She shut her eyes and tried to put her confused thoughts into words.

'Wind from the west at fifteen metres a second. Rain in the south turning to sleet as we move north. In the south and east, a yellow weather alert. Gusts will grow stronger toward evening. Large trucks should stay off the road.'

Hildur found the meteorologist's monotonous voice soothing. She pinched her eyelids together and scrunched her toes under the table. Both helped her focus.

'I have ... I have this awkward feeling that I don't know everything I ought to know. I was so young at the time, but I remember some things. I remember moments and words, visitors sitting at our kitchen table, heads hanging. But I know there's something I'm not remembering.'

Now it was Tinna's turn to close her eyes. She took two deep breaths and began. 'A couple of people driving through town saw two girls walking in the snowstorm, but for some reason, they'd both kept going without stopping.'

Hildur remembered all this. She'd read it in the police notes.

'The search for your sisters lasted for days, but no trace of them was ever found. No belongings, no clothes, nothing. A lot of people believed they'd died in the mountains, lost in the snow,' Tinna continued.

'I think that's a strange conclusion,' Hildur snapped with such unexpected venom she startled herself. 'Why would they walk into the mountains in such awful weather? I'm sure they entered the tunnel even though it wasn't open to traffic yet. Everyone knew the tunnel was finished. The grand opening had been celebrated in town the summer before. They had a hot dog stand at the square, and a band played Icelandic oldies. The kids got balloons and popcorn.'

Tinna shrugged and looked helpless. 'Yes. The search-and-rescue dogs were brought in, but the girls' scent vanished at the mouth of the tunnel.'

Hildur looked at her aunt's face. The passing years had left their traces. The furrows at the corners of Tinna's eyes had deepened and her jawline had softened. Ageing had touched them all.

'The mouth of the tunnel. That's what everyone kept saying. The mouth of the tunnel.'

Tinna shook her head apologetically, and her eyes grew moist. Hildur felt sorry for her aunt. She felt sorry for herself. She shouldn't have come here to talk about unpleasant things but to spend a carefree evening and enjoy her aunt's stew.

But today she had to talk, because the topic wouldn't leave her in peace, and her unease had increased lately. 'The police didn't know either. At least I didn't find any indication in the old notes.'

The same details had been spinning through Hildur's head for years. The story seemed to repeat itself the same way every time. It was devastating, but it never went anywhere. It was like waking to the same nightmare every night. Her sisters had vanished without a trace. The locals suspected they'd got lost in the storm and died in the mountains. But the dog hadn't smelled any tracks leading there.

Hildur glanced at the dessert plate with the gold rim set out on the table. A heap of gnawed bones had formed there. When you looked more closely, you noticed how small and delicate they were, like the bones of children. Lambs were slaughtered at the age of six months or so.

Hildur turned away and reached for her glass of pineapple juice.

'I remember that dog,' Tinna said. 'It was this bitch with sad eyes. Lísa. There was a picture of her in a newspaper story about the search. Everyone said she was a gentle, hard-working animal.'

Hildur thought about Molli, the dog who'd participated in the avalanche searches at Fjallavegur. 'Who was Lísa's handler?' she asked.

'A bald, beardless man named Magnús. He met some woman from the capital at search-and-rescue training and moved to Reykjavík before the turn of the millennium.'

Hildur's interest was instantly piqued; it was as if she'd been zapped by an electric shock. She remembered the dog she'd seen at the avalanche zone the week before; she was sure the handler's name had been Magnús. And he hadn't had a beard. Had Magnús moved back to the fjord? Hildur sank into her thoughts. She decided she'd question the handler in more detail first thing in the morning. She didn't really know Magnús at all. He wouldn't necessarily be able to tell her anything new about such an old case, but she would check.

'Do you want dessert? I made baked pears,' Tinna asked, despite knowing Hildur always ate dessert if it was offered.

As her aunt fussed over the next course, Hildur's phone beeped.

Hi cupcake. Join me for an evening run? An easy five k. maybe a little stretching after . . . ;)

Hildur smiled to herself. She'd already worked out once today, but another round wouldn't hurt.

'Is that that nice PE teacher?' Tinna asked. She pulled the pears from the oven and set a generous bowl of whipped cream on the table.

Hildur grunted and kept tapping.

Sounds good. I walked here to my aunt's. Wearing my running gear. See you at the old factory in an hour?

The reply arrived immediately.

See you. Kiss. – F

Hildur lowered the phone and let her gaze slide to the kitchen window. It was dark outside. Then it struck again: the

178

unpleasant, familiar pressure gradually fell over her like a black, weighted blanket.

As she stared out into the streetlamp-dotted darkness, she knew. She knew something unpleasant was coming, but she never knew where to place it on a map or timeline. Something was seriously off.

Maybe an exhausting run was the perfect way to end the day after all. It would tire her out and help her breathe more easily.

Chapter 27

Ten seconds at a good clip, picking up speed toward the end. Thirty seconds steady jogging. Fifteen seconds fast, picking up speed toward the end. Thirty seconds jogging. Thirty seconds fast. Thirty seconds jogging. The familiar burn in the lungs. A spiking pulse, a breaking sweat from interval training on the snowy path.

The route through the recreational area above the terraced houses followed tracks trampled by dog walkers. Off the path, the snow was knee-deep, but the path had been tamped into a solid base. Even so, running on it was surprisingly laborious. Every footfall meant sinking in a few centimetres.

A moment to catch a breath and pick at chunks of snow packed between shoe-soles and traction cleats. A glance down at the village, where streetlamps set the snowy scene aglitter. Some people had already strung Christmas lights along windows and gutters. Simple white Christmas stars hung in the windows of the nursing home. A glowing red Santa Claus scaled the wall of one house. The Christmas lights were a weapon against the darkness. The houses of Ísafjörður were festooned with colourful strings in early November, and it wasn't until the sun had returned and rescued the world from darkness that the last of the waving snowmen were taken down to make way for Easter decorations.

Running was always a release. A patch of melancholy had hit recently, but luckily exercise helped. It was too bad work had interfered with running together today. But that was life.

Work was important to both of them, and they both wanted to do their jobs as well as possible. Saying no to work was especially hard because it was so wrapped up in the wellbeing of others. Sometimes students called in the evening and asked for advice, or child protection services needed help with an urgent home visit. Dealing with people was both heavy and rewarding. Sometimes it was possible to help, sometimes not. But sometimes was enough.

A moment of deeper thought devoted to the two of them. It was time. Telling could wait no longer. Today was supposed to have been the day. It would have been a lot simpler while they were both moving. It was easier to raise difficult subjects when you didn't have to look the other person in the eye. Now the conversation would have to happen face to face. Well, that would work too. It would have to.

For the next kilometre, a slow, steady jog. A few arm circles and shoulder shakes.

One last interval training before a slow jog home at an easy pace. The path rose up to the avalanche barrier. The two of them had run past this spot together last time. The route had been covered in snow, so they'd circled the barrier and continued on flat ground. But someone had opened the path. The thrill of exertion was like an electric charge that filled the body. The spurt up the hill would put the finishing touch on the run. The barrier was so high the lights of the village didn't reach the top, but that wasn't an issue. A headlamp and traction cleats were all that was needed.

Stumping up the hill. Right, left. Right, left. A clipped gait preserved strength. The burn in the quads. Another ten metres to the flat crown, where it would feel nice to pick up the pace for a few hundred metres before the return descent to town.

A satisfied glance over the terrain. The wind had blown the loose snow from the path, and the base looked good for running.

Someone else was already there; the winter night had lured another soul out to exercise. It was too dark to make out the other person clearly. They weren't wearing the usual running gear and didn't seem to have a dog. Running frequently meant you recognised most people you came across by their clothes or the dog at the end of their leash.

But the other person wasn't worth a second thought. *Just keep going.*

The newest avalanche barriers had been erected over a decade earlier to protect the town. Made of small rocks and soil, the barrier was a few dozen metres tall at its highest. The eastern edge dropped gently toward the village. In summer, the slope was covered by grass and lupins. Now it was blanketed by snow so deep the local kids would be able to go sledding.

In contrast, the western edge of the barrier was steep. The sheer wall was held in place by a massive structure of metal mesh drawn across the full width. The purpose of this massive wall was to prevent any snow from the mountains from sliding down and destroying the town. A fence over a metre tall ran along the steep western edge.

Or should have.

For some reason, the fencing had been removed for a distance of at least twenty metres. The missing fence was perplexing. Had the village technical department not finished repair work on it? Some blockhead must have forgotten to put up a warning sign about the missing fence at the base of the rise.

The figure in the long coat was slowly approaching. They didn't show any indication of making room on the path. Slow down and make sure not to run too close to the barrier's edge.

Annoying. Yes, the path was narrow, but it should always be shared with others.

Tomorrow morning would mean a call first thing to City Hall to give the technical department an earful. Insist they come fix the fence right away or at least put up the appropriate warnings.

Then, suddenly, so fast there was no chance to register it, the passing figure abruptly turned and did a full-weight body slam. If there had been time to prepare, it might have been possible to tense before the moving mass struck, or maybe even dodge it. But now the blow was inevitable.

There was no time to react. A lifetime first: complete loss of physical control. Like a newborn foal whose long legs floundered and tangled when it tried to stand. Hands raked the air but made no contact with anything. The ground underfoot had vanished.

Make that call first thing in the morning. Call City Hall. First thing in the morning.

The last thought before slamming into the ground.

The headlamp continued to burn a hole in the darkness.

Chapter 28

The spoon had clinked against the glass bowl when Hildur's phone started ringing insistently. Hildur immediately recognised the number. It was Tumi Jónasson, from the Reykjavík Police Missing Children's Unit. Hildur was finishing the dinner her aunt had prepared, spooning the last bite of dessert into her mouth. A baked tinned pear drizzled with melted After Eight chocolate mints had been a trendy dessert in Iceland back in the 1980s. Hildur didn't know anyone except her aunt who still made it.

'This is Hildur.'

'I know. You're the person I'm trying to reach. Any news worth sharing?'

When Icelanders asked each other how they were doing, they often asked if they had 'any news worth sharing'. It was a fun custom. Did Tumi have something urgent to discuss? Hildur had just spoken with him that morning.

'Yes, it's urgent. I wouldn't be calling when normal people are eating dinner if it weren't.' Tumi's jovial voice drew out the vowels.

Tumi was Hildur's favourite colleague in Reykjavík. No, he was probably Hildur's favourite colleague in the world. They'd got to know each other years before, during Hildur's tenure in Reykjavík, when they'd both worked on child protection matters. Tumi was the one who'd coaxed Hildur into getting involved in the missing children's unit. After their pilot project had been granted continued funding, Hildur had taken responsibility for special child protection cases in rural Iceland. Tumi handled all of Reykjavík on his own. He'd once done some statistical calculations regarding his work and concluded that at any given moment, an average of nineteen Icelandic children were on the run from home or the authorities' supervision. Tumi knew them all by name.

Tumi had done pioneering work with the country's youth. He drove an old, unmarked car and wore civilian clothes. He roamed the streets of Reykjavík, looking for teenagers who'd left home or rehab and did all he could to maintain contact and help them. He'd never broken a young person's trust.

Hildur remembered an instance when the two of them had been called in to a drug den where they found a teenage boy suspected of car theft. When he saw the police, the kid had run onto the balcony and threatened to jump if they took him back to rehab. Tumi hadn't stooped to lies; he'd kept his face neutral and admitted the next stops would be the police station and then rehab. The boy had eventually relented and agreed to leave with them. Hildur had never forgotten the kid. As a matter of fact, she'd seen him at Keflavík airport not too many years back. He'd become a bus driver.

Tumi's dogged, unrelenting solo efforts had probably prevented more juvenile crime than all of Reykjavík's police units put together.

Tumi was calling from the job. He'd been keeping an eye on two teenage girls who were almost of age, and their school had informed him a few days ago that they hadn't been seen in weeks.

'I went to their homes, but no one there had even noticed they were missing.'

The same old mess, Hildur guessed. Parents with serious substance abuse problems and no grasp of the day of the week or the time of day: from a child's perspective, the polar opposite of equal opportunity.

'The entryway was strewn with rubbish bags and dog shit. I took the dog to an animal shelter, but I couldn't find the girls. I asked around my contacts and was able to track them to a drug den near the Mjódd bus station. I found them, but they weren't in the mood to talk. Their exact words were: "Fuck off, boomer."'

Even so, Tumi had kept an eye on the girls. Sometimes he was able to reach them by phone, but when he did, their responses had been curt. He had no reason to arrest them: they weren't in acute danger and hadn't been suspected of any crimes. 'And we don't have room in the holding cell to bring in people for drinking beer or skipping school.'

Hildur liked talking to Tumi, but she was eager to get to her run and erase work from her mind.

Tumi explained the girls had somehow got their hands on a car and driven out of the city. Neither had a driver's licence, which meant they were considered a danger to traffic. 'I lost them here at the petrol station at Staðarskáli. The only places they can go from here are north or the Westfjords.'

Hildur shook her head. Tumi had followed the girls for a couple of hundred kilometres and was now calling from a service station in the middle of nowhere passed by two of the country's biggest roads. One led north from Reykjavík, the other from Reykjavík to the Westfjords.

'Can you check the traffic police cameras to see if you spot a white Subaru estate? If not, I'll continue north from here.'

Of course Hildur would help her colleague. Driving around rural Iceland hunting down the girls seemed like a wild goose chase, but there didn't appear to be an alternative. There were few police officers in sparsely populated areas, and Tumi knew the history of the case. He wanted to help the girls before things got any worse.

Hildur heard music in the background. She could make out the words. It was 'Þú og ég,' 'You and I,' the biggest hit by the '60s rock band Hljómar. Hildur remembered Tumi always listened to Icelandic oldies in the car.

'I'll go do it right now. I'll call you soon. Why don't you go in and have a coffee while you wait.'

'Here? No way. I have a Thermos with me. Petrol station coffee is so corrosive my stomach would be a mess for days afterwards.'

Before Hildur slipped her phone back into her pocket, she tapped out a text to Freysi.

Something came up at work, have to skip the run. Shouldn't be long. I'll come by later tonight. – H

Chapter 29

Her elasticity and strength had vanished. As if one sharp axe-blow had severed every supply line in her body. Hildur tried to run faster, but her legs refused to obey. They wouldn't bend the way they should. She'd heard people who'd experienced sudden trauma say their legs grow incredibly heavy.

She'd never experienced anything like it, at least not since her sisters had disappeared. She'd felt completely powerless then, too. But she'd been a child. There wasn't anything she could have done; she couldn't have participated in the search parties or otherwise been of assistance. Now she was grown.

She felt like she was in a videoclip being played in slow motion. Her lungs were burning as she made her way to the car park of the only apartment building on Urðarvegur.

Urðarvegur was a short street on the outskirts of town, on the steep side of the fjord. It was the last street before the avalanche barriers. Lined primarily with single-storey houses and two-storey terraces, it ended at an apartment building owned by the council. Turnover among renters there was high; most occupants were students or workers from the fishing vessels whose stays in Ísafjörður were temporary.

Hildur knew the building: she'd been inside its units countless times when a loud house party or escalating argument required police intervention. Fists flew in the single-family homes, too, but there weren't neighbours on the other side of the wall to hear the violence.

When she reached the car park, Hildur saw the first sign that what she'd just heard over the phone was true. Her heart was pounding hard; the lights of the police vehicle cast their blue glow into darkness at the same frenzied rate.

Hildur ventured behind the building, as the shortest route to the avalanche barrier began from the backyard.

Just a moment ago, Hildur had been sitting in Freysi's kitchen reading old running magazines. After waiting for an hour, she'd grown concerned. Freysi didn't usually go on such long runs at night. She'd tried to call him several times. When Hildur's phone had finally rung, the message had been curt and harsh.

Freysi was dead, and Hildur needed to attend the scene.

Her friend was dead. A couple of days ago they'd been running together. They'd just been texting each other. And now he was gone. It felt impossible to believe. Like a tasteless joke others would be laughing at soon. But it wasn't. Hildur had instantly known Beta was serious from the sound of her voice.

Hildur had rushed out the door then and there. Clearing the snow from the car would have taken too long, so she ran the whole way.

Hildur pulled out the headlamp she'd kept in her pocket, turned it on, and stepped under the crime-scene tape set up by the patrol. As she approached the avalanche barrier, she realised what she'd just heard on the phone was true.

She saw a mound on the snow a few dozen metres away. It reminded her of a dead seal in the shallows, belly bloated. The figure was twisted in an unnatural position. The headlamp strapped to the head still burned, its wedge of light stabbing the darkness.

A grave-faced Beta walked up to Hildur and slowly shook her head. She raised both arms to signal for Hildur not to come any closer.

Hildur looked her boss dead in the eye, then stared into her face. Beta's mascara had smeared from her lower lids, emphasising

189

the sadness of her expression. Then Hildur's attention was drawn to Beta's scarf: it was folded the wrong way and had bunched up under Beta's hood. Hildur's eyes surveyed the folds one at a time.

Hildur's attention caught on Beta's make-up and scarf because that was all her mind was capable of taking in at the moment.

'I'm going to hug you now,' Beta said, stepping closer.

Hildur leaned into her much-shorter boss and breathed. In, out, in, out. They didn't speak. Around them, snowflakes drifted to the ground. Some caught in their hair.

'Is he . . .' Hildur whispered.

'Yes. I'm sorry; Freysi is dead. I checked.'

Hildur took a step backwards and tried to focus her vision beyond Beta. 'The doctor is coming, then the forensics team. Let's not go any closer.'

'What if he can still be resuscitated? Maybe he just needs more oxygen.' Hildur knew her questions made no sense, but she couldn't stop herself from voicing them. It was as if she were watching herself, Beta, and the whole situation from outside her body. She saw and heard everything but wasn't a party to it.

Beta shook her head.

That's when the blow fell. Hildur tried to gasp for breath, but the effort felt pointless. Her lungs emitted the same rattle she remembered from childhood when she'd fallen stomach-first from the back of a horse to a mountain path. The pain had been so intense she hadn't been able to scream.

Breath rattling, Hildur fell to her knees. She could feel herself shaking. Beta crouched at Hildur's side and wrapped her arms loosely around her subordinate. Hildur clenched her fists inside her gloves, digging her nails hard into her palms. Localising the pain helped; it drew her attention elsewhere.

Hildur shivered as she rose to her feet. Her breathing gradually steadied, and she let her nails retract from her skin. She looked up at the starry sky. It was still tinged by the flashing emergency lights of the police vehicle in the car park below.

'I'm so sorry I had to call you in. When I realised who'd been found here, I didn't want to. But I had to. I couldn't leave,' Beta said calmly.

'I know, I know . . .' Hildur turned away. She wished tears would come, but they didn't. At least not yet. 'I know there . . . there isn't anyone else to call. I'm the only detective here.'

She knew police weren't supposed to investigate crimes involving those they were close to, but she and Freysi hadn't been married. Nor had they been a couple in the traditional sense.

'We weren't close that way. I mean, we weren't family. I don't see a conflict of interest.'

But Beta sounded like she meant business: 'You're not staying at work.' She insisted on taking Hildur home and spending the night. 'He was your friend, after all. This is a big deal.'

Hildur looked at her boss, and something inside her erupted. She wasn't sure what it was. A flash of injustice and anger? It was her friend who'd died, so she'd be the one to decide what she did next.

'I'm staying at work.'

Beta didn't want to give in; her body language said as much. Her gaze had slid seaward, to the shores where houses sought safety in numbers and only the odd car disturbed the quiet. Beta's arms were clasped tightly at her sides, and the parka hood pulled over her head emphasized the cocoon-like effect. She surveyed the town as if searching for an answer.

Hildur had one ready for her: 'I'll rest tomorrow, but not today.'

Hildur didn't know if her decision made any sense, but she didn't care. She simply didn't have a choice. Freysi was dead and would stay dead. All Hildur could do now was figure out what had happened here. The weights that had dropped from her legs, and she felt more alive. 'Tell me everything you know.'

Beta seemed to deliberate a moment longer, then made her decision. She looked up at the avalanche barrier rising before them and said the fence had been removed.

'But Freysi and I were running here just a few days ago. The fence was there then.' So someone must have made a hole in it and knocked Freysi off the edge. 'Freysi always used cleats when he ran in the winter. I'm sure he didn't fall by accident.' Hildur shot her boss a look; she knew Beta was considering the possibility of suicide.

Iceland saw very few homicides but plenty of suicides. They generally involved substance abuse or mental health problems that had gone untreated. To escape a dead end, people took their own lives by hanging, intentionally crashing their car, or overdosing. The majority of those who killed themselves were men in their thirties. Men Freysi's age. Over the course of her career, Hildur had delivered numerous notifications of suicides to families. It was awful every time. Sometimes family members guessed why the police were standing at the door. In other cases, news of their loved one's death came without warning. Either way, the news elicited the same bottomless dread on the faces of loved ones, quickly followed by sorrow and disappointment, or in some cases anger and bitterness.

'I know it wasn't suicide. Freysi and I were supposed to go running. I had to cancel because of work.'

Homicides committed in the heat of the moment usually took place out of the public eye, and often victim and perpetrator alike were heavily intoxicated. Or else an aggressive speed freak with a knife thought someone had cut the snaking line outside a bar and lost his cool.

This was neither. And the breach in the fence and the isolated location indicated planning.

'Someone must have known his running routines. There aren't any random passers-by on this dark hill.'

Hildur didn't have a clue as to why anyone would have wanted to kill Freysi, a gym teacher in early middle age whose only vice was smoking. Freysi didn't have any jealous ex-wives hunting him down or drug debts, and he'd never mentioned problems any more significant than lower back pain.

A chilling thought forced its way into Hildur's mind: 'Over the past three weeks, we've seen three bizarre homicides . . .'

She turned to Beta, who finished the thought: '. . . that don't seem related in any way.'

That would mean stirring panic, vast media attention, and perfectly justified fear that more cases might follow. The press didn't know about the hair found in mouths of the avalanche-scene and parking-garage victims, but it was only a matter of time before the information leaked. What was going on?

A forensics team had just set out from Reykjavík. The weather was good, so their chopper would be landing at the airfield in under an hour. Beta had also called in a canine with a handler. So little time had passed since the killing that it might still be possible to catch a scent.

'I also called in a patrol to keep an eye on the scene until forensics arrives,' Beta said. 'Cancel it. I'll stay.'

Beta shrugged in surrender. 'Fine. I'm going back to the station. The dog-walker who found the body said he'd come by after he took his dog home.'

Hildur nodded and watched her boss's back recede as Beta made her descent to the car park.

Once Beta had gone, she turned toward Freysi's sprawled body. She wanted to go closer. Look and touch one last time. Say goodbye.

She didn't, of course. Doing so could have contaminated the scene and complicated the investigation.

She and Freysi were supposed to have watched a movie after their evening run. Snuggle on the couch under a white lambswool blanket and have a beer. Now she was looking at his body, and everything around her felt like a film whose plot was impossible to grasp.

A few teardrops, the first of the evening, squeezed out between Hildur's eyelids and fell to her cheek. The cold wind instantly carried them off. It had stopped snowing. The mountain rising at her side felt bigger than usual. As if it had spread its shoulders to shelter the solitary figure in the dark night.

Hildur had never had anyone. No one close, the way most adults did at some point in their life. They had spouses and children, or at least boyfriends or girlfriends. She didn't, and she'd never missed it in the past.

Now it felt as if she'd lost something she'd never had.

Chapter 30

Jakob leaned against the car in the airfield car park. He gazed at the empty runway, arms folded across his chest. The helicopter ought to be arriving soon. He'd been called into work half an hour earlier; the phone had rung just as he and Guðrún were showering. They'd spent the evening fooling around on the couch before moving from the living room to the bedroom. Then they'd got peckish and gone into the kitchen to fix sandwiches. After Jakob finished making them, Guðrún had sat on the kitchen table and suggested he might butter her next ... Jakob laughed out loud. What was going on? Who was this amazing woman he'd met?

Guðrún was an incredible package. The adventure that had lurched into motion at the yarn shop had stretched to several days. They hadn't left her place except to go to work and the supermarket. They'd spent the rest of the time exploring each other's bodies. It was a new situation for Jakob. Sure, he'd had all sorts of relationships besides Lena, a couple of the more serious variety and a slew of one-night stands; a police cadet had no trouble getting attention in the bars of Tampere. But he'd never experienced anything like this before. It was as if he'd been airdropped into paradise.

He also felt conflicted. His happiness felt inappropriate in the circumstances: their little police department had another seemingly complex homicide under investigation.

As an intern, he didn't have any major responsibilities to shoulder, and his limited language skills prevented him from contributing as much as Hildur and Beta. Even so, he'd tried to do what he could to be of assistance. He'd scoured the holding tanks, organised the storage room, and subbed for a patrol officer who was on sick leave for a couple of days. Riding around in the patrol car had given him some exposure to the customs of the small town.

They're going to take some getting used to, he reflected. When breathalysing drivers, his senior partner had stopped everyone except a grey-haired man in a red Toyota. When Jakob had asked about it at the end of his shift, his partner had looked perplexed. The guy at the wheel had been his uncle. And evidently his uncle never drove drunk.

But after tonight's call, things had grown even more complicated. The number of homicides under investigation had doubled, and if Jakob had understood correctly over the phone, the victim was Hildur's friend. That felt incredibly unfair. He was living his best life while his closest colleague was experiencing another big loss.

His closest colleague. Jakob considered the words for a moment. Hildur was more than a colleague, there was no denying it. Even though they hadn't known each other long, he considered her a friend. He didn't have many close friends, and none of them had succeeded in getting him to open up about Lena and Matias the way Hildur had.

The sound of a helicopter approaching from the sea brought Jakob out of his reverie. This day had come to an unusually wretched end. A dead man had been found at a recreational area in the heart of town, and forensic investigators had had to be called in from the capital. Beta had asked Jakob to escort the team from the airfield to the scene.

Jakob turned toward the water and the racket. The sound of the helicopter grew louder as it closed in. A few minutes later, the chopper arced from the sea toward the airfield wedged between the fjord and Mount Kirkjubólsfjall. As it landed, the blades of the rotor emitted such a powerful chopping noise that Jakob had to hold his hands over his ears. The wind whipped by the helicopter kicked up the fallen snow. For a moment, Jakob was standing in the middle of a blizzard.

After the aircraft came to a rest on the pad, three taciturn-looking men climbed out. Each carried a large black equipment bag. Jakob waved at the men to draw their attention. After introducing himself in English, he opened the boot and began working out how to get the bags to fit. The first two slid in neatly side by side. The third required a brief game of Tetris. Jakob turned the bag sideways, and then he could push it into the remaining space.

As the boot clicked shut, Jakob took a closer look at the men. The biggest one was the first to open his mouth: 'I'm Jónas Ingimarsson. This is Sveinn Þórsson and Hörður Arnarsson from the forensics unit. They were just here, poking at that guy buried in the avalanche.'

Now Jakob remembered the men from the previous week, and they seemed to recognise him, too. He had even exchanged a few words with them while they were combing the crime scene. One was into Krav Maga, and the other volunteered as a children's handball coach during his free time. The two of them climbed in the back, while Jónas, who was the most senior, sat in the passenger seat.

'So you guys need forensics again, huh?' Jónas said. 'What the hell is going on out here?'

Jakob heard the arrogance in Jónas's tone but didn't let it get to him. In all likelihood, it was just a matter of the 'bigger budget, more resources' syndrome: a city cop visiting his country cousins to clear up messes he felt they couldn't sort out on their own. Jakob had witnessed the same phenomenon in Finland, where experts from the south all too often demonstrated the same 'I'm here to save the day' attitude as the guy sitting next to him.

'Why don't we go find out,' Jakob simply said, then started the car. This Jónas must be the unpleasant character Beta and Hildur had been talking about at the station.

Jónas confirmed Jakob's suspicions by launching into a long monologue: 'So I'm not from the forensics unit. I'm a lead investigator from Reykjavík criminal police. I came here to keep an eye on the kids and figure out what the hell is going on. A second homicide in two weeks! I hope it's not because the crooks up here are smarter than the cops.'

Jónas slapped his thigh at his supposedly funny quip and guffawed.

Hörður and Sveinn merely looked weary. The surprise night shift in a remote fjord didn't provoke similar squeals of delight from them. They looked like they'd had zero interest in flying here to collect samples into sealable baggies. Either that, or they were suffering from the same headache as Jakob: the loudmouth in the passenger seat.

Jakob steered out of the car park and onto the road leading to town.

Jónas's jaws didn't stop moving. '*Jæjja*, kid. How did you end up in a godforsaken place like this?'

Jakob didn't feel like engaging in this particular conversation but had little choice: the guy at his side would be there for the next few kilometres. So he recited the lines he'd been regurgitating over and over the past few weeks, performing them for everyone from the lifeguard at the swimming pool to the cashier at the post office and anyone he met on the job. *From Finland, training to be a police officer, international exchange, internship here at the local police station, drawn to the quiet and nature of Iceland.*

'Doesn't sound like your plan worked. It's been a year since I've been here, but now that you showed up, forensics is here for the second week in a row. You're not the murderer, are you?' Jónas said, bursting into a loud belly-laugh.

Sveinn and Hörður didn't join in. They stared out into the night without saying a word. Jónas turned his head so he could see his colleagues in the back seat and encouraged them to loosen up.

'After we're done, we'll hit the pub for a nightcap. Small towns like this have their advantages. Men from the capital are a welcome change of pace from forklift drivers who work at the seafood plant. Believe me, boys, I've made my rounds of these fjords in my day.'

The car filled with Jónas's irritating laughter again. Couldn't the guy shut up, even for a second?

'I'm driving us over to the avalanche barrier,' Jakob said, gesturing toward town. He hoped talking about work would get the detective with the verbal diarrhoea to stuff it, and so he shared what he knew about the case. A local man, about thirty years old, had been jogging on top of the avalanche barrier at night and fallen. A hole had been made in the fence.

The irritating investigator from Reykjavík rubbed his stubbled jaw and said in a knowing voice: 'Are you guys sure he didn't liberate himself from this world? Folks fall like frozen grass when the dark time of year begins.'

Jakob understood the death could easily be considered a suicide. He also knew it wasn't true. The gap in the fence was the strongest argument against it. Someone committing suicide would have just climbed over the fence, which wasn't much more than a metre tall.

'Besides, the guy was known to us. The victim was supposed to meet our detective after his run.'

Jónas sat up straighter and laughed again. He pulled his black beanie lower and talked to himself in a knowing tone: 'Well, well. So Hildur's fella kicked the bucket.'

Jakob glanced at the back seat through the rearview mirror. The faces of the forensic investigators said it all. Although they looked ashamed of their colleague's behaviour, they didn't comment.

Jakob shook his head and allowed himself an expression that did nothing to conceal his frustration. 'We're just hoping you'll do your work quickly and without any delays,' he said drily, then gritted his molars, deciding he wouldn't say anything for the rest of the drive.

Jakob pulled into in the apartment building car park, climbed out of the car, and opened the boot. Jónas pulled out one of the bags and strode off toward the police cordon. Hörður and Sveinn took their bags and thanked Jakob for the lift.

'That guy is a total asshole. We're really annoyed that he invited himself along,' Sveinn said apologetically. 'But Jónas is convinced the lawyer who was killed in the parking garage, the paedophile buried in his summer cottage, and this jogger are somehow linked to each other.'

Jakob had come to the same conclusion during the drive: no criminal investigator from the Reykjavík homicide unit would care about a small-town gym teacher who slipped and fell. Jónas had joined the forensic team so he'd get first crack at the most recent crime scene.

Jónas wanted to be the one who caught the serial killer.

Chapter 31

The north wind picked up as evening turned to night. At first it loosed tender sighs from the sea on the deserted town centre, gently shifting the fallen powder across the road and back again. After taking some time to gather its strength, it followed with pitiless punches, like a sledgehammer striking a windowpane. The wind set the streetlamps shivering and pushed packed snow from the roofs to the street. The unpredictability was what made the weather so harsh.

Hildur shifted her weight from foot to foot and circled her arms to stay warm. She'd been standing in this spot for almost an hour, waiting for the arrival of the forensics team. The avalanche barrier sheltered her from the wind, but it couldn't keep the cold at bay. The freeze was gradually invading her body.

She heard a car approach and stepped over to where she had a view of the car park below. The car looked familiar: the local police force had leased a few vehicles from the local rental agency. They were all white Škoda Octavias.

Hildur saw Jakob walking in the direction of the avalanche barrier. The other passengers had gathered to collect their bags from the boot and now started pulling on their coveralls. The gear was a must for forensic investigators, who couldn't afford to contaminate the scene.

The investigators endeavoured to collect as many samples as possible that might prove useful in identifying a perpetrator. The samples would be delivered to the laboratory in Reykjavík for analysis. One of the key samples taken from a crime scene were fibres, and the investigators would be looking for them in places where the murderer's and the victim's textiles had come into contact. In this case, the murderer had presumably pushed the victim over the edge, at which point the murderer's and victim's clothes would have rubbed against each other. The fibres were too small to be detected by the naked eye, so chances were high the investigators would have to take Freysi's coat to the laboratory.

Jakob greeted Hildur with a discreet nod and stopped to scan the snowy terrain. As he studied Freysi's sprawled body, a shiver ran through him. Then he fixed his gaze on Hildur. Nor did he shift it away, even when Hildur turned her face a little in the other direction. He just stood there, looking at her.

'I'm sorry,' he finally said. Hildur shrugged.

'Beta told me you were friends.' Hildur shrugged again.

The two of them stood there in silence. They both knew what was said now made little difference. What made a difference was standing there together.

Hildur flipped up the collar of her coat and forced herself to keep going. A little longer. A few more hours. She figured the collapse would come later. She considered the likelihood analytically, wondering when it might hit and whether she'd be able to delay her drop into the abyss. She wanted to put her imminent implosion in a paper bag and set it on the shelf to wait for a better moment. Right now she had to concentrate on her work.

She saw the trio in white protective suits approach with their equipment bags.

Goddammit.

'What's Jónas doing here? He's not a technical investigator.'

'He pushed his way into the helicopter at Reykjavík airport,' Jakob explained.

Of course he did, Hildur thought. *He's here to get information and further his career.*

There was no way Jónas would work overtime to travel to this distant fjord unless he figured it would be to his advantage somehow. He was a Reykjavík man through and through and looked with amusement and contempt at anything that happened outside the capital. As far back as Hildur could remember, he'd told the same story about his retirement plans at police events: he was going to move to Florida to play golf and they'd never see him in these frozen fjords ever again.

Why don't you do us all a favour and go chase golf balls? Hildur thought to herself as she gave Jónas a neutral hello.

She provided a step-by-step summary of the evening's events, progressing systematically and calmly from fact to fact. She showed the suspected site of the fall, the gap in the fence, and the location of the body. She advanced cautiously, as if on thin ice, and tried to keep her mind steady.

'Judging by the footprints, only three people approached the victim: the first officer to arrive at the scene and the doctor who declared the victim dead.' Then she nodded at the biggest footprints and paused. She felt nauseous. Her mouth grew moist, and the acid bubbled from her stomach into her oesophagus. She took a piece of gum from her pocket and popped it in her mouth. 'That third set of footprints, the big ones, may be those of the perpetrator.'

The depressions were clearly visible in the snow. As a foot pushed into the soft, malleable base, it formed a three-dimensional track. The investigators would photograph the footprints and make moulds of them.

'Who found the body?' Jónas asked.

'A local out walking his dog,' Hildur replied, without looking at Jónas. 'He didn't approach the body and immediately called the police. He's providing a statement now.'

Jónas shot a querulous glance at the dog handler who'd just arrived, the dog sitting obediently at his side. 'OK. We'll let the pup have a go first.'

Hildur felt the irritation inside her swell. Although Icelandic police officers weren't limited to acting within their home districts, it was unacceptable to show up at another officer's workplace and throw your weight around. The Westfjords were Hildur's, and she was the only detective in the region. But actually, the irritation was welcome right now. It focused her attention elsewhere and helped her concentrate on her work.

'No, what we'll do is let me call the shots.'

Hildur kept her voice cold and calm, but even so, she seemed to have struck a nerve. She noticed her colleague's eyes narrow and his jaw tighten. But she just turned to the dog and its handler and began giving instructions.

In all likelihood, the suspect had descended from the avalanche barrier to the car park and proceeded to the road. The big footprints were distinct in the snow, but on the road, they would have mingled with other tracks. Hildur wasn't sure the canine would be able to catch the scent anymore, but it was worth trying.

'Magnús, let's let the dog try first. My guess is the perp was here at most two hours ago.'

'Come on, Molli, let's go,' Magnús said, tenderness in his voice. He led the dog to the footprints made by the big shoes, speaking calmly the whole time.

Molli spun around in place and wagged her head alertly from side to side. Then the exhilaration hit. She seemed to catch hold of an invisible thread and took off after it, engrossed in her task.

'Call when you find something,' Hildur shouted to Magnús's receding back. He answered with an affirmative wave of his hand as Molli trotted toward the apartment building, nose to the snow.

The men from forensics and Jónas had started assembling lighting at the scene, up at the broken fence and at the site of the fall. They photographed the area, examined the footprints and fingerprints, moulded silicone to capture any potential marks made by tools and anything else that could tell them anything about the murderer who'd just been there.

Hildur watched the forensics team from a short distance away; she wanted to give them room to do their work. She wasn't needed, nor did she want to go any closer. She saw the two men bend over the contorted body. They touched the victim's head and talked. They started by looking for traces of blond hair. Hildur did her best to gather important details from what she heard while shutting out everything personal. She tried to imagine it was an anonymous corpse, not Freysi, lying there in the snow. Even so, it was gruelling listening to the men.

'The body is still slack,' said the investigator named Hörður. 'Less than three hours have passed since he died.'

'Yup, mouth pops right open. I need more light here in the cavity. OK, now I'm going to lift the tongue.' A gloved hand sank into the corpse's mouth. Nimble fingers spent a moment probing the sides, palate, under the tongue. For a moment no one spoke. The wind wailed softly. The lamps sizzled, and the instruments clinked against each other.

Then the look of concern on Sveinn's face was swept away as if by a wingbeat. It was replaced by a small smile completely inappropriate to the moment.

'There's a tuft of blond hair here,' he said, holding it up before sealing it in a baggie. The hair would be analysed more closely in the lab.

Hildur felt a nasty lurch inside her. As if a big rock had rolled from one side of her chest to the other. A particularly abhorrent thought occurred to her. It hurt badly, but it was true.

This was her fault. She had failed.

The murderer had struck three times, and this time the murder had happened in her home district. If she'd caught the perpetrator earlier, her friend would still be alive.

Hildur's phone rang. It was Magnús.

'Molli came straight down to the marina. The tracks end at the harbour's edge, next to the sailboat dock.'

Chapter 32

The harbour was deserted. The boats' cabins were dark. Large fishing vessels stood still, waiting for their next expedition to sea. Smaller boats rocked with the rhythm of the waves. A few large sailboats reposed majestically in the dock, masts stripped.

Magnús was standing at the edge of the harbour basin, hands in his pockets. Molli the border collie sat faithfully at his side.

This breed of dog was exceptionally popular in Iceland. Eager, alert, and smart, border collies were used nearly as much for sheepherding as the island's native breed. Many of Iceland's sheepdogs were actually crosses of Icelandic sheepdogs and border collies. Hildur guessed Molli was purebred, but she wouldn't bet on it. Besides, it wasn't as if she cared what breed the dog was.

The warm glow of the streetlamps turned the surrounding snow orange. A passer-by could have mistaken Magnús for an ordinary dog-walker who had stopped to admire the harbour lights.

There was a fascination with the waterfront at night. Countless people had come and gone, reached for the railing, bringing goods, taking memories. But at night everything stopped, and peace fell over the harbour. Only the sea continued its eternal movement.

Hildur didn't know whether Molli liked being scratched by strangers, so she settled for merely praising the dog. Molli glanced at her indifferently, then continued to stare at the sea.

'You use the same dog to track on land and snow?'

Magnús nodded. He was visibly delighted that, judging by her question, Hildur appeared to have some understanding of search-and-rescue dogs. Avalanche dogs were used to search for missing people under snow. Led by their sense of smell, tracker dogs followed a route taken by someone who'd left a scent behind. Disaster canines were able to move in exceptionally difficult terrain to locate, for instance, injured people trapped in ruins after an earthquake. Some dogs and their handlers had mastered one type of search, others multiple.

'Molli has a keen sense of smell, and I've tried to bring myself up to speed. Training the dog isn't the hardest part about this job,' Magnús said, giving his border collie a gentle pat on the side. 'Training the handler is.'

The Icelandic police had their own canines, but there wasn't a single one in the Westfjords. Here, as in sparsely inhabited regions in general, search-and-rescue dogs belonged to civilians.

Hildur turned to the water and stared into the blackness. The sea slapped the dock with its small waves. *Freysi's murderer was here*, she thought to herself. This was where the tracks had ended. Straight from the avalanche barrier to the harbour's edge.

'Whoever she was tracking either fell into the water here or had a boat waiting,' Magnús said, stroking his dog under her chin. Molli stretched up her neck, clearly relishing the scratching.

'I'm going to call in divers and talk to the harbour master,' Hildur muttered to herself. 'Marine traffic is monitored.'

Magnús shifted his weight and rubbed the beanie that had slipped nearly into his eyes. The dog looked at her master as if asking when they could go. 'I have an early morning tomorrow. I'm driving north to train avalanche dogs,' Magnús said, by way of explaining his eagerness to be on his way.

'Of course. Thanks for coming.' Hildur tried to squeeze out something resembling a smile before she continued: 'Listen, Magnús. Before you go, there's an old incident I'd like to ask you about.'

Magnús's whole being tensed. For a moment he looked as if he'd give anything to be able to sink into the ground. A dark shadow fell across his face, underscoring his weary bearing. 'Yes . . . I know. The speeding ticket. I just haven't had time to pay it . . .'

Hildur waved his worries away. 'It's not about fines; I don't know anything about that. I'm talking about a much older case.'

Hildur told him about her sisters who had disappeared on their way home from school twenty-five years before. Of course Magnús remembered the case. Everyone did. News of the two girls' disappearance had been unavoidable.

'My aunt remembered you participated in the search parties. You had a dog with a sad face at the time.'

Magnús nodded. A smile rose to his face as he remembered the dog. 'Lísa was gentle and hard-working. Molli is one of Lísa's pups. They have a lot in common.' He looked proudly at the dog sitting patiently and faithfully at his side. 'The fact that your sisters were never found was a terrible tragedy for the whole town. I can't imagine how hard it must have been for your parents. And for you.'

Hildur nodded. Magnús turned his kind eyes to her. He stroked his dog with steady, controlled movements. His presence radiated calm. He may have been in a hurry, but there was no visible sign of it. His lack of hair, eyebrows, and eyelashes made him look somehow ageless.

'Do you happen to remember exactly where my sisters' tracks ended?' Hildur asked.

Magnús didn't immediately reply. Looking thoughtful, he stared at the sailboat swaying slowly at the end of the dock. 'I remember it vividly because I thought it was so strange.'

Something inside Hildur shifted. She felt like she was being administered tiny electric shocks as she listened to Magnús's account. She wanted every last detail she hadn't heard or seen yet.

Magnús said Lísa had followed the girls' trail into the tunnel. She had tracked the scent from the centre of town to the tunnel's mouth, where it abruptly ended, as if it had hit a brick wall.

'How deep inside the tunnel were you?' Hildur felt this detail was particularly critical because there was no mention of it in the police reports.

The dog had stopped right at the mouth. Magnús was sure it was no more than ten metres in.

'Did the tracks loop around or anything?'

'That was the strange thing. They didn't continue anywhere. They just stopped. I remember Lísa sat down and hung her head, staring at her paws. That's what she did whenever she felt like she had failed.'

Hildur considered this and asked if the girls might have turned around and gone back out.

Magnús stared out to sea as if giving his response serious consideration, then said in a confident voice: 'Lísa would have picked up on that. The tracks . . . they just stopped.'

Molli shifted restlessly, and Hildur suggested she walk Magnús to his car so they could keep talking. It didn't take long for the cold to work its way in when you stood still.

They passed huge light-brown plastic containers stacked in towers a few metres high outside the harbour offices. There was a fishy smell in the air. The containers were meant for storing seafood. Fish stayed fresh longer on ice.

'If you ask me, clear tracks suddenly stopping was too strange.'

Hildur let Magnús continue. He seemed pleased to have a captive audience.

'The scent that led to the mouth of the tunnel was forgotten pretty quickly, because most of the searchers believed the girls had started walking home over the mountain pass.'

Hildur noted the use of the phrase *most of*. She clung to it. *Most of. Most believed.* 'You didn't?'

'No. But it didn't matter what I said. Others wanted to send the searchers into the mountains, so that's where we went. The tunnel didn't interest them because everyone assumed no one used the tunnel. But I didn't believe that either. Workers who'd helped build the tunnel were using it. The tunnel was finished the previous summer, and the road was ready by autumn. The tunnel hadn't opened to traffic because it hadn't passed its final inspection. Big metal gates kept cars from entering.'

'What workers?' Hildur asked. 'Work on the tunnel had been completed long before.'

'Not exactly. There was a waterfall in it that hadn't been dealt with.'

Hildur's fingertips began to prickle, and it wasn't from the cold. What was this waterfall Magnús was talking about? She knew Ísafjörður got its drinking water from a spring that welled up inside the mountain, but she'd never heard about a waterfall.

Magnús told the story. When the workers had started digging into the rock, they'd come across huge amounts of water inside the mountain. There was a waterfall there. Its force had surprised all the engineers involved in planning the project. The blasted wall had to be repaired to prevent the water from flowing into the tunnel.

'Those responsible for moving the rock didn't make much noise about the water damage so as not to kill the whole project. There were all sorts of other problems with it too.'

Back in its day, the tunnel had faced impassioned opposition. Conservationists felt the blasting would cause harm to the surrounding nature. Those commissioned to handle the earth-moving equipment were suspected of paying workers under the table, and later the local labour union had taken a few of the subcontractors to court over unpaid overtime compensation.

'The main contractor repaired the wall without subcontractors, and no mention of the waterfall was ever recorded anywhere,' Magnús said, shaking his head. This was the traditional Icelandic way of doing things: permits weren't requested, work was wrapped up quickly, and questionable incidents were allowed to sink into the shadows of history.

Hildur and Magnús had arrived at the hospital, where Magnús had parked. He opened the back and let Molli jump in her cage. He started up his vehicle and began scraping the windows.

'How do you know about all this?' Hildur asked.

Magnús broke off scraping, stood up straight, and looked Hildur in the eye.

Two decades ago, Magnús's life had looked pretty different to how it did now. He'd drunk away his money and lost his apartment over rent arrears. A friend of a friend had rescued him from the streets by letting him stay at the family cottage one winter. And so Magnús had been cottage-sitting at Ögurvík when the flaw in the tunnel's construction had been detected. Ögurvík was located a good hour from Ísafjörður on the road to Reykjavík.

The winter my sisters disappeared, Hildur thought, a longing gnawing at her from the inside. She wasn't sure who she missed so acutely: Freysi, who'd died today, or her sisters, who'd disappeared almost a quarter of a century before? Anyone Hildur loved fled from her, and she felt partially responsible. She didn't know how to explain her sense of guilt. She didn't know where it came from. She just felt it.

Hildur tried to shake off the unpleasant thoughts and focus on what Magnús was saying. There had been a farm next to the cottage at Ögurvík, and the owner ran a small masonry business. This stonemason left before six every morning to work in Ísafjörður. Magnús said it was easy to remember such details when no one else lived within a hundred-kilometre radius.

'One October morning, this neighbour's truck got stuck in the snow outside my place.'

It was an unspoken social contract in Iceland that one always helped neighbours and those in need. So Magnús had started up the tractor parked at the cottage and pulled the neighbour's truck out of the snow.

'He thanked me over and over and bragged about doing some secret repair work in the tunnel. Apparently, a hole in the wall that could eventually cause water damage. He told me he was fixing it. Then he drove off to work, and I don't think I ever saw him face to face again,' Magnús said, rubbing the driver's mirror clean with his sleeve.

So someone had had access to the tunnel. Someone who'd been paid to fix a flaw no one was ever supposed to know about. Hildur felt a chill go through her. She was angry. Why hadn't she been told about this before?

Magnús sighed deeply. He seemed to empathise with her fury. 'No one cared. With two local girls disappearing without a trace, patching some hole in the wall wasn't very high on the list of priorities. There was no one in the tunnel, period. I was drinking too much back then and owed everyone money. No one was going to listen to the ravings of a man like me.' Magnús climbed into his car and buckled his seatbelt. By now Hildur was cold, too, but she was thirsty for more information. The tunnel was supposed to have been empty, but it turned out some mysterious stonemason had been roaming around, patching walls. She stared Magnús in the eye and waited for him to tell her more.

If two strangers in Iceland met, they immediately started to figure out what connections they shared. They went through relatives, schools, and summer jobs. Some link was inevitably found that turned the stranger into an acquaintance. One of us. Shared acquaintances created a shared context that put both parties at ease.

Hildur, like all Icelanders, had asked the question dozens if not hundreds of times. But never before had the answer felt so momentous: 'Who were his people?'

Magnús looked helpless. He had no reply. And as he didn't know the answer, he resorted to a description: 'Kind of a strange guy. Unkempt, kept to himself. I'd never seen him before.'

He was still holding the scraper he'd just used to clean his car windows. Now he raised it and used it to tap his forehead lightly a couple of times.

'He had a big scar right here.'

Chapter 33

Stars shimmer in the sky like diamonds on black cloth. Some have already died, but they all twinkle. There's something beautiful about being able to see the ones that no longer exist. A star doesn't die immediately. Nor does a dandelion disappear by being snapped; you have to pull it out by the roots. And pulling out the roots is the hardest task.

People like to talk about how far they're willing to go on another's behalf. How helping others gives so much meaning to their lives. It's all lies. Nothing but the mutterings of the lazy. They're not up to it.

Most people aren't.

I've proved it to those closest to my heart, and in doing so I've helped many. Everyone. I've helped everyone. I've accomplished a lot.

My plan worked. It succeeded almost perfectly. I was in a hurry at the shore, when the waves struck because I had to manage on my own. There was no one to help.

Except those two. In my heart, now and forever.

Oh, if people only knew the whole story, they'd understand! If they felt this same flame searing their breasts, this wind blowing from the empty highlands, they'd understand me. They'd encourage me. They'd cheer me on. They wouldn't want me to get caught.

Predator and saviour. They're one and the same.

The good book says: He also that is slothful in his work is brother to him that is a great waster.

I don't tolerate such sloth. I've proved it to everyone. I've proved it to the two of them, those most precious to me. I love them. I love you both.

There's one final task left for me to complete. It's the hardest of all, as it will be the last. But I'm not afraid.

Chapter 34

November 2019, Ísafjörður

It was so quiet, that the breeze blowing in through the window that was ajar in the vestibule could be heard distinctly. Its faint hum reached the furthest corner of the dim dwelling; the corner where Hildur sat. She'd been watching the floor-length curtain in the living room sway in time to the wind for a while. Maybe half an hour. Probably longer. The curtain billowed in the middle and flared out at the sides. The seawater-soaked wetsuits had been waiting in a black garbage bag for days. They were still there. First, Hildur hadn't had time to hang them to dry. Now she didn't have the energy. She stood and moved the rubbish bag into the bathroom. There was a loud squelch as the heavy sack hit the tiled floor.

Hildur glanced around her messy home and took satisfaction in the grey winter light. It was merciful. It revealed some of the coffee stains on the counter and the cheese left out on the table but didn't expose the full extent of the neglect.

She dribbled water from the tap into a mug she found on the counter and peered inside the fridge. She wasn't hungry, but she knew she ought to eat.

The chime of the microwave pierced a hole in the silence. Hildur instinctively hunched her shoulders to her ears and shivered in disgust. She felt the sharp ping down to the pit of her gut. The sides of the microwave were crusted with crud, and the rim of the rotating tray was chipped.

She sat on her old chair to eat. The leather upholstery at the rear of the seat was worn, and she could feel the heavy tape there through her thin trousers. Hildur had covered the holes a few months before with sports tape designed to withstand aggressive chafing. As her former martial arts instructor at the police academy used to say during pre-training taping of wrists and finger joints: 'You can fix anything with sports tape except a hangover, heartache, and misunderstandings.' Hildur dragged her backside to the chair's smoother, less worn front edge.

She sat there staring at the chicken she had heated up in the microwave and considered her situation. This moment wouldn't last. She knew it because she'd experienced similar collapses over and over. You just had to tolerate the pain.

Usually it was minimal, and pain of a different sort would help it pass. Disciplining her body in the waves or at the gym often offered relief. But sometimes it was so heavy it drained her of her capacity to act.

The previous instance of such darkness had occurred several years before. Hildur had spent a couple of days at home, helplessly climbing the walls. She'd been nauseous the whole time. Her legs had been heavy, her vision blurred.

And then the news had come.

A family from the island of Heimaey had driven to Reykjavík to run some errands. On the way back, as the car was boarding the ferry that would carry them home, the weather had been catastrophically bad. A strong wind had lashed the country for days; the ground was sheathed in ice, the snow coming in flurries. The driver had lost control at the harbour, and the car had slid from the pier to the bottom of the frigid sea. Rescue divers had found the parents and a baby in its car seat inside. By the time help arrived, they were dead.

This accident at the harbour had had a particularly strong effect on Hildur, had dragged her into the depths of despair. And as she read news articles about the accident, she'd grasped why.

There was a family member who hadn't been in the car. A pre-school-aged child had been left with neighbours when the rest of the family made the trip to Reykjavík. The fate of the surviving child was the worst because it was so familiar. She'd been spared but had lost everything. That little one and Hildur shared the same fate.

Hildur didn't see this side of herself as strange, but she wasn't disturbed by those who might. No one but Aunt Tinna knew about her premonitions. And Tinna knew because the gift of foresight had been passed down in the family.

Hildur had never told anyone else. The whole thing was so hard to explain. She wasn't a clairvoyant or a fortune-teller, but her awareness that something bad was about to happen, followed by her powerlessness in the face of this knowledge, sucked the strength out of her.

Hildur knew a lot about mental illness. She'd read books on the topic and followed diary-style blogs.

But her distress never lasted long. She felt better after the misfortune had taken place or the crime exposed. Then her strength would return, and once again she was able to focus on resolving matters and helping others.

When she'd come back from the harbour the night before, the oppression had weighed on her heavily. She'd experienced it as a headache, a pain that eventually slid down into her chest and abdomen.

Jakob had helped her home and offered his company, but Hildur had wanted to be alone. She had silenced her mobile phone, closed her laptop, and told Beta she was going to take the day off.

She knew she would be OK. She'd been through this before and survived.

The food vanished from Hildur's plate at a steady pace. She had no choice: she knew if she didn't eat now, it would take longer to get her strength back. The sooner she ate, the sooner she'd be able to sleep, too, and the sooner she'd be herself again.

Hildur wanted to regain control over her thoughts, get her muscles moving. She craved it more than ever. She had to figure out what had happened. What had happened to Freysi? What had happened to her sisters? Based on the description Magnús had provided, she had recognised Jón as the stonemason working in the tunnel. The mark on the face was an unmistakable identifier. Who exactly had Jón been, with his scarred face and secret repair work?

Hildur glanced out the window, then looked at the large cross-stitch hanging on the wall. Aunt Tinna had given it to her on the occasion of her eighteenth birthday. Her name had been embroidered into the cross-stitch, with a description from ancient Nordic mythology beneath it.

Hildur. Battle. A Valkyrie in the service of Ódin. Spirit of war and mistress of death, charged with deciding whose time it was to win in battle – and whose to die.

A gust of wind blew a curtain across the cross-stitch. Hildur laughed. A Valkyrie, huh?

Chapter 35

The little conference room at the police station felt cramped. Usually it held two, at most three people. Now five attendees were packed around the round table. The window had to be kept open to ensure a sufficient supply of fresh air.

Jakob sat at the window end of the table; Sveinn and Hörður, the forensic investigators who'd arrived from Reykjavík the previous evening, had seated themselves across from him. Jónas sprawled in his seat, taking up space for two. Beta had brought in five cups of coffee on a tray. She set the tray down but couldn't muster the will to elbow herself a seat at the table. Eager to get the meeting out of the way, she simply pulled a stool over to the flipchart.

Jakob reached into his backpack and retrieved two rustling paper bags: croissants and cheese sandwiches from the bakery. Sveinn and Hörður were delighted by the breakfast their colleague had conjured up, but Jónas looked as sour as he had the previous day. He'd been scowling all morning.

Apparently, Jakob stirring sugar into his coffee was the last straw. 'Who puts sugar in their coffee?'

Smile glued to his face, Jakob held out the bag of croissants to Jónas. 'I'm a sweet guy.'

Jónas shook his head and muttered something to himself, but that didn't stop him from shoving his hand into the bag and taking a big bite of a flaky croissant.

Beta had decided to hold a meeting before the team from Reykjavík set out for home. She would have to manage the meeting with Jakob, as Hildur had taken the day off. She sipped at her coffee and decided she wouldn't stand for any showboating today. The case warranted their full attention.

It was becoming clear a single perpetrator had killed Heiðar, Jón, and Freysi. That was unusual. Beta wrote the three victims' names on the flipchart.

'Freysi. The fence had been removed, and he was pushed off. The perpetrator's tracks led to the harbour. Did we find anything there?'

Jakob had brought out his needles and started knitting. He retrieved more yarn from the bag under the table as he eyed the notebook in front of him. Hildur had called in divers the night before, but they hadn't found anything of interest in the harbour. Jakob had visited the harbourmaster that morning, but the control room had noticed nothing out of the ordinary. 'They did point out that the control room won't catch movements of the smallest craft. The suspect might have come in on a small boat without anyone noticing,' Jakob said, letting his gaze scan the room.

Veins bulging from his forehead, Jónas stared back at his knitting colleague. He could no longer conceal his ill temper. 'We're investigating a murder and you're knitting baby booties over there.'

'A sleeve, actually,' Jakob replied. He'd decided not to let Jónas get on his nerves today. 'Luckily I'm capable of doing two things at once.'

Beta gave Jakob an approving nod and briskly changed the subject: 'What did you two find at the scene yesterday?'

Sveinn shook his head in dissatisfaction. The discoveries had been slight. The cuts in the fence were neat; a heavy-duty tool had been used. He and Hörður had photographed the edges and taken mouldings with silicone mass. When they got back to Reykjavík they'd compare the markings to the most common tool models; it was possible they'd be able to identify the implement used. No fingerprints had been found. Either the perp had been wearing gloves or the prints had been wiped. But the fence was clean.

'As of now, the footprints are the most important evidence. The perp is pretty big, shoe size is forty-four. The print is presumably from a hiking boot. I'll do a more detailed comparison when we get back to the city.'

'What about the fibres?' Beta asked.

'We removed the deceased's outerwear for examination at the lab.' Sveinn added they'd been to the deceased's home that morning to retrieve samples from home textiles and clothes for comparative purposes.

Beta wrote, *Big perp, 44 shoe*. In terms of facts, this was very little to go by, but it confirmed Siggi's description.

'Any new developments regarding the lawyer?' Beta asked.

Jónas shook his head. Some dark fibres had been found in the vehicle that hadn't come from Heiðar's clothes, his wife's clothes, their home, the hotel, or his workplace. The only fingerprints found in the car were Heiðar's. The surveillance cameras in the parking garage had been out of order. The recordings from CCTV cameras in the vicinity had been reviewed, but no suspicious or solitary figures had been spotted.

Last of all, Beta reported what she knew about Jón, who'd been murdered in his cottage.

The case was still a mystery. No murder weapon, no fingerprints, no nothing.

The sum total of evidence from all three cases was a vague eyewitness account of a large figure in dark clothing and blond hair in the mouth of every victim.

'We have an old paedophile, an asshole lawyer, and a sweet-heart PE teacher,' Jónas said, eyeing the room.

Everyone present was thinking the same thing: what or who was the common denominator in this circus?

Jónas tapped the table with his forefinger. 'Let's sift through all possibilities. Hobbies, schools, childhood summer camps, sites of families' summer cottages. There must be a common thread; we just have to keep scratching until it's revealed.'

Jakob set his needles down on the table, glancing first at Jónas and then Beta. 'Might the common denominator have something to do with familial background? Correct me if I'm wrong, but I get the sense a lot of people here are related to each other somehow.'

Beta twirled the marker in her hand. Jakob's idea wasn't half bad, and as a matter of fact, had already occurred to her. Beta explained that she'd pored through Jón and Heiðar's family backgrounds without finding any commonalities.

'Let's do some DNA tests. They'll tell us,' blurted Hörður, who'd been listening quietly from the side.

Jónas pushed his chair away from the table and leaned back. He seemed impatient: 'Sure, why not? But it'll take a long time before we have any results.'

Beta knew that. There was a perpetual backlog at the forensics laboratory. Even if there weren't, it still took a few days to perform the DNA analyses.

She stood and stretched. Sitting in a meeting wasn't going to make them any wiser; they'd have to keep poking under rocks and see if anything turned up. 'So we'll be exchanging information if we find anything?' she confirmed as she shut the window. The room had grown chilly.

The group exchanged a few more words about the upcoming days before the team from Reykjavík made ready to leave. Their southbound flight was scheduled to depart in an hour.

Freysi's body would accompany them in the hold. The autopsy would be performed later that afternoon.

Leaning against the doorjamb, Beta offered to see the men out.

'I'm pretty sure we'll be able to find our way out of this, umm, police station on our own,' Jónas said, shooting an amused glance around the premises. 'I assume you have an indoor toilet?'

Beta indicated a door down the hall that was ajar.

Then she remembered the text message she'd received from the post office that morning: the ceiling lamp she'd ordered online was ready for pick-up. The post office was open, and now she had a free minute. She decided to walk the men out and pop around the corner.

The teams exchanged gloomy farewells at the door and promised to keep each other up to date. The men from Reykjavík marched off toward the service station car park, where a patrol car was waiting to take them to the airfield.

Beta saw they meant to cut across the car wash. The snow there covered a sheet of mirror-smooth ice, and locals knew to avoid the spot. The owner of the service station had even put up a sign warning the unsuspecting, but the men had walked past it.

Beta waved and shouted: 'Walk along the other edge; it's really slippery there.'

Jónas turned back, a crooked smile on his face: 'Yes, Mummy.'

Beta couldn't believe her ears. What a jerk! She'd tried to be helpful, and all the guy could do was mouth off. She didn't understand Jónas's behaviour. He'd been a pain in the butt for as long she'd known him. Really damn annoying. It was unfortunate they had to deal with such troublesome types, even in their profession. She watched the trio's backs recede. 'So he thinks he's too good to take advice? Let him look after himself, then,' Beta muttered to herself as she waited for the inevitable to occur.

Jónas was trying to look important, taking long, fast strides toward the patrol car. Apparently, he was in a hurry to get back to the capital. Halfway across the car wash forecourt, he slammed to the ground on his left side. His face twisted up in an agonised grimace as the snow kicked up by his plunge drifted down over him.

Beta was alarmed: it looked like a pretty bad tumble, and the man on the ground didn't seem to be able to get up. Sveinn and Hörður had rushed over to help, but Jónas shooed them away. The look on his face spoke of intense pain.

Beta pulled out her phone, called emergency services, and introduced herself to the dispatcher. 'An elderly man slipped in front of the Ísafjörður police station just now. It looked like a bad fall. He slid onto his side and doesn't seem to be able to get up. Hopefully his hip isn't broken.'

Beta thanked the dispatcher, returned the phone to her pocket, and glanced back at where Jónas lay on the ground. She tried to maintain a serious look on her face but was sure the secret satisfaction she felt was evident in her gaze.

Chapter 36

November 2019, Reykjavík-Ísafjörður

Lian was nervous. She held her phone firmly to her ear. The thumbnail of her free hand scratched at some yoghurt crusted to the table, and she was surprised by a smear: the yoghurt wasn't dry after all. All she did was spread the room-temperature gloop around. Disgusted, she wiped her thumb on the side seam of her jeans and waited for someone to pick up.

Lian had meant to call the police a few days before, but her shift that night had rearranged her plans. One of her patients had slipped on the way to the bathroom and fallen on Lian, who hadn't been able to move out of the way. Lian had hit her head on the floor. Luckily things hadn't been any worse. Lian had suffered a mild concussion and spent the next couple of days resting at home. The evenings had been the typical hubbub with the kids, but she'd been able to enjoy some quiet during the day. The rest had done her good. This morning, she'd felt strong again and told the head nurse she'd be coming in for the day shift. During her sick leave, Lian had put everything work-related out of her mind, and that included Jón Jónsson and Heiðar Arason, the men she'd read about in the newspaper during her lunch break. When she got back to work, she remembered: she needed to immediately tell the police what she knew. It was possible the detail she'd recalled was meaningless.

Maybe the detective would just grunt politely, thank her for being an active citizen and sharing her concerns, and then hang up, shaking her head.

Finally, someone answered. Lian introduced herself in the Icelandic fashion, first by wishing the other party a good morning, telling where she was calling from, and giving her first name. Upon moving to Iceland, Lian had quickly learned people introduced themselves by first name only. Traditional surnames were rarely used because every Icelander was someone's son or daughter. Initially, it had felt odd to make an appointment at the salon or introduce herself to the tax authorities in such a familiar manner. Nowadays if felt totally normal.

Lian launched into an explanation for her call. She spoke with a slight accent but felt she had done a fair job of mastering Icelandic. She avoided words she found difficult, preferring to use expressions she knew well. Now she explained that she worked as a nurse at Kleppur, even though her real title was psychiatric nurse. But 'nurse' was a lot easier to pronounce, and a call from Kleppur meant no explanation was required. It was the only psychiatric institution of its type in the country.

Lian said she'd read the news about Jón, who'd died in Ísafjörður, and Heiðar, who'd died in Reykjavík.

But the police officer who answered didn't reply. Lian frowned. 'Excuse me, can you hear me?'

The man at the other man started speaking, but Lian understood nothing of what he said except 'in English'.

Speaking more slowly now, Lian asked if the man spoke Icelandic. She spoke Filipino, Spanish, and Icelandic, but had never mastered English. But strangely enough, the police officer who answered the phone didn't seem to understand Icelandic.

'*Hablas español?*'

There was a heavy sigh at the other end of the line. Lian took this to mean no. She and the police officer didn't have a language in common.

She tried to explain to the policeman that she'd call back later. She assumed he was working the shift alone. Lian's matter could wait until an officer who spoke Icelandic arrived at the station. It wasn't as if anyone's life was in danger. Then again, how did she know? Either way, she had to return to her duties. The patients were waiting. As she ended the call with a familiar goodbye, she smiled to inject some goodwill into her tone.

Jakob stared at the wall in frustration. He was annoyed that he'd had no choice but to hang on the line like an idiot without understanding a word and put the other party in an equally awkward position.

He'd experienced the same sense of helplessness back in Norway, when, after a brief exchange of greetings and 'how are yous' in English, his ex-wife's Norwegian friends had inevitably switched to Norwegian. Jakob had felt like he was regressing, like a child who wasn't being included in the grown-ups' conversation. As soon as he learned the language, the sense of being an outsider had eased.

And now he'd have to face the same slog again. It was a long way from simple two-word sentences to meandering dialogues. He knew he'd learn Icelandic, but it would take time.

The woman who just called had sounded pleasant, and even though she didn't seem to be in a hurry, Jakob had come away with the impression she was calling about something important. But Beta was in a meeting and Hildur had stepped out.

Jakob looked at the terms he'd plucked from the call. He'd made a note of the woman's number, which he'd seen on the screen of the phone, and the words *Kleppyr*, *Jón*, *Heiðar*, *Satan*, and *blessing*. He shook his head and laughed. *Satanic blessing*. Hildur would have to call the woman back.

Jakob continued reviewing Jón's phone logs. He'd already gone through them twice, but he was checking the numbers one last time. Maybe he'd spot something out of the ordinary. Staring at the numbers gave him a good opportunity to knit. The calm, steady repetition of hand movements helped him focus on reviewing the long series of numbers.

Guðrún had left yesterday for Reykjavík and would be staying there for a couple of days. Jakob had spent the evening alone and had had plenty of time to knit. He'd finished the sleeves and the body of the sweater, slipping them onto the same circular needles. The part he enjoyed most was coming up: knitting the pattern. He'd designed it so there was no need to narrow it with rows of two colours, rather all the narrowing around the yoke would be made with single-coloured rows. That made knitting faster and resulted in fewer mistakes.

Jakob was almost at the end of the first such row when the phone rang again. This time the caller recognised him immediately, and when they heard Jakob's name switched to English. It was Hlín from the Westfjords public broadcasting desk. She and Jakob had met in passing at the ruins of Jón's home after the avalanche.

'You reported the death of that runner a couple of days ago.' Hlín sounded friendly, but the sharpness of her tone indicated she wasn't calling for a leisurely chat. Jakob asked how he could help her.

'I've understood it was neither an accident nor a suicide. Can you confirm this?'

Jakob quickly collected his thoughts. He had no intention of lying to the journalist, but he wasn't going to tell her anything either. Beta and Hildur had decided there would be no public announcement regarding the suspected homicide yet. Heiðar's death had so clearly been a murder that it had been reported relatively quickly after the event. The same went for Jón and his slit throat. If the journalists knew all three cases were linked and started writing sensationalist stories about a serial killer on the prowl . . . Jakob didn't even want to imagine the ensuing chaos. Hildur and Beta hoped for more information before they let the reporters have the story.

'He fell from the avalanche barrier and died from injuries sustained during the fall. The investigation is still underway, so there's no more to tell at this point.'

Hlín took a deep breath and said in a voice a degree more forceful: 'People have a right to know.'

Jakob tried to placate her by telling her that, as in all cases where death occurred outside hospital conditions, an autopsy was being performed. The results hadn't arrived yet.

'Shall we agree that I'll call you when I have something to report?' he said, jotting down Hlín's phone number. He promised he'd get back to her as soon as possible.

'*Jæjja*. All right, fine. But remember to call. Because I'm not going to forget,' Hlín said, then hung up.

Chapter 37

November 2019, Ísafjörður

Hildur pulled on a pair of wool socks and brought her foot up to her chair. She leaned her chin against her knee and opened the files on her laptop screen. With the assistance of the friendly staff member at the museum, she'd quickly found all the material she needed.

The municipal archive was one of Hildur's favourite buildings in town. The large windows of the white stone structure gave onto the sea, the mountains, and the cemetery. In summer, the place was bright, and in winter cosy and softly lit. The tall rooms created an open space that supported reflection. Ísafjörður's most handsome stone edifice had originally been built in the 1920s as a hospital. When the patients and caregiving staff decamped to more modern facilities in the 1980s, the old hospital had been rededicated to history and culture. In addition to the municipal archives, a library and a photography museum were housed inside. Hildur could have studied the digital archival material from the station, but she preferred to come here, where she would be surrounded by old books, stacks of paper, quietly humming computers, the tick of the wall clock, and the slow shuffling of the museum staff.

The ambience here was much more atmospheric than at the police station. Wool socks and the museum's high ceilings and big windows helped Hildur think more freely; it was the easiest place to link one-off events into stories. It was Hildur's belief that understanding the story behind the crime facilitated unlocking its secrets. If you didn't know your history, you couldn't understand the present day. She didn't make much noise about her method at criminal investigator retreats or in professional training. It was her odd little habit, and she preferred to keep it that way. Luckily, being the only detective in the region meant there was no need to try and blend into the masses.

And so Hildur was more than familiar with the archives' light-yellow carpet and mid-century wood furniture. She'd spent dozens, probably hundreds, of hours on the premises. She'd investigated the background of and motives for crimes by digging into the details of the involved parties' pasts. Most of the details she'd found, even the interesting ones, had proven useless in her criminal investigations, but now and again she'd caught something while sifting through material that had led her to the motive for a crime. In a couple of instances, she'd solved tricky cases thanks to information found in old documents.

She remembered one extortion case from a few years back. The police had been tipped off about a brazen sheep farmer who'd been blackmailing large sums of money from his elderly neighbours. The neighbours' daughter had contacted law enforcement when her father began to suffer from a surprising shortage of funds. The old man had refused to say anything about the affair, and the entire investigation was on the verge of drying up until Hildur found some crumbs of information in decades-old city council minutes. By putting two and two together, she'd learned about suspicions of insider trading and divined why the neighbour was being extorted.

Twenty years earlier, the neighbour had been on the city council and had bulldozed the council into selling off a piece of land at a fire-sale price. His wife then bought it. The council members had been aware of the council's need for a new fire station. The wife had purchased the property at an exceptionally low price, refurbished it, and a few years later rented it to the municipality as a fire station for a substantial monthly payment. Several tens of millions of krónur of taxpayers' money had been burned.

Such insider trading was nothing new in local Icelandic politics. It was usually swept under the rug, and then the rug and the rubbish beneath it were destroyed. But that hadn't happened in this instance. The sheep farmer had found out about the insider trading, and when the elderly neighbour's adult son had announced he'd be running for mayor, the sheep farmer had promised to expose the fraud and smear the family's reputation unless the neighbour paid him off.

No charges of insider trading were made, as the statute of limitations had expired. But the sheep farmer received a sentence of a few months' probation for extortion.

Hildur returned her gaze to her computer screen and focused her full attention on the material in front of her. She wanted to dig up details on Jón, Heiðar, and Freysi. She was determined to find something that would offer even the tiniest clue as to the murderer's motives.

An archive employee had helped her look up all potential material including mention of the men's names. Newspaper articles, official municipal documents, obituaries. She browsed through old newspaper reports about Jón's crimes, but they contained nothing she didn't already know. Heiðar's name appeared in dozens of articles, in nearly every instance as his client's legal representation. Hildur muttered to herself as she read the articles. She remembered many of the trials covered thanks to her police work. How many white-collar criminals had this guy represented over the course of his career?

Next, her eyes alighted on a personal profile of Freysi published in the local paper when he began teaching physical education at the grammar school. I LOVE EARLY MORNINGS, read the headline. Hildur allowed herself to study the photo at length. Freysi looked so young and sweet. Apparently, it had been windy the day the picture was taken because his hair was sticking up in front. Hildur felt a lump form in her throat. She forced herself to gulp it down. Her cursor moved over to the red X and closed the file. She couldn't let herself drown in memories now.

She stood and walked over to one of the big windows. She rested her forehead against the window frame and looked out. The children from the daycare next door were outside. Toddlers in winter coveralls wobbled through the snow like little boats on the waves. Their falls didn't seem to bother them, in fact, the opposite. The puffs of powder provoked them to run even more wildly through the drifts. The museum's thick walls blocked sound effectively, so Hildur could only imagine the shrieks of joy. No plan, no logic; just doing what feels fun in the moment. Hildur got a kick out of watching the spontaneous play. Although she liked children, she didn't want any herself. The thought of being a parent felt foreign to her.

She returned to the computer. Her next task was reviewing obituaries. They often contained much more information than official documents or articles polished by professionals.

The memorials to the dead published in Icelandic newspapers were bursting with stories. These obituaries were not only homages to the heroic deeds of famous or professionally successful Icelanders; they were also accounts of completely ordinary people and their lives. The texts spoke about the deceased's homes, childhood years, hobbies, friends, and sometimes even favourite football teams or vacation destinations.

An obituary described an individual's history from the personal perspective of the author. Sometimes multiple obituaries were written about a single person, as siblings, parents, children, schoolmates, and colleagues wanted to share their own memories of the deceased. Comparing the informal obituaries created a multidimensional image of a person. Hildur was interested in whether Jón, Heiðar, or Freysi had ever happened to have written an obituary or if they were mentioned in anyone else's memorial. So little time had passed since the men's deaths that no obituaries about them had been published yet. They often weren't until after the funeral.

A newspaper's obituary supplement could sometimes stretch to twenty pages because all submissions were printed, even those that had little to offer in terms of literary value. The memorials crystallised something about the essence of Iceland: every person's life was a story worth telling, and every story was important. Stories about Iceland's inhabitants had been told since the island was settled in the 800s. The first Viking adventures inspired the Icelandic sagas, the crown jewels of medieval European history.

Hildur browsed through the obituaries offered by the search engine. A glance was all it took to show many of them were irrelevant. After all, Jón Jónsson was one of the country's most common names.

One obituary was found under Freysi's name. It was dedicated to Rúnar, a friend from his university days. A young man who was also studying to be a physical education teacher, Rúnar had died in a traffic accident on the road leading into Grindavík. Freysi had signed the obituary along with a few of his fellow students. Rúnar was described as a reliable friend, a well-liked

student, and a competitive volleyball player. The obituary said
that he had met his girlfriend Helga on the job, after which he
suddenly hadn't had any time to play volleyball.

This put a smile on Hildur's face. Friends who'd found themselves coming in second place to a girlfriend were still ribbing
Rúnar, even in death.

Hildur brought up the next search result. Another obituary,
dedicated to a dead man named Jón Jónsson. Once again, the
text was not about the Jón who'd just been murdered. This Jón
had died of cancer at the age of ninety-six in Egilsstaðir in the
east of Iceland.

But something else caught Hildur's eye: her attention was
drawn to an unusually short text at the bottom of the page.
Obituaries were typically at least a quarter of a page in length.
This was only two paragraphs. And there wasn't even a photo.

My eyes and your eyes
O, those precious gems
What's yours is mine and what's mine is yours,
You know my meaning.
I'm sorry for everything. We never even met. Heiðar.

Hildur recognised the first part of the text; many Icelanders
would. It was one of the country's best-known odes to love, the
first verse of a poem written by the nineteenth-century Icelandic
poet Rósa Guðmundsdóttir. The narrator speaks to her love in
beautiful terms.

But the end of the obituary was curiously formulated. This
piqued Hildur's interest. Why on earth was Heiðar the only
signee? No one ever signed an obituary with their first name

alone; they used their whole name and title or relationship to the deceased. There was nothing here. As if the author hadn't wanted to reveal any more than his first name.

The information provided on the deceased was scant. There was no photo. The obituary had been written in October 2012 for a woman named Valgerður Indriðadóttir. She had died very young, at the age of twenty-one. No mention of the cause of death, but there wasn't necessarily anything unusual about that. Some obituaries divulged the cause of death; others didn't. Life was more important. What the deceased and the writer had experienced together.

Hildur reached into her pocket and pulled out the little notebook where she recorded random observations. Things that didn't directly relate to any criminal investigation but around which a heavy, tattered curtain of fog seemed to hang. Hildur jotted down Valgerður's name, birth date, and date of death. She saved a copy of the obituary on her laptop, slipped the notebook in her pocket, and decided to return to the police station.

The area in front of the museum had just been ploughed, and the snow squeaked under Hildur's shoes. The sea wind snatched at her hair, then flung it in her face. It was coming up to noon, but there still wasn't much light. The sky was so murky with clouds that there wasn't enough sun to reach the town. Hildur lifted her hood to protect her head and strode more briskly.

She found the obituary she'd just read jostling around in her brain. The signee nagged at her. Hildur knew there were hundreds of men in Iceland named Heiðar, not just the lawyer who was mangled in the parking garage. One *Heiðar* under an unusual obituary didn't necessarily mean anything.

But more than the single-name signature, she was intrigued by the contradictory nature of the text. Why did the author say he'd never met the deceased? Obituaries were only written about relatives, friends, and other loved ones. What exactly had the writer meant?

Hildur didn't mean to leave the matter there. She would have to poke around some more.

Chapter 38

Hildur's teeth sank into the mouth-watering pizza; the combination of peppery cheese and spicy pepperoni was superlative. She left the crust uneaten and set it down on the edge of her plate. She grabbed the next piece and bit down again. So much had happened over the past two days that her body constantly demanded more food. Her hunger felt bottomless.

The food served by the grill below the police station wasn't the healthiest in the world, but it tasted good and killed an appetite. Hildur gazed out the restaurant window. Snow-covered, flat-topped mountains rose skyward at the town's edge, beyond the last residential streets. At this hour, the sun just grazed the peak, setting the upper slopes glittering. The sky was blue, the sea mirror smooth. Perfect weather for enjoying the outdoors. If she lived the eight-to-four life most people did, she could go for a run after work. But just now, a leisurely afternoon run felt like as remote a dream as a surfing vacation in Morocco.

Hildur's day hadn't been as beautiful as the weather. She'd taken yesterday off to gather her strength. Today she'd spent this morning perusing old documents. When she returned to the station, she'd asked everyone to not ask how she was holding up. She wanted to keep working, and that was that.

Jónas, who had slipped in front of the police station the day before, had been taken to the local hospital, where he'd been diagnosed with a static hip fracture. He wasn't going to be walking anywhere for the next few weeks. The forensics team from Reykjavík had flown south with Freysi's body.

Hildur stared at the mountains. Ages ago, this hunk of lava at the seam of two tectonic plates had been covered by a sheet of ice kilometres thick. New land formed through volcanic activity, of course. But when volcanoes erupted below heavy masses of ice, the mountains ended up with flattened crowns. The thought of ice-flattened heights felt comforting. The mountains had formed with a weight on their backs, but they still formed. They just turned out a little different.

'Hildur, are you listening?'

Jakob was staring at her from across the table, a questioning look on his face. Hildur pushed away her empty plate. 'I'm sorry, I wasn't.'

'I asked if you could help me.' Jakob told her about the strange call he'd received that morning, of which he'd understood almost nothing except the words *Satan* and *blessing*. He showed Hildur the words he had written down:

Kleppyr, Jón, Heiðar, seitna, bles.

Hildur broke out laughing. The burst of joy felt good. The laughter relaxed her. After catching her breath, she took the note and looked at it a second time, interpreting the text for Jakob.

'*Bles* doesn't mean "blessing". It's used when saying goodbye. And *seitna* doesn't have anything to do with "Satan"; it means "later". Kleppur is a psychiatric hospital in Reykjavík,' she said. 'So who was it who called? One of the patients?'

'I'm not sure. She sounded totally sane. The only problem was I didn't understand what she was saying.'

They both knew the police got a lot of prank calls. Some people just wanted to talk: if there wasn't anyone else to talk to, at least the police would pick up. Some calls belonged in the whacko category. People called in about radiation they'd seen or a murder they'd witnessed that had been reported in the previous day's newspaper.

Jakob pointed out the phone number at the bottom of the note. 'Could you call her back so I can stop worrying about it?'

Hildur pulled her phone out of her coat pocket, tapped at it, and lifted it to her ear. The phone rang once, twice. After the sixth ring, Hildur gave up. She would try again soon.

Winter coats under their arms, the duo stepped out through the grill's sliding doors and headed toward the rear of the building, which was where the entrance to the police station was. Beta was in her office on the phone. There was a half-eaten packet of cookies on her desk and the steady voice of the news anchor was coming from the radio.

Jakob and Hildur sat at their desks and started tapping at their computers. Hildur recorded her observations about the previous days' events. Jakob was engrossed in the telephone data. He was comparing the calls made and received by Jón and Freysi, looking for numbers in common, checking the call times.

Suddenly, Hildur slammed down the lid of her laptop and stood. 'Listen. I've been thinking about one thing related to Heiðar. Let's go to Reykjavík for a couple of days. We need to dig up more information on our dead lawyer.'

Hildur had the sense the only way to make any progress in the investigation was to visit the capital. The obituary signed by the mysterious Heiðar was troubling her; it gave her an ominous feeling. And what Jónas, the detective from Reykjavík, had said about Heiðar's widow was odd: apparently she hadn't seemed shocked in the least by her husband's death. Hildur wanted to talk to her. The widow had to know something about her deceased husband's movements. Something the others hadn't had the sense to ask her. Besides, Jónas was lying in the hospital, so the Reykjavík investigation would be advancing at a slower pace for the next few days.

'You have to see a little bit of Reykjavík during your internship. If the trip ends up being a bust in terms of work, at least you can say you've been to the northernmost capital in the world.'

Jakob had no reason to protest. He tidily wound up the charger cord for his laptop and gathered up the essentials from his desk to pack along.

'I'll pick you up in half an hour. Go to the bathroom before we leave. It's a two-and-a-half-hour drive to the nearest rest area.' Hildur glanced out the window. Dark clouds were gathering. 'Or three. It's going to be coming down hard soon, and I don't like speeding in sleet.'

Hildur marched into Beta's office and informed her of the field trip to Reykjavík. The boss approved the idea; it was important to dig up all possible information on the victims' backgrounds.

Hildur liked Beta's management style. Experts knew best what was relevant to their work and what wasn't, and that was why they were allowed significant freedom in deciding how they spent their time. They didn't need to report every last move to the boss. What mattered were results.

Hildur headed home from the station. She would have to warm up the car, pack running clothes, toothbrush, face cream, and a change of underwear into a bag, and make some coffee for the Thermos. She cast a critical eye over her high-topped, shabby winter running shoes and decided to toss her nicer low-top autumn trainers in the bag, too. There wasn't as much snow in Reykjavík as there was here. Lighter gear would see her through.

She suffered no pangs of conscience even though she hadn't told her boss – or Jakob, for that matter – the whole truth about the trip they were about to make. It wasn't that she had lied. She had merely left something unsaid. Because there was a certain place along the way where she had to make a stop.

Magnús's words about a mysterious stonemason were still eating at her. He hadn't remembered the stonemason's name, but when he described the man's appearance, Hildur had instantly known who he meant.

Jón had been in the tunnel where her sisters' tracks had ended. Jón had lived on the farm next door to Magnús. And that farm was where Hildur had to go now.

Chapter 39

November 2019, Ísafjörður-Reykjavík

Hildur's premonition proved accurate. The weather had taken a turn for the worse. The windscreen wipers toiled away at the sleet falling from the sky, but their impact remained minimal at best. It was raining icy slurry so hard that the instant the wipers swept the landscape into view, it was blanketed under grey slush again. Visibility was poor, and Hildur drove with an excess of caution. She remained within the lane lines, maintaining a speed of under eighty and keeping her eyes glued to the road.

The weather was bad for driving, and the temperature on the mountain roads crossing the highlands had dropped below freezing. The sleet came in snow form up there, and the traffic police ploughs wouldn't necessarily be keeping the road open this late in the day. Hildur and Jakob had hit the road in Hildur's personal vehicle; Brenda's mascot shook her hips steadily in time to the SUV's movements. When the weather was bad, Hildur preferred to rely on her own vehicle. She had customised her four-wheel drive with forty-inch tyres. There had to be a lot of snow on the road before Brenda's undercarriage would get stuck in it. Besides, using her personal vehicle allowed her to claim decent kilometre-based compensation for the trip. The tax-free income was a welcome addition to her salary.

'Luckily it'll be dark soon,' Hildur said with a sigh, both hands on the wheel.

'Tell me about it. It's nicer to drive in the dark when it's coming down hard. You can see the reflectors on the snow markers better,' Jakob said. He was perched in the passenger seat, knitting needles in hand; his bag of yarn had been firmly wedged between the seat and the handbrake.

'Is the weather often this bad in Finland?' Hildur asked. She glanced at the sweater in Jakob's hands out of the corner of her eye. Guðrún must still have been out of town, seeing as he'd had so much time to knit. The sweater looked like it was almost finished. The pattern was going to be spectacular: long, graphic lines and earth tones. Although it was contemporary, it somehow reminded her of the old cross-stitches hanging on her Aunt Tinna's walls.

'We have snow, ice, and darkness. It doesn't come down this hard very often, though,' Jakob said.

They drove past Súðavík. The grey surroundings made the village look, if possible, even more miserable than usual. Small houses huddled side by side and roads drowning in slush, not a tree in sight. The finishing touch on the eerie ambience was the abandoned service station; sheets of plywood had been nailed over its long-shattered windows. The plywood had been soaked by precipitation over the years and wouldn't stay in place much longer.

The winding road followed the shoreline. In this part of Iceland, the roads had been intentionally built at the foot of the mountains, right at the water. Maintaining roads up in the highlands was expensive in the wintertime, as huge amounts of snow might fall over the course of one night, and the big ploughs couldn't manoeuvre across the steep, hairpin terrain. Many of the region's most dangerous mountain roads were closed in winter. But land was flatter at the shore, making it possible to plough there.

The Fjord of Swans was followed by a small fjord, less than ten kilometres long. Then the road turned into narrow Horse Fjord, named after Hestur – or horse – mountain. It rose a good half a kilometre in altitude on the fjord's northern edge, where it was lashed by the Atlantic.

Hildur nodded in the direction of the broad, flat-topped peak. 'That's where I go in the autumn to pick crowberries.'

Hildur could enjoy complete privacy and peace there. She had never seen other berry pickers in the area, because there wasn't a single road leading to the mountain. Picking there meant a several-kilometre walk with one's pails, and not many had the condition or the time to devote to it.

Hildur dedicated a couple of weeks every September to berry picking. She would put her training on pause and head out with her buckets whenever she had a free moment. Sometimes she picked blueberries and even bog bilberries, but she preferred the slightly tart, tough-skinned crowberries. Back at home, she would clean them of the worst leaves and twigs and boil them for juice. She usually ended up bottling more than necessary for her own needs, so many of her acquaintances had grown accustomed to getting Westfjords berry juice as a Christmas or hostess gift. Her pathologist friend Axlar-Hákon was the biggest fan of her homemade present. On this occasion, Hildur had packed a few bottles wrapped in newspaper in the back of the SUV. She brought Hákon some every time she visited Reykjavík. She did it because she enjoyed it, but it didn't hurt to have the country's only pathologist feel like he was perpetually in her debt to the tune of a few bottles of juice.

That's how everything worked in Iceland. Someone knew someone who was prepared to help them. Everyone scratched everyone else's back and exchanged favours.

Jakob looked over at the mountain and nodded approvingly. For a first-timer, the drive ahead was a long one. The more you drove these roads, the shorter the trip felt. With every pass, the fjords grew more familiar, the curves grew less dramatic, and the more one had the urge to stop and study the increasingly distinct details in the surrounding mountains.

'This is the fourth fjord now. How many do we have left?'

'Three deep fjords and one mountain pass to the first service station. Then we'll be halfway there.'

Neither the car radio nor their mobile phones had any reception in the remote fjords, but the clack of Jakob's knitting needles and the squeak of the windscreen wipers created a cosy ambience in the car. Hildur and Jakob continued their journey in silence.

Hildur flicked her right turn signal and pulled off the highway onto a dirt road leading to an old farm.

Jakob shot Hildur a questioning glance. 'What are we doing here?'

'There's one thing I want to take care of really quickly,' Hildur said.

The track was bumpy, and Hildur decelerated. When she reached the farm, she pulled up in front of a barn that had seen better days. It didn't look like sheep had lived there for years. It was dark by now, but Brenda's headlights illuminated the property. Sheets of wood had been hung over the barn's windows. The roof had collapsed at one corner.

Hildur turned to the main building. The façade was in a sorry state, but otherwise, the place looked habitable: the paint was peeling, and the gutters dangled, but the walls were straight and the windows had panes. The ground-floor lights appeared to be on, and a van was parked out front. After hearing Magnús's account, Hildur had studied the map and was sure she'd come to the right place. This was where Jón had lived back in the 1990s.

She'd been compelled to come to this place. She'd had to see it in person. She'd driven past this lonely farm dozens, probably hundreds, of times when travelling between Ísafjörður and Reykjavík. The derelict property had caught her eye, but she'd never driven onto it.

However, after what Magnús had told her, she hadn't been able to get the farm out of her mind. Hildur didn't know if anyone would be home or if the place was even inhabited. No one was registered as living at the address, and it wasn't linked to any people or phone numbers. But it looked like there were lights on inside. And that gave her hope.

Hope for what? she thought to herself. She didn't really know what she expected. But she knew if she didn't stop here, it would continue to trouble her. She hadn't wanted to say anything to Jakob about the stop in advance because she hadn't known what she could have said without sounding completely insane.

Knitting needles in hand, Jakob continued looking questioningly at Hildur.

'Wait here. I'll explain later.' Hildur slammed the car door behind her and strode to the entrance of the main building. There was no bell, of course, so she knocked on the glass pane in the door. The freezing rain was soaking her hair. She'd tried to retreat beneath her hood, but a hood was no use against Icelandic sleet. The strong wind flung the precipitation at will, and at times it flew horizontally, straight into her eyes. She dried her face on her coat sleeve and knocked again, this time a little harder. A moment later she saw movement in the entryway, and someone grabbed the door handle from the inside.

As is customary in Iceland, the door opened inward. The amount of snow that packed in front of doors would make them impossible to open outward. An inward-opening door guaranteed a quick exit, even during the winter.

There at the door stood a friendly-looking woman Hildur's age. 'Car trouble?'

In these sparsely populated regions, residents were used to occasional requests for help. If you ran out of petrol or had a flat, there was no way to call for help. You had to turn to the nearest habitation, and it might be dozens of kilometres away.

'No, nothing like that,' Hildur quickly answered. She said she was a police officer and on her way to Reykjavík for work. 'I wanted to stop here on the way. Um, hm, could I come in?' The mention of the police put the woman on edge. She wrapped her long sweater around herself more tightly and sank her hands into the deep side pockets of her cardigan.

Hildur was used to this reaction: a police officer at the door didn't usually bode well. 'What I'm here about has nothing to do with you. It's about this old farm.'

The woman still looked sceptical. Nevertheless, she invited Hildur in and led her to the kitchen table. She suggested a cup of coffee; Hildur declined. Hildur wanted to keep the visit short. Jakob was waiting in the car, and they were supposed to stop at the kiosk in Hólmavík for coffee.

The woman poured herself a cup anyway. She introduced herself as María Jónasdóttir, a ceramics artist from Reykjavík. María had bought the farm a couple of years earlier from an estate. She explained she was renovating it into a studio, but the project was advancing slowly, mostly during vacations and on long weekends. She hoped to be finished by summer. María said she planned on turning the old barn into a ceramics workshop. Her dream was to install a kiln in there. 'Now I have to drive my pieces back to Reykjavík for firing.'

Hildur smiled. This was exactly what the ceramicists of her imagination looked like wearing a colourful, long-sleeved dress, a long cardigan, a big brooch, with curly hair pulled back with a silk scarf.

Now Hildur got down to the point: she wanted to know something about the farm's past that wasn't in official sources of information. 'Did you know the previous owner?'

'Unfortunately. I bought the place from a family that was arguing over an inheritance. The estate agent said the estate had been waiting for decades to be distributed. The farm wasn't sold until the most antagonistic characters involved had died. I can dig up the information on the previous owners if you want.'

Hildur thanked María but said it wouldn't be necessary; she could find that information from the census with a couple of clicks. 'But tell me who lived here before you did.'

María shrugged and apologised for not being able to answer. She didn't know. 'If I understood correctly, the estate had been renting it under the table.'

This news came as no surprise to Hildur. She had looked up the farm on the national register. According to the official records, no one had lived here in over three decades.

'When I first came here a couple of years ago, the place looked abandoned. The windows leaked, and it was overrun with mice. The roof repairs alone gobbled up a fortune,' María said. She had wrapped her fingers around her coffee mug. Old houses could be chilly. 'May I ask why you're interested?'

The ceramicist seemed curious.

I wonder if this visit is going to be any use, Hildur thought to herself. 'It's related to a crime under investigation,' she answered vaguely.

María turned up her nose. She seemed offended. 'I haven't noticed anything illegal going on around here.'

'No, this is related to a really old case.' Any excess patience vanished from Hildur's voice. 'When you moved here, what did you do with whatever had been left behind?'

María didn't have to think long. The estate had emptied the property and buildings of all belongings; clearing the house and its surroundings had been a condition of the sale. The place had been full of junk. The old tractor tyres, broken-down machines, rusty oil barrels, and heaps of fishing nets had been a terrible eyesore, a mountain of debris visible to the road. Hildur felt a pang: it was her spark of hope dying. It had been ignited when Magnús told her about the scarred stonemason who'd lived on the property around the time her sisters went missing. Hildur had hoped to find something on the farm that would shed even the tiniest bit of light on their disappearance. Despite the sting, her disappointment wasn't outwardly visible. She thanked María for the information, stood, and began moving toward the front door. 'How's the berry picking around here, by the way?'

'There are a lot of blueberries out back; I picked a few buckets this autumn. They were small but incredibly flavoursome.'

'The smaller the better. Even if they are a nightmare to wash,' Hildur said, sitting on the stool in the entryway.

Waterproof winter shoes didn't let water in, but they didn't let it out either. That meant sweat had an unpleasant tendency to collect inside footwear. Hildur caught a pungent whiff as she pulled on her shoes. Damned winter conditions.

María folded her arms across her chest and leaned casually against the frame of the door between the vestibule and the house. The big eyes of the owl brooch pinned to her cardigan were staring straight at Hildur.

Suddenly, María looked as if she remembered something. 'As a matter of fact, something just occurred to me. I doubt it's important, but . . .'

Hildur stood up and shifted her gaze from the owl to María's face. 'Go on.'

María wrapped her cardigan more tightly around herself again. She said she'd been renovating the barn last summer. The kiln would be going in as soon as she'd saved enough money for it. Big ceramics kilns were major investments.

'There was this odd mound behind the barn. It really stood out against the flat terrain. At the time I thought maybe people believed that elves inhabited it, and that's why no one had touched it.'

Hildur knew some folks left mounds and stones on their property undisturbed because they believed the hidden people lived in them. The afterbirth of cows and horses were left as gifts at the mounds of the elves, and the grass next to them was never scythed or mowed with loud mowers.

The elves of old Icelandic folktales were unseen human-like beings who could become visible at will. Elves generally kept to themselves in the natural world but made visits to ordinary people at whim. They punished those who misbehaved by lighting mysterious fires or breaking things. For good people, elves performed favours, for instance helping those lost in the fog find their way home or ensuring a good harvest for those who respected nature.

'Could you show me the spot?' Hildur asked. The sleet had turned to rain. Both she and María had pulled up their hoods to shield their faces and walked at a hunch, heads drawn down to their shoulders. María stepped behind the barn and stopped next to the wall, in the shelter of the roof. The effort was pointless, as the rain was cleverer than they were. It always knew how to come at them from an angle that offered no protection.

'This is what I meant,' María shouted over the rain, gesturing around the corner. She flicked on the torch she was carrying and aimed it at the wall.

Hildur stepped up right next to María and let her gaze search the torch's beam. She shivered. There was a big mound that clearly stood out from the otherwise flat yard. Hildur felt the soft soil shift underfoot, and the air smelled of wet earth. The rainwater reverberated against the barn roof like a men's choir echoing in a chapel. The light from María's torch turned the stalks of grass into fine strands of hair standing on end.

Recollections of the places Hildur had been with her sisters and moments they'd shared flashed through her mind. She'd had only a few memories of them, and some of those had already faded. She remembered one year when each of them got a water-powered toy car for Christmas. The girls had raced them from the kitchen doorway to the armchair in the furthest corner of the living room. Rósa had won, and there had been no limit to her delight.

Hildur remembered Rósa's broad smile but not the year or if there'd been snow.

A lurch of María's torch brought Hildur back to the present moment. She eyed the formation María was pointing at. It appeared manmade. A clearly raised area a couple of metres long and a metre wide next to the sheepfold wall. At first, she thought it might be a dung heap, but rejected the idea after a moment's consideration. No farmer would locate a dung heap right next to a barn, for fear of pests.

It wouldn't be hard to believe the mound was a sacred spot inhabited by elves – if you believed such stories, that is. For Hildur, they were merely old folktales people had made up to entertain and comfort each other in the days before computers and smartphones.

Water streamed down her face, along her skin, in at her collar. Rain.

Or maybe tears.

Maybe they were the same thing.

The mound was too symmetrical. A couple of metres long, a metre and a half wide, half a metre tall. Some faint voice whispered inside her. Deep down, she knew she was right.

What she was looking at was a grave.

Chapter 40

After the final fjord, the road turned up into the mountains. Steingrímsfjarðarheiði was a mountain pass about forty kilometres long that linked the area of Strandir on the eastern shores of the Westfjords with the Ísafjörður basin. The route hadn't opened until the mid-1980s. Before that, the only way over the highlands had been a tiny footpath.

At its highest, the pass rose to half a kilometre above sea level. That was nothing for a mountain road, but the conditions made it challenging. In the summer, the nearby sea frequently pushed a thick fog into the area. Many people had got lost in its black depths. Some had never been found.

The narrow, winding track demanded skill of drivers. Everything was more merciless in the winter up here than down in the villages. Snow was frequent, and strong winds lashed it into motion. The road had to be closed now and again due to blizzards. But today the big iron gate had been turned aside, and the way was open.

Hildur glanced out of the corner of her eye at the big digital weather sign on the right shoulder. It said the air temperature in the highlands was a little below freezing and the wind was blowing at a maximum of twenty-two metres per second.

She tried to keep her face neutral, even though she was roiling inside. Her head teemed with incomplete thoughts. A connection existed between her missing sisters and Jón. Jón had been living at the old farm and working in the tunnel when her sisters vanished. Now Jón had been murdered. As had Freysi

256

and Heiðar. There was no rhyme or reason to the big picture. Even so, she got the sense a big picture existed; she just didn't know which pieces fitted together.

She also felt bad she hadn't been able to tell Jakob the reason for her stop at the farm. He'd sat waiting and knitting in Brenda. When Hildur had returned to the SUV, drained, Jakob had offered to drive the rest of the way, but she had refused. She said she preferred to drive the difficult stretch of mountain road herself.

'OK.' That was all Jakob had said. *OK.* And continued clacking his needles. The hill rose steeply, and Hildur gave Brenda more gas.

Eventually Jakob broke the silence. 'Are there any of those trolls around here?'

Brenda's windows gave a view of a seemingly endless lava plain. Black formations thrust through the snow where the wind had blown off their veil of powder. The rolling fields of lava went on as far as the car's headlights reached. In the darkness, it was hard to know where sky began and earth ended. The terrain looked like a bedsheet with a repeating weave of black and grey tones.

Hildur grunted. 'Some of those stories are totally made up. The inventions of marketing men.'

Tourists were told stories about trolls who inhabited the highlands. When the trolls cooked inside their mountains and the porridge boiled over, there was a volcanic eruption. And then everyone would laugh. Oh, these silly Icelanders!

Some of the troll stories had been used to explain the formations rising from the terrain and the origins of the world.

'The old stories say the route through these mountains rose when a troll named Kleppa rode through the area on his steed, Flóki.'

'Is it possible to still catch a glimpse of that steed?'

257

'Sure. It's just as likely as getting good coffee from the kiosk in Hólmavík.'

As always, the coffee Hildur pumped from the Thermos was atrocious. Judging by the burned smell and the grease floating on the surface, it had been made around lunchtime. In addition to the coffee, they bought hot dogs with all the toppings, two containers of vanilla *skyr*, and a big bag of candy. Hildur and Jakob sat in the furthest corner of the dining area to eat their modest meal.

When they reached Hólmavík, their mobile phones had started working again. As she spooned her *skyr*, Hildur pulled out her phone and decided to get the most unpleasant matter out of the way. She needed her boss's permission to dig.

'Hey, it's Hildur. The trip is going fine. We're drinking disgusting coffee in Hólmavík . . . Listen, I need an excavator at Ögúrvík.'

Hildur explained to Beta about the man with the scarred face Magnús the dog handler had told her about, the farm at Ögurvík, and the grave-like mound she'd just discovered.

Beta was sceptical.

'Goddammit. Take it out of my pay, then,' Hildur snapped and hung up. She'd guessed Beta wouldn't look favourably on her hunch regarding the importance of excavation. So what? This wouldn't be the first time she acted in opposition to her boss's point of view.

Jakob looked at Hildur serenely over his hot dog but didn't comment. Apparently, he was politely waiting for her to address the topic of the stop they'd just made.

'You have mayonnaise on your chin.' Hildur took a napkin from the stand on the table and handed it to her colleague.

Jakob crammed the rest of the steaming hot dog into his mouth, wiped away the mayonnaise that had dribbled into his beard, and tossed his wrappers in the rubbish.

The two of them walked back to the car, buckled their seatbelts, and started off down the next mountain road, Þröskuldar, which would take them south. They still had a little under three hours to Reykjavík.

'Will it bother you if I use this?' Jakob had put on a headlamp and pressed the button to set it to minimum intensity.

I guess that's what happens when you start knitting, Hildur thought to herself, amused. 'Just don't turn this way and it'll be fine.'

They drove the rest of the way in silence. When the mountain road reached Route 1, the main highway around Iceland, radio reception returned, and their mobile phones worked normally again. At first, Hildur listened to the evening news broadcast from Icelandic public radio, followed by a music programme, *Kvöldvaktin*, 'Swing Shift'. After the obituaries, 'Swing Shift' was one of her favourite radio shows. In every episode, the hosts played music, discussing the songs and the meaning the music held for them. Hildur wasn't particularly interested in music; she found sitting in concerts incredibly boring, and she didn't even go to gigs where the audience packed in front of the stage to dance as the band played far too loudly. She couldn't imagine an activity more uncomfortable than dancing in public. But 'Swing Shift' was excellent. She found it relaxing listening to people who knew a lot about music converse and play songs she never would have heard otherwise.

By the time the lights of Reykjavík began to appear against the dark sky, Jakob had finished the pattern for his sweater.

Chapter 41

November 2019, Reykjavík-Garðabær

The next morning, Hildur was up by six. She and Jakob had booked single rooms at the Grand Hotel, near Laugardalur Park. The Grand was one of the state-owned hotels, and government officials who lived outside Reykjavík frequently stayed there during work trips to the capital. Hildur assumed Jakob was probably still asleep, but she wasn't tired. She pulled on her running clothes and tightly knotted the laces of her running shoes. As the temperature was well above freezing, the streets were free of snow and cleats were unnecessary.

She headed south toward the seashore. She and Jakob had agreed the night before to meet at breakfast at eight. Hildur glanced at her watch. An hour and a half would give her time to run to the lighthouse at Seltjarnarnes and back. The paved pedestrian-cum-bike path was lit the whole way, and Hildur knew the route well. When she lived in Reykjavík, she'd often run the city's shores, and the route around the Seltjarnarnes headland had been one of her favourites.

The air smelled of the sea, and her hair tossed in the wind. She passed the Viking boat sculpture erected in honour of the capital's two-hundred-year-anniversary, the luxurious waterfront concert hall, and the old harbour, where passenger boats took tourists out to go whale watching. Now and again she stepped off the pavement when the tarmac felt unpleasant underfoot. The soft, grey, winter-ravaged grass offered a gentler surface.

The longer Hildur had been gone from Reykjavík, the less eager she was to return. Everything in the city was too orderly somehow. The roads were straight, there was concrete everywhere, the green spaces were carefully situated, and in summertime, the flowers grew exactly where they'd been planted. The place needed a touch of wildness, some lack of discipline. Hildur missed that already, although fewer than twelve hours had passed since she'd left home.

The stark white lighthouse at Seltjarnarnes was only accessible at low tide. Today Hildur was out of luck: the rising tide had swallowed the neck of land that led to it. She took a short break to catch her breath and settled for admiring the illuminated tower from a distance.

She glanced at her sports watch again to make sure it wasn't too early for the first call of the day. She reached into her jacket pocket for her phone and dialled the number of an excavator operator acquaintance of hers, gave him instructions on how to reach the farm, and made him promise to wait for her. She would stop by that evening to show him the exact spot. Then she sent Beta a text message:

I'm sorry I lost my temper. But I'm bringing in an excavator – Hildur.

Before long, her phone pinged with a curt reply: *Jæjja.*

Hildur shrugged. She interpreted the reply to mean Beta had approved her request.

Bellies full of the hotel breakfast's scrambled eggs and semi-thawed berries, Hildur and Jakob drove to the forensics facility downtown and left the bag of crowberry juice bottles in Axlar-Hákon's office. After that, they made for the city of Garðabær, just south of Reykjavík.

Morning traffic into downtown Reykjavík was at its worst. Every single one of the capital's two hundred thousand residents seemed to be commuting along the broad thoroughfare of Kringlumýrarbraut packed into cars and SUVs. Luckily, Jakob and Hildur were travelling in the opposite direction. Their destination was the peninsula of Arnarnes, the most expensive neighbourhood of the garden city of Garðabær. Its waterfront villas weren't gated off from the rest of Iceland yet, but Hildur guessed it wouldn't be long before the millionaires who called the area home had their way. They'd already stopped a public bike and pedestrian path from being built across the peninsula. Some wanted to completely close off local traffic to anyone not driving to and from their residences.

Hildur pulled up in front of a white stone villa. With her patches of rust, Brenda stood out against the Teslas and Range Rovers that generally slid along the well-groomed stretch of street. Hildur slammed Brenda's door behind her and, with Jakob at her heels, marched across the neatly trimmed garden to one of the property's many entrances. The doorbell next to the oak door suggested it was the main one.

A tired-looking woman in a knee-length robe and fuzzy slippers answered. 'The cleaning company wasn't supposed to send you until the afternoon. I was still asleep,' she snapped, pulling the door shut.

Hildur stuck out her hand to block the door from closing. 'You must be Kolfinna Daníelsdóttir? We're from the police. I'm Detective Hildur Rúnarsdóttir, and this is Jakob Johanson. We'd like to talk about Heiðar.'

'I've already talked about Heiðar. As a matter of fact, I've spoken with several police officers over the past few days.'

Kolfinna Daníelsdóttir seemed ill-tempered, which was no wonder under the circumstances: she'd just lost her husband. She gripped the edge of the door firmly with both hands. Hildur noticed her knuckles were turning white.

'We have a few more specific questions.'

'You don't seem to have any idea what it feels like to lose a spouse,' Kolfinna wailed. Her voice cracked as she explained she simply didn't have the energy to talk to anyone else.

Hildur had the impulse to say she understood; after all, she'd just lost a friend who meant a lot to her, too. But, at least in the eyes of outsiders, that wasn't the same as a spouse.

'My condolences. And I have no interest in bothering you, but some things have come up we need to ask you about. We're doing everything we can to complete this investigation as fast as possible.'

Kolfinna sighed and moved away from the door, beckoning the visitors in with a lethargic wave of her hand.

Hildur was embarrassed to have left her indoor socks at home. Her sweaty running socks would no doubt leave toe-shaped tracks on the herringbone parquet.

They sat down on couches of cognac-coloured leather arranged in the middle of the living room. Kolfinna sat alone on a narrower one; Jakob and Hildur sat side by side on the larger, which faced the water. The north-facing wall was all glass, and the sea views from the living room were spectacular. Old Reykjavík was silhouetted against the horizon. There weren't many furnishings, but Hildur guessed each piece cost more than all the furniture in her house put together. Valuable art was showcased on the walls. Hildur recognised at least one Kjarval expressionist landscape and a couple of postmodern pieces by Ragnar Kjartansson. Hildur had never been in a home with a genuine Jóhannes Kjarval hanging on the wall. She was only used to seeing the works of Iceland's most famous twentieth-century painter in museums.

'Can you tell me anything about your deceased husband's movements over the past few weeks?'

Kolfinna looked Hildur dead in the eye. 'Do you really think he told me what he was up to?'

Hildur had heard about the couple's cool relations, but even so, the answer caught her off guard. Kolfinna had seemed distraught with grief when she opened the door, but the mood had quickly turned. Kolfinna now seemed frustrated.

'But you both lived here. Did any of his routines change?' 'If they did, I didn't notice.'

Not long after her wedding day, Kolfinna had come to learn the real reason her husband stayed in the marriage. Heiðar had always wanted money, and her family had it. A lot of it. She spoke in a steady voice, like a CFO reporting on her company's most recent quarterly results. 'He was after the money. He didn't want me; he hasn't for years.'

She described her deceased husband as a cold social climber incapable of displaying empathy. Which was no doubt a useful trait in his chosen profession.

'It's tragic he died that way, of course. It's a big loss for our children, and it's causing me all sorts of headaches. But I don't really miss him. I don't know what he was up to when he wasn't at home. And he wasn't home often.'

Hildur nodded and let Kolfinna continue. 'He never spoke to me about his women,' she said, gazing off into the distance.

'Were they ever the source of any trouble, in your experience? Did they come here? Or call the house?'

'Are you saying some jealous mistress might have killed him?'

Hildur dodged the question: 'We don't have any suspects yet.'

This was true; they didn't have any suspects yet. Hildur wanted to dig into Heiðar's past to gain some understanding of his life. She'd heard from her colleagues in Reykjavík that on the night of his death, Heiðar had been at a hotel with a girl-friend. The frightened young woman had been fingerprinted and swabbed for DNA samples.

Hildur tried to formulate her words as carefully as possible: 'Do you know if your husband had any longer-term affairs? Any, um, more serious ones?'

'He was a very impulsive person. I don't believe he loved any-one except himself. Himself and the feeling of falling in love. His affairs usually petered out within a few weeks. When there was a new girl in the works, he'd be cheerful at home. The thrill generally lasted several weeks, then Heiðar would get bored, and the relationship would end.'

Kolfinna shifted in her seat and looked as if she'd suddenly remembered something. Her manicured hands fingered the hem of her robe. 'I do remember one girl. It was an awfully long time ago, though. Heiðar was in an unusually pleasant mood one year, from spring to autumn. Then he suddenly changed, became closed off and cantankerous.'

Kolfinna had tried to ask her husband what was bothering him, but he hadn't replied. He'd just sat in silence on the couch, drinking calvados and staring out the window.

'I was taking clothes to the dry cleaners when I found a funeral programme in the breast pocket of his dark suit.'

Hildur's ears pricked up. She eyed Kolfinna. 'Whose funeral was it?'

'Her name was Valgerður. There was a photo on the programme. A beautiful blonde.' When Kolfinna uttered the name, a shock-like sensation ran through Hildur's body.

Blood surged to her head, and her palms prickled. *Valgerður.* It had been a grind digging up the details of the victims' lives, but that one curious obituary had stuck with her. Hildur's instincts had told her it was relevant. At first it hadn't made any sense. And now it did. Like a piece that hadn't originally fit anywhere. A young woman. Valgerður.

My eyes and your eyes. O, those precious gems!

The widow of the man who'd authored the obituary was sitting right there. Heiðar had written it for his secret girlfriend. Which was why it was only signed with a first name. He hadn't wanted anyone to know.

'How did your husband explain the funeral programme?'

'The way he always did when confronted with something unpleasant. He denied it. The story was a friend had borrowed the suit for his cousin's funeral. I could tell he was lying, but I didn't care enough to keep pestering him about it. A few days later, I checked the suit pocket. The programme was gone. I guess he got rid of it.'

Hildur wished she and Jakob could make their exit. The ambience in the house made her uneasy. But she wanted to know if Heiðar had travelled recently or had any visitors at the house.

'We went to the south of France in August to buy wine, but nothing since. At least nothing I knew about. His business acquaintances would sometimes come over for dinner.' Kolfinna described how these dinners typically progressed. First the cleaner would come, then the chef. Colleagues in elegant, understated suits and their well-heeled wives would gather around the table to enjoy the multi-course dinner conjured by the chef. The topics of conversation would range from cars to summer cabins and cryptocurrency investments. The evening would end with vintage whiskies.

'Did he have enemies?'

'Did he have enemies? Half of Reykjavík hated him, and the other half kissed up to him but secretly wished for his downfall. It would be hard to find anyone in the city who liked him.'

Hildur shivered. Heiðar clearly hadn't been ideal son-in-law material.

'But,' Kolfinna continued, 'I'm not sure any of them had it in them to kill him.'

Hildur studied Kolfinna where she sat on the couch. White robe and red slippers, aged by exhaustion. The widow struck her as an actor in a supporting role, surrounded by a stunning set but forgotten by the director.

'Were your families close?'

Kolfinna quickly shook her head. 'My father saw Heiðar for the climber he was and couldn't stand him, and my mother goes along with everything my father says. We usually only saw them at Christmas, even though they live in Hafnarfjörður.'

The families lived ten kilometres apart but only saw each other at Christmas. *Families sure can be complicated*, Hildur thought to herself.

'What about Heiðar's family?'

'Now that was the strangest thing. I've never met them.'

Hildur consciously held a long pause so Kolfinna would continue.

'I tried to ask him, but he just kept saying he didn't have a family. That he'd always looked after himself. We'd argue whenever I asked about them. He refused to discuss the matter.'

267

Hildur nodded. She'd discovered two cracks in the hotshot lawyer's façade: the blonde Valgerður and the secrecy surrounding his birth family. She would have to keep tapping away at both, hoping more would be revealed.

She stood, took a folded business card from her pocket, and set it down on the mahogany coffee table. But before her fingers released it, Hildur glanced at Kolfinna and cleared her throat.

'This doesn't have anything to do with our investigation, so you don't have to answer. Based on what you told us, your relationship wasn't the best. Why didn't you just divorce him?'

Kolfinna laughed hollowly and smoothed the hem of her robe. 'Because I was so foolish I didn't insist on a prenup before marriage. He didn't want to get divorced, and divorce made no sense for me. We settled for sharing an address, but we were like strangers in each other's lives. I didn't want him to get a penny of my money.'

Kolfinna plucked the business card from the table with her lilac-coloured nails and studied it closely. 'Westfjords? Why are you investigating the case?'

'The government's decentralisation policies,' Hildur said with a shrug. Jakob, who'd sat silently on the couch throughout the conversation, shook Kolfinna's hand goodbye.

As Hildur U-turned the clunky Brenda, she nearly toppled a gold giraffe outside the house opposite, just dodging the sculpture at the last minute. She hit the accelerator, and a cloud of heavy black diesel exhaust slowly descended over the golden statue as they sped out of upper-class Arnarnes. It looked like Brenda's air filter needed changing.

'Money and taste don't go hand in hand,' Hildur reflected, as she turned from the traffic circle onto the main road leading to Reykjavík.

She explained the contents of the conversation to Jakob and told him about the old obituary she'd stumbled across. Jakob took a moment to digest what he'd heard. The windscreen wipers cleaned the view, and the air was on full blast, preventing the windows from fogging up.

'Maybe I'm a little naïve, but it sounds to me like the heartless lawyer was in love for once in his life.'

Hildur smiled. She'd suspected the same thing. The present crime spree felt too bizarre to be something as mundane as debt collection that went too far or a settling of scores on the drug-scene. The victims hadn't belonged to the same group of barflies or rival criminal gangs. The murderer's motive had to be sought elsewhere.

Only two true alternatives remained: hate and love. And they couldn't always be distinguished from each other.

Hildur eased off the accelerator and moved into the right-hand lane. She selected Route 1 and turned north at the intersection. Beyond Reykjavík's city limits, the landscape changed dramatically: within fifteen minutes, she and Jakob had left the small apartment buildings, clusters of terrace houses, and neighbourhood-linking thoroughfares far behind. The view out the windows was of shaggy Icelandic horses huddling in wet fields, taking security and warmth from each other. They all faced the same way, rounded backsides and thick tails to the wind.

Jakob had lifted his bag of yarn into his lap. The snarled ends needed untangling and the skeins rerolling. He picked a grey yarn and slipped it onto his needles. All he had left to knit were the collar and the extra rows at the back. A traditional Icelandic sweater was the same front and back and could be worn either way. But the human collar-line was almost always lower in front than in back, and Jakob didn't like it when sweaters that fit well at the nape were too high at the throat. So he'd decided to break tradition in the service of a snugger fit and add a couple of centimetres to the back.

'Hildur, there's something I have to ask you.'

Hildur turned down the radio. She glanced at an approaching service station, then the petrol gauge. They had enough diesel to make it to the next town, so she kept driving.

'That farm yesterday. Why did we go there?'

Hildur knew the matter was bothering Jakob. She had no doubt seemed distracted and unusually quiet after the stop. It wasn't that she'd wanted to keep anything from Jakob; she'd just been too drained the day before to discuss the matter with anyone. Plenty of people were aware of her sisters' disappearance, but she was the only one who had to live with the trauma on a daily basis.

'I wanted to check up on something I'd heard.' It was getting hot inside Brenda. Hildur unzipped her parka and turned off her seat warmer. She told Jakob about Magnús, the clandestine masonry work done in the Ísafjörður tunnel, and the farm.

When she reached the end of her story, Jakob set down his knitting needles and stared out the windscreen. He was surprised by what he'd heard. 'So you think this Jón who was murdered in his cottage had something to do with your sisters' disappearance?'

Hildur shrugged. That was her hunch, but of course there was no way she could be sure. She had no proof, just the report of a dog handler who, at the time of her sisters' disappearance, had been living in a booze-fuelled haze.

'I wanted to see where Jón used to live. I guess I hoped I'd find something there that would be of some significance.'

Then Hildur told Jakob about the mound and the excavator she'd called in to turn over the yard. 'I get if you think I'm weird for digging holes in strangers' backyards to find answers to something that happened a long time ago,' she said, accelerating to ninety kilometres per hour.

The road ran near sea level in southern Iceland, crossing the lowlands and circling the brown giants of mountains. It hugged the shoreline until Whale Fjord, where it plunged Jakob and Hildur into a six-kilometre tunnel that led from one shore of the fjord to the other.

Jakob reached over and turned off the incoming air. 'I don't think anyone is weird. Our problem is we try too hard to pretend we're normal. We think everyone around us is logical and rational, but it's not true. We're all thinking the weirdest things all the time. But most of us don't have the courage to do anything about those thoughts. We just settle for acting, well, normal.'

Hildur's eyes were glued to the grey tarmac. She had to blink a few times. For some reason, she was touched by Jakob's words.

A good hour later, they reached Búðardalur, where the locals' livelihood came in large part from a big dairy. All the mouldy cheeses eaten in Iceland were manufactured there.

'I have to pee,' Hildur said, steering off the road into a big car park. 'I'll get us some coffee and pastries for lunch while I'm at it.'

The centre of the village was tiny. It consisted of two buildings housing a small supermarket, a restaurant, an ice cream stand, and a service station.

At the supermarket's self-service counter, Hildur chose two delicious-looking wheat rolls drizzled with a thick layer of chocolate. The supermarket also had a coffee machine. She filled two to-go cups to the rim and put three sugar cubes in one. Then she briskly returned to Brenda with the coffee cups in her hands and the pastry bag in her teeth.

'These should tide us over till we get home. But before that, we have one more stop. The excavator operator just called. He opened that mound and said he found something.'

Chapter 42

November 2019, Ögurvík

The snow had melted, leaving the farm a muddy waste that seemed to have no end, making it somehow disconsolate. Just the night before, snowfall had drawn a cold white blanket over the terrain, giving it clarity and structure. For a moment there had been snow, cold, and blue skies. Then what happened every winter happened: a wet south wind warmed by the Gulfstream swept over Iceland. It coughed a couple of times and melted the snow, pushing it into the rivers and back to the sea.

The excavator wasn't running, but its powerful work lights still burned. The wedge of light drew out the surroundings from the darkness, its unnatural yellow glow exposing the barn's derelict condition. The mucky yard was dotted with puddles of various sizes, excavator lights shivering in their surfaces.

Hildur registered the water droplets falling into her eyes but didn't feel them. Her skin was numb. She clenched her fists in her coat pockets and leaned into the wind. As she approached the hole, she felt small and shy.

For some reason, she thought of an old folk tale about a fearful woman who'd lost everything. Hildur felt her back was as hunched, like the woman from the story, who'd given birth to a child, wrapped it in a rag, and left it in the mountains to die. That was what people did in the old days if they had children they couldn't take care of. Later, as the woman sat in the barn with the animals bemoaning her poverty and how she couldn't even go to the dance at the neighbouring farm because she had nothing to wear, she heard a child whisper from the wall.

Dear mother in the barn,
in the barn do not weep.
I will loan you my rags
to dance the night away in,
dance the night away in.

Hildur shook the awful poem from her mind. Why had it even occurred to her just now?

The operator sat in the excavator, puffing on a cigarette. The smoke he exhaled between his thin lips floated inside the cab before eventually finding its way out the door. He was staring ahead, bored. He didn't step out to greet Hildur and Jakob. 'I've been waiting here for a couple of hours.'

'Visibility was poor in the highlands,' Hildur explained without apology. Everyone around these parts knew poor visibility meant a slower journey. She took a closer look at the operator's furrowed face. He seemed tired.

'There's something there,' he said, flinging his butt to the ground. It fell at Jakob's feet, and Jakob stomped it out under his rubber sole.

Hildur stepped up to the hole and peered in. Nothing but darkness. She clenched a miniature torch in her pocketed fist. A click of its side, and it was on.

'I'd only been digging for fifteen minutes when I hit some plastic bags. I stopped so the scoop wouldn't damage anything,' the operator shouted from the cab. He was already rolling his next smoke. Thick fingers rolled the fine paper around the loose tobacco without the assistance of a rolling device.

The beam of Hildur's torch struck the bottom of the hole. Rain had pooled there, and yellow plastic was visible beneath the muddy swill. The operator had mentioned plastic bags. Hildur put on her gloves, pulled on her hood, and descended into the hole. Luckily the operator had dug a generous area, and the hole's gently sloping sides were easy to navigate. The final step was going to be steep. Hildur steadied herself against the side of the hole with one hand as she held her torch in the other. She told Jakob to stay up top and give her more light.

She stood there, not moving.

And then the fear evaporated, and she stepped to the bottom of the hole. The unknown no longer frightened her. All she had to do was dig, finish the task before her.

Hildur used her hands to brush the soil off the plastic. Swipe by swipe, the dirt moved aside, and a supermarket bag emblazoned with a pink logo of a pig came into view. She put the torch between her teeth and carefully lifted out the brittle bag with both hands so it wouldn't fall apart. There was a second bag next to the first one, and she lifted it out of the ground as carefully as a newborn as well. The plastic had weakened but hadn't split.

The yellow bag had faded, but the pink pig still stood out clearly. Every Icelander recognised the iconic logo. Iceland's first chain of bargain grocery stores had been founded in the late 1980s and was now the biggest supermarket chain in the country.

Hildur's hands trembled as she began expanding a tear in the first bag. She knew it might be better to let forensic investigators comb the site, but she could wait no longer.

She slit the bag as if gutting a fish and held up the contents so she could see them. 'More light,' she mumbled, torch in her mouth. Jakob brought his light closer.

Hildur pulled a small parka from the bag. Long ago, it had been pink. Now it was wet and smelled bad. In the beam of light, she could see the fabric was covered with black spots. Remnants of fur clung to the edge of the hood.

There wasn't much left of the coat, but Hildur still recognised it immediately: it had been her winter coat during her first year at school. The coat with the fur collar she'd been especially proud of. It had been expensive, and their family had never had any extra money. All her clothes had been passed down to her little sisters. The coat had gone first to Rósa, then to Björk.

Björk's coat.

Hildur slipped the coat under her arm and took a second look inside the bag. There was a little red My Little Pony backpack at the bottom.

Hildur took the torch from her mouth and aimed it back at the spot where she'd just fished out the plastic bags. She knew what she'd seen out of the corner of her eye, but she wanted to be sure. Surer. As she moved the mud away, her hand touched the hard, pale objects.

Tiny, delicate fragments of bone.

Chapter 43

November 2019, Ísafjörður

Next weekend would be Father's Day in Finland. It was the heaviest day of the year for Jakob. Once again, he wouldn't be getting some funny card made at daycare.

What did Matias make of all this? The thought frequently crossed Jakob's mind. Was Jakob fading into a question Matias wasn't allowed to ask anymore? A man who would be forgotten? A stranger who would be vaguely familiar for a little while but who no longer clattered about the entryway? Who didn't have an address or phone number? From whom no package arrived to open with his other birthday presents?

It would be reasonable for Jakob to be able to see his child. And Matias ought to have a right to his father.

Jakob brought up Skype on his phone, and it took a moment for the white letter S on a blue background to load. He only had one contact in the app: Lena.

He swiped Lena's photo with his forefinger and pressed the purple video camera icon.

The phone rang, and the ringtone echoed in Jakob's empty apartment. After the fourth ring, there was a rustling, and Lena appeared on the screen. Her face exuded relaxation and joy until she realised whose call she'd answered. At that point, her expression turned stony. Not that this was anything new. Their conversations always began the same way these days. Lena erected a wall between them and refused to talk.

'What do you want now?'

'Hi, Lena. I just thought I'd call. We were cut off last time.'

After the separation, Jakob had been in shock. At first he'd been afraid, and then he'd started to hate. As the process advanced, he'd felt powerless. It seemed as if Norwegian society had turned its back on him – a foreigner, and a man. Every demand of Lena's had been met. She'd got custody, her lies had been believed, and Jakob had been forced to step aside. He'd been granted visitation rights, but even his visits hadn't been honoured as intended. Lena seemed to enjoy tormenting him by making up reasons why Matias couldn't talk with him on the phone or see him at the times set by the courts.

Lately, Jakob had made a serious effort to understand his ex-wife. Was she somehow sick? Was she angry with him for reasons he didn't understand?

'Oh, you just thought you'd call,' Lena said, mimicking him. She looked past the camera. 'You can't just call. Calls need to be scheduled in advance. You know that. I have a ruling by the courts that states all—'

Jakob had to interrupt, even though he knew it would just worsen the deadlock between them. 'I know. And my call last time was based on that decision. We had a call scheduled, but you cut it short,' he said, trying to keep his voice steady. 'I didn't get a chance to speak with Matias.'

'Can you hear yourself pressuring me again?'

How are we right back here? Jakob thought to himself. He hadn't meant to put any pressure on Lena, despite having plenty of reasons to. The situation seemed hopeless. He felt the impulse to roar into the phone, shout at Lena for estranging a child from his father, but he knew that would be a losing game. He had no doubt she was recording the calls. If he raised his voice, that would just give her more evidence against him in future trials.

In future trials . . . The notion made Jakob start. Had he actually just thought that? He'd promised himself not to continue the torturous court battle. He didn't even have the money. But what if there were no other way? At this rate, he'd keep on losing. It wouldn't be long before Matias didn't remember him at all. He would fade from his son's life, and Lena would have complete say over everything. Maybe pushing back and getting a lawyer was the only way to turn things around.

'Lena, don't be offended by my asking this.' Jakob brought every last poker skill into play and tried to sound as calm, as neutral as possible. 'Is everything OK? I know things are bad between us, but I still care about you. I want you to be as happy as possible. For Matias's sake.'

For a moment there was no response. Then Lena's face disappeared. She must have set the phone down on the counter, as all Jakob could see on camera was the hood above the stove. He heard the refrigerator door open, followed by Lena's voice in the distance.

'For God's sake. You're so pitiful.'

Jakob shut his eyes. It wasn't that Lena's cruel words hurt; he just needed a second to gather his resolve.

And then, hating himself for begging, he said: 'Could I please speak with Matias? It's Father's Day this weekend. Is he nearby? Could you maybe even just show him for a second?'

Lena sighed and turned the phone's camera toward Matias for an instant. A blond boy in blue fire-engine pyjamas was playing intently with his dinosaurs on the living room floor. When he heard his mother's voice, the boy looked up from his toys and turned to her. He stood and walked over to Lena holding a Tyrannosaurus rex missing its tail. The boy's eyes twinkled with curiosity.

'Who's calling?' Jakob heard Matias ask in Norwegian. He saw his son reaching for the phone. The hand was no longer tiny and round. His fingers had grown. They looked more slender than last time. *A big boy's fingers*, Jakob thought to himself.

Jakob's longing took the form of physical pain. He wished he could scoop up Matias in his arms, blow on his neck, and take him outside to throw snowballs at tree trunks.

His child was both there and not there.

'It's nothing, honey. Nothing. Some man dialled the wrong number by mistake,' Lena said in a tender voice before hanging up.

Jakob pinched his thigh until it hurt. Making the pain physical helped him tolerate it. He couldn't fall apart now. He typed out a Skype message.

I hope you're both doing well. I'll be there after Christmas to see Matias. The court papers say I have three days with him.

Jakob turned off his phone and lay down on the living room floor next to his basket of yarn.

He'd made up his mind. He wasn't giving up. There was no way.

Chapter 44

Freysi's cause-of-death report was finished by Monday. No surprises had arisen during the autopsy. He'd died from the fall: his neck broke when his body struck the ground. The hair in his mouth was from the same individual as that found in the mouths of the other victims.

The forensics investigators had also come across black wool fibres at the abdomen of Freysi's athletic jacket. The fibres had presumably ended up there when the murderer pushed him, as no similar fibres were discovered on Freysi's other clothes or textiles when the investigators searched his home. The only other item of interest discovered there were Hildur's fingerprints in copious quantities. She'd felt obliged to explain their presence to the Reykjavík police over the phone. The results of the DNA analyses weren't in yet.

Jakob dribbled coffee from the station's single-serve machine into a to-go cup, poured in lots of sugar, and pressed a compostable lid over the top. He'd promised to chat with Freysi's colleagues while Hildur and Beta continued their work at the station. He pulled on his winter coat and grabbed his coffee in apparent satisfaction before leaving for the local school.

The yellow schoolhouse had multiple entrances; Jakob picked the one where he saw the caretaker's glass-fronted cubicle inside. The enormous, whiskered man filling the cubicle reminded Jakob of a walrus. He sat at his desk, eyes half-shut, before lazily leaning his head in the direction of Jakob's voice.

'The teachers' lounge? Up the stairs, follow the fish.'

'The fish?'

'The fishy smell. The teacher's lounge is next to the lunch-room, and there's cod for lunch today.'

'I see. Thank you.' Jakob turned from the counter to the stairs.

The whiskered walrus hoisted himself up and poked his head out of the cubicle. 'Don't you know how to read? Take off your shoes and put them on that shelf. We don't want mud on our floors.'

Jakob spun back around, placed his winter shoes on the top shelf, and started up the stairs in his stockinged feet. A steady murmur of voices carried from the teachers' lounge. Jakob knocked and entered.

Twenty people of various ages turned toward him. The air in the room was stuffy and smelled of coffee. The beige curtains at the windows looked like they'd been there for decades.

'Good morning. I'm with the police. My name is Jakob Johanson.'

The mention of the police inevitably sent an electric current through those present, and this encounter was no exception. The teachers sat up straighter and tried to hide the curiosity a police presence inevitably sparked.

'We're investigating the death of Freysi Gunnarsson. I'm sure you've all heard about it.'

Jakob let his gaze circle the room. The faces there eyed him with friendly curiosity. The police had informed the media that Freysi's death had been a homicide.

'It's so terrible. I read about it in the news,' said a woman in glasses and a long plaid skirt. Jakob guessed she was the handcrafts teacher.

An older man lowered his newspaper to the coffee table, looking lost: 'How could something like this happen here? I never would have believed it.'

'Is there anyone here who knew Freysi well?' Jakob asked. 'I'd like to talk, off the record.'

A flustered exchange of glances and mumbled words Jakob couldn't catch. But he was in no hurry. He finished his coffee and tossed the empty cup in the waste basket under the counter.

A young man raised his hand and cleared his throat. 'I wouldn't say we were close, but we played badminton together.' He came over to shake Jakob's hand. His name was Anton, and he was a maths and chemistry teacher. Jakob suggested they go somewhere more private to talk.

'It's my lesson prep hour,' Anton said. 'We can go to my classroom.'

A periodic table hung on the wall of Anton's class. Instead of individual desks, there were long tables surrounded by adjustable stools.

'We're investigating Freysi's murder, and this is just an unofficial conversation,' Jakob said calmly. 'I'd like you to tell us everything you know about Freysi. Any detail might end up being useful.'

Anton seemed like a perfectly nice guy, but he also seemed a little nervous to be talking to an officer of the law. It occurred to Jakob that if he revealed something about himself first, it might ease the tension. 'I assume it's OK if we speak English? I'm here on a police exchange and haven't learned Icelandic yet.'

From his seat at the head of the table, Anton gave Jakob a friendly smile. 'I lived in the United States for a long time. English is like a second language to me.' He took a deep breath and appeared to consider his words. He twisted his wrists and looked uneasy. 'How can I put this without sounding too dramatic . . . I think Freysi had some sort of, hmmm . . . secret.'

Jakob started. It sounded like Anton was jumping right in at the deep end. 'A secret?'

'Yeah, I'm not 100 per cent sure, and I get the sense he told me by accident. But what he said struck me because he was in such incredible physical condition. He beat me at badminton almost every time.'

Jakob urged Anton to continue.

'I was going to reserve us a badminton court for next year, but Freysi said there was no point. He said he wouldn't be in any condition to play.'

This slip of the tongue had compelled Freysi to offer Anton an explanation. Freysi suffered from a rare disease. Anton didn't remember what it was called, but it had something to do with the brain. And it meant Freysi would probably be facing paralysis soon.

Jakob listened to Anton's account with growing incredulity. Hildur's boyfriend was on the verge of being paralysed? Jakob's impression based on what Hildur had said was that Freysi had been a long-distance runner in his prime.

Anton must have sensed Jakob's doubts. 'I don't think anyone else knew. He didn't want to risk his job by speaking publicly about it. And I promised not to tell anyone.'

Freysi had said the illness would progress either quickly or gradually. The only thing that was sure was he was sick and didn't have many years left.

The last time they'd played badminton, Freysi had told Anton he was seeing a woman he liked. Evidently, Freysi had meant to talk to her about his illness. But he hadn't wanted to tell anyone else. 'At first I thought it was suicide. That he couldn't stand the idea of being paralysed.'

'It wasn't,' Jakob said. 'For investigative reasons we can't share the details, but we're absolutely sure it wasn't suicide.'

Anton nodded, then seemed to remember something. He glanced at a second door at the back of the room. 'We shared an office here so we wouldn't have to take lesson prep work home. Freysi was working on some other project there, too. You want to take a look?'

Jakob nodded, and Anton opened the door. It gave onto a windowless room less than ten square metres in size and lit by a fluorescent tube and desk lamps. The tiny cubbyhole's walls were lined with books, folders, and stacks of papers.

'Those books are mine,' Anton said.

Then he pointed at a white Ikea bookcase in the corner. 'That's Freysi's archive.' The shelves were overflowing with papers and notebooks. Jakob spotted a couple of familiar biology textbooks among the paper. The spine of one orange tome read GENETICS in big block letters. Jakob picked it up and gave it a cursory browse.

'I can leave you to look through things if you want,' Anton said. 'I'll be in the teachers' lounge if you need anything.'

Jakob started going through the papers spread across Freysi's desk. Exams waiting to be corrected, travel compensation forms, a few running magazines. The plastic file organiser at the corner of the desk was filled with sheafs of papers and documents in plastic sleeves. Jakob reached for the topmost sheaf.

It didn't take him long to grasp its contents. He used to be a biology teacher, after all. The pages contained handwritten notes on heredity. As he read on, a frown formed on his face. Family trees and random phrases about hereditary illnesses. How strange. Jakob scooped the papers into his satchel. He wanted to take a closer look at the station.

Then he started going through the bookcase. Blank paper, receipts, lecture notes. And at the bottom of the bottom shelf,

Jakob found a tattered blue notebook. By all appearances, it had been used frequently. There was only one word on the cover: *dagbók*. Diary.

Jakob opened the notebook and turned on the desk lamp. The first pages of the diary were filled with entries in ballpoint pen, but they were all in Icelandic. Jakob packed the diary into his satchel too. He would have to give it to Hildur to read.

Chapter 45

The children had built snowmen during break. One wore a red beanie and had a pencil for the nose. Jakob strode across the schoolyard, noting the kids had migrated from the snowbanks to the jungle gyms. You couldn't make balls from new snow. That morning, big cakes had clung to shoe-soles; now the snow underfoot felt a lot harder. The freeze was deepening.

Anton had offered Jakob lunch in the school lunchroom, but Jakob had declined. He had to get back to the station as soon as possible and talk to Hildur.

The hot dogs at the grill downstairs were tasty, so Jakob ordered one with all the toppings to tide him over. He was shoving the tail end in his mouth as he stepped in through the station doors. He glanced in the entryway mirror to make sure he didn't have mayonnaise in his beard.

Before Jakob could make it into his office, Hildur hurried up to him. Judging by the look on her face, the matter was urgent. He took off his coat, hung it on the rack, and changed his heavy winter footwear for lighter indoor shoes.

'That nurse who didn't speak English just called back. She had some interesting things to say,' Hildur said, as they sat down at their desks. Hildur's was covered in print-outs. A quick glance revealed them to be photocopies of old newspaper articles.

The nurse, Lian, had apologised for not being able to answer earlier. One of her daughters, a gymnast, had fallen during practice and been taken to the hospital for surgery. The girl would recover, but Lian had taken a few days off work to tend to her child.

'Lian works at a psychiatric hospital. She told me about a patient they had a few years ago.'

Jakob glanced through the old newspaper articles as he listened to Hildur's story. The further she got, the more frustrated he grew. He felt like he'd made a huge mistake. Why couldn't he have understood the woman when she'd called?

'I'm sorry. The investigation could be so much further along if I'd understood what she was trying to say.'

Hildur lowered her hands to the desk and looked Jakob dead in the eye. 'Stop that. Not another word. If anyone's to blame, it's me or Beta, since we weren't here to take the call. We shouldn't have left you on your own. Besides, we have all sorts of tip-offs and theories being offered all the time, and you have to let their nonsense go in one ear and out the other.'

Hildur told Jakob to listen to the rest of the story.

Lian had been working at the hospital for a long time. Several years ago, a woman in late middle age, Marta, was admitted after a family tragedy. The trauma had broken Marta's mind, and she'd ended up in chronic care. Lian hadn't offered any more details about the nature of Marta's illness, as she was bound by an oath of confidentiality: she wasn't allowed to deliver medical records to outsiders without official permission, and the police didn't have such permission yet. As a matter of fact, Lian suspected she'd exceeded her authority simply by virtue of making this call. But after seeing the reports on the deaths of Heiðar and Jón, she'd felt it was important to share what she knew.

'I promised her our conversation never happened,' Hildur said.

Marta had received psychiatric care at the hospital for several years. The staff had been convinced she'd never recover. Then suddenly, a couple of years ago, Marta had improved. Lian had been her nurse at the time. Marta found religion and began attending the hospital's Bible study as well as the church service held every week. Apparently, Marta never missed a Sunday. Her health had improved markedly. Finding religion had been good for her. Eventually, Marta's condition was deemed so improved that she no longer required hospitalisation. She'd been released from the hospital about a year ago.

Now Hildur reached the point in the story that explained the reason for Lian's call. 'Hospital staff are used to seeing all sorts of things on the job. The patients' rooms are always cleaned carefully, but personal belongings are not touched.'

Some patients were in the habit of collecting rocks in the yard and keeping them inside their mattresses. Others cut ads from magazines and organised them into envelopes. Lian had cleaned Marta's room thoroughly after the latter's discharge. In the corner of the wardrobe, she'd found a big black bin bag full of papers that were apparently meant to be recycled.

Lian told Hildur she'd taken a look at the papers tossed carelessly in the bag. 'Apparently, out of sheer curiosity,' Hildur said.

Marta's notes were detailed records: names, addresses, genealogies, maps, dates, times of day. Lian had taken them for fabrications and ultimately tossed them in the recycling bin.

'But one article Marta saved had stuck in Lian's mind,' Hildur said. She reached over and handed one of the printouts to Jakob.

The old article Lian had come across in Marta's closet had a big photograph of Heiðar and some other man. Lian remembered it so clearly because it was about fraud perpetrated by the former CFO of the Icelandic Gymnastics Federation. Lian's daughters were gymnasts, which was why she'd paid close attention to this news. Heiðar had served as the defendant's lawyer.

'Lian told me Marta had written *Jón* in big letters in the margins of the article, and under Jón's name, *Heiðar*. Apparently, the handwritten notes were hard to misinterpret.'

Jakob didn't grasp Hildur's meaning.

'A family tree,' Hildur explained. 'Marta had drawn a family tree. And in the drawing, Jón was Heiðar's father.'

'I don't understand,' Jakob said, confounded. 'We checked the population register. It said there was no relation.'

Hildur grunted. 'Do you think everything it says on official documents is true? The DNA analyses could easily indicate something different.'

The image of a wealthy, successful lawyer was a total disconnect from that of the paedophile skulking in the tiny, derelict cottage.

'At first it seemed impossible to me, too,' Hildur said, rapping her fingernails against the wooden tabletop.

Jakob remembered what Kolfinna, Heiðar's widow, had told them while ensconced on her sumptuous sofa at Garðabær. Her husband had never spoken about his parents. Heiðar had wanted to keep his parents as far away as possible.

Jakob scratched his beard and thought. 'So, someone murdered father and son. That can't be a coincidence.'

Hildur's eyes searched her desk for another clipping. She took a fresh print-out of an October 2012 article and handed it to Jakob. 'The pieces are falling into place now. The only thing that's still unclear to me is where Marta is, or if she's been murdered too.'

Jakob studied the announcement Hildur had circled with a red marker. He didn't understand the text, but from the photo, the cross and the dates, he gathered it was an obituary. The woman in the photograph looked young and happy. Vibrant. Her long blonde hair had been stylishly cropped at the front.

Jakob checked her years of birth and death. She'd only been twenty-one when she died. He shot Hildur a questioning glance over the print-out he was holding.

'This is Marta's daughter, Valgerður. She died seven years ago.'

Chapter 46

The New Testament says: If any man will come after me, let him deny himself, and take up his cross daily, and follow me. For whosoever will save his life shall lose it: but whosoever will lose his life for my sake, the same shall save it.

I lost my life, but I saved all those who remain. I turned people away, but I saved those who would have followed them.

I caught the mistake and put an end to it. Now I must go.

Chapter 47

November 2019, Ísafjörður

The mood in Jakob and Hildur's office was electric. Now that they'd found the connection between Jón, Heiðar, and Valgerður, the pieces that had been floating around had begun to settle into place.

While Jakob had been chatting with Freysi's colleagues at the school, Hildur had reached out to the parents named on Heiðar's official records. They'd been living in the United States for some time. Heiðar's mother told Hildur that she and her husband had adopted Heiðar as an infant. When Heiðar turned eighteen, his parents had moved abroad for work, and Heiðar had moved out on his own in Reykjavík. Since then, communication between the parents and their child had dwindled; it had been sporadic at best over the past twenty or so years. Apparently, at least five years had passed since they'd last been in touch. The parents had been informed by the police of their adopted son's death and were flying in from Boston the following week for the funeral.

At the time of the adoption, the mother hadn't known the details about her adoptive child's biological parents. That information had been confidential. But in a country the size of Iceland, no secret remained secret for long, and this instance had been no exception. The adoptive mother had later heard from friends of friends that the woman who'd given birth to her son had been a drug addict, not even twenty years old. She'd left her child at the maternity ward and walked out the hospital's front

293

doors headed who knows where. She'd been found dead a few weeks later at Kjarvalsstaðir Park in downtown Reykjavík. The child's biological father had been a binge drinker whose place on Hverfisgata the biological mother had occasionally bunked at. Heiðar had been placed in an orphanage, and she and her husband had adopted him not long after.

The child's biological father had been Jón. Hildur had verified it: in the 1980s, Jón had been on the books at the same address as Heiðar's biological mother.

Hildur returned to the office with two cups of coffee. She handed one to Jakob, who stirred the sugar that had sunk to the bottom. Beta had joined them a moment before.

They studied the diagram they'd just sketched on the flip-chart. 'So somehow Marta figured this out,' Beta said.

Jón was Heiðar's father. Valgerður was Heiðar's girlfriend. Marta was Valgerður's mother.

Determining kinship in Iceland required nothing more than an internet connection. Everyone with an Icelandic social security number is listed in the country's digital family tree, the Book of Icelanders. Anyone can look up information on anyone's parents or parents' relations. When entering your own social security number, the site presents your family tree all the way back to the first Icelander. With a couple of clicks you can bring up the family tree of, say, the president of Iceland, a sheep farmer from the next fjord over, or your spouse. Of any Icelander at all.

'Figuring out the adoptive relationship must have been trickier,' Jakob said.

Hildur shook her head lightly. She disagreed. 'It took me half an hour to get the information, and it wasn't even hard. The adoptive mother was eager to talk about the past. You'll come to find the inhabitants of this little island are a nosy bunch. We have a saying that's truer than you'd think: when three people know, all of Iceland knows.'

Hildur took another look at the diagram on the flipchart and stepped backwards: 'OK, so we have in-laws and lovers. And everyone's dead except Marta. Where's Marta now? And what does Freysi have to do with this?'

Jakob opened his satchel and arrayed its contents on the table. He placed the blue notebook and loose papers so Hildur and Beta had a good view of them. He explained he'd been to the school and spoken with Freysi's colleague, who'd given him some interesting information.

'Did you know Freysi was sick?'

Hildur was running her hand across the cover of the dog-eared diary. The movement came to an abrupt stop. 'Sick? What are you talking about?'

So Hildur didn't know. Jakob took a moment to gather his thoughts. He would be the one to tell her. 'Freysi hadn't wanted to renew their badminton court reservation for next year, because he suspected his illness would prevent him from playing. It sounds like he'd been meaning to tell you, but I guess he didn't have time . . .'

Hildur crumpled the diary in her fist. Her chair squeaked as she scooted closer to the table. She opened the diary, leaned her hands against her cheeks, and began to read.

The first pages were filled with text handwritten in ballpoint pen. The entries were mundane: running schedules, records of what he'd eaten, weather observations. As they went on, they grew more diary-like. Observations about how he was sleeping, thoughts about his energy levels. Feelings about his illness. Hildur recognised the handwriting. It was Freysi's typical scrawl: half cursive, half stick letters.

The most recent entry was from a few months ago. Hildur scanned the text. The further she got, the more unbelievable it seemed.

I don't have much time left to live.

When I write it down like that, it feels so final. The end of my life.

My symptoms, which have been increasing in intensity lately, finally have a name. This hereditary cerebral haemorrhage is treacherous. Even though the symptoms just started, the possibility of illness has existed inside me since I was born. And the probability that I'd be one of the ones to develop symptoms was laughably small!

But I'm not laughing.

There are only a few families in Iceland who carry the gene. And apparently, this is the only place in the world where the disease exists. My neurologist told me it developed about ten generations ago, in the 1500s. That's when the south Icelandic and west Icelandic gene pools mingled, causing a dangerous genetic mutation.

The disease didn't really spread in the old days because everyone died so young. Life expectancy was so much shorter that there was no way a hereditary disease could spread into the common gene pool. But those who lived longer spread the gene without knowing it.

There's a 50 per cent chance of the gene being passed down from parent to child . . .

These days the disease is better understood . . .
Not everyone who carries the gene develops symptoms . . .

Hildur's thoughts were racing faster than her eyes could read. She had to look up from the text. What genetic mutation? And what neurologist? Freysi had been seeing a neurologist? She had a hard time internalising what she was reading.

Hildur beat Freysi at weightlifting, but when it came to speed and endurance, Freysi ran rings around her. He jogged and played, trained and took his multivitamins every morning. How could he have been seriously ill?

Freysi's diary entries felt surreal. Why hadn't she known any of this? She thought they'd been pretty close. They'd dated and enjoyed each other's company. But on the other hand: she hadn't told Freysi everything about herself either. Apparently that's how it went: you thought you saw a big part of the people you knew. But actually, you only saw what you'd decided to look at, what the other person had wanted to show you.

I don't know whether I should congratulate myself for having made it this far or give in to the fear and mourn the fact that I contracted this disease. I don't know if I got it from my mother or my father. They both died so long ago. It doesn't even matter. Either way, I feel like a walking time bomb. The only positive aspect of this is I never had children. Good thing I didn't want them when I was younger.

It's also a good thing I didn't meet Hildur when I was younger. She's different. And things might have gone a totally different direction with her. Even kids.

Goddammit, this is so unfair! I'll have to tell her soon.

That was where the entries ended. Hildur flipped through the remaining pages, but there was nothing else in the diary. She found herself feeling something odd and inappropriate: a flash of happiness. Her reaction scared her. Her joy felt completely wrong in the circumstances. How could she feel happy if the admission of love had come from beyond the grave? Was she allowed to take joy in it?

She looked up from the notebook and stared at the wall opposite. Her colleagues looked at her questioningly, but she couldn't get a word out.

'I also found these in his office,' Jakob said, showing the notes he'd brought.

Hildur took the sheaf of papers and quickly flipped through them. She recognised them; she'd seen them in Freysi's kitchen a couple of weeks before. Freysi had wanted to talk to her about genealogy then, but they'd been interrupted by a call she received and the assignment at Súðavík.

Beta peered over Hildur's shoulder at Freysi's strange scribblings. She couldn't make head or tail of them.

'So that depicts heredity. Genes,' Jakob explained before either woman could ask. 'I was a biology teacher before I went to police college. I've seen this stuff before.'

Jakob explained that he'd taken a superficial look at the images. Based on his interpretation, Freysi appeared to know the gene had a 50 per cent probability of being passed down from parent to child. Freysi had gotten it from one of his parents.

Although Jakob hadn't specialised in genetics, as a biologist he'd gained a general understanding of the unique characteristics of hereditary diseases. 'We have a few hereditary regional diseases in Finland, too. They're caused by genetic mutations like these.'

Genetic mutations have always existed, but it's been possible to study them more closely in countries like Finland and Iceland, where the gene pool is extremely homogenous in certain areas. When a population has a limited number of antecedents, it's easier to pinpoint genetic mutations. And Finland was just as isolated as Iceland back in the day; people had lived in very small groups for centuries.

'There's a municipality in northern Finland where part of the population carries a gene that strongly increases the risk of schizophrenia. If a child inherits the gene from their mother or father, the child's chances of developing schizophrenia doubles. Freysi's disease was related to the circulation in the brain.'

Hildur felt restless. She stood and walked over to gaze at the blue vista beyond the window. There was no wind. The mountains rising from the fjord were reflected in the glassy smooth sea. The mirrored surface repeated the shapes of the mountains and the colour of the sky. As she saw the two identical realities at the same time, she mused:

'Freysi died prematurely. Was it because of his genes?'

Chapter 48

November 2019, Bolungarvík

It was as if a giant had taken a huge mallet and knocked a dent in the mountain. First there was a low rush that gradually intensified in speed and volume. Then absolute silence and . . . bam! The hollow thud echoed from the rocks until it faded and eventually dissipated into the sea. About ten seconds passed, and then the faint rush began again.

Hildur's entire body felt the force of the wave. If she wandered into the wrong spot and was caught in the undertow, she'd be crushed by the shoals hidden below the surface. But she wasn't scared. The frigid water was nothing to be afraid of. She knew she ruled it. She had mastered waves, currents, the wind, and the movements of her surfboard.

She'd stayed late at work the previous night with Jakob and Beta. They'd looked up Marta's information because they wanted to establish contact with her. She might have some information on the murders – or be in danger herself. After all, her child, her child's former boyfriend, and the boyfriend's father were all dead.

But they'd had to take a break from the murder investigation when they received a call from the local bar. An argument had escalated into a fistfight, and the police were needed on the scene. The three of them had gone because neither patrol had been free: one had been dispatched to handle a domestic incident, the other to tend to a fender bender in the neighbouring fjord.

By the time Hildur and her colleagues finally headed home, it was nearly two in the morning. They'd agreed to get a proper night's sleep and continue their investigations in the morning.

Hildur had had to come to the sea this morning to clear her thoughts. She didn't want to imagine what might still be to come. Three people had experienced violent deaths. She'd lost her friend. Hope about discovering what had happened to her little sisters had kindled in her breast. It was the tiniest flame, but it fluttered, and Hildur meant to keep it alive. Beta had given her permission to continue her investigations. Because of the bones, there was good cause to suspect the hole excavated at Ögurvík was a grave, and evidence of the long-missing children had been found at the site. Beta had been surprised, almost shocked, by the discovery. She'd been vaguely familiar with Hildur's sisters' disappearance, of course. Beta had promised that if further developments turned up, the money would be found to investigate. A case over twenty years old wasn't at the top of the list of priorities, of course, but Hildur would be allowed to spend some of her work time on it. Hildur had accepted Beta's conditions and sent the bones and contents of the plastic bags to Reykjavík for Axlar-Hákon to analyse. He'd promised to look into the matter as soon as he had a quieter moment at work.

Upon waking, Hildur had checked the weather forecast and then the wave conditions from the marine forecast site maintained by the Road and Coastal Administration. According to the site, the waves would be a good metre tall. If waves were too big, they broke too far offshore, and the surfing was no good. The best surfing weather in the fjords was when the wind was calm and the waves were small.

Hildur had strapped her surfboard to Brenda's roof, tossed her wetsuit in the back, and headed west. As the darkness relented and shadows began to emerge, she'd grabbed her board and stepped into the sea.

It wasn't a good idea to go surfing alone, of course. Anything could happen: Hildur might hit her head on the board, swallow too much water, or misjudge the force of a wave. If something did happen, there wouldn't be anyone around to help. Danger was constantly present.

Maybe that was the reason Hildur loved surfing so much. When she was able to control danger, she was able to control herself, too.

The lights had come on in a fishing village in a nearby cove. A few big ravens had perched on the shoreline rocks and were looking in Hildur's direction. Further out, a pair of fishing vessels were headed out to open sea. She could hear the rush of the sea through the neoprene hood she'd pulled over her head to keep it warm.

She saw the perfect wave approach. She judged it to be no more than a metre tall, but it was deliciously long. Hildur turned the nose of her board shoreward and started paddling hard. The crest of the wave drew closer, and she hopped nimbly to her feet on her board.

Her only thought just then was dominating the wave.

Right foot forward, left foot back. She always assumed the same stance. The wave started carrying her along, pushing her gently onward, semi-parallel to shore.

The wave was powerful, and there was nothing she could do to stop it. But for a brief moment, she could master it. For a few dozen seconds, she steered it exactly where she was headed.

If you ended up in an argument with the sea, the sea inevitably won. If a big wave caught Hildur off guard and engulfed her, the only thing she could do was calm herself. Being still was often the greatest power.

In that instant, the rising November sun stretched its rays, illuminating the snow-covered mountains across the bay. The beams of wintry light from beyond the sea made the snowy heights of Hornstrandir unusually bright. They stood out against their dusky backdrop like immense white spectres.

And then an idea crashed into Hildur's consciousness like a wave.

She turned her board shoreward and paddled furiously. She glanced back and saw a wave coming in. It was small, but it would speed her along to her destination. Hildur rose onto her board. She had to get back to Brenda fast.

She had suddenly remembered something important.

Chapter 49

November 2019, Ísafjörður

Hildur changed out of her wetsuit and into dry clothes in Brenda's back seat, then drove from Bolungarvík to the station by the straightest route. She turned on her computer, logged in, and soon found what she was looking for.

Yes. She'd remembered correctly.

The previous summer, a young woman had died in the Hornstrandir wilderness area. Hildur had read an article about the incident at the time but hadn't given it any more thought. Now she read the article again. There wasn't much information. The young woman had been hiking solo and died in her sleep. She'd been staying at a wilderness guesthouse, an old summer cottage in the vicinity of Hesteyri. She'd suffered from apnoea, and the suspected cause of death was an apnoea-induced disturbance of the cerebral circulation. The body had been transported to Reykjavík by helicopter.

Hildur left the site and looked up the autopsy report from the national police database. Before she reached the end of the pathologist's notes, she knew what she would find. A few blond hairs had been found in the woman's mouth. Hildur checked to see who had performed the autopsy. Hildur didn't recognise the pathologist's name, but it wasn't Axlar-Hákon. Daníel Hilmarsson.

Hildur glanced at the date. The autopsy had been performed mid-July, so probably a summer locum. Most Icelanders vacationed in July. Hildur brought up Axlar-Hákon's number on her phone. After the fifth ring, he picked up.

'Hi, Hildur. I haven't had time yet to look at that stuff you sent in,' he immediately said. Hildur put his mind at ease: 'That's not why I called.'

'And thanks for the crowberry juice. Exceptional, as always.'

Hildur would have been happy to chat at length with Hákon, but this time her matter was pressing. 'Did someone called Daníel sub for you last July?'

Her inference had been correct.

'An intern, very nice guy, enthusiastic about his work. Hopefully he'll pick up where I leave off when I'm granted my freedom.'

'I just read one of his reports again a second ago. Guess what? Blond hairs were found in a woman's mouth.'

'Damn. Seriously?'

Axlar-Hákon sounded surprised, and it was no wonder. Chances were they'd just found another victim. Hákon promised to get in touch with his stand-in immediately and call right back.

Hildur sat there, waiting for the minutes to pass. She leaned her forehead against her office window, felt the coolness against her skin. The weather had done a 180 since morning. The wind had picked up from the south, piling the sky heavy with grey clouds. A southerly wind meant temperate, overcast weather. It wouldn't be long before sleet started falling again.

Hildur rose onto her tiptoes on a slow, silent count of three. She paused, then lowered herself again on a three-count. She repeated the movement twenty times.

Jakob spun his chair around and watched her. 'Are you OK?'

'I'm training my calf muscles.'

Hildur thought it made sense to put any free moments to use. Twenty calf raises three times a day got the blood in her legs circulating and built up the strength in her legs.

Jakob shook his head and turned back to his computer.

Hildur finished her set and fetched herself more coffee. Her phone rang.

'I got hold of Daníel. He remembered the case clearly. Lísa was the only young adult he performed a post-mortem on last summer.'

Daníel hadn't paid any particular attention to the hairs he'd found in the mouth. Because Lísa had been blonde, he'd assumed they were hers, that a few long strands had got in her mouth while she slept. That didn't sound so odd, especially as she'd died in her sleep.

After the call, Hildur relayed to Jakob the information about this new victim. Lísa had died during a summertime trek.

The finished sweater was folded on Jakob's desk, and he was sorting through the remnants of yarn at the bottom of the bag. Hildur loved the pattern. The overall effect was delicate, but the pattern itself was exceptionally strong.

Suddenly, Jakob seemed to remember something. He stood and gestured for Hildur to follow him. They walked down the short hall from their office to the station lobby. A map of the Westfjords hung on the largest wall. Jakob scanned the map for the place Hildur had just been referring to and jabbed a finger at it.

'I remember you mentioned this area in passing once. You went there on summer vacation with your aunt or something. I was just thinking . . .' Jakob rolled up the sleeves of his sweater and eyed the map even more closely, '. . . you can only get there by boat, right?'

Hildur nodded. You couldn't get to the nature reserve by car, and landing an aircraft or helicopter there was forbidden except under very rare circumstances.

Hildur grasped Jakob was driving at. 'You're right, damn it!'

Lísa had spent the night in a guesthouse. There were only a few guesthouses for hikers in the wilderness area, and in high summer, when the place was overrun by vacationers, they were fully booked. Someone else must have spent the night at the guesthouse, too. Whoever it had been needed to be questioned.

'Sailboaters, Gunnar's Boat Taxi, SeaLines, and Northern Lights. Those four companies operate all the tourist boats between town and the nature reserve.' Hildur wrote the phone numbers for the boat companies in her notebook, ripped out the sheet, and handed it to Jakob. 'Ask for lists of all passengers from the days preceding Lísa's death. Let's start calling through the names. Someone must have seen her.'

For the next hour and a half, Jakob and Hildur sat at their phones. According to the passenger lists from the boat companies, about fifty tourists had spent the night at Hesteyri on that date in July. Hildur and Jakob called every single one. The majority said they'd followed the same route Lísa had: they'd taken a boat to the Fljótavík coast and hiked over the pass into Hesteyri, where the largest cluster of houses in the area stood. No one had lived in them for decades; the last residents had moved away in the 1950s. Nowadays the little wooden buildings were kept as summer cabins. There was no electricity, no plumbing, and no mobile phone coverage there.

Just about everyone Jakob and Hildur spoke with remembered the incident: word of the dead tourist had reached the other hikers in the area. But most said they'd slept in tents and didn't remember having seen Lísa at all.

The phone on Jakob's desk started to ring. Hildur grabbed the receiver.

'Ísafjörður police.'

'Hi, this is Margrét. Did you say police? Did you just call me?' A child's voice could be heard faintly in the background. 'I'm at home with sick kids; I couldn't answer right away.'

Hildur introduced herself and said she was investigating the death of the woman who'd died at Hornstrandir the summer before. 'According to the passenger lists, you were in the area at the time.'

There was a moment of silence at the other end of the line. Apparently, Margrét was moving to another room so she could talk out of earshot of the children.

She told Hildur she'd been on her annual summer hike with her sisters. 'We wanted to see those cliffs.'

'Did you come across Lísa, this dead woman, during your trek?'

'Yes. We stayed at the same guesthouse as she did. My sisters and I. There was fish soup for dinner. Or she'd already eaten by the time we arrived. I remember the soup because it was so delicious.'

The sisters had left early the next morning to continue their hike to the next fjord. It wasn't until later they learned the girl they'd met at the guesthouse had died during the night. The four of them had meant to share a four-person room furnished with two bunk beds, a small nightstand, and an armoire. But that evening, the host had come into the room to warn them there were bedbugs in one of the bunks and sleeping in it wasn't a good idea. The bunk in question had been Lísa's.

'We thought it was a little strange, but it didn't occur to us to say anything.'

'What was strange?' Hildur asked.

'Well, that the woman offered Lísa a bed at the other end of the house, in her bedroom. Lísa was pleased she'd been warned about the bedbugs, but it sounded a little strange to us.'

So Lísa had followed the woman to the other end of the house, and the sisters had never seen her again.

'Do you remember what this host looked like?'

Margrét answered in the affirmative, then held a slight pause. She seemed to be trying to recall the event from the previous summer in as much detail as possible.

'She was surprisingly strong for a woman her age. She pulled the boat up on shore by herself and was laying a wall of big rocks around the house. My sisters and I were impressed by how strong she seemed. I think she was about my mother's age, around sixty. Big, and, well, sort of, well, bedraggled. Hair uncombed and clothes a little shabby.'

'Do you remember her name?'

'Yes. Her name was Marta.'

Chapter 50

Hildur could feel Brenda trembling in the wind. The captain who'd agreed to ferry them to Hornstrandir had assured her the wind would drop by two that afternoon. At that time, they could set out across the strait for Hesteyri, a voyage of a little over half an hour.

Hildur, Beta, and Jakob had tried to discover Marta's whereabouts, but she hadn't had a permanent address since she left the hospital. She didn't have a contract with an energy supplier, or a vehicle registered in her name. She didn't use a credit card, online banking, or a mobile phone. It was as if she'd ceased to exist after her hospital stay.

Margrét had mentioned a four-person guesthouse. They needed to see the place as soon as possible, but the captain at the harbour had postponed their departure due to strong winds. They could have requested assistance from a coastguard vessel. That seemed like overkill, though, as they had no cause to suspect anyone's life was in immediate danger. The captain had indicated departure would take place in two hours' time. They would have to settle for that. The weather always had the last word.

While they'd waited for it to improve, Hildur and Jakob had driven to Aunt Tinna's place at the fringes of Ísafjörður.

Tinna knew Hesteyri well. Hildur had been nine the first time Tinna had taken her to the Hornstrandir Nature Reserve. She would probably remember that summer forever; it had been the first summer after her sisters went missing. And the week-long trip to Hesteyri had kicked off a summertime tradition for her and her aunt that had continued until Hildur went off to the university.

Hildur had fallen in love with Hesteyri at first sight. As she'd stood at the edge of the lush valley, taking in the green grass blowing in the breeze and sensing the presence of the majestic mountains, nature had spoken to her. And she'd wanted to listen. She no longer felt lonely or unlucky there in that landscape. It had been a moment of personal empowerment, during which all other matters had felt trivial.

Tinna and Hildur had travelled to the nature reserve from Ísafjörður by boat. They'd stayed at a place Tinna's good friend had access to, an old wooden house on the water. Tinna knew the homes in the area better than Hildur did.

'Hi, Tinna, we're here,' Hildur called out. The aroma of fresh coffee filled the entryway.

'Come in. I'm just setting out the cups.'

Tinna clicked on the coffeemaker and wrapped Hildur in an embrace. Then she hugged Jakob and took his cheeks in her hands. 'You seem like a handsome boy,' Tinna said, not bothering to conceal her enthusiasm.

'This is my colleague,' Hildur said. 'Jakob, the Finn,'

'Oh, I know that. I'm just being silly. Please sit.'

Hildur noticed her aunt had set out the nicer coffee cups. Tinna poured the coffee and offered her guests Christmas cake, a cinnamony, sugar-dusted confection with white cream filling. Supermarkets only carried it in the middle of the winter, and the season always began with a bang in November. The cakes in green wrappers were a sure sign of Christmas's approach.

'What prompted you two to come all the way out here?' Tinna asked.

Hildur told her they wanted to talk to her about Hesteyri. 'Listen. Do you happen to remember a woman named Marta?'

Tinna groped at the table. Jakob helped by pushing the cake server toward her. Tinna sliced herself a thick slab of fragrant spice cake and pondered.

'It's for our work,' Hildur continued. 'We'd like to get in touch with her.'

'Marta . . . Yes, I remember her. Her family's house was right next to my friend's. They shared a water pipe.'

When the last of the residents had moved away from Hornstrandir in the 1950s, the houses had been left behind for summer use. Most didn't have running water. A few cottagers had built an above-ground plumbing system that conveyed water directly indoors from mountain streams.

'When Marta's parents died, they left the house to Marta. She spent summers there and started renting bunks to tourists at a pretty young age.'

Tinna remembered the guesthouse as having been a popular place to lodge. It was never advertised anywhere; people just knew about it and made their reservations through the boat transport company.

Tinna stood and went into the living room. The television was playing a rerun of some reality show that took place on a tropical island. Tinna opened the drawer under the TV stand and bent over it, apparently searching for something.

Jakob leaned toward Hildur and asked in a voice barely louder than a whisper: 'Why didn't you tell me your aunt was blind?'

Hildur didn't understand his point: why should she have mentioned it? She was so used to Tinna's inability to see. Tinna's vision had started to weaken noticeably a couple of decades earlier, and before long she had completely lost her sight.

'I don't know. Should I have warned you that she's a brunette?'

Jakob seemed to get the point. He smiled at Hildur, poured more coffee, and dropped the issue.

'You might want to have a look at these,' Tinna said from the kitchen doorway. She was holding a brown photo album, its cover emblazoned with a silver rose and the word 2000. She sat back down and handed the album to Hildur, suggesting she turn to the pictures from the summer of 2000.

Time had glued the album's plasticky pages together. Hildur pulled them apart, making sure not to tear the delicate membranes that protected the photographs. It had been ages since she'd last looked at traditional printed photos.

The summertime shots were at the back. Hildur held the album up to her face and studied the images at close proximity. They exuded a carefree warmth: the sun was shining, the sea was blue, and the people in them looked relaxed and happy. Some of the photos were overexposed, but even so, she could still recognise Hildur and Tinna.

'Wow, is that you?' Jakob asked, pointing at the picture Hildur was looking at. In it, Hildur was wearing denim cut-offs and a blue-and-white striped flannel shirt tied at the navel. Her hair had been knotted in two side buns.

Hildur grunted. 'Distinct Spice Girls influences.'

She continued flipping through the images: her and Tinna in a boat en route to Hesteyri, her and Tinna sunbathing in their T-shirts out in front of the cottage.

'There should be a picture of four women in front of the cottages. We were cleaning rhubarb when some passer-by asked to take a photo of us with your camera.'

Hildur found the photo. She and Tinna were sitting on a bench that had been carried outside, and the two big plastic bags in front of them were filled with sliced rhubarb. Big leathery leaves had been piled next to the bench. Hildur had her sleeves rolled up; she was just stripping the leaf from a stalk. Tinna sat at her side, hand raised to shelter her eyes from the sun.

'Who are these two women next to us?' Hildur asked.

There was a woman Tinna's age laughing and looking straight at the camera. Her sleeveless T-shirt revealed muscular arms. She had two long stalks of rhubarb in one hand and a sharp-looking knife in the other; her large palm was wrapped around the handle. The woman looked both very strong and incredibly gentle. A school-age girl sat on the grass at the women's feet. She was holding a rhubarb leaf over her head like an umbrella and cackling.

'That's Marta and her daughter Valgerður. They spent a summer at Hesteyri at the same time we did,' Tinna said, lifting the coffee cup to her lips. 'It was a nice summer for all of us.'

Hildur pondered. She didn't remember having met the women in the photograph, but that was no surprise. Hesteyri was packed with Icelandic tourists in the summertime.

Tinna said Marta and Valgerður had been exceptionally close. 'They were somehow more than mother and daughter. Their relationship was very intense. They went everywhere together and finished each other's sentences and had kind of grown together at the hip.'

Hildur's attention was drawn to the little girl's luscious hair: it reached halfway down her back. It was as thick as a waterfall and as blonde as just-ripened oats.

There was a delicate tinkle as Tinna lowered her cup to her saucer. She grew serious. 'Then that terrible thing happened. I think you were living in Reykjavík by then. You probably don't remember.'

Much had happened over the course of a single year: Valgerður had had a child with a man from Reykjavík. He'd been married and had promised to leave his wife once Valgerður gave birth. But the child had died very young, under the age of two. The poor thing had been diagnosed with a rare hereditary brain disease. The young mother took the child's death so hard she never got over it, and eventually, she committed suicide.

'The daughter's suicide and granddaughter's death drove Marta over the edge. She spent a long time at a psychiatric hospital. I haven't heard anything about her since. Her house at Hesteyri was left empty.'

Silence fell over the table. The clock ticked. The tropical island show had ended; now the afternoon weather forecast was blaring from the television. A storm warning for the north-western seas starting late that evening.

The child was diagnosed with a hereditary brain disease, Hildur repeated to herself. Valgerður and Heiðar's child. And in that instant, the meaning of the obituary that had troubled her was clear.

My eyes and your eyes
O, those precious gems
What's mine is yours and what's yours is mine,
You know my meaning.
I'm sorry. About everything. We never even met.

Now Hildur grasped the obituary's curious formulation. Heiðar hadn't been referring to Valgerður, but to his child! He'd never met his own daughter. In his obituary, he was apologising for having brought about her death. By passing down his genes to her.

Hildur stood and pulled on her coat. It was time to pay a visit to Hesteyri.

Chapter 51

November 2019, Hesteyri

The captain cracked the window a few centimetres to let in fresh air and keep the cabin from fogging up. It was a small boat. Hildur, Jakob, and Beta sat packed side by side on the artificial leather bench running along the wall. Between the bench and the captain was a compact table with a map of the Ísafjörður Strait displayed under transparent contact paper. Hildur unzipped her parka; she was getting uncomfortably warm. Beta said she and her family often went hiking in the Hornstrandir Nature Reserve in the summertime. Her husband was an enthusiastic photographer and enjoyed taking photos of the Arctic foxes that inhabited the reserve.

Although the cabin was too hot, sitting outside wasn't tempting. The little vessel was ploughing into a headwind, and even small waves were flinging frigid water across the deck.

'We have about four hours before the wind picks up again,' said the captain. He manned the wheel in a heavy sweater, jeans, and cap.

The further the boat moved from the harbour, the more it lurched. Their stomachs were going to suffer in the billowing sideways motion. Luckily the shuddering voyage would only last a good forty-five minutes.

'I wonder if it would have been possible to spot the pattern earlier,' Hildur pondered audibly. The trails of all the victims had ultimately led to Jón. 'Most of all I'm frustrated I didn't see

Freysi's role right away,' she sighed, drawing lines on the table in front of her with her forefinger.

Hildur had known Freysi's parents had had their only son at an older age and had been dead for some time by the time she and Freysi met. That was the sum total of what Freysi had revealed about his family. Hildur cursed herself for not having grasped that Freysi's father Gunnar was Jón's brother. There was nothing surprising about two residents of the same town being related. What was surprising was it hadn't been general knowledge.

'There's no point beating yourself up,' Jakob said, gazing out at the sea. 'There have been so many twists in this case. Maybe Freysi's parents intentionally kept their distance from Jón, because he had an unsavoury reputation.'

Hildur glanced at her colleague. Jakob's empathy felt good.

'Lísa's medical records indicated she'd suffered from apnoea. I just had a quick look at information on cerebral haemorrhages and found a study indicating that those suffering from the disease exhibit above-average rates of apnoea. Lísa probably carried the same gene as Freysi,' Jakob said. 'The same one Heiðar had. And Valgerður's child.'

Suddenly, Jakob's face went green. The boat's rocking motion was getting to be too much for a landlubber. He took a bag from a box on the table, opened it, and retched.

Soon after, the boat slowed and approached the shore. 'End of the line,' the captain said laconically, pulling down his cap.

Hildur and her colleagues wanted to have a look at Marta's old cottage, the one that had appeared in Tinna's photograph. The one where Lísa had died the summer before.

Beta climbed out of the boat, followed by Hildur and Jakob. The wooden dock was weathered; seaweed clung to the pilings like fur. A small motorboat had been pulled up on the shore nearby and secured to big rocks with rope.

The three of them stood there for a moment, taking in their surroundings.

A strip of flat land no more than a few hundred metres wide ran between the shore and the snowy mountains beyond. The terrain was treeless and bare. The wind had banked the snow, and some of the houses were buried. The blanketed structures bulged from the ground like boils swelling randomly along the waterline. Most were wooden buildings, painted white, with red metal roofs. These homes were heated with oil; few could have afforded heating with wood, as it was expensive and transporting it by boat onerous.

Tinna had said Marta's cottage was black and stood on a gentle rise. Hildur scanned each house carefully until she found the one she was looking for. 'Third house from the right,' she said, leading the way through the snow.

As they approached the cottage, a pair of big ravens took to the wing. The birds had been pecking at food scraps; the snow behind the cottage was littered with potato peelings and carrot tops. Out in front of the cottage, there were footprints. Footprints made by big hiking boots. None of them were carrying a service weapon; they'd assumed their pistols wouldn't be necessary. Even if someone were at the cabin, there were three of them. Hildur knew guns would be useless under the circumstances.

She reached for the door's fat wooden handle. She glanced at her colleagues and gave it a firm tug. The door creaked. The entryway was small and narrow. One wall was draped with a fishing net; at the other, long-legged waders hung by the suspenders from a nail. A photograph, a metal box, and a Bible had been set out on a yellow wooden stool in the vestibule as if to welcome the visitors.

The photo was bleached by time and brittle from the damp. Hildur picked it up and took a closer look. A woman, about twenty, was squinting and smiling at the camera. It was summer, and the sun was shining brightly against a black backdrop. It must have been taken against the cottage's southern wall. The woman had a little girl about a year old in her arms. There was a resemblance. Both had incredible blonde hair. The girl's hair was long for her age, lovely long hair tied up in a high ponytail with a red bow. Both the woman and the girl were laughing.

Hildur immediately recognised the woman: it was the photo from Valgerður's obituary, only that time it had been cropped tight to the face.

Hildur handed the picture to Jakob and picked up the metal box. It contained a white card from the maternity clinic, on which the midwife had written the baby's gender, time of birth, weight, and length. The newborn's footprint had been pressed to the front of the card. The foot was tiny, and delicate, but all the toes were distinct. Beneath the card, at the bottom of the box, Hildur found a tress of fine blonde hair tied with a red ribbon. A child's hair.

Hildur reached for the Bible on the stool and flipped through it. There were several bookmarks, and Hildur stopped at the last one and read. The Gospel of Matthew. After finishing the final lines, she was certain of what she'd already intuited in the boat. They wouldn't be finding anyone here who would prove a danger to them.

He that findeth his life shall lose it: and he that loseth his life for my sake shall find it.

Hildur didn't need to look through the pane of glass in the inner door to know what had happened. After her stint in the psychiatric hospital, Marta had come home.

*

A pair of heavy-looking hiking boots dangled at Hildur's eye level. They'd once been black and shiny; now the greying footwear was scuffed at the tips and flattened at the heels. It was clear they'd been in heavy use. Now they dangled in the air, free. Swayed slowly, like lupins in the summer breeze. An aluminium stepladder lay on its side on the floor beneath them.

Hildur opened the door and stepped into the cottage, only to be greeted by a strong, foul smell. Based on the odour, the body had been hanging from the roof beam for some time. Hildur stepped past it and into the dim living room. She registered a faint rustling. The small ventilation window high above the snowline was open, and the breeze that entered through it was rattling sheets of paper tacked to the wall.

Hildur heard Beta exit the house, presumably to walk back to the boat. They'd need assistance moving the body.

All the furniture in the small cottage had been pulled away from the left-hand wall. What Hildur saw there made her freeze: dozens of sheets of paper arranged in bullet-straight rows. They were filled with sketches and text written in a small hand. It didn't take Hildur long to grasp that the phrases, times, and dates scribbled on them formed a timeline of sorts.

Freysi runs in the evenings > 8 p.m. Alone when?
Hverfisgatan parking garage, Reykjavík + keys
Drive to Ísafjörður 5 p.m.
Tuesday pizza delivery (check timing!)
10 p.m. arrival Reykjavík
Cameras (done)

A second cluster of notes bearing names had been tacked up beneath this timeline. An arrow from each note led to the other notes. Hildur remembered what Lian had told her over the phone: Marta had produced detailed genealogical diagrams during her stay at the hospital. That's exactly what these notes in front of Hildur were.

A family tree.

Hildur focused on it. Two arrows descended from Jón: *two children*. Heiðar and Lísa. Father and children. All dead.

Next to Jón, his brother Gunnar, and below Gunnar a name that made Hildur flinch.

Freysi. Brothers and nephew. Every single one dead.

In the diagram, Heiðar was linked to Valgerður, and arrows from their names pointed to a child. That made them father and mother. Valgerður and Heiðar had had a child that had died in infancy of a hereditary cerebral haemorrhage. Valgerður had committed suicide, and Heiðar, who carried the gene, had been murdered.

As she studied the family tree, Hildur grasped the pattern. The entire family from Jón down had been erased, one name at a time. Marta had murdered everyone related to Jón. All those who had a 50 per cent probability of carrying the gene. Marta had ensured no one would have to ever go through what she'd been through: the premature death of a child and grandchild.

Jakob had quietly entered the room. He walked up next to Hildur and studied the notes on the wall.

Hildur gulped audibly. 'In the end, it wasn't complicated at all. Just the opposite. It was so simple. See? There was a woman who was robbed of everything, and eventually, she lost her mind,' she said, bringing Marta's story to its conclusion.

Chapter 52

November 2019, Ísafjörður

Golden liquid slid down the rim of the pint glass, and a centimetre of soft foam formed on the surface. The latest beer from the local brewery, a dark lager flavoured with orange, had just been launched. Hildur, Beta, and Jakob had ordered it at the bartender's suggestion.

'It's on me,' Beta announced, flashing her Visa at the payment terminal.

Jakob carried the glasses to the most private table in the place. Hildur brought over a basket of nachos with spicy sauce.

The establishment in the white wooden house on the main street was the only pub in Ísafjörður open seven days a week. The menu boasted fresh fish, juicy burgers, and salads. On weekends local bands would play in the back room, but tonight songs from Sigur Rós's third album were coming from the speakers. A television usually blared in Iceland's small-town pubs, so armchair athletes could watch football over a pint. The ambience in this place was quiet because the televisions were in an annexe out back. All possible football games were shown on the big screen out there and one could make as much noise as necessary.

The trio hung their coats on a nearby coatrack made of old horseshoes.

'Cheers!' Hildur said, raising her pint. Three glasses came together with a clunk.

This year's seasonal brew was tasty; the bitter orange gave it a pleasant aftertaste. The three of them sat in silence, sipping their beers and gazing out into the dark November night. It was raining. Once again, the streets were clear of snow. It came and went. The same pendular movement would continue all winter.

Hildur eyed her companions. These were the people she was closest to. The people she spent the most time with. The only one was missing was Tinna. Freysi was gone.

Beta would have two beers, maximum, before heading home. Her husband frequently travelled for work, so feeding the children and reading them a bedtime story often fell to her. She didn't seem to mind. She said she preferred spending her free time at home. She was clear about doing her work well, but she refused to stay and work overtime except in the most unusual of circumstances. And Beta practised what she preached, which meant those who worked under her didn't have to prove their excellence by working overly long hours.

Right now all three of them were tired. The trip to Hesteyri the day before yesterday had stretched to over twenty-four hours. They'd needed a helicopter to move the body, but the helicopter had been busy transporting two patients in urgent need of surgery. And so Hildur, Jakob, and Beta had cut Marta down, performed a preliminary cause-of-death examination, and covered her body with a sheet.

Marta hadn't wanted for anyone else to suffer the same agony she had. She'd planned everything out down to the last detail to ensure no one else would experience a similar loss. By the time the helicopter finally picked up Marta's body, the weather had deteriorated.

Crossing the strait at that point would have been too risky. And so the three of them had sheltered in the cottage for the night with the captain. They'd found pre-packaged fish rolls in the kitchen cupboard and heated them up on the gas stove for their supper.

The link between the girl who'd died the previous summer at Hesteyri and the other murders had been confirmed by the papers found in Marta's cottage. Lísa's birth certificate indicated Jón had been her biological father, too. Lísa's biological mother had been no more than a child herself, only sixteen, when she gave birth. They didn't know how Marta had got her hands on the birth certificate. Another mystery was how Jón, who'd fathered two children, had become a paedophile who preyed on teenage boys. Lísa and Heiðar had been half-siblings unaware of each other's existence. They'd lived and died without ever knowing about each other.

Some things remained mysteries forever. The whole story was never revealed. There were questions to which the answers would no longer be found.

Hildur, Jakob, and Beta had gathered all possible materials from Marta's cottage, down to the paperclips, and organised them in piles in the station conference room. They would spend the next few days reviewing everything and finalising the investigation. Beta had received a call from the forensics lab in Reykjavík that morning, reporting the results of the DNA analyses. The results confirmed what they already knew: Jón, Heiðar, and Freysi were related.

None of them were in a particularly celebratory mood, but taking a moment to share a pint in the town's sole pub had seemed like a good idea tonight anyway.

Hildur thought about the funeral coming up that Saturday. Freysi was to be laid to rest at the local church. Beta had promised to join Hildur if she didn't want to go alone. Hildur had appreciated the gesture of support. But even though she knew it would be hard, she wanted to go alone. She meant to attend and sit in the back row. That way she'd be able to see everything without having to deal with looks from the other mourners. That would be easiest.

Hildur pulled the nachos closer and dipped her chips in the cheese sauce. She'd gone for a short run that afternoon and hadn't had time to eat afterwards. Corn chips and beer were a fine stand-in for dinner.

Jakob finished his pint and offered to get another round. But before he made for the bar, he reached into his satchel and pulled out a bundle wrapped in paper.

'I had time to finish the armpits yesterday. I named the sweater *Hildur*, so this first test version belongs to you. I think it will look good on you.'

Hildur accepted the package and opened it right away. She was delighted: a light-brown sweater with a simple, striking pattern was revealed. It was the one Hildur had been admiring. Jakob had created the design himself, and it was stunning. She unfolded the sweater and stroked its smooth surface.

'Thank you. It's really beautiful,' Hildur said, choking up. She put it on then and there.

Jakob soon returned, carrying three pints. Hildur took a moment to study him where he sat on the couch. She and Jakob hadn't known each other long, but he'd become a good friend. She enjoyed his company. It was like a refreshing glass of water: no constant misunderstandings, no hidden messages, no surprises. Jakob didn't try to always be funny or otherwise the centre of attention. Presumably, the outward calm he projected resulted from all the things he'd been through over the course of his life. Knowing the extent of what could happen had a tendency to put small setbacks into perspective. Hopefully he wouldn't be returning to Finland right away.

'Do you have any plans for Christmas vacation?' Hildur asked.

'As a matter of fact, I do. I'm flying to Norway.'

By decision of the Norwegian courts, Jakob had been granted monitored meetings with his son over the week between Christmas and New Year's. 'I'm not sure I'll actually see him, but I'm going to go try,' he said, sipping at his overflowing pint. 'After that, I'll come back here, of course. I still have a few months of my internship left.'

Just then, the restaurant door was yanked open. Guðrún. A shock of blonde, wind-tousled hair exploded from under her loose beanie. Her long cardigan was unbuttoned, and she was wearing the perfect shade of lipstick. She quickly pulled the door shut behind her and took off her rain-soaked hat.

'I was on my way to the shop and saw people I knew through the window. I'm not intruding, am I?' she asked, taking a seat on the couch next to Jakob before anyone could respond. Guðrún nudged her bottom right next to Jakob's and possessively stroked his beard. Jakob turned toward her and pressed a light kiss to her lips.

No, Guðrún wasn't intruding, just the opposite. Jakob's eyes were twinkling with laughter. It warmed Hildur's heart to see him so genuinely happy.

'That sweater fits you like a sliver in the ass,' Guðrún said. It was an old local saying used to express two things that went together perfectly.

Hildur thanked her and nodded in Jakob's direction. 'He's a really skilled knitter.'

'He's a real sweetheart,' Guðrún said, lowering her hand to Jakob's thigh and giving it a squeeze.

Hildur chuckled, rolled up the sleeves of her namesake knit and walked over to the bar. As she leaned against it, she saw herself in the mirror hanging on the wall. She took a second look and liked what she saw. Then she called to the bartender over. She would be getting the next round.

Chapter 53

November 2019, Ísafjörður-Hnífsdalur

Hildur was having a hard time opening her eyes. The surrounding muscles functioned, but her lashes resisted. They were glued to her lower lid. She felt around the nightstand for her water glass, dipped in two fingers, and wiped away the biggest specks. One of her eyes opened enough for her to glance at the screen of her phone. Seven fifteen. How frustrating. She'd meant to sleep until nine.

Her body was weighed down with exhaustion, but she knew from experience that she wouldn't be able to fall back asleep. Once her brain was awake, quieting it was impossible. There was a groan, and the covers flew to the floor.

She stared at the ceiling and performed a silent body scan to see how she felt. Her head ached a little. She could still taste nachos and cheese sauce. The sweater Jakob had given her was rolled up under her head, and she could smell the lambswool. It was a safe smell; she liked it.

As expected, Beta had refused a third pint and headed home to cook dinner. Hildur had stayed a little longer with Jakob and Guðrún. After the three of them had tasted their way through every beer in the bar – luckily there were only five – Jakob and Guðrún had left for Jakob's place entwined in each other. Hildur had returned home alone. And apparently passed out without removing her make-up or brushing her teeth.

She turned on her electric toothbrush, drank a big glass of cold water, and ate a banana. She didn't have to be at work for three hours, so she'd have time for a run first. She felt a painful pang inside when she caught her hand automatically reaching for her phone. Who exactly was she planning on texting? She would be running alone.

In the dim entryway, she pulled on her running clothes, slipped into her running shoes and cleats, and attached her headlamp. A long, slow jog in the fresh air couldn't make her feel any worse. Ten kilometres wouldn't erase the events of the past few weeks, but it would make them more tolerable. If a collision was unavoidable, she'd make sure the surface was as soft as possible.

Hildur knew she was a little hungover and understood the risks of exercising in such a state. But if a minute chance of a heart attack and massive anxiety were hanging in the balance, she'd rather take the first.

When she stepped outside, she deliberately looked in the opposite direction. Freysi's place was empty now. She picked up the pace and forced herself to look forward. Onward.

There's nothing I can do about it, so I'm not going to think about it anymore.

The spikes of her cleats sank into the surface of the path, keeping her on her feet. The tiny metal balls pushed the ice out of their way, and the rhythm produced by the crunch accelerated with every footfall.

The illuminated pedestrian path ran alongside the road. To the left rose flat-topped Mount Eyrarfjall. It hadn't chosen its site. It was just there. Through wind, rain, and blizzard. On the other side of the road, the dark sea roiled. Hildur couldn't see the waves, but she heard them crash against the stone breakwater protecting the road. She could make out two shivering lights advancing across the sea. Boats. Twenty years ago, they would have been humble fishing vessels heading out early in the morning to see whether the sea had anything to offer. Now they were food taxis. They were carrying feed to the fish that circled the pens sunk out in the middle of the fjord.

Hildur's pulse rose. After a few kilometres of running uphill, her legs were heavy, but she felt light. She'd get in five kilometres if she circled the edges of Knife Valley and stop at the gates of the little cemetery there. That way she could turn around and still make it to work by ten.

A little over fifteen minutes later, she paused at the cemetery. The night still hadn't relented, and she couldn't see where the gravestones ended and the sea began. There was one powerful spotlight. It was trained on a statue erected at the edge of the graveyard in memory of Icelandic sailors lost at sea. There the sailor stood, back to the waves, sternly eyeing all those who entered the cemetery. The illuminated, furrowed face under the fishing hat stood out clearly against the dark sky. She stared at the fisherman's proud gaze for a moment, then turned to head back.

Hildur felt her phone vibrate in her pocket. The number flashing on the screen was Axlar-Hákon's.

'Good morning. Did I wake you?' asked a calm male voice.

'I'm on my way to work,' Hildur said, climbing the slope to the pedestrian path that would take her back to the village.

'I'm calling about those bags you sent.'

For a moment, Hildur felt weightless. She'd couriered the plastic bags and bones she'd found in the hole at Ögurvík to Reykjavík for further examination. They didn't have anything to do with any criminal investigation presently underway, so they hadn't been a priority.

Even so, Axlar-Hákon had promised to take a look as soon as he could make some time. Hildur heard him flip through his papers as he reviewed his findings.

The bags had contained one backpack and some articles of clothing. The fibres had been very fragile, but based on what he'd been able to retrieve, Axlar-Hákon ventured to guess they were from two different layers of clothes. There'd been an old nametag in the backpack, and the name Rúnarsdóttir had still been legible on it. *Rúnar's daughter.* Hildur listened with her eyes shut.

Axlar-Hákon held a slight pause before he continued: 'Hildur. I remember this case, of course. Rúnar. That was your father's name, wasn't it?' He didn't appear to expect an answer.

'The bones? What about the bones? Did you look at them?' Hildur asked in a barely audible voice. She gripped her phone so hard its sharp edges dug painfully into her fingers.

'I did. They're not human bones. They're pieces of a calf's leg bone. My guess is they're really old. Of course, we'd have to conduct much more detailed testing to establish a more definite time frame, but my guess is the bones are much older than the contents of the bags.'

Axlar-Hákon continued talking, but Hildur didn't hear anything else he said. The hand holding the phone dropped.

She opened her eyes and gazed across the water at the mountains to the east. The sky behind them had brightened from black to purple.

A Word from the Author

Hildur entered my life unexpectedly. As unexpectedly as Iceland.

I moved to Iceland twenty years ago. I was studying economics at the Helsinki Business School at the time and had the opportunity to go abroad for a year-long exchange. I picked Iceland for selfish reasons. I wanted to bathe in hot springs and ride Icelandic horses! And instead of macroeconomic theory, I studied Icelandic culture and folklore. I had some explaining to do regarding these idiosyncratic course selections, but luckily my professor at my home university was an understanding woman and said curiosity was a good thing.

I'm still on that idiosyncratic path. I met a handsome man at a bar in Reykjavík, talked him into a relationship, moved my things into his place, and now we live here in Iceland with our two children. It's probably worth clarifying I'm not keeping my husband hostage: luckily he gradually warmed to my idea of us sharing a life together.

A couple of years ago, I made an imaginary friend. An Icelandic woman named Hildur began to take shape in my mind. She simply came for a visit and refused to leave. I would imagine Hildur surfing the waves of the Atlantic, see her running the mountain slopes. She became an acquaintance I spent time with when I was alone. She was someone whose company I enjoyed. Ultimately I had to start writing down her stories. As I kept writing, I realised I had so much to tell about Hildur there was no way one book would suffice. I was going to have to write more about her.

The Clues in the Fjord is fiction. Even though some of the places mentioned in the book exist, the events and characters are fictional. Any possible similarities between fiction and reality are happenstance.

I want to thank all those helpful people who supported me during the writing process. Thank you, Ingibjörg Elín Magnúsdóttir and Aldís Hilmarsdóttir, for having the patience to answer my questions about police work. Thanks to my Instagram followers, who helped me with my questions about search-and-rescue dogs. Thanks to my fellow coworking space member, the knitwear designer Sigríður Sif Gylfadóttir, for helping Jakob knit Hildur a sweater. It turned out beautifully. Any errors that have made their way into the book are mine alone.

Thank you to my superb publisher, WSOY. Anna-Riikka Carlson, publisher of domestic fiction: thank you, thank you, thank you for having the patience to listen to my overly long voice messages and read my emails and for sharing my enthusiasm about Hildur. Executive editor Hanna Pudas – the biggest thanks in the world to you! I don't know what I'd do without you. I know writing wouldn't feel as nice. Thanks to editor Lea Peuronpuro for your steely professionalism as I completed the manuscript. Thank you WSOY brand manager and fellow Satu, Satu Sirkiä, for the superb marketing.

The most important thanks come last: thank you, family and friends.

Ísafjörður, April 2022

Satu Rämö

Don't miss out on Hildur Rúnarsdottir's second case . . .

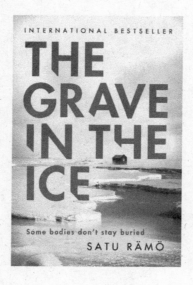

Detective Hildur Rúnarsdottir and her trainee Jakob are plagued
by their own demons while working on the chilly west coast of
Iceland: Hildur by the disappearance of her younger sisters
twenty-five years ago and Jakob by a custody battle that
has left him unable to see his son.

When a local politician is found shot dead on a ski trail, the two must
put aside their personal problems to investigate the murder. While
initially thought to be a crime of passion, there are much darker
secrets hiding beneath the surface. Hildur and Jakob soon realise
that even the dead can't stay buried forever.

COMING SPRING 2025
AVAILABLE FOR PRE-ORDER NOW

Don't miss out on Hildur Rúnarsdottir's third case . . .

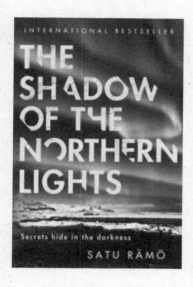

As Christmas comes to the west cost of Iceland, a corpse is found in a fish farming pond. Detective Hildur Rúnarsdóttir and trainee Jakob Johanson barely have time to start their investigation before another body is discovered. And soon a third.

While investigating the case, Hildur's lost sister weighs heavy on her mind. Meanwhile, Jakob travels to Finland for the hearing of his fraught custody battle, that leaves him facing dire consequences. As the number of deaths continues to grow, Hildur and Jakob are desperate to catch the killer before they strike again.

COMING AUTUMN 2025
AVAILABLE FOR PRE-ORDER NOW